8/31

D0290139

The Spoils of Eden

THE
DAWN *of* HAWAII
SERIES

Book One

The Spoils of Eden

LINDA LEE CHAIKIN

MOODY PUBLISHERS
CHICAGO

© 2010 by
LINDA CHAIKIN

Editor: Paul Santhouse
Interior Design: Ragont Design
Cover Design: Studio Gearbox
Cover Image: girl: bigstockphoto.com; beach and trees: www.photos.com;
    fisherman, boat and other guy on the beach: istockphoto.com

Library of Congress Cataloging-in-Publication Data

Chaikin, L. L.
    The spoils of Eden / Linda Lee Chaikin.
        p. cm. — (The dawn of Hawaii series ; bk. 1)
    ISBN 978-0-8024-3749-5
        1. Missions to leprosy patients—Hawaii—Fiction.
    2. Leprosy—Hospitals—Hawaii—Fiction. 3. Adoption—Fiction.
    4. Hawaii—History—19th century—Fiction. I. Title.
    PS3553.H2427S66 2010
    813'.54—dc22

                                        2010003493

We hope you enjoy this book from Moody Publishers. Our goal is to provide high-quality, thought-provoking books and products that connect truth to the challenges and opportunities of life. For more information on other books and products written and produced from a biblical perspective, go to www.moodypublishers.com or write to:

Moody Publishers
820 N. LaSalle Boulevard
Chicago, IL 60610

1 3 5 7 9 10 8 6 4 2

Printed in the United States of America

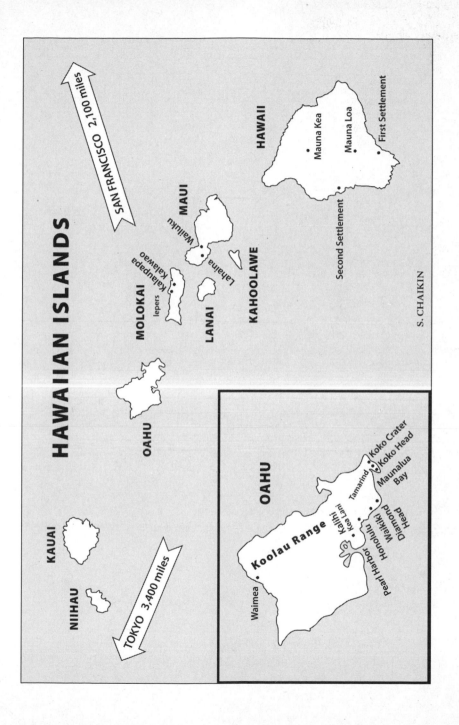

HAWAIIAN ISLANDS

NIIHAU

KAUAI

OAHU

MOLOKAI

Kalaupapa
Kalawao
lepers

MAUI

Wailuku

Lahaina

LANAI

KAHOOLAWE

HAWAII

Mauna Kea

Mauna Loa

First Settlement

Second Settlement

SAN FRANCISCO 2,100 miles

TOKYO 3,400 miles

S. CHAIKIN

OAHU

Koolau Range

Waimea

Kalihi
Kea Lani

Pearl Harbor

Honolulu

Waikiki

Diamond Head

Tamarind

Koko Crater
Koko Head

Maunalua Bay

Contents

HISTORICAL CHARACTERS AND TERMS

Many of the characters who appear in *The Spoils of Eden* are not fictional. Woven into the story of the Derrington and Easton families are real people who played an important role in the history of nineteenth-century Hawaii. The following lists include several of the more important characters and terms from Hawaii's colorful past. (Not listed are historical locations, buildings, and objects.)

CHARACTERS

Claus Spreckel — the sugar king from California.

Hiram Bingham — one of the first missionaries to Hawaii who helped create the Hawaiian alphabet, which was used to translate the Bible into Hawaiian.

John L. Stevens — American Foreign Minister (political) to Hawaii.

Kamehameha I monarchy — Kamehameha the Great conquered the other independent island kingdoms around him to form one kingdom, which he named after his island, Hawaii.

King David Kalakaua — who ruled over Hawaii for seventeen years until his death in 1891; the second elected monarch and the first to visit the United States.

Lorrin Thurston — member of the Hawaiian league and a grandson of pioneer missionary Asa Thurston.

Priest Damian — a Belgian priest who was ordained in Honolulu and assigned at his own request to the leper colony on Molokai in 1873, where he died in 1889 after contracting the disease.

Queen Liliuokalani — the last reigning monarch of the kingdom of Hawaii, who was deposed in 1893; a musician and songwriter, she wrote Hawaii's most famous song, "Aloha Oe."

Walter Murray Gibson — King Kalakaua's controversial prime minister, who was eventually run out of Hawaii and died on his way to San Francisco.

Queen Emma Kaleleonalani — who in the 1870s had a cousin who was a leper at Molokai.

TERMS:

alii — chief, princely

aloha — love, hello, good-bye

auwe — an expression of lament; alas!

haole — foreigner, especially white person; Caucasian

hapa-haole — person of mixed race; Hawaiian-Caucasian

hoolaulei — festive celebration

kahu — caregiver or nurse

kahuna — sorcerer or priest of the ancient native religion

kokua — helper; a person who would live with and assist a leper

lanai — porch, terrace, veranda

luna — overseer

makua — parent or any relative of one's parents

muumuu — gown, Mother Hubbard gown

Pake — Chinese

wahine — woman

Derrington Family Tree (Fictional Characters)

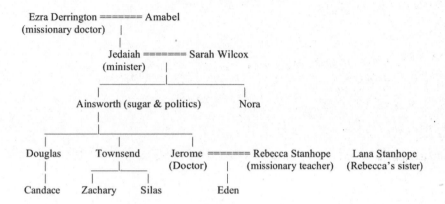

```
Ezra Derrington ======= Amabel
(missionary doctor)   |
                      |
           Jedaiah ======= Sarah Wilcox
           (minister)     |
     _____|_____
     |                                      |
  Ainsworth (sugar & politics)            Nora
     |
  ___|_____
  |            |                      |
Douglas    Townsend        Jerome ======= Rebecca Stanhope    Lana Stanhope
  |            |           (Doctor)  |   (missionary teacher)  (Rebecca's sister)
  |       ____|____                  |
Candace  Zachary  Silas            Eden
```

Easton Family Tree (Fictional Characters)

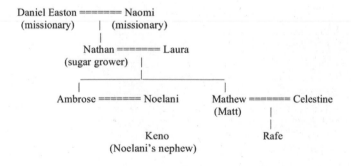

```
Daniel Easton ======= Naomi
(missionary)   |    (missionary)
               |
           Nathan ======= Laura
        (sugar grower)  |
       _____|_____
       |                              |
   Ambrose ======= Noelani      Mathew ======= Celestine
                                 (Matt)   |
                                          |
              Keno                       Rafe
         (Noelani's nephew)
```

Chapter One
The Board's Decision

Honolulu, Hawaii
June 1891

*S*unlight filtered through leafy palms as Eden Derrington walked the path to Kalihi Hospital. Birdsong filled the trees while crimson and lime hummingbirds fed among deep-throated flowers. Nearby, the white sand glistened as waves gently stroked the shore. Small ivory clouds moved lazily across the powder-blue sky . . . though an ominous sense of trouble shadowed the tropical morning. While appreciating the beauty around her, Eden considered the darkness that lay ahead.

Somewhere ahead a bird shrieked in unexpected fright, reminding her of the presence of evil. Once, in an even more glorious garden than the tropics, evil had brought spiritual and physical ruin to its inhabitants.

As Eden visualized Satan entering Paradise as a serpent, she quickened her pace through a dusky grove of palms and came into the sunlight. *Father God, how beautiful that garden must have been!*

For even now, with the curse of thorns, thistles, death, and decay, the beauty of Your creation still remains.

Later that morning at Kalihi Hospital, Eden slipped unseen from the Hawaii Board of Health meeting and quickened her steps down the hall. She could hear the doctors' muffled voices in continued discussion as she approached the sunny waiting room near the front of the hospital. Wearing an ankle-length, gray cotton dress overlaid with a traditional nurse's white pinafore emblazoned with a red cross, she stepped outdoors and hurried down the steps. In her bag were official documents, signed by the Board, and she was determined to present them at Hawaiiana Plantation as the Board had charged her.

Eden's dark, winged brows came together. The two influential doctors who had arrived late for the meeting worried her. Entering somewhat distracted, they soon realized their colleagues had already decided the matter at hand. At first they seemed amenable to the majority decision, but looking toward her, they'd hesitated. The younger doctor had drummed his fingers on the desk with disapproval, while the older gentleman kept sliding his spectacles up and down the narrow bridge of his nose.

Eden had the distinct impression the esteemed doctors thought her too young. If they had only known she'd once been engaged to the man the Board was making an inquiry about, they *certainly* would not have entrusted her with this task.

The tropic sun now blazed from a clear sky. She breathed in the fresh trade wind that kept the kingly palms swaying. It cooled her face and ruffled her wavy dark hair, partially pinned up off her neck in Victorian fashion and graced with a perky white nurse's cap.

Hurrying past the familiar shrubs of massive red and yellow hibiscus, her senses were filled with the heady fragrance given off by the clusters of pink flowers on the jacaranda trees. Insects buzzed and tiny finches twittered from the branches. Together they wove a chorus of praise to their Creator.

The hospital's flower bed, ablaze with color, reminded her of a

Fourth of July celebration in the States. *No*, she scolded herself. Don't even think about independence right now. Was there not enough to concern her already without more discord between her and Rafe Easton, the ambitious young man she'd so recently been engaged to marry?

The issue of independence hovered in her mind. Grandfather Ainsworth Derrington was soon to return from Washington D.C. Upon his arrival she would be called to account for her continued support of the Hawaiian queen. Grandfather was a firm annexationist, and joining other prominent sugar growers in Hawaii, he had been meeting with sympathetic members of the U.S. Senate hoping to garner support for making the Hawaiian islands a territory of the United States. Cousin Zachary Derrington, who ran Great-aunt Nora's newspaper, the *Derrington Gazette*, had been castigated in public for writing in favor of Queen Liliuokalani.

What if that incident were only the beginning? Where the discord would end was anyone's guess. Matters were coming to a climax, and it wasn't likely to end without bloodshed. Already there were wounded hearts, broken friendships . . . and broken romances. She glanced at the empty ring finger of her left hand.

Nearing the road she paused, lifting a hand to shield her view. Yes, he was there. Ling Li, the Chinese driver of a horse-drawn hackney, was parked beneath some palms, waiting. Ling was a well-known driver who catered to the Kalihi staff. Eden always tipped him well, knowing there were ten youngsters in his family hut at Kea Lani, the Derrington family sugar plantation. Today, however, she was going to Hawaiiana Plantation to meet with Rafe Easton about Kip, the baby boy he was planning to adopt.

As she approached Ling's hackney, a voice called out. "Eden, wait!"

Recognizing the voice of Lana Stanhope, the chief nurse in the leprosy research department—and also her aunt—she tensed, suspecting the worst. The two influential doctors must have changed the Board's decision. Distressed, she clutched her bag and turned.

Aunt Lana had arrived from San Francisco some months ago, after resigning her head teaching post on tropical diseases at the nursing school where Eden had graduated. When Lana, after much prayer and heart searching, accepted the position of working with Dr. Bolton in his quest to control the spread of leprosy in the islands, Eden had greeted the decision with joyous satisfaction. For, while her aunt would be working with Dr. Bolton, Eden, hired as her assistant, would be furthering her own knowledge as well.

Matters were coming together so well, Eden had thought at the time, until the man she loved, Rafe Easton, threw down the gauntlet in frustration. Was she to become his beloved wife and mother of their children, or risk her life as a nurse in the infamous Molokai leper colony?

Eden was dismayed. She had quietly planned during her nursing studies to work at her father's side when he returned from his world travels researching a cure for leprosy. Her beloved father, Dr. Jerome Derrington, was on extended leave from his staff position at Kalihi. The Hawaiian king, Kalakaua, had generously sponsored her father's travels, but after Kalakaua's death, the sponsorship revenue had dried up. Now the king's sister, Liliuokalani, was on the throne, though it was doubtful news of this had reached Dr. Jerome.

Rafe was right about one thing—she could not fulfill the roles of two women. Rafe was not a doctor, and he would not be living on Molokai. *His* ambitions lay elsewhere. She knew she should either follow his lead in marriage or remain single, and so she and Rafe had mutually agreed to end their engagement. A smile graced her lips as she remembered that warm, romantic evening when they'd walked the sands of Waikiki and he'd placed the diamond ring on her finger. The fact that it no longer sparkled there pained her. Confused at times, Eden struggled with her heart, and with her faith. A day did not go by without her asking God for guidance. There were times when she could not sleep at night for fear of losing the one man she had loved and wanted since she was a young girl. And there the conflict stood, unyielding; and while they knew of their love for one another, the emotional tension between them remained.

Eden's emotions churned as Aunt Lana hurried down the hospital steps. She should be the one to meet with Rafe over the Board's decision. If she could not show her concern now, he might become convinced that her professed feelings for him were shallow. She must not allow him to believe that!

Lana Stanhope, now in her thirties, had remained unmarried after a bitter disappointment with Dr. Bolton many years earlier. Eden believed, or at least hoped, that the old love between them had not truly perished amid the struggles of life and might still emerge like a seed during springtime thaw. Perhaps she was a sentimentalist. Perhaps she wanted to believe this of Lana and Dr. Bolton because they alerted her to what might be awaiting her and Rafe. She longed for happy endings, but knew enough Scripture to know there can be no happy endings apart from yielding to God's greater purposes. One could not sow seeds of willfulness and expect a harvest of purpose and peace. She also knew that a decision to obey God did not always bring a bountiful harvest in this short life, but sometimes awaited that hour when believers were rewarded at the *bema* seat of Christ.

Lana hurried toward her, carrying a small parcel. She was a tall, willowy woman, with thick honey-colored hair rolled up at the back of her neck. As she approached, Eden sympathetically noticed lines of fatigue at the corners of her hazel eyes.

"What a morning," Lana moaned, pushing strands of hair back into place. "My mind's in a whirl. This humidity is wilting me." She thrust the small parcel, tied with string, into Eden's hand.

"Since you're going to Hawaiiana, bring this to Great-aunt Nora, will you? It's her prescription from Dr. Bolton. She'll be at Rafe's, visiting with his mother."

Eden stared at the parcel, then cast a glance toward the hospital. "Great-aunt Nora's prescription? That's all?"

"Yes. That's all—for the moment. After you left, there was some discussion as to whether it was appropriate for you to represent them. Dr. Bolton won them over, however reluctantly. Eden, I don't like the situation you're facing. It might be wiser if I go as the Board's representative. Rafe Easton will be angry about what's happened and it's best if you're not associated with it."

"Lana, please don't. We've already been over this. I've explained to both you and Dr. Bolton how I must be the one to see Rafe about Kip. If I don't go to explain, he'll believe I don't care. I need to handle this." Though Eden kept her voice professionally calm, there was no way to fool Lana about her feelings for Rafe. The matter at hand was tearing her in two, and Lana knew only too well the signs of an injured heart—since she herself had carried one for years.

"I won't let them down," Eden assured her. She tightened one hand into a fist behind her back. They believed she lacked the professional fortitude to send a baby to the leper colony. Were they right? *Could I really send Kip back to the leper colony?*

"Of course you won't let us down," Lana said. "Dr. Bolton made it clear to them that you can be trusted. After all, if you're willing to work with your father when he returns from India, you surely have the courage to follow through on this."

Eden felt a prick. Her aunt's boast might not be as correct as they both hoped.

When her father returned, Lana had said. More like *if* her father returned!

Her heart thumped with emotion. Yes, he would return to Honolulu, just as she had always believed he would. How she had longed for and cherished those few letters he had sent from faraway places. Upon his return, she wanted Dr. Jerome Derrington to become in actuality what he was to her genetically. A father. *Her* father!

"You know, don't you, that Rafe will insist on knowing who informed the Board that Kip came from the Molokai leper colony?" Eden said.

Lana shook her head with frustration. "I know. But you saw the message that arrived for Dr. Bolton. We both did."

Yes, and she'd written the words down. Even so, Rafe would not let the matter end there. Of that Eden was certain.

When Rafe's merchant ship, the *Minoa*, had anchored in Honolulu last year after a two-year voyage to French Guiana, few knew there was something even more valuable than prized pineapple slips on board. *A baby boy*. Rafe had kept Kip alive by instructing the cook to prepare a canteen with the thumb from a leather glove tied at the opening, with a hole poked through it, so the baby could drink milk supplied by the ship's goat. Once safe in Honolulu Rafe had allowed a story to circulate that baby Kip was his nephew.

At the time, Eden had been distraught over the new child and could not accept Rafe's explanation. Later, asking for her avowed silence, Rafe secretly informed her Kip came from Molokai. Rafe had put in there to rendezvous with her father. Her father did not arrive for the meeting, however; a baby did. It was left abandoned on the beach.

Unable to walk away and leave the baby to the incoming tide, Rafe checked him all over for leprosy, saw no visible signs, and brought him aboard his vessel. Now Kip was like a son, and Rafe planned to adopt him. Yet, Kip posed a risk, and she must be the one to deliver the Board's decision that Kip must be returned to . . . a fate so heartbreaking she could not bear the thought.

"All right then, Eden," Lana was saying. "The matter about Rafe and Kip is in your hands. And remember," she added, tapping the parcel, "make certain your great-aunt takes her prescription this time. The directions are inside. It's just the regular dosages at morning and bedtime."

One of the nurses came out from the hospital and called for Lana, saying that Dr. Bolton needed to see her. As her aunt hurried back to her duties, Eden walked to the hackney that would bring her to Hawaiiana . . . and her meeting with Rafe Easton.

⸙

Ling Li and his ramshackle hackney sat waiting by a line of coconut palms. Of slight build, and wearing a straw-colored tunic and knee-pants, he climbed down from the driver's seat as Eden approached and offered her a cheerful grin and several short bows. His sing-song greeting seemed as cheerful to Eden's ears as the trill of the tropical birds. He knew many of the hospital staff from driving them around Honolulu.

For months she'd been planting seeds of Scripture in his mind, offering prayers that Ling would come to trust the only One who could save his precious soul. So far, her seed-sowing had not borne fruit.

"You have happy day, Miss Eden," was his usual pleasant greeting.

"Thank you, Ling. Please bring me to the mission church. From there I'll walk to Hawaiiana."

Eden lifted the hem of her gray dress from around her high-button shoes and stepped up into the hackney. As she sank onto the sagging, horsehair-upholstered seat, the old sway-backed horse moved slowly down the street in the direction of Pearl River.

Above the clocking of horse hooves she began her conversation with a few scriptural truths. She had grown attached to the good-humored old man and was anxious about his soul. Ling would merely grin and taunt her with his light-hearted dismissals. "Woman preaching. Woman preaching no good."

"Then when will you come to the mission church to hear Ambrose teach the men?" she asked. "They meet in his hut each Monday night at seven. He tells them many important things from God. Don't you want to know what they are?"

Eden smiled at the old man when he rubbed his nose. "No food there," he said, his eyes twinkling. "Noelani not cook like wife."

Noelani, Ambrose's wife, was a *hapa-haole*. Her father had been a Yankee whaler out of New Bedford, and her mother claimed a relationship with a royal cousin, though that could never be proven.

Eden knew that Ling Li was teasing her about Noelani's cooking, for she was known as a most excellent cook, and on Monday nights she served the most delicious coconut cake in the islands.

"You fib, Ling Li. You come on Monday. And how are all your children? Are they and your wife well?"

He wrinkled his brow, shaking his head. "Mother of Ling Li's sons is well. Youngest son, he not well."

Eden came alert. "What's wrong with number seven son?"

"Number seven son have bad pain in head, and he hot with fever. Sick since he go to Rat Alley."

Rat Alley, the area in Honolulu where the Chinese sugar cane workers lived, packed together in lean-to shacks, had rats in abundance. They came from the wharf's shipping business and had the potential to spread sicknesses from all ports of the world.

Eden tensed at this news. "Where is he now? I will come see him. Bring me to him."

Ling Li shook his head. "Can no do, Miss Eden. He go to Rat Alley to be with Great-uncle Woo. Woo good doctor. Great-uncle take care for number seven son. He have ancient medicine from Shanghai." He added slyly, "Much older than *haole* medicine."

"Nevertheless, I should look at him too. Maybe the haole medicine can help your son get well. You bring your son to Kea Lani this afternoon."

He sucked through his teeth as he considered. "He with Great-uncle Woo. Have plenny work. I come tomorrow morning. Mebbe."

She decided she would send a message to Lana to follow through, just in case Ling didn't bring his son to Kea Lani.

"Number seven son not have *mai Pake*," he said, meaning leprosy.

She understood why he would try to assure her of this. Native Hawaiians called leprosy by the Chinese name, *mai Pake*. Since the disease had at first been associated with the arrival of Chinese workers on the sugar plantations, the native Hawaiians called leprosy a "Chinese curse." The Chinese sugar workers preferred to be left to the ancient wisdom of their medicine men, who sold treatments to the afflicted, usually herbs or Black Rhino horn ground into a powder. The rhino horn cured nothing, but it did require the death of an African rhino for nothing more than his horn!

As for blaming the Chinese for bringing leprosy to the Hawaiian islands, Eden believed this was probably unfair, since the medical profession did not know for certain where the first cases had come from. All they knew was that the disease had been on the islands before the first missionaries arrived from America. Such diseases had a way of traveling from port to port around the world. She was well aware that there was ample sin for the blame to be shared by all, for the Scriptures clearly taught that all have sinned and fallen short of God's righteousness.

"Like all disease, it touches the innocent and the guilty," she told Ling Li. "Even little children get ill, and babies die at birth. They've done nothing wrong; it's just that we're all born into Adam's fallen race. Disease is not usually caused by individual sin, although we have all sinned in God's sight."

"I no sin."

"Disease, death, and sin is a 'family' affair, touching all in Adam's race."

"Adam? Nobody to me."

She smiled. "Without *our* father, Adam, you would not be here, Ling."

"Eh, so *you* say."

"All of Adam's children are born spiritual lepers."

He looked at his hand, without lesions. "I no leper. Ling Li all clean, see?" He lifted his rough calloused hand with knotty knuckles. "Clean," he repeated.

"One day the Lord will win you over and make your heart clean."

"One day Miss Eden win over everybody. Because Miss Eden very nice girl." Then, seeing her smile, his eyes twinkled again. "Wife say so about you—not me. Ling Li never be won over. Ling Li very bad."

"True. Ling Li, is *very* bad," she retorted, in a teasing tone, "and that's why you need a *very* perfect Savior."

"I think about it. But I think more some other day. Head very tired now."

Eden settled in for the short ride as the hackney jolted along the narrow street. The morning had proven demanding, just as Aunt Lana had said. Eden was grateful for a reprieve and leaned back into the seat for a few undisturbed minutes. She loosened a wooden button near her throat and relished the trade wind blowing warm and moist.

The Pacific came into view and she could just make out the greenish-blue haze she knew to be the glove-shaped island of Molokai with its leper settlement, Kalaupapa. Once again the tragedy of her mother, Rebecca, came to mind, bringing feelings of regret and wishful thinking.

If only she could have known her mother.

Though her mother had been incarcerated at the settlement for years, Eden had learned of the tragedy only two months ago from Grandfather Ainsworth, and only because of Rafe's insistence. "If Eden is not told the truth, I'll tell her myself," he told Ainsworth. "She actually suspects her mother was murdered."

The Derrington family, with her Grandfather's permission, had kept Rebecca's condition a secret for over a decade because the pervading culture of business and society shunned anyone connected with the sickness. Uncle Townsend in particular wanted the matter hidden because he was running for the Hawaiian legislature, and he had warned, "It will give my opponent something even *more* devastating to use against me." Even so, her uncle's political race had not gone smoothly, because of his own moral leprosy. He'd been young at the time, politically inexperienced, spoiled, and unfaithful in his marriage.

It had been the Derrington name that helped Uncle Townsend win his seat in the Legislature. Now, many years later, he still held it, though he hadn't changed for the wiser, and his sinful ways were occasionally mentioned in the small Honolulu newspapers that opposed his political views.

Eden bristled over the fact that the family had concealed her mother's condition. Since childhood she'd naturally accepted what she'd been told—that her mother was dead. Then, as Eden matured, there had been several bewildering contradictions that caused the story to unravel. In her confusion she began to suspect that Rebecca may have been murdered. Meanwhile, during Eden's troubling years of doubt, her grieving father, driven by some haunting passion that savaged his strength, had traveled the exotic world seeking the cure that would set his wife free. *If there was any shame, it was that the truth was kept from me all those many years.*

Ling Li pulled to the side of the road, bringing the hackney to a shuddering halt.

"What is it? Why are we stopping, Ling?"

He hissed. "Must stop. Stay in seat."

Eden leaned forward and looked across the road. She recognized a group of islanders being escorted single file from the quarantine station to the wharf where they would board the *Kilauea*, a steamer licensed by the Board of Health to transport lepers into forced exile at Molokai. For all the times she had witnessed this tragic scene, she could never look upon the lepers with the professional detachment of the Board of Health doctors. For the most part these lepers were without faith in God, without hope of ever returning to home or family, and doomed to a solitary life of hardship ending in dismal death.

On the deck of the steamer were rows of cages where the lepers would be confined for the fifty-eight-mile voyage. Once the steamer reached Molokai and neared the section of beach where the lepers were to be left, they would be given a bundle of meager supplies allotted to them by the Hawaiian government. Then the landing boats would be lowered into the sea for the perilous ride through the surf to the rocky shoreline. High waves had on occasion caused some to drown before reaching land. The lepers would be off-loaded near the rocky shore, or directly into the sea if rough breakers prevented a landing. Those that reached the beach often died within a few short years from health complications, such as pneumonia, during the rainy season. The huts they lived in were leaky, and when the patients grew weak from their disease, they were unable to go out and gather wood for warmth and cooking. Though the government gave them taro roots for planting, not all had the strength to do so, and many wasted away. Still, others lived on for many years.

Is there not some better way? she thought again. Surely there must be, but the Board of Health was out of money. The past king had squandered finances on his extravagant lifestyle, and now his sister, the present queen, insisted that conditions on Molokai would not be improved because Hawaii was deeply in debt. *If only someone could tour churches in America,* thought Eden, *telling Christians of the dreadful fate of the Molokai lepers and raising money for assistance and better dwellings.* She would be willing to go, especially if Lana or Dr. Bolton could accompany her.

Eden was especially grateful that her father had arranged for her mother to have a bungalow at Kalaupapa. He had also paid for a *kokua* woman to live with her. A kokua was a servant who did not have leprosy, but was willing to risk the disease to care for the person. Many times they ended up with leprosy as well, but it was part of the grave risk they knew they were taking. Eden had tried to discover the name of Rebecca's kokua, but no one in the family apparently knew. It was a sad statement on their lack of interest in Jerome Derrington's wife, an ordinary teacher at the Royal School.

Eden was still trying to discover the kokua's identity. She wanted to reward her, if alive, with whatever she and her mother needed. Eden considered that no one in the Derrington family actually knew for certain if Rebecca was still alive. She had personally done what she could to learn of her mother's condition, but the matter remained hazy. She had written her father, telling him she'd learned about her mother, but hadn't heard back from him yet. He was due to arrive back in Honolulu within the year, however, and then she would know everything. She would even make the trip to Molokai —something she now dreamed about—with Dr. Jerome Derrington leading the way.

As the group of lepers marched to the pier, they were followed by great wailings of lamentation from family and friends. The Hawaiians going about their normal business drew away from the pier when they recognized the wailing, as though they expected poisonous vipers to lunge out and sink sharp fangs into their legs. Some of the lepers had been in hiding until bounty hunters tracked them down. These were far enough along in the crippling disease to offend the sensibilities of the crowd. They hobbled up the ramp on feet with rotting toes, using canes to achieve an awkward balance. Others had only recently contracted the disease and were still whole except for a missing earlobe or a bright spot on the cheek. Many of them wept in despair, seeing what they would become in time. Still, there were those who boarded the ship with dignity, shoulders back and heads held high. One young man smiled as he waved a salute to family. "Only for a short time," he called, "and then I'll be home with the Lord." His family waved their good-bye, then bowed their heads in prayer.

The guards kept their distance, using long poles to urge the line up the ramp, as though prodding cattle. Their faces were as stoic as the medical practitioners.

No matter how many times Eden viewed this tragic scene, she could never keep the professional lid on her emotions. These people once had hopes and plans, and now their lives had come to this. Those sent to Molokai never returned.

"It's the hopelessness of their situation that's so dreadful," she told Ling. "Leprosy in the Bible is a picture of incurable sin. Lepers would stand far off and cry, 'Unclean! Unclean!' so that others would not come near. Only the sinless One, Jesus, was able to touch and cure a leper."

Eden watched with deep emotion as men, women, and even two children were hurried toward the gangplank. She remembered the two children. Dr. Bolton had spoken of them with sorrow and frustration. "What could I do? It pains my heart. If I'd left either of them with their mother, the disease could contaminate her and break out among relatives. Where they came by it, no one knows."

The children's mother, wearing a yellow *muumuu*, followed barefoot in the wake of the guards, wailing inconsolably.

"*Auwe! Auwe! Auwe!*" the pitiable cry continued.

The two children, huddled together, captured Eden's attention. Scared and bewildered, they clung to each other like Hansel and Gretel, looking back over their shoulders at their wailing mother. The pathetic sight tore at Eden's heart.

The other lepers seemed not to notice. Like men already dead, forever separated from their mournful relatives, they shuffled up the gangway to board the *Kilauea*.

Eden grasped Ling's shoulder. He flinched, startled. "Drive me closer."

He moaned his displeasure.

"You're safe," she assured him. "Doctor Bolton's staff examines lepers every day. Please, Ling."

He did so, the horse walking slowly nearer.

A larger throng gathered along the wharf now, watching. More wailing filled the air. The two children kept crying and looking back as the guard hurried them up the gangway. The woman tore at her hair with a wail and broke through the onlookers, running toward her children.

"I go with them," she cried. "I die with them—be their kokua."

The stone-faced captain shook his head. "Nay, woman, ye make a big mistake. Go and you'll never come back. You'll become a leper. Return to your husband."

"Husband gone, and my little flowers are still buds. I go with them."

As she screamed and pleaded, a Hawaiian guard rushed forward to restrain her. The captain spat tobacco juice and lifted a silencing hand. "You cannot come without legal papers. I've no time to wait."

"I cannot leave them!" she cried. Struggling, kicking, and screaming hysterically, she managed to twist free from the guards and clawed her way past the others. By this time the two children were wailing as loudly as she. The guards caught her again, this time roughly holding her arms behind her. She fell to her knees weeping.

Eden glared, climbing down from the hackney in order to reprimand the guards in the name of the Board of Health. At that moment the captain intervened. In a loud voice he shouted, "Do you vow before these many witnesses ye want this damnable fate?"

"I go with my children!"

"As ye will, then, woman. Come! Ye'll soon be numbered among the lepers."

Eden stood there, numb. The wind shook her straw sun hat. She watched the woman run to the children and gather them to her bosom like two trembling chicks, now safe beneath her wings. The throng fell silent.

Eden's thoughts flashed to the only one in all recorded history who could touch a leper and say, "Be clean." Jesus came as the spotless Lamb of God to a world of spiritual lepers, who in God's holy view, were as loathsome as these physical lepers. But Jesus, who cleansed physical leprosy, thought it more important that men be cleansed from spiritual leprosy. Sinful men who believed in His atoning death and resurrection became purified children of God, without spot or blemish. She remembered what Jesus had spoken to Mary Magdalene in the garden after His bodily resurrection: "I ascend unto *my* Father, and *your* Father." *Now*, Eden thought, *because of Jesus, God can be my Father.*

Chapter Two
Cousin Zachary...and Silas

*T*he sprightly beat of horse hooves cut through the sobering moment at the pier. Eden turned toward the road to face an oncoming buggy, a smart new one, with leather seats and crimson fringe. The driver, a haole, maneuvered his horse up beside Ling's dilapidated hackney.

Cousin Zachary Derrington was splendidly fair, and his white shirt, rolled up at the sleeves, displayed strong, tanned arms. The cleft in his chin was nearly as pronounced as his father, Townsend's, and his eyes were a pale blue, as cool as a glacier and dusted with gold lashes. Eden lamented that Zachary's scandal-ridden father, Townsend Derrington, with his seat in the Hawaiian legislature, had done little to lead his son Zachary down the right and honorable path.

Zachary's golden hair showed beneath his taupe-colored hat with its silk ribbon band. He clutched the reins of a sleek and restless auburn horse. The Pacific breeze caught the canopy's gaudy crimson fringe and sent it shivering. For two months now the brash, toothy smile on her cousin's face had been replaced by an expression of gloom and resentment. She braced herself for an onslaught of anxious concerns.

"Eden! I need to talk to you."

Stepping down from the seat, wearing fawn-colored riding habit and shiny boots, he winced when his weight shifted to his left leg. Had he injured himself?

He left his buggy and came around to where she stood beside the hackney. Maybe he'd hurt his leg riding one of Rafe's new horses. The men did share one interest in common. Both loved purebred horses imported from California—and sometimes risked their lives to tame and ride them!

Zachary's brows were furrowed. Since childhood he'd manifested emotional disturbances of one sort or another, some so troubling he'd been under a doctor's care in a home. It wasn't until she'd had the recent privilege of leading his troubled soul to faith in Christ that he'd become a more genial personality. Even now there were times when he became so emotionally upset he'd take the medication prescribed by Dr. Bolton.

Eden had a special sympathy for Zachary. He'd become the brother she'd never had. Zachary had become amenable to the relationship, though at one time he'd refused to believe she was a true Derrington and contested Rafe for her attentions. All that was past; he understood she was his blood cousin and treated her so. He often confided in her to share his frustrations with his father, Townsend, Eden's uncle.

"Are you going home to Kea Lani?" he asked, taking her bag from the hackney. "I've a meeting there—with—*my father*," he said, choking on the word as though it were bitter.

She looked at him, uneasy. *Trouble again.* No doubt over his half-brother, Silas. "I won't be going to Kea Lani until this evening. Right now I'm on my way to the mission church for a chat with Ambrose, then over to Rafe's. Great-aunt Nora is there. I've a new prescription for her."

Zachary nodded, but his thoughts appeared to be elsewhere.

He was only half attending to what she said.

Eden paid Ling Li, and the hackney clattered back toward Kalihi Hospital. Then she walked with her cousin to his buggy. He stowed her bag and helped her in, then went around and swung himself into the seat, wincing slightly.

"How did you injure your leg?"

His jaw tightened as he touched his left knee. "Oh, it's nothing. I must have twisted it a little the other day."

Eden scanned his features. He was behaving oddly. She wondered why.

With a flip of the reins Zachary guided the fancy buggy down the palm-lined dirt road. "Since you're going to stop at the little church, I'll bring you as far as the turnoff to Kea Lani. I can't be late for my meeting." Zachary's scowl deepened. "Besides, I'd just as soon not accompany you to Ambrose's."

She removed her wide-brimmed hat and pulled her dark hair away from her neck, where it had come loose from the roll. "An odd admission to make. Why wouldn't you care to visit our beloved Ambrose?"

He scowled. "It's not Ambrose, but . . . well, okay, I'll tell you. Remember the Bible study he started for several of us young men a few months back?"

"Yes, of course. You, Rafe, and Keno. I've been urging Ling Li to join you, even though he's older. Not that it should matter, except he'll feel out of place."

"Ling *who?*" he scowled, his brows twitched in a nervous habit.

"Ling Li. You know, the dear old Chinese hackney driver. He's pretty much of a set piece around Kalihi grounds."

"Oh, him." Zachary sounded distracted.

"Well, Ling Li isn't young, as I said," she went on, "and he'd likely stand out, but—"

"Never mind *him*, Eden. He's just a coolie." He frowned at her. "You're always preaching to people. Women aren't supposed to do that sort of work."

The Derringtons can be such awful snobs, she thought.

"Anyway," and he moved a shoulder impatiently, "I've been too busy to attend a study on Monday nights. He left off in the Bible somewhere in an uncomfortable chapter—I think it was Romans chapter one. I suppose Ambrose will call me on it. My not being at the meetings, I mean."

"Oh come," she said with a laugh. "As if Ambrose carries a whip! You know very well he's one of the warmest, most fatherly pastors we've had since we were children. If anything, he'd welcome you back like the prodigal."

Zachary cracked a smile as if his face hurt. "Oh I know. Actually, I haven't been away *that* long. Just since April."

She recognized the defensive tone in his voice. *April? What happened in April?* Then she remembered. Silas Derrington, Zachary's half brother, had arrived from Louisiana in April.

"I'm not the only one who's been absent from the Monday meetings." He shot her a glance, as though about to reveal something. "Rafe hasn't been showing up either."

She refused to respond. Ambrose was Rafe's blood uncle. They were close, and Rafe supported his missionary endeavors. *So why hasn't Rafe been attending?*

They rode in silence. Zachary glanced at her. "I'd better get on with the *real* news. Cousin Candace is over at Rafe's new plantation, isn't she?"

"Yes, she's visiting with Rafe's mother. Why do you ask?" She scanned his tense face with curiosity.

Rafe's mother, the ailing Celestine, widowed after the accidental death of Matt Easton, had made a great error some years ago when she agreed to marry Zachary's father, Townsend Derrington. The marriage had swiftly turned unhappy for Celestine, as many feared it would, and it had made Rafe and Zachary stepbrothers. It had also given Townsend Derrington rights over Easton property.

Rafe and Zachary were related through the mismatched marriage of their widowed parents, and though they'd spent much of

their growing-up years on different plantations, they had often quar-
reled, their temperaments and plans being worlds apart. As Eden
well knew from past experiences, Zachary was usually at fault.
Thankfully, the two men were friendly now, and she attributed the
change to Zachary's conversion.

Silas Derrington, on the other hand, had been a total stranger
to Zachary and Rafe until his staggering arrival in April. Rafe had
seen Silas a few times at some of the festive plantation gatherings
held by the bigger island families like the Derringtons, Hunnewells,
Judsons, Landrys, and Eastons, but recently Rafe claimed he was
too busy with the new pineapple plantation to spend much time on
festivities. Even Eden hadn't seen Rafe since they ended their
engagement two months ago.

"Great-aunt Nora's also at Rafe's," Eden emphasized, wondering
where Zachary's uneasy expression was trying to lead her. "If you
think Candace and Rafe are—"

"No, not at all." Zachary waved an impatient hand. "It's clear
what woman Rafe wants." His mouth twitched.

Eden looked away. She wished she could be as certain. He'd ended
the engagement at her request readily enough. She frowned to herself.
She would have expected him to at least protest or to again vow his
undying love, but he hadn't. If she would permit her heart to brood
over another woman, it wouldn't be Candace that concerned her, but
Bunny Judson, Parker Judson's niece in San Francisco. She'd best
not mention Bunny now—Zachary had fallen for her during the
holiday season last year.

Continuing, Zachary observed, "Grandfather wanted Rafe to
marry Candace last year, but Rafe, in his distinctively polite but
blunt way, said no."

Eden remained inscrutable, and switched topics. "Even though
Celestine hasn't been well lately, Great-aunt Nora is at the planta-
tion to gain political support for Queen Liliuokalani." She looked at
Zachary, studying his troubled face.

His shoulder jerked in frustration. "Of course she isn't well.

What woman could be at peace in mind or soul married to *my* father, roustabout of the islands?"

Eden was sadly accustomed to Zachary's bitterness. The problems between son and father had raged for many years, extending well beyond Townsend's immoral reputation to include the criticism he'd heaped upon Zachary since childhood. And now, ever since Townsend's illegitimate son, Silas, had appeared two months ago, Townsend praised Silas's abilities at Zachary's expense.

Zachary flicked the reins, frowning. The horse trotted at a faster clip.

"A cable came this morning from San Francisco. Grandfather Ainsworth should be arriving today."

"*Today?*"

"Yes, this afternoon."

"But Cousin Candace is at Rafe's!"

"Exactly. Since Grandfather asked Candace not to see Keno while he was away in Washington D.C., there will be trouble if he arrives and finds her at Rafe's. You'd better warn her."

Candace's love for Keno was known by the family, and, like Grandfather Ainsworth, they disapproved. The fact that Keno was a steadfast Christian would not change Grandfather's mind, "though I like the young fellow for it," he had faintly offered.

Eden had been present on several occasions when their Grandfather had gently but firmly reminded Candace that, "such a marriage was not plausible."

"You're the only child of Douglas," he'd said of his firstborn son, who'd drowned at sea together with Candace's mother in a shipping accident. "I've placed you as my primary heir, Candace my dear, and you simply must live up to the honor of your father, Douglas A. Derrington."

The "better" plans Grandfather Ainsworth had made for his favorite granddaughter did not include her marriage to the *hapa-haole* Keno, even if he did have an "Englishman from a good family" for a father. The Englishman had left for England without a backward glance, even before Keno's first cry was heard.

Grandfather had replaced the loss of his firstborn son, Douglas, with Candace, often smothering her unintentionally with family plans. "You're a fine Derrington," he would say.

Candace complained, "The shoes don't fit, Grandfather, and they never will." But Ainsworth merely smiled. He believed that if they didn't fit now, they eventually would.

Zachary shook his blond head. "That's not the worst of the news. Grandfather isn't returning alone. There are several people from San Francisco in his party, including Oliver P. Hunnewell. This is going to be Candace's dark hour, I'm afraid."

Oliver P. Hunnewell was Ainsworth's choice to become Candace's husband. Several years ago, their grandfather began forging an alliance with the highly respected George F. Hunnewell of San Francisco and Honolulu with this in mind. The Hunnewell family was well known in society and respected by others with wealth and power. George F. Hunnewell was one of the mighty sugar kings in California, along with Parker Judson and Eden's own family, the Derringtons. Certain newspapers had named them "the Big Three."

"Candace thinks she can avoid this marriage," Zachary said, gloom returning to his voice. "She'd like to love and live unpretentiously with Keno in a little grass hut. I told her she doesn't realize what she's coming up against when the Derrington patriarchs want to expand the sugar industry and enter politics."

"I believe she does know," Eden said. "Candace is no girlish simpleton. She's not after a 'grass hut' as you suggest, but a man who is a strong Christian. She's already told me she won't marry a man, no matter how wealthy and important he is, if he's not a believer."

"Well, Oliver *is* a believer. So she has no recourse where Grandfather's concerned. All the Hunnewells are Christians. They come from missionary stock, same as us—and Rafe Easton, for that matter. His father just lost his wealth, that's all, and now Rafe's planning on getting it back. As for Oliver, he even goes to church most Sundays."

"Unless it's raining, or too hot, or he'd rather sleep late," she said lightly.

"When he's home in the islands, he does go to Kawaiahao." Kawaiahao, the historical missionary church was across the street from the royal Iolani Palace.

Eden grew serious. "Candace doesn't think he's sincere, Zachary. He's what she calls a nominal Christian, whereas Keno is genuine."

"And, she loves him. I know." He grew quiet a moment. "Well, she knows I'm all for her. And she knows she can count on you, too. The thing is, her simple piety just won't work in this situation. Not with Grandfather. Wait and see."

"It's not just piety. She wants a firm foundation to build her life and family on, not piles of sugar-gold."

"Oh I know, I know. It's just that Derrington marriages have always been this way—first approved by the patriarchs. Except for Uncle Jerome's, that is." He glanced at her. "When he married your mother it was against all the family rules—and he's paid, too."

Yes, he paid in full, Eden thought, refusing to take offense from Zachary's thoughtless words. They had all paid. Her father, her mother, and she herself.

"And what about me?" he added. "Candace is not the only one whose marriage is prearranged. It's my duty as a Derrington to marry Claudia Hunnewell, Oliver's sister!"

Eden couldn't help but laugh, for he looked so self-sacrificing. "Poor Zachary. It's your *suffering duty for the Derrington name* to marry Claudia, who at one time you wanted more than all the gold in the world."

His face showed humor for the first time. He was boyish and handsome when he relaxed.

"Well, maybe Claudia Hunnewell *and* piles of gold. As a matter of fact, I'd take Bunny Judson for nothing, though I haven't seen her since she was out here visiting her uncle Parker for Christmas." His smile vanished. "And she hasn't answered my letters."

Eden recalled that Bunny Judson went home to San Francisco

to stay with her ailing mother. She was surprised, though, that Parker Judson's beautiful niece hadn't answered Zachary's letters. She had given the impression that she enjoyed his attention—along with Rafe Easton's.

He looked over at her. "What will Grandfather say when he learns you and Rafe Easton have parted ways over your plan to work with lepers?"

Eden's smile faded and she became uncomfortable. *Yes, just what would Grandfather Ainsworth say?* In the past he'd had disagreements with Rafe and the Easton family, but matters were at last coming to a peaceful end, though Rafe still awaited the rightful return of Hanalei, his father's Kona coffee plantation on the Big Island. At least her grandfather and Rafe had settled upon a truce before the trip to Washington D.C.

"I was wrong about Rafe," her grandfather had told her reminiscently, rubbing his goatee. "I'm pleased you want to marry him. Rafe's bringing those prized pineapple slips from French Guiana was quite a feat. Shows real spunk. I wish I'd made amends with him before he partnered with Parker Judson on that new plantation. If I'd been wiser, I'd have seen it coming with Rafe. He's like Matt Easton," he said of Rafe's deceased father. "Rafe will be one to reckon with. Yes, he'll make me a strong right arm."

What would she say? Glancing down at her empty ring finger made her uneasy. Had she made a foolish mistake?

She broke the silence without answering Zachary's question. "Maybe you could go to Candace and explain about Grandfather and Oliver Hunnewell. I need to stop at the church first to speak with Ambrose." She, too, had troubling news to deliver—to Rafe. "Can you bring Candace back to Kea Lani before Grandfather arrives?"

He shook his head, looking gloomy once more. "No, Townsend's at Kea Lani waiting for me right now. I dare not show up late. I'm headed straight there once I bring you to Ambrose's."

The tension in his voice was unmistakable. Zachary rarely called

Townsend "Father," a sad result of their failed father-son relationship.

"Silas is there, too," he added. "Townsend demanded a meeting between the three of us."

The cause for the meeting was no secret to Eden. Grandfather Ainsworth hadn't been pleased with Zachary's behavior. Although her grandfather was a moral man who had not forgotten his missionary roots, he was also one of the most politically influential planters in Hawaii, and a comrade to Claus Spreckels and Parker Judson, two of the California sugar kings. Grandfather Ainsworth and Townsend had expected Zachary to become a strong leader so he could one day take over the Derrington sugar enterprise. Eden believed their expectations were unfair, and she knew Zachary felt the weight of their disappointment.

Eden also understood Zachary's hostility toward his father and Silas. Silas had appeared at Kea Lani plantation one morning while the family was gathered on the lanai for breakfast. Walking right up to the table, he calmly introduced himself as Silas *Townsend* Derrington, placing great emphasis on that middle name.

As Eden remembered that life-altering scene on the lanai, she could still feel the appalling emotions that settled over those seated around the breakfast table. It seemed as though a full minute passed before anyone spoke. Townsend appeared as though he might fall out of his cane chair, but then his bravado pulled him through the moment, and he took control, boldly addressing the boy. "Well, well, Silas. When did you arrive in Honolulu? You should have let us know. I'd have had someone meet you and bring you here to Kea Lani. So, what do you think of the Derrington sugar plantation?" He acted as if the young man's appearance was no more than a family member dropping by unexpectedly.

With the arrival of Silas Derrington, Townsend began making public overtures that Zachary found alarming. Who knew which way the family winds would blow? It would depend on Grandfather Ainsworth's reaction when he returned. Grandfather had been in

Washington D.C., when Silas arrived, so he too would be in for a surprise that afternoon. He now had another grandson—an *illegitimate* one. How would he respond to Silas? The injustice Townsend had done to both Zachary and to Silas had angered Eden.

Silas was perhaps the one who had suffered most for his father's sin, though Zachary would certainly disagree. Townsend, meanwhile, continued to show himself calloused enough in conscience to proceed on his life's journey without apparent guilt toward God, his wife, or either of his two sons. How that was possible, Eden often wondered.

"'A real *man*, my son Silas,'" Zachary mimicked Townsend's voice. "'Takes after me, his father.'"

Eden, incredulous, looked at him. Had Townsend actually said this in front of Zachary? The anger on his face confirmed it.

"That's what he said," Zachary choked. "Said it right in front of me to some of the legislators at the Iolani Palace dinner meeting last night. And all I could do was to stand there embarrassed, my feet glued to the floor. He boasts of the relationship growing strong between him and his 'firstborn son,' Silas." He gritted. "It brings him pleasure, he said. And Silas *illegitimate*. But me? Oh, no. Not a word, even though I've been loyal to him all my life."

Eden was aware of Townsend's favoritism toward Silas, and flaunting it publicly was unwise, serving only to feed jealousy and competition between the brothers. She could see jealousy, like an adder, sinking poisonous fangs into weak human flesh—Zachary's. The tensions were increasing with time, and she saw no promise of resolution. If her uncle Townsend acted with impatience and recrimination, as he was likely to do, he would be adding fuel to the fire.

Was any good to come from Silas's return to Honolulu? Perhaps Grandfather Ainsworth's forthcoming response would put an end to Townsend's behavior.

"I'll try to warn Candace about Grandfather's arrival as soon as I leave Ambrose," she said.

Eden gazed off toward the pale blue water and clear sky. The palms rustled lazily in the tropic breeze beside the road. Just beyond the horizon a storm appeared to be building. Eden sensed that trouble would indeed come to test them all.

Keep thy heart with all diligence; for out of it are the issues of life, she quoted from Proverbs 4:23. *Lord help us Derringtons,* she prayed. *We are all walking the cliff's edge, where our hearts and convictions are concerned. To accomplish Your purpose for our lives is the true cause that will matter in the end.*

Chapter Three
Ambrose

*Z*achary drove along the narrow dirt road toward the little missionary church established by Eden's parents. The familiar bungalow for Ambrose and Noelani stood nearby, a welcoming sight for Eden. Noelani would be up at Hawaiiana caring for baby Kip while Ambrose was home preparing for the Sunday service.

Her cousin halted the buggy near the roadside and was about to climb down to assist her, but she remembered his injured knee and stopped him.

"Zachary, before I go . . . don't think I'm trying to interfere, because I understand how you feel. But saying too much to your father in Silas's presence can't strengthen your cause. Wait until Grandfather is home, then tell him how you feel about Silas. Remember, Grandfather doesn't yet know."

His face was glum. "Sometimes I wonder. Grandfather appears to know more than he ever expresses."

"Yes, but he's never approved of your father's ways with women. Let Grandfather handle Townsend *and* Silas."

He nodded. "Don't worry. I won't go after Silas with flying fists."

Under his breath he added, "Though sometimes I'd like to teach him a lesson."

She winced. Silas looked as though he might be able to defend himself too well. She could have reminded her cousin that he was a Christian now, and Christians did not use their fists to settle family disagreements, but Zachary often told her she was too preachy. As far as she was concerned, it just made good sense to remind him of what the Scriptures taught. . . .

"Remember," he asked. "Try to get Candace and Great-aunt Nora here before Grandfather arrives this afternoon, will you?"

She dismounted from the buggy, feeling a warm gust of moist Pacific air rustling her gray nurse's dress with its red cross. She watched soberly as Zachary turned the horse and buggy onto Derrington property, where a secondary road led to the plantation house built in the days of Grandfather Ainsworth's father.

As Zachary rode away, her restive mind could envision strife personified as jackals running close at the buggy's wheels, nipping and snarling as Zachary set out to keep the meeting. "We have your emotions," she imagined them boasting. "You'll soon be ours to parcel out like a dead rabbit."

The mission church spoke to her of peace, for within rested the treasure chest of truth that would answer all debates and silence the quarreling voices of strife. The wooden building stood across the road on a gardened plot of land once owned by the Derringtons but now part of a larger acreage sold by her uncle Townsend to Parker Judson. When Rafe had agreed to a partnership with Parker Judson to develop the pineapple plantation using the prized slips Rafe brought from French Guiana, he'd gone out of his way to negotiate with Parker Judson to allow the historical church to remain untouched on its own special plot of ground, along with Ambrose's house. For that act of faith and devotion on Rafe's part, she loved him all the more.

Eden quickened her steps, turning her thoughts to the new problem she must deal with. Ambrose could advise her, as he had been doing since her childhood, and he would pray for her when she went to speak with Rafe about Kip. Ambrose was a bedrock in her life. He had always been there for her while her father, Dr. Jerome, was away on his quest.

She hurried along the path past the pearl fishery once belonging to Matt Easton, but now controlled by uncle Townsend since he'd married Celestine.

The sun was warm, and she resettled her fiber sun hat while the trade wind, smelling of the sea, stirred around her and flirted with the tropical foliage, weaving mysterious patterns and hinting of many adventures yet to come. She smiled, wondering what those adventures might be.

Eden neared the church, nestled among the palm trees and topped by a white cross. The cross beckoned to the weary and sin burdened, and the door was placed perfectly in the center, for "Jesus is the true door that opens to forgiveness and access to the Father," her father had said.

Inside there were no fancy furnishings or stained glass murals, only wooden pews and plain, square windows. As she stepped onto the bare wooden floor, the familiar grit of beach sand greeted the soles of her shoes. Somehow the sand always found its way inside. It did not matter, though, for in this little church amid the soft rustle of palms and the distant breaking of waves, Eden felt a fellowship with heaven. She suspected she was sentimentally inclined toward the church as a link to join her heart to her parents because they had established it before her birth.

When several Hawaiians working for the Derrington family in the pearl fishery had made professions of faith and were baptized— in the pearl fishery—her father, Jerome, had requested land from his father, Ainsworth, to build the church. A missionary friend of Jerome and Rebecca had served as pastor until the American mission board transferred him to the Big Island.

Jerome, with Rebecca's help, had managed to keep the church open until the tragedy of leprosy struck Rebecca and she'd been sent to Molokai. Her father, a broken man, had then departed the islands in search of a cure.

After that, Ambrose had stepped in to carry on the work as lay minister. The Bible teaching had borne lasting fruit when a nearly blind Hawaiian woman became his first female convert. That woman had been Noelani's mother. The entire family had turned to the Lord, and Ambrose eventually married Noelani.

Now that Eden knew Rebecca was a leper on Molokai, she understood why her father had immersed himself in his work of trying to find a cure. His dedication to all the lepers on Molokai had spurred him on to travel the world doing medical research for Kalihi Hospital. Despite his prolonged absences—she had seen him only a dozen times since Rebecca's incarceration at the leper colony—there remained a special connection between them.

He had not written much to her in those early years, but later, as she grew older, his letters would arrive filled with news of the world's medical needs. Eden found them anything but dull. As the years continued his fiery, John Brown–style passion for his cause inspired her to share his feelings. Perhaps it had been his fascinating letters, written from steamy jungles in South America and the Far East, that helped forge her decision to enter the medical profession. Joining the Kalihi staff at the hospital had been her choice, and now more than ever, knowing her mother yet lived, she was determined to follow her father from Kalihi Hospital to Molokai if given the opportunity.

Eden walked the narrow aisle toward the cubicle that Ambrose used for his office. The enclosure was piled with pulpit commentaries, some of which she'd bought for him in San Francisco and sent by steamer, and it provided a quiet place to pray. He needed the solitude, for Noelani's many Hawaiian brothers and sisters and nieces and nephews loved to call on them, so their small house was often hectic with visitors.

Ambrose must have heard her steps, for he stood up in the cubicle and looked out into the small sanctuary.

He was a big man, and at age sixty had developed a rounded middle, but unlike her tall, slim Grandfather Ainsworth, Pastor Ambrose's stolid stance and dark, smiling eyes brought her a sense of paternal security. Ambrose's usually sleek silver hair was tousled, as though he might have been praying on his knees with his head in both hands, as he often did.

"Well, Eden, my dear, come in, come in. I guess you know Noelani's up at the big house? Nora and Candace are there also."

"Yes, I know, but I wanted to talk to you first if you have time."

"There's always time for what matters most. Come up to the bungalow, and we'll enjoy some of Rafe's Kona coffee. He brought a load of good beans back from Hanalei yesterday and dropped some off here for the Monday meeting."

She followed him through the church door and out along the flowered path toward the bungalow where she'd lived her childhood under his and Noelani's compassionate patronage.

"I hear Rafe's too busy to attend those Monday night meetings," she said casually.

"Zachary tell you that? Well, Zach's the lad I worry about. That's not to say Rafe isn't causing me a few sleepless hours lately, but Zach's behaving strangely this past month or so."

"It's Silas," she said quietly as they walked along. "Uncle Townsend's been boasting about his firstborn son and dismissing Zachary."

"Yes, a pity for both young men." He shook his head sadly. "Unless something changes in the near future with Townsend, I'm afraid there's real trouble ahead. And Zachary isn't alone in it."

She thought of Celestine and wondered how the matters between her and Townsend could be solved, when Townsend remained unrepentant.

"I can't help thinking that Townsend's boasts of Silas are another insult to Celestine. He's a selfish fellow and needs all the prayers we can muster, Eden. He's at the top of my list."

She had sometimes wondered who was first on Ambrose's precious prayer list, but knew it was a holy matter between him and

God. Hearing this brought a twinge of conviction. She rarely prayed for her uncle Townsend. To be truthful, she didn't like him. It was easier to pray for lepers she didn't know than a man who gloated over his shameful affairs. *This is something I need to deal with,* she thought.

"About Zachary." He looked down at her. "Did you notice he'd hurt his leg?"

"I can't help noticing such things. It's the nurse in me," she jested. "But he didn't say how it happened. Why do you ask?"

"Perhaps it's nothing. As I mentioned, Rafe dropped by this morning. He merely asked if Zachary had been here last night."

She paused on the pathway, and searched his gaze, wondering what was on his mind.

"Why would Rafe ask such a thing? Zachary lives at Kea Lani, so he would come by almost every day." She stopped, remembering how Zachary hadn't stopped at the church to see Ambrose since April. Even so, Zachary lived at Kea Lani, which was within walking distance of Ambrose's house and Rafe's new pineapple plantation.

"True, my dear, but Zachary isn't usually in the habit of prowling about after midnight, then running when a member of the family recognizes him."

"Is that what happened?" Her curiosity sparked to life.

"It's likely inconsequential, but, yes, Candace thought she saw him last night on the lanai near your Great-aunt Nora's guest room. When she called to him, he left in a hurry. She mentioned it to Rafe at breakfast and thought Zachary might have injured himself. Rafe knows I'm often up late at night working, so when he stopped by this morning with the Kona beans, he asked if Zach had come by to see me last night on his way back from Hanalei."

She considered as they came to the bungalow. "Did Rafe think Zachary hurt his leg leaving the lanai?"

"Candace did, I gather from what she told him. I don't know what any of this means."

She glanced at him. He wore a troubled look, so she remained silent as they walked on together. Zachary's behavior made no sense, and when they arrived at the comfortable bungalow, the puzzling incident was dropped.

Ambrose's horse and buggy were still out front from some earlier calling. Her favorite hibiscus bushes were growing vigorously beside the wooden steps that climbed up to the latticed lanai. She remembered them from childhood, when she'd lived in this love-filled home.

Even though she now lived at Kea Lani as a Derrington, there were still so many prized memories here that whispered to her heart. She'd grown up believing her mother had died, and Grandfather Ainsworth and Great-aunt Nora had told her there was no one in the family to properly care for her at Kea Lani. Jerome had taken Rebecca's death extremely hard, it was said, and he had left Oahu to voyage to Tahiti, Bora Bora, and eventually as far away as India until his loss was assuaged. She'd accepted this story as a girl, but even then it hadn't been satisfying. "Why couldn't Jesus heal his hurting heart?" she'd asked as a child, and received only a sad silence and the admonition that her father thought it best that she be cared for by Ambrose and Noelani.

Noelani, who had worked for Rebecca at the Hawaiian Royal School, had been pleased to become Eden's nanny. Even after Eden reached her young teens, the family had appeared in no hurry to bring her to Kea Lani to be raised with her two cousins, Candace and Zachary.

"You fit in so well with 'Uncle' Ambrose and 'Aunt' Noelani," they had commented, although Ambrose and Noelani were not actually her blood uncle and aunt. They were Eastons, which meant that Ambrose was Rafe's blood uncle, while Townsend was Eden's. Eden had wondered if she would ever move to the plantation house.

Then, when she'd turned fifteen, Grandfather Ainsworth, without advance notice, sent for her by carriage and brought her to Kea Lani as a rightful member of the prestigious Derrington family.

Eden had never resented those early years with Ambrose and Noelani, for they'd been happy ones. She loved them as fully as any Derrington and, in some cases, perhaps even more. It was through Noelani that she'd learned to love the native Hawaiian people and to understand their Polynesian culture. And Ambrose, *dear Ambrose*, had brought her to faith in Christ and taught her to appreciate the missionary endeavors that were so much on his heart.

After returning to Kea Lani, Eden had settled into the comfortable life of being a wealthy Derrington, receiving her higher education along with Candace and Zachary, and moving among the elite families of the islands and the influential planters and members of the Hawaiian monarchy. Through Great-aunt Nora, who was a friend of the royal family and especially of the present queen, Liliuokalani, she attended dinners and balls at Iolani Palace in Honolulu, and met dignitaries and ambassadors from England and America.

"I'm on my way to Hawaiiana, Uncle Ambrose, so I can't stay long," she said as they entered the front door. She explained the expected return of her grandfather on the afternoon steamer, then said, "Zachary is concerned for Candace. Oliver P. Hunnewell is in the party that voyaged from San Francisco with Ainsworth."

"Oh he is, is he? Zachary does well to be concerned for Candace. No doubt your grandfather wishes the marriage to take place between her and Oliver this year."

"Is there any way you can convince him that she's better off marrying Keno?"

"No, but I will use our most powerful resource—the matter will go on my prayer list. Candace asked me to speak to Ainsworth before he went to Washington D.C. Unfortunately, he doesn't see the need for her to marry any man other than the Hunnewell boy. Ainsworth's a fine man, but when his mind's made up on a matter, he can't—*or won't*—be swayed. I've little doubt, though, that Keno, while lacking in this world's treasures, would be the better choice for Candace."

Eden stood on the woven palm fiber rug. It was stained blue-green. The rattan furniture throughout the room was padded with soft, indigo cushions, and on the wall hung one large painting that always made her smile: a replica of a fox hunt in Tudor England, with lords and ladies wearing massive white wigs. Though out of place in a Hawaiian bungalow, it had hung there since her childhood.

On a small stand under the painting were woven baskets of coconuts and bananas, and next to these were a fire-darkened coffeepot that had seen many years of use and a certain brown-stained mug that Ambrose refused to yield for a chinaware tea cup from Shanghai. On a wooden table was a collection of his papers and books, an inkhorn and pen, and a worn leather Bible smudged with yellowing margins. Everything was old, but cherished because of memories of blessings and prayers answered, and verses that had comforted and warned. Yes, *this* was home to her. These things were more valuable than Kea Lani's thick French carpets, mahogany furniture engraved with pineapples, fine damask divans, Vienna chandelier, and expensive figurines from Europe.

Ambrose sat at his desk, and Eden noticed for the first time that his breathing appeared to trouble him. For a moment she forgot about Candace and her grandfather. She remembered how Ambrose had hoped to turn the church over to the Hawaiians and retire, but there was no one willing to take his place as its busy lay-pastor, and certainly no one as spiritually capable. Ambrose once had held high hopes that Noelani's nephew, Keno, would become a minister, but Keno had never felt it was his spiritual gift or calling to serve as pastor.

"Is that why you're here, Eden? To discuss Candace?"

She walked around the room. Now that she was here with the unpleasant news about Kip, she wondered if she shouldn't have left the matter to Aunt Lana after all. Then, squelching her inner doubts, she faced it head-on. "No. It's not about Candace. I only learned about Grandfather's arrival a short while ago. It's Rafe that brings me here, and baby Kip."

His gaze searched her face. "Rafe and Kip?"

She sighed and walked up to the desk. "I've been sent here by the Board of Health to bring Kip back to Kalihi for quarantine. The Board learned about Kip being born on Molokai to lepers. You know the law. It's forbidden to keep Kip until the Board certifies that he doesn't have leprosy. And even then—" her voice trailed off.

"Even then, it's not at all certain a baby from Molokai can be adopted."

"Yes," she breathed and sank into the chair. "There's a ruling that may require Kip to be placed in a hospital-run home for children born on Molokai. Oh, Ambrose! This will be difficult to explain to Rafe. Even so, I've arranged with Dr. Bolton to be authorized to examine Kip."

Ambrose stared at her, his own concern bringing furrowed lines to his tanned forehead. "This is ill news for Rafe, no doubt about that. Are you sure it's wise for you to be the one to inform him and claim control of Kip? It won't go over well, Eden."

She rubbed the back of her neck, her head aching. "You're voicing the same concerns as Lana. All I can say is what I told her. I feel responsible for this tragedy. And I do see it as such. Kip is not a leper. I'm sure of that. I examined him myself after his arrival last year. And Noelani knows what to look for. She agrees he's clean and has been all along. But I feel I must be the one to explain the situation to Rafe because I—I'm connected with Kalihi Hospital. If someone else brings him the news I fear he'll think I don't care. And I do! Oh I do, Ambrose!"

"Of course you do," he said gently. "I'm sure Rafe will see it that way in time."

"In time?"

"He's very attached to Kip."

"I know that. But so am I!"

"Yes, but Kip is even more special to Rafe now that you and he have ended your engagement. Kip is all he has."

She jumped to her feet and turned away. "Oh, Ambrose, don't

say it that way. It makes me feel as though I've done him dreadful harm." She turned quickly and faced him. "It so happens Rafe was quite willing to end things for the present. He took the ring back quickly enough."

"I'm sure he had his reasons, but I don't believe that was the resolution he wanted."

"You said yourself he's been difficult to get along with. Well," she said, suddenly defensive, "he was that way even before I told him I had a calling to work at Kalihi and Molokai. He hasn't been happy in months."

"I doubt it had to do with you, my dear Eden. He thinks highly of you and your strong motivations. He always has. I believe he's frustrated over needing to surrender his plans for the pineapple plantation to Parker Judson. As we both know, he's indebted to Judson for a good deal of money. Until he's made Hawaiiana successful, he'll not have paid his debt. It's Hanalei on the Big Island he's working to get control of from Judson. Hanalei has always been his home, and the plantation he grew up on. Matt established it," he said affectionately of his deceased younger brother. "And it's a precious thing to Rafe. It was tragic when Celestine made the error of turning its management over to Townsend."

Eden calmed herself and walked over to the window to look out. "Yes," she said quietly, "I know. I've discussed it all many times with Rafe." She rubbed her fingers together and became aware it was her bare ring finger she was rubbing. Placing her left hand inside her pocket, she turned and looked at Ambrose.

"Ambrose, I'm the one to tell Rafe, and I'll need to take Kip back with me to Kalihi. But I can promise Rafe that I'll not leave Kip any longer than absolutely necessary for me to eat and sleep. I'm going to stay there with Kip day and night."

He was quickly beside her. "My dear, you can't do that. It's too much of a risk for you."

"No, I'll be all right. I know how to protect myself. Besides, if I go to Molokai one day when my father comes home, I'll be with lepers every day. This is a call upon my life. Rafe must understand this before he and I can decide on any future together. I need time . . . and I need him to wait."

Ambrose took both her hands into his and looked at her. His eyes were kind but firm. "Eden, you're asking a great deal of him. Don't be disappointed when he proves himself only too human."

She said nothing for a long moment, then turned her head away. He released her hands.

"I'll do all I can to help you," he said. "Both with Rafe and Kip, and the calling you believe God has laid so indelibly on your heart."

She threw her arms around him, and he patted her head as though she were a child. "I knew you'd understand. If only Rafe would," she said, with a slight tone of resentment.

Ambrose was quiet for a moment. "Rafe has his own struggles. He too, is trying to come to peace with certain issues."

"Yes, and one of them is his father. Rafe has always believed his father's death wasn't an accident," she said bluntly.

Ambrose gave an agreeing nod. "That's one of his issues and why he wants to control Hanalei. But he has another problem with you, Eden."

She lifted her gaze and saw his sobriety. "With me? It looks as if our biggest problems are each other. Maybe we weren't meant to marry after all," she said in frustration.

"Rafe saw in you a woman to stand beside him as he confronts the giants keeping him from attaining his father's stolen dream. He looks upon running Hanalei as a dream. He wants your love displayed in a commitment to *follow him* wherever *he* goes."

"A bit selfish, isn't it?" she found herself saying.

"No. Not selfish. It was God's way from the beginning, Eden. A woman follows her man, not the man his woman. If it's seen differently nowadays, it's because culture is walking away from God's plan for marriage."

"Oh, Ambrose, I'm sorry." She turned, placing palms to her temples. "I know, a woman was created to be the helpmate, not the leader. I've said so to myself many times, and I've said so to Candace. It's one of the main reasons she doesn't want to marry Oliver. She isn't at peace with the idea of following his leadership. And the real reason I gave the engagement ring back to Rafe is that marriage wouldn't be fair to him right now. I simply can't release the longing I've had since childhood. That's why I can't commit myself just yet."

He patted her shoulder. "Don't get yourself too upset. Life is a struggle, and marriage is a struggle. It's uphill all the way. You're upset right now, and you've too many worries on your heart. This matter of Kip is alarming, and this goal of yours to find your mother and work with your father among the lepers on Molokai—do you believe doing so will release you from this longing you say you've had for so long?"

"Oh yes, yes it will. This is what I want, Ambrose. Except—" her voice trailed.

"Except your heart is divided because you also want Rafe. You're in love with him and have been for years."

She nodded. "Yes. You know me well. You and Noelani both."

"You were a daughter to us," he said kindly. "When Ainsworth sent you here after Jerome went away, we saw you as the answer to our prayer for a child of our own. We've never regretted those ten years you lived with us."

She smiled. "I was thinking when I entered this house that it will always be *home*. And I'll always be grateful for your guidance and Noelani's mothering."

"Well, just remember you're not the only one who faced the loss of a father," he said gently. "From your earliest years, you longed for Jerome, and he wasn't here. Rafe, too, was dedicated to his father, and then Matt was taken away, suddenly and unjustly. Then Matt's plantation at Hanalei was taken away. Stolen, is the way Rafe views it."

Eden understood Rafe's resentments—or believed she did. Perhaps she'd not taken them to heart. There had always been her own goal to think about.

"I've been doing much thinking about fathers recently," he

mused. "I've come to the conclusion that the father image has strong spiritual implications."

"Spiritual?" She looked at him quizzically.

"Yes, because in the end, the quest for the deepest relationship we seek can only be fulfilled in God. Who was it that came to the garden of Eden in the cool of the evening and called for Adam, to walk and commune with him as a father walks with a son?"

She thought about Adam meeting and walking together with God in the garden. What did Adam say? Could he ask God questions as a child does his father? How wondrous it must have been to walk and talk with his Creator in the cool of the evening, among the fragrance of the flowers and greenery, the animals in perfect harmony. Did some gentle lion or elephant follow close behind as their voices carried through the trees?

"And then the serpent entered and destroyed their fellowship," she said wearily.

"And *then* God came and made redemption possible for those who accept the remedy of the cross of Christ. Adam and his fallen sons and daughters can be restored to an even higher position of fellowship with God as Father. *Now* we can call Him Abba, *Father.* Ah, what a privilege! We *do* have a Father, my dear Eden. We have a family. We *belong.* And you and Rafe included will never tremble alone or have Him taken from us in death or, like Zachary, know the stab of rejection."

She stared out the window. The hibiscus flowers were visuals of the Father's care, brightly colored and basking in the warmth.

Ambrose said no more. His reassuring pat on her shoulder told her their conversation would be kept between them. "Take my buggy to Hawaiiana," he said. "The horse is hitched."

Several minutes later Eden became aware she was alone at the window and that Ambrose had quietly gone about his business. She picked up her sun hat from the table where she'd laid it, tied the ribbon under her chin, and went out the front door. Onward to Hawaiiana . . . and her meeting with Rafe.

Eden drove the horse and buggy up the half-mile dirt road toward the Hawaiiana plantation. This fledgling plantation, if all progressed as planned, would one day become Oahu's largest pineapple plantation, boasting the largest, sweetest, and juiciest pineapples on the islands. With a nostalgic smile, Eden recalled tasting sections of such a pineapple while on board the *Minoa*, anchored in San Francisco Bay. She could still remember the sweet golden flesh and the warm juice that seeped through her fingers when she bit daintily into the section he had handed her.

The breeze tugged at her dark hair beneath the sun hat. The road narrowed when she turned onto a well-used section leading toward the building and planting now underway. It was a hard-pressed volcanic dirt path, lined by trees and ferns, and presenting a view of an unbounded blue-green sea beyond the cliffs.

The Hawaiiana Great House had been started during her engagement with Rafe, and its wondrous lanai remained under construction, but there were sections already completed that housed Rafe's mother, Celestine. The nursery, too, was in use, and it was there that Noelani cared for Kip. With Ambrose's approval, Noelani remained at Hawaiiana five days a week to care for the baby, then returned to her house and Ambrose from Friday through Sunday night, where she assisted Ambrose with his preparation for the worship service.

Eden understood that, with the engagement between her and Rafe broken, it was likely she would never live at Hawaiiana as they'd planned. If she allowed her emotions to reign, dwelling on the loss could be overwhelming. She was not blind to Rafe's dependable Christian character, his intelligence, and yes, his obvious good looks. She was at the age when romance, love, marriage, and a family of her own were desires yearning for fulfillment. The loss was especially painful to her heart when she felt weary, alone, and disappointed. Quite suddenly the thought of seeing him again after two months unnerved her. She fought an almost overwhelming urge to turn back and ride instead to Kea Lani. She must have been dazed with arrogance to think she could simply walk back into the fire and not be tested! Maybe Lana was right after all about who should meet with Rafe. Yes, she should turn back. Turn back now. Go home to Kea Lani where she would be safe. Safe, because Rafe wouldn't come there to confront her love for him. As long as they kept apart and put up a front, they could pretend they didn't need each other.

Grandfather Ainsworth will be home this afternoon, she thought, sitting in the buggy, clutching the reins. Maybe she should go home and wait to welcome him back from the States. After all, she could always send a message to Lana at Kalihi to call on Rafe Easton about Kip.

Eden stopped the buggy on the side of the road and sat listening to the sigh of the tropic breezes in the palm trees and breathing the fragrance of wild orchids.

*R*afe Easton stood in the bungalow doorway as the breeze blew in and cooled him. His shirt was off, and he wore white cotton trousers. Tan and muscled, with dark eyes and hair, he watched his friend, ally, and chief foreman, Keno, speak with a Hawaiian woman.

He had raised this temporary bungalow in the midst of the new pineapple plantings. Hawaiiana lands covered over a thousand acres stretching from the old Easton family pearl beds, by Pearl River, all the way to the rim of the Koolau mountain range.

Parker Judson, his partner on Hawaiiana, was one of several sugar magnates with political influence in both Hawaii *and* San Francisco, where he kept a second home on Telegraph Hill. Many claimed that he stood on an equal footing with the biggest sugar king of them all, Claus Spreckels. Parker had no son or daughter, and after a meeting with Rafe in San Francisco, he'd taken an unusual liking to him—or as Rafe would clarify, "an affectionate liking for my French Guiana pineapple slips that I risked my neck to smuggle out." And so, Parker had backed him in the establishment of a new pineapple enterprise, which Parker owned.

Rafe, in return for selling Parker the rare pineapple slips and developing the plantation's lands, earned the right to manage the Kona coffee plantation, founded by Rafe's father on the Big Island of Hawaii. Matt Easton had died there during Rafe's boyhood, and though the authorities considered his death an accident, Rafe had never accepted that explanation.

Matt's death not only robbed Rafe of a close relationship with his father, but matters turned darker still when Townsend Derrington married Rafe's mother, Celestine, and wrangled control of the Easton plantation away from her. While still a youth, Rafe had lost not only his father, but the land that would have become his inheritance. Townsend, ever looking for new ways to pay down his persistent gambling debts, had leased the Easton lands to Parker Judson. But now, Hanalei would be run by Rafe, and it was for this prize that he worked such long, demanding hours for Parker Judson.

Rafe used the bungalow for his field office and general habitat when working late, often well past midnight. It was a ready place to eat and rest rather than having to return to the main house, though it offered little comfort in the heat of the day when the sun beat relentlessly on the palm frond roof.

Keno turned away from the Hawaiian woman who'd been seated beside the road and walked toward Rafe, carrying a large *ahi* tuna. Nearing the bungalow, Keno held up the slippery fish, its scales glinting in the sunlight.

Leaning in the doorway, eating an overripe melon with a wooden spoon, Rafe shot Keno a quizzical look. "What's that all about?"

Keno gestured toward the lingering woman. "She wants you to buy this."

When she grinned at Rafe, he smiled and looked back Keno. "I don't like fish, so you buy it and send it over to Ambrose."

Keno thoughtfully stroked the slippery fish with one finger. "Hawaiian *wahine* has heard how poor, handsome *makua* Rafe is heartbroken over haole girl with green eyes."

Rafe flicked away some melon seeds and narrowed his gaze as Keno continued. "Hawaiian woman says her own eyes are black, but she can cook an *ahi* great and delicious. She wants to come inside and comfort you."

Rafe didn't so much as bat a lash. "Tell her that poor, heartbroken makua Rafe cannot be solaced. He only wants 'green eyes' in his little hut."

Keno dug in his pocket for some change. "I'm broke." He held out his palm. Rafe dug into his own pocket but also found nothing. Rafe gestured. "Bring the fish back."

Keno, a strongly built pearl diver, trotted down the slope to where the woman waited, seated by the narrow road with her basket. He shook his head no, firmly handed her the *ahi*, made negative gestures with his hands—then pointed down the road. His voice carried on the breeze: "Go up to the big house, ask for Noelani. She'll buy the fish. *Rapidamente!*"

Rafe turned his mouth. *Spanish?* Of all languages to use with her.

The woman walked away in the direction of the Great House, and Keno trotted back toward the bungalow.

Finishing the melon, Rafe wiped his hands on a towel. The one woman he wanted, he couldn't have, even after offering her everything—his heart and his life. No small offering as far as he was concerned. He would never understand women. One brought him a big smelly fish, anxious to stay, the other kept him dangling on a line while she awaited the return of her long lost father, daily risking her future to leprosy at Kalihi Hospital.

Keno came inside, brushed past him, and sat down by a desk cluttered with papers, books, and a Bible. He reached for a pencil.

Rafe tilted his head. "You were a little brusque with her, weren't you? '*Rapidamente!*' he mimicked good naturedly.

"If I wasn't firm with her, she'd camp out there. Gotta be careful, ol' pal. Remember that divorced lady, the haole? She kept coming to see Ambrose, wanting to tell him all about how lonely she was for a fellow and how she needed 'counseling' to deal with her temptations?"

"I remember. He learned his lesson and got rid of her in a hurry. Told her that Noelani would be happy to counsel with her . . . a woman's heart to a woman's heart. Wise, isn't he?"

"Safest place for you, my friend, is to get you on board the *Minoa* again," Keno said, finally finding Rafe's map. He reached over and spread it across the desk. "No sooner will you board ship for French Guiana than 'Miss Green Eyes' will pine for you, weeping tears into her lace hanky. She will bemoan how she lost you, and become pale and wan. Then, Dr. Jerome will realize how he's manipulated her to support his work, send for you posthaste, and have Ambrose perform an immediate marriage—" Rafe promptly muffled Keno's mouth with a towel.

"You talk too much, Keno." Rafe smiled at him maliciously. "I think it was you whom Fishy Wahine had her eyes on. Yes, that was it, you conniving hapa-haole. I had best speak to Candace about this. Let her know how the adoring island women hang around my office making a nuisance of themselves, anxious to cook you little coconut cakes while you're supposed to be working."

"Alas, you pine for green eyes . . . and I for red hair. We both should take to sea again and forget our misery."

"It's wiser you stay in Honolulu this time, Keno. And seriously," Rafe said, looking down at him, "Ambrose is right. You should become a lay pastor. The little group we've started here on Hawaiiana needs you. Later, when Ambrose retires, you could take his position at the mission church. You need to begin teaching our group at least once a month, though, just to get over your fear of speaking before people. Then if you want to go to seminary, I can arrange for it."

Keno frowned. He ran his fingers through his dark hair. "I can't do it. It makes me nervous." He laid a hand against his stomach. "When I stand up to teach, I forget everything. It's best if you help me the way you said you would. A plantation of my own. Then, maybe, Makua Ainsworth would think me respectable enough for his granddaughter."

"He already thinks you're respectable. It's your lack of money and blood ties that keeps him aloof. I've told you a dozen times, Keno. There's no way he'll bless a marriage between you and Candace. Look at all I went through before Ainsworth would agree to a marriage with his Eden."

"Yeah, and you a big Easton, too. And even a big missionary heritage."

"Big, nothing. Not enough for Ainsworth until Parker Judson decided my slips would produce pineapples of gold. Then he suddenly decided I might be good enough for his granddaughter after all."

"At least you were finally able to bargain with them."

Rafe gazed out the door thoughtfully. "There's still something sinister about the way my father died. I haven't forgotten, and I plan to get the truth one day, even if someone big gets hurt. His death wasn't an accident."

"I always thought you were right about that, but it might be wiser to leave the ugly matter to God and go on with your life. You have a good future. Eden is bound to come awake one of these happy mornings and realize what she truly wants. She's too smart a woman not to, if you want my opinion."

Rafe kept silent. Eden was indeed intelligent and beautiful in his view. That she was devoted to principles he honored and admired didn't mean that she would join him in marriage. Her desire to bring the hope of Christ to hopeless lepers stirred his heart and made him love her all the more. Considering the tragedy that had struck her mother Rebecca, he could fully understand her dedication. She was convinced of her calling, and he was willing to see her continue her work at Kalihi, even though it presented a great risk. The last thing he wanted was to become the foolhardy man who tried to end God's calling on her life. And he desired the will of God for his own life as well, even if it included a break in their engagement. "'How can two walk together except they be agreed?'" he had quoted to her from the prophet Amos when he received his ring back.

He was also aware there was more on her mind than her work at Kalihi Hospital, and it was this more dangerous plan that worried him. Dr. Jerome had written her a poetic letter of his noble goal to open a research clinic at the Kalawao leper colony on Molokai, and he'd suggested she work with him, alongside his research assistant, Herald Hartley. Jerome had spoken of Herald in such glowing terms, it had become plain to Rafe that her father had plans to see Herald and Eden married. Such a union would fit perfectly into Jerome's plans. Together, the three of them would find the cure for leprosy and rescue Rebecca from the dreaded final stages of the disease.

And Eden warmed to the letter like a fragile moth to a searing flame.

Rafe respected Dr. Jerome's dedication, but he had little confidence in his questionable research, most of it conducted over the past two years in China and India. Rafe also knew for a fact that Rebecca had long passed the early stages of leprosy, where even the faintest hope of a cure was possible—except if touched by Christ. Jerome was deceiving himself, which was tragic enough. But to draw Eden into his dream was even worse, for it was a dream that Rafe believed would end badly.

Rafe turned back to Keno, who was still talking. "I can't teach, let alone *preach*. What if I forget what I planned to say?"

"You don't need to memorize the entire message. You make notes and keep them in your Bible."

"What if I drop the notes or get them in the wrong order or lose my glasses?"

"Since when do you need glasses?"

"That's just it, pal. One never knows. I might need them tomorrow or even next week. Then what?"

Rafe frowned. "What does Candace see in you?"

Keno slapped a hand against his chest. "She sees a friend and the handsomest hapa-haole in the islands! And the man she trusts."

"Anything else?" Rafe asked dryly.

Keno pretended to think hard. He snapped his fingers. "It was I, Keno, who led her to know the Savior."

"Yes, exactly." He pushed a thumb against Keno's chest. "That's why you should listen to Ambrose. Become a Christian leader, and I'll back you all the way."

Keno looked at him askance. "And you? It was you, pal, who led *me* to the Lord. So you, too, should be a big pastor. I'll be your assistant pastor. Yes, that's the answer. That could work."

"I'll grow the best Kona coffee in the islands, produce the sweetest pineapples in the world, and have many sons with Green Eyes to help you around the church. I'll keep one son in seven to carry on the plantations."

Keno whooped in laughter, and Rafe returned to the doorway, looking out at the mountaintops with their blue, green, and purple hues. Clouds were gathering, and there was the feel of more than the usual afternoon mist in the air. Right now, despite his finest intentions to show himself magnanimous toward Eden, he *was* angry. Angry that she had placed their lives on hold while she put Dr. Jerome ahead of him.

Rafe touched the diamond ring in his trouser pocket. He carried it around, still feeling emotional about his loss, yet knowing emotions would not solve his deep dilemma. He was a practical man, and his practicality always rose to the top. The ring was worth thousands of dollars. And she *had* worn it. For three weeks and five days . . . or was it six days? Well, she had worn it either way, and there had been tears in her soft green eyes when he had put it there, and tears when she had taken it off. He could still feel the warm splash of her tears against his wrist as she returned it to his palm and walked away. A ruddy mess!

Relish your freedom, he told himself. *Get out of here, Easton. You need the cure! The sooner you get away, the better off you'll be! Then, maybe in a couple of years . . . No. Forget it. Not again.* If he learned to get over her, it would stay that way. Permanently.

"Yes," Keno was saying, "it is time you mollified your wounds with salt water." He stared at the map. "The sea!" He lifted his hands above his head. "The blessed sea. A strong ship. And a long, *long* voyage."

Rafe laughed. "Stop staring at that map, will you?"

"Why should I stop when this wondrous map holds the answer to our misery?"

"You know what you remind me of?" Rafe gritted. "A *kahuna*. Gazing into the innards of a rotting *ahi* trying to figure out my future." He walked to the table and tapped his finger on the outline of the Caribbean. "If I go back to French Guiana as Parker Judson wants, you're not coming with me. Candace or no Candace, you're staying with Ambrose."

"Oh, no, pal. You and me are partners, remember? You'll need plenty of help with another load of slips. You don't know anything about nursing them down in the deep, dank hull, and I do. Then, as part of the bargain, you'll stake me in my own plantation as we agreed." Keno scowled. "But saying good-bye to Candie will be bad."

Candie, was it? How the dour Ainsworth Derrington would bloat like a toad to hear a "Hawaiian boy" call his favorite niece, chosen from childhood for the golden crown of inheritance, "Candie"!

Rafe laughed. "Ah, we men are such fools. Poor, lovesick Keno." He patted his head. "Your misery makes me feel better already."

"As they say, misery loves company."

Rafe was still smiling when he stepped outdoors to the barrel of water standing under a coconut palm. Scooping the chipped ladle into the water, he drank. *Did she really enjoy hurting him like this?* He tossed that self-pitying notion aside almost at once. He'd been raised to take it on the chin, not to whine and fuss. Eden wasn't trying to hurt anyone. She was too innocent for that. But she *would* end up hurting herself. That was what bothered him the most. She didn't think he understood her reasons for delaying marriage, but he did.

Very clearly. *Too* clearly, actually. In many ways she was still a little girl working through the hurts of childhood. She wanted what she'd been denied—a close, loving relationship with her father. She would have him at last, or so she told herself, and she wouldn't allow anything or anyone to interfere. Right now, Rafe himself had become the "other man" by demanding she be his alone.

Eden was wise in so many things, yet she refused to see that her father was like a drowning man. Rafe feared that once Jerome discovered he could not cure his wife, he would pull Eden under the waves with him.

The secret no one else appeared to understand was that Dr. Jerome blamed himself for Rebecca's sickness. When Rafe was a boy, he had heard Jerome and his father, Matt, arguing about Rebecca Stanhope, as she was then called. Matt said something like, "You'll end up taking her from the Royal Hawaiian School to work with lepers, and the day will come when she'll end up one of them." Strangely, she had.

Keno folded the old map, whistling. "We will survive. We are already on our way to recovery. As soon as we feel the pitch and roll of the ship, the water slapping on its sides, and the smell of salty wind, we will be healed."

"That's the old spirit," Rafe said. "Run up the flag and beat the drums." Absently he removed the coconut shell canteen hanging by a strap from the tree. Then he noticed Keno staring down the narrow road. Rafe followed his gaze.

A woman was driving a familiar buggy along the track in the direction of the bungalow. The horse and buggy belonged to Ambrose, and the woman . . . was Eden. He could recognize her anywhere, the nurse's uniform, the red cross, the toss of her dark hair shimmering in the wind beneath her hat.

His eyes narrowed. Unplugging the coconut, he took a swallow—and spat it out, choking and coughing and tossing the canteen aside!

Keno dove to save the liquid from draining out.

"What is that?" Rafe choked.

"My new invention . . . made from rotting pineapples."

"It's rotten, all right."

"I've been experimenting," Keno said proudly, putting the stopper back. "If I could make a pineapple wine—an *innocent* wine, you understand—"

"Innocent wine!"

"And, well, convince old P. J. to market it in San Francisco, I'll become rich. Then I'll win Makua Ainsworth's respect. Money will do it every time. You said so yourself. He'll let me marry Candace."

Rafe shook his dark head wryly. "Forget what I said about taking Ambrose's place. You need to go back to the foot of the mourner's bench."

"What! I'm saved in three tenses, pal. Past, present, and future. And I'll learn to say them in Greek too."

"If Ambrose finds out you're making wine with rotten pineapples, hoping to get rich, he'll bar the door on Monday nights. And your Aunt Noelani will keep you in back doing the dishes."

Keno looked worried. "You think I made it too strong?" He looked at the coconut shell.

"You've got to be kidding, Keno," he said hoarsely. "That stuff is poison."

Keno slapped his forehead. "Of course! That's it. *Poison!* Horticultural poison for the bugs eating the pineapple slips—don't you see? That's even better!"

Rafe shook his head and let his marveling gaze drift from the coconut to the road. "Eden's coming."

Keno looked down the track. "Sure enough. I'll get rid of this," he said, nodding at the coconut, "and I vow to quit the rotting pineapple business." He burst into the bungalow, returning a few moments later with a bowl of Kona coffee. "This should clear the poison. Drink it up, pal, and I'll keep her busy."

"I can deal with her," Rafe growled. He drank the coffee, pushed the bowl against Keno's chest, glaring, then entered the bungalow.

He snatched his shirt from the peg and slipped it on, followed by his beat-up Panama hat, then went to his horse.

Keno folded his arms across his chest. "She's just as smitten as you are," he said cheerfully. "She just doesn't know it."

"Brilliant deduction."

What had caused her to come see him after two long months? *Surely not love*, he thought cynically.

Somehow, I have an uneasy feeling about this . . .

Chapter Five
Firestorm

*E*den saw in the distance perhaps a hundred men, digging, cultivating, and planting. Most were of Chinese ancestry, but there was a second group off to themselves, which she recog nized as Japanese. Having grown up around Grandfather Ainsworth's massive sugar plantation, she was used to seeing men working. They came from China and Japan of their own will, signing contracts to work for a certain wage and a certain length of time. When the contracts ended, many of them set up their own little shops in Chinatown and other neighborhoods. Others continued working in agriculture. Ambrose would reach out to the various language groups, begin tiny assemblies of believers, and train them to reach their own people.

She could see the green shoots of pineapple plants growing abundantly and assumed the French Guiana pineapple variety had taken to its new home.

Pulling the horse and buggy to one side of the road, she stopped. Across the sun-drenched acreage she fixed her gaze on the lone shady oasis, a singular palm-thatched bungalow. "Like Jonah's gourd," she thought with a smile.

Rafe stood outside the bungalow door, while Keno rushed about, in and out of the bungalow, but she couldn't tell what he was doing. It was clear they had seen her, so she remained in the buggy. A moment later Rafe went to untie his horse. Mounting, he settled his hat lower and rode slowly to meet her, the wind ruffling his shirt.

She clutched the leather reins tightly. Meeting Rafe again after their stormy parting two months ago was in itself stressful, but representing the Board with the kind of news she had on Kip was certain to bring a tropical storm.

She noticed his masculine looks that at times made her uneasy, even though she knew they shouldn't. There was no sin in a fine appearance. It was what one did with the God-given asset. What she admired most about Rafe were the Christian principles he adhered to in keeping himself under discipline. She respected him for his restraint. She had never seen Rafe use his appearance to take advantage of vulnerable women. Such could not be said of her Uncle Townsend.

She waited, still wondering how to greet him after all this time. Their love for one another, she believed, was still unwavering, even though conflict had delayed their marriage. Noelani had said it was best to lay conflict to rest before marriage rather than be joined in a struggle once married. Eden wondered if any marriage, at any stage of life, was without its conflicts. "Conflict can be healthy and make us grow," Ambrose often said. "The tree that's buffeted by winds can develop stronger roots. What we need is to make certain our relational conflicts are dealt with according to the teachings of the Bible."

Should she smile casually? Act grave and sophisticated? Businesslike? *I'll wait and take the cue from him*, she thought.

He brought his horse alongside the buggy and looked down at her, his eyes smiling under dark lashes as he studied her with a faint smile.

"Can it be?" he jested lightly. "What fortune is this that shines upon my path, bringing such fairness to brighten my bleak heart."

He removed his Panama hat and bowed his dark head with hand at chest. "Welcome to Hawaiiana—though we have a long way to go before it competes with Kea Lani."

His lightheartedness brought a reprieve to her fears, and she was able to smile. "Hello, Rafe."

Almost at once, aware of her vulnerability, she resumed her previous solemnity. Would it be wise to come straight out with the truth about Kip? Or would she appear insensitive? Kip had come to mean so much to him. His attachment to the baby boy over the past months surprised her. Not that she wasn't attached herself, but somehow she hadn't seen Rafe as the sort of young man to bond so quickly with a baby. There was much about Rafe she still didn't understand, even though she'd known him since childhood.

Oh, she groaned to herself, *this is going to be one of the worst moments of my life.* Worst, except for that tumultuous meeting they'd had when she'd taken off the engagement ring and he'd accepted it with devastating calmness.

"I hope you don't mind my coming here like this," she began awkwardly.

"Mind? Now, why should I?" came his suave tone, as though their hearts were as disengaged as east from west. "To what do I owe this privileged attention?"

So. He'd chosen to play down what to her was a breathless moment. To keep the affections they had for each other tied up, like a dog on a leash, she thought, offended over his casual indifference. Though considering the degree to which their emotions could reignite, perhaps he'd taken a safest approach after all. She ought to be grateful for the latitude it afforded her.

Then I, too, shall be casual and friendly, as though nothing in all the world has happened between us.

"Dr. Bolton requested that I deliver Great-aunt Nora her new prescription. Then I happened to meet Zachary on the road. He had news about Grandfather Ainsworth. He's returning from San Francisco this afternoon."

"Ainsworth?" He frowned.

"Yes. Candace should be told, and I'm hoping to get her to come with me to Kea Lani before he arrives."

"Is that what you wanted to see me about?"

"Well, there is more I need to speak about," she said, unable to veil the note of concern in her voice.

Rafe sat on his horse looking down at her, toying with the leather reins, but beneath the casual manner she read an alertness.

"Then why don't I bring you up to the house to see Candace? You can give Nora her medication as well. I imagine they've got Kip up by now, playing in the nursery."

Eden tensed at the mention of Kip, struggling with the main reason for her visit to see Rafe. Conflict loomed like a shadow cast over the future, and her brightened spirits, enlivened by seeing Rafe, sagged. Their first meeting in months had been so pleasant, and now her dreadful announcement would surely separate them again in mind and heart.

He swung down from the horse and gave a swat to its hip. The horse trotted back toward the bungalow, and Eden inched sideways to make room for him on the seat beside her. As he stepped up she handed him the reins. He gave them a flip, and the horse started down the path.

Eden scanned the distant hills of green foliage contrasted with dark boulders, streaked with garnet and mauve.

"You know the difficulty Grandfather has with the idea of Candace and Keno getting married," she said. "There's going to be trouble because Oliver P. Hunnewell is returning with him. The engagement Ainsworth wants is no doubt at hand."

"Candace's bound to dig in her heels," Rafe agreed. "Even so, she's not been here the last few weeks just to spend time with Keno. She's been teaching some of the wives and children of our workers who've recently become Christians. Keno and I are going to build a another bungalow to meet in and put a cross on top," he said simply.

She stared at him, surprised that he'd been active in church planting when she knew of the eighteen-hour days he'd been keeping to get the pineapple plantation established.

"Why—that's wonderful, Rafe! Does Ambrose know? He didn't mention it to me."

"Keno was talking about it with Noelani, so she'll pass it on to him. I'm trying to get Keno to become the lay pastor, but he's got cold feet."

"Then who's been doing the teaching?"

"Candace," he said. "She's been teaching the women."

She hadn't known; she was learning some things.

"We also need a good interpreter. What do you know about Ling Li?"

"Strange you should mention him. I've seen him just this morning. Yes, he might be helpful, though his youngest boy is ill. I'm hoping to see him, and I may need to contact Dr. Bolton."

He turned his head. "You're taking too many risks, Eden." His resonant voice was calm, but with a note of purpose.

"I'm a nurse. It's my calling."

Under his scrutiny she felt suddenly uncertain. Tension seemed to rise between them. After a moment he went on. "Your women's class at the mission church has been successful." He looked at her evenly. "Maybe you'd consider helping us here? Taking Candace's place for a while? We meet on Thursday nights."

Eden realized she must have been looking at him with her feelings written on her face. She turned her eyes away. "Yes, I think I could manage it. Thursday nights?"

"Yes, around seven."

Eden looked toward Mauna Loa. A haze robed the mountain with mixed shades of charcoal, purple, blue, and green. The palms and ferns rustled alongside the road.

Grandfather Ainsworth's return to the islands had apparently seized Rafe's attention, for he returned to that topic as he drove the horse and buggy toward his plantation house. "So your Grandfather's back in Honolulu," Rafe said. "I'll be interested to hear what's developed from his meetings in Washington D.C."

"Don't tell me what I've heard about you is true after all."

He lifted a brow. "What have you heard?"

She toyed with her sun hat. "Oh, just that you're beginning to be swayed toward annexation. That you're a member of Loren Thurston's Honolulu Rifles. That you attend their secret meetings."

"If you know that much, it doesn't speak well for their secrecy, does it?"

She glanced at him and saw a smile.

"Who's been depicting me as this dark conspirator? Zach?"

She didn't want to make trouble between the two men she cared most about, so she shrugged gracefully.

"You know the political situation. As you say, there are many hotheads. Seems everyone's talking revolution."

"And choosing sides like children in a game."

"Surely you're not saying there won't be a revolution?"

"With the foolish standoff between Liliuokalani and the Legislature? I'd be the last one to suggest otherwise." Unfortunately, I don't think she understands the genuine convictions of men like Thurston. It's too easy to underestimate their sober opinions. They won't have their individual rights and property subject to the whims of absolute sovereignty, not after her brother's faulty reign, giving too much power to a fraud like Gibson."

Eden did not favor Gibson, but she was concerned over what Rafe believed. "You've always supported the Hawaiian monarchy," she reminded him.

Three years ago, when Rafe had first planned to enter a life of journalism, he'd written well-researched articles for Great-aunt Nora's *Gazette*, all of them fully supporting the Hawaiian monarchy.

"Unless Thurston's group has managed to persuade you otherwise," she wheedled.

His smile was indulgent. "You'd make a good spy. Are you sure you're not working for the monarchists? Have you considered changing your profession?"

"Very amusing. I shall never give up medicine."

"Never?"

She smoothed the ribbons under her chin, looking straight ahead.

"If I'm to be swayed toward annexation of the islands," Rafe went on, "I'll decide for my own conscience. I won't need Thurston and Dole. As a matter of fact, though, you're wrong about those two. They're decent men, conservative in their politics, and they have the future of Hawaii in mind."

"I don't believe I'm wrong. Nora's told me so much about them. Facts that she's dug out of the cave, so to speak."

"Sounds dangerous."

Eden folded her arms and ignored his comment. "Thurston desires a revolution at any cost, even bloodshed."

"Nora has convinced herself of that. Once she's convinced, it's easy to pound the drums to win others."

"So, you do support annexation!" she said almost indignantly.

"Thurston's not one of the hotheads pushing for annexation, but there are prominent men on both sides of the issue, by the way. Nora lacks some incontestable facts; what she does have is an over-supply of zeal for Liliuokalani."

"I shall be sure to tell her that."

"One thing is certain, you won't find me out front leading the charge like a General Lee. I may support the birthright of Lili-uokalani to the Hawaiian throne, but that doesn't mean I'll put my head on the chopping block for her royal cause again."

Again, because, as Eden well remembered, before he'd embarked on his voyage to French Guiana, he'd written on the right of Lili-uokalani to reign after her brother, who was childless. While his article had upset Grandfather Ainsworth, her Uncle Townsend became enraged. To this day, Townsend believed that he'd fright-ened his rebellious stepson Rafe out of Hawaii. "If the need arises," Townsend boasted, "I'll do it again." Eden knew her uncle was deceived. Rafe had planned his trading voyage on the *Minoa* almost a year before leaving Honolulu with Keno and the others. He had chosen a rigorous captain, "a seasoned man of the sea," as Rafe had called him, who had vowed to "indoctrinate" Rafe in the ways of a ship. The voyage from Honolulu took over two years, and when he and Keno returned, Rafe was the Minoa's new captain, with a highly prized cargo—the new variety of pineapple slips.

"Nora's urging me to resume my old journalistic position at the *Gazette*," Rafe was saying with a faint smile. "In my spare time, that is."

"Well, I hope you stay too busy with Hawaiiana," she said candidly. "Zachary's passionate about his work at the *Gazette*, as you know. Great-aunt Nora has all but promised him control of her newspaper if he's successful. It means everything to him."

"Zach doesn't need to concern himself with me taking his place. As you so aptly put it, my hands are full at present, nurturing sweet, glorious pineapples *and* Kona coffee, I might also add, if I regain control of my father's plantation on the Big Island."

She knew Hanalei was Rafe's supremely desired treasure. As yet, it still dangled like a pearl before his eyes.

"It's Silas who has an eye for position as Nora's editor-in-chief," Rafe said.

The disclosure rendered her momentarily speechless. Had Silas worked in journalism before coming to Honolulu?

"I'm certain that will astound Zachary. He thinks of Silas as a gambler."

Rafe looked thoughtful. "So Zach's told me. The truth is, I've been so busy here at Hawaiiana that I haven't spent more than a few minutes in conversation with Silas since he arrived in April."

"Silas's interest in running Nora's newspaper won't make things any easier between Zachary and Silas."

"Zachary is insecure," Rafe said quietly and uncritically. Eden recognized in Rafe the same protective attitude that he'd had for Zachary since boyhood. She thought of Zachary's injured leg, and how Ambrose told her that Rafe came by the mission church that morning to ask whether he'd seen Zachary the night before. Had

Candace really seen Zachary on the lanai after midnight? If so, why had he chosen to flee? Candace certainly had a clear mind; was there some misunderstanding?

Hawaiiana Plantation House emerged, a handsome white structure in full sun surrounded by sage-green palms and a wide lanai. She had little time left alone with Rafe and knew she must grit her teeth and accomplish the task if it was to be done. She smoothed the edge of her nurse's pinafore and gave him a glance.

"Rafe . . ." she began, clearing her throat delicately. "I was on my way here to see you before Lana Stanhope gave me Great-aunt Nora's prescription, and before I ran into Zachary on the road."

He turned toward her.

"This is not going to be easy for me to tell you," she began again, "or for you to receive." She straightened her shoulders and stared ahead. "You see, I've been sent by Kalihi Hospital's Board of Health. It's about Kip."

There. She'd opened the dread door that would lead to *trouble.* A moment of stark silence followed and she let out a quiet breath. His tanned hands tightened their grip on the reins. Although Rafe was a solid Christian, she knew he was sometimes like a restrained volcano. Several years ago she'd watched in horror on the beach as his stepfather, Townsend, struck his face several times with fists while Rafe kept his arms loose at his sides. But she'd also seen him flatten Zachary—no easy task—when Zachary had tried to embrace and kiss her. Zachary hadn't understood that she was his blood cousin.

Rafe turned to look at her. Though she stared straight ahead and refused to meet those dark, energetic eyes, she could *feel* his gaze.

"You have my full attention, Eden. What about Kip and the Board of Health?"

"Rafe, first I want you to understand how I went out of my way to try to get the Board members to change their decision, and that I also requested to be sent to you as their representative. Lana thought I should have let her do it. Maybe she was right, but I had my reasons. I know this won't make you feel any better toward me."

Rafe stopped the buggy where there was shade under several large crape myrtle trees in full magenta bloom. With the plantation house directly in front of them, he dropped the reins, jumped down, and walked around to her side. Before speaking another word, he lifted her down, held her shoulders and faced her. Their eyes locked.

"What about Kip?"

"I wanted to bring the news because I couldn't bear the thought that you might think I was indifferent to the Board's decision."

His gaze narrowed intently. "What decision?"

"I—I almost feel a certain responsibility over what's happening. Because I'm part of Kalihi, of the medical group who has made these laws. But Rafe, we must enforce them! I have no choice—"

She saw the small flame come to life in the depths of his eyes. And yet his voice came with utter calmness.

"What about Kip?" he repeated.

She drew in her breath and forced her emotions to stillness. She nodded and swallowed.

"Someone, I don't know who, alerted the Board of Health regarding Kip's birth at Kalawao . . . and now you can't adopt him, Rafe." In a monotone she continued, "I've come to take him back to Kalihi."

A moment elapsed. The breeze rustled the nests of purple flowers, and the leaves swayed.

"No one is taking Kip to Kalihi, Eden. Not even you."

His response did not surprise her, but his deadly calm affected her more than a swell of outrage. She would allow the grueling moment to ease a little before going on with her mission.

"Tell me how the information reached the Board," he said, his jaw clenching.

"Yesterday, a message arrived for Dr. Bolton. It would have been at noon when he was alone in his office. Lana and the others had taken their usual lunch break out on the lanai."

"Yesterday . . ."

"I only learned of it this morning from Lana," she explained, lest he misconstrue her delay in coming to inform him of anything so tragic.

"It was a letter to Bolton?"

"Not a letter. A sheet of ordinary paper, the words printed in ink, not pencil. The paper was folded neatly in half, and there was no envelope. Dr. Bolton said a Hawaiian boy delivered it to his office. I saw nothing familiar in the writing or in the spelling. All was correct."

"No pigeon English?"

"No."

"What were the exact words, if you can remember?"

She reached for her medical satchel. "I can do better than that. I wrote them down. I've brought you my copy." She handed the note to him and watched as he read the words, which she now knew from memory.

The baby boy named Kip held by Rafe Easton on Hawaiiana was born of a leper on Kalawao. You must do something. It's illegal. The baby is a leper.

"Dr. Bolton's sympathetic," she said quickly, hoping to convince him he had friends at Kalihi. "He and Lana are on your side of this issue. They tried to talk the Board into ignoring the message, but the others refused. The law is clear as they see it. I don't think they'd have permitted me to represent them if they knew we'd been engaged."

"Just what does the Board think they're going to do about Kip?"

"You know the law as well as I. That's why you kept Kip's birth a secret when you brought him here. Most people think he's your nephew. The truth is known, Rafe. I must bring him to Kalihi."

"For how long?"

She hesitated. "It's—the time can be rather indefinite. At least until they know he doesn't have leprosy."

His discerning gaze made her uncomfortable, and she looked away.

"And after he's cleared?" Rafe persisted.

He already knew the answer, as did she. He was forcing her to admit to the painful reality about Kip's future.

"I've already said the law won't allow adoption," she confessed miserably. "He'll need to remain on the Kalihi premises, or . . ." She could not go on.

"Or be sent to Kalawao," he said brutally. "Isn't that the true situation, Eden?"

She remembered the tragic scene she'd witnessed earlier that morning as the lepers boarded the steamer for Molokai. She could envision little "Hansel and Gretel" holding hands to comfort one another and looking with frightened eyes back at their wailing mother. But Kip was still a baby and wouldn't know why he was being taken from the warm, happy arms of Noelani and sent away to strangers at the leper camp. The thought was unbearable.

"I'll never let him go to Molokai!" she cried with strong revulsion. "I promise you he'll remain in the Kalihi ward."

Rafe gave a stiff shake of his head. "You won't be able to stop it, Eden. That decision will be left to the Board. I'm going to find out who it was that meddled in my private affairs. And when I do, he'd better slink away unseen for the first boat to Shanghai."

"Rafe, please. Let me handle this."

"Just what do you think you can do?"

"I can protect Kip at Kalihi until it's proven he doesn't have the disease. Then, we'll find a way to . . . to release him to better circumstances." She didn't think he was still listening.

"There were just a few of us who knew about Kip's beginnings," Rafe was saying pensively. "That gives me a good start where to begin asking questions. From there I'll talk to Lana Stanhope and Bolton and anyone else at Kalihi who might remember something. I'll not give up till I track him down—if it was a he."

"You don't think that Lana would do such a thing!"

"Lana?" For a moment it seemed he'd never heard her name before. "Lana didn't know where Kip was born. Did you ever mention it to her?"

"I've never mentioned Kip's birth to anyone, not even Ambrose and Noelani."

"I know it wasn't them or Keno. They'd all die at the stake before harming Kip's future."

Eden waited, but he said no more. She formed fists in her lap. "Why didn't you include me in those who would 'die at the stake?'"

"Do you need to ask me that, Eden?"

She remained silent, mollified, then tore her gaze from his.

"Does Zach know where Kip came from?" he asked.

"Not through anything I've said. I don't believe he'd do anything so low. Maybe in the past, but not now. There must be someone else. Someone here at the plantation? A worker who may have overheard something?"

Rafe shook his head, looking at the message again. "The English is too good." He paused, thinking. "Someone on the *Minoa*, perhaps. Though I doubt it. They're all loyal. I've known them for over a dozen years. They're paid well, and there are no grudges. I'll make sure about it, though."

"Rafe, whoever did this is either afraid Kip actually carries leprosy or else has a grudge against you. Either way, it won't change the results, even if you discover who notified the Board. You know what I must do."

Rafe's gaze sharpened. "And what do you *think* you must do?"

Reluctantly she turned back to the buggy and retrieved from her medical satchel the legal document, endorsed by the Board, that awaited Rafe's cooperative signature. With her back toward him she bit her lip. Then, in a professional tone, she said, "I'm sorry, but Kip must be put under indefinite quarantine at Kalihi."

"No one is taking Kip."

She turned quickly to face him. "No baby born of a leper can be adopted—"

"You've told me that."

"He'll need to stay in a bungalow at the hospital grounds with some others in his situation—"

He deftly lifted the legal document from her fingers and crumpled it, his gaze meeting hers, and tossed it back into the buggy.

"Kip isn't going to Kalihi, Eden."

"But Rafe—"

"And he is *certainly* not being sent to Kalawao. He doesn't have the disease. He's as clean as a lily, and you know it."

"Of course I know it. I'm a nurse, remember? And a student of tropical diseases under Dr. Bolton."

"You have my highest regards, Miss Eden," he said with a small bow. His next words came with blunt precision. "Even so, Kip isn't going to any holding station, not if I can stop it."

She went to the buggy to retrieve the wadded legal paper, smarting under his retort. Sometimes his wry little remarks about her work infuriated her. He was jealous, that was all. Jealous because she wanted to excel in the study of tropical diseases so she could one day work with her father. Why couldn't he understand that she loved her father?

"The Board of Health has already made laws that can't be altered without the Legislature changing them," she said, briskly smoothing the wadded paper to cover her misery.

"Our brilliant Legislature doesn't even know what it's doing half the time. The only thing they care about is keeping their power base. Look, Eden. You've already examined Kip for yourself. He's clean. Noelani cares for him every day. So does Celestine. Placing him at Kalihi in quarantine will only increase his chances of contracting leprosy."

Her heart melted. She couldn't help herself. "Oh, Rafe, I'm so sorry. This is such a dreadful situation. When Lana told me this morning about the message, I didn't know what to do. I'll make you a promise. I'll be there working nearly every day, sometimes late into the evening. I vow I'll not let Kip out of my sight for longer than absolutely necessary. I'll even put a bunk in the children's room and sleep there. I'll protect him, I promise—"

His reaction was sudden and startling. She was in his arms, and his heated gaze wouldn't let go.

"Do you think risking both yourself and Kip in any way solves my dilemma? Don't you understand yet, Eden? It's your protection that I worry about, as well as Kip's. My mind was made up months ago. I'm going to adopt him. He's *mine*. The moment I took him aboard ship, I made a commitment. No one is going to thwart me now. Once my heart is committed to someone, I won't quit trying. Not with Kip—and not with *you*."

She lowered the side of her face against his chest and closed her eyes, relishing if only for a moment what seemed a restoration of their relationship, but in reality she knew that it was far from settled. She raised her face to look at him. The intensity of his gaze warmed her.

He lowered his head toward her—stopped abruptly, and then stepped back.

"I prefer to wait until you're sure your own sweet little heart is committed—not to Kalawao or to your honorable father, but to *me*."

She came rudely awake. "Committed? I've been committed to you since you were seventeen, and you know it! But I have a calling . . . and I must go through with it to see where it leads me."

"It will lead you to greater risk. Was Priest Damien able to escape leprosy during his service on Kalawao? Do you think Doc Bolton will escape as he handles diseased limbs and fingers day after day?"

She turned away, plucking some of the nearby purple blossoms. "We're all very careful. We're trained."

"Never mind. The Board's in error if they think sending you here with soft talk will cause me to sign Kip over. If Bolton wants to discuss the matter with me, he can come here himself."

Soft talk! She whirled. "It won't be Dr. Bolton who comes. It will be a Honolulu policeman! They arrested a man just last week for trying to run away with his wife. He'd been told to bring her to Kalihi, but he refused. Now she's in quarantine and he's being held at the police station."

"Very merciful of your kindhearted doctors and nurses to use health laws to intimidate and force cooperation. There's something to be said about the power to imprison people in outdoor cages while it's decided whether or not they're lepers."

Eden was stung into silence. How true! She could not endorse the corruption that occurred, as in past days under Arthur Murray Gibson, "the one-man cabinet" of King Kalakaua. Even now, injustice was displayed in certain decisions made by both the Board *and* the throne. Eden was offended by the "bounty hunters" who were rewarded financially for reporting anyone they could find who might have a visible sore, wound, or lesion. And if those reported didn't turn themselves in to the leper station at Kalihi for quarantine, the Honolulu police would arrive at their huts with rifles to arrest them. Eden found it distasteful to see frightened people locked up at the leper station for weeks and sometimes much longer, on the mere suspicion of having leprosy. If the lesion in question were designated leprosy, then papers were issued by the Board and the new leper was banished to the Kalawao colony, near Kalaupapa on Molokai Island.

Eden had never been more shocked than when she first arrived at Kalihi and met the leprosy patients she wished to help. They were not typical hospital patients, but internees. Many of them were being held against their will, men taken from families, women from young children. They weren't kept in comfortable, clean hospital rooms, as she'd thought, but in wired huts, like prison cells. Some were in actual metal cages on the grounds of Kalihi. Ethnicity appeared to have nothing to do with their treatment. Whether the suspects were Hawaiians, hapa-haoles, haoles, or Chinese, the law prevailed. Men and women, old and young, married and single were incarcerated. The first time she'd seen the situation—especially the small children taken from parents—it had broken her heart. In her mind these children were already doomed to die, which actually seemed more merciful than years of dreadful existence on Molokai.

Some of the apparent hardness of the Board of Health could be traced to certain Honolulu businessmen working on the mainland to promote sightseeing holidays amid Hawaii's tropical beauty. These businessmen, fearing that growing publicity over leprosy in the islands would hinder annexation, had urged King Kalakaua and Walter Murray Gibson to purge Hawaii of every known leper.

Firmness came into Rafe's voice. "Is this what it means to live in the Kingdom of Hawaii—to have a few greedy haoles manipulating weak kings who'd rather gamble and drink than rule with authority and wisdom? I, for one, don't care to have a pack of laws, rules, and regulations that benefit the few in power. I'll take a republic where individual rights are protected by a constitution. Where the freedom exists to protest self-imposed authorities who want to ramrod their wills through the Legislature."

Eden turned away.

"You can tell the Board what I said when you go back there tomorrow. If it's the last thing I do, Eden, I'll fight that law of non-adoption until I see it discarded. It's a law that needs to be booted out of Hawaii and anywhere else that claims to be a civilized Christian community."

It hurt deeply as she realized he saw her as siding with the enemy, infringing on individual rights, taking away the baby he had learned to love. Even her role as a compassionate nurse with the red cross proudly displayed on the front of her pinafore no longer merited his respect. Mention of helpless children taken from parents and placed in perpetual quarantine made her feel she was becoming stern and pitiless. Was this how he saw her, then? And the work she'd been proudly engaged in?

Eden's resolve tightened. "You seem to have forgotten," she choked, "that I am a victim of this same law. My mother was taken from me, from my father, and from the safety of her home. She was forced onto a boat to Kalawao. For years I never knew what had happened to her. Don't think that I have no compassion for the weak and abused." She whipped around to run toward the house when he overtook her.

"Eden, darling, please forgive me."

Once again, as in the past, she was in his embrace, and this time she clung to him, holding back tears, wanting him to understand and support her, yet knowing that she must not lose control of herself and be left vulnerable to every sentiment that could come sweeping her way.

"I know you're on Kip's side." He spoke warmly into her hair. "I only wish you were on mine."

Oh Rafe, but I am! she wanted to cry out. *I am!* And yet the words she believed and wanted to say were held bound and chained.

Someone was coming, riding the lane from the plantation house on horseback to where she and Rafe stood beside the buggy. Rafe released her, and Eden turned to see who it was.

Zachary rode up and drew his reins. He looked from Eden to Rafe and must have recognized that matters between them were strung to the breaking point. Rather than looking satisfied over Rafe's difficulties as he would have two years earlier, he looked genuinely disheartened.

"Oh," he said wearily, "sorry to interrupt like this." He looked over at Eden. "Grandfather's already arrived. He's up at the house now and sent me to call you up."

Eden stood, numb.

Zachary refocused on Rafe who stood with hands on hips. "Hope you don't mind, Rafe, but your plantation house seems to have been commandeered as the meeting hall."

For a moment Eden felt as though a storm had swooped through her mind, scattering her wits to the four winds as she remembered with a jolt, Candace, Keno, Grandfather, and Oliver P. Hunnewell. She had failed to warn Candace in time.

"Already arrived?" She put a hand to her forehead as if she could make herself come up with an answer to the dilemma. "But you said he wasn't arriving till this afternoon."

"The steamer must have arrived early. He surprised us all."

"But I never warned Candace," she said. "I needed to speak with Ambrose, then Rafe, and . . ."

"Let's not worry about it," Rafe said calmly. "Candace is mature enough to hold her own with Ainsworth. She's not a child, and Eden isn't responsible for making matters work out for everyone. Is Townsend here with you?"

Eden believed Rafe was thinking of his mother, Celestine, having to face Townsend. She was reluctant to legally end their marriage, despite Townsend's widely known infidelities. After his son Silas arrived, shining the spotlight on Townsend's earlier sins, her acquaintances advised her to divorce him, but she believed that something drastic could still happen and change him. "Life is meant to be endured," she often said. "Not every heartache can vanish with a magic wand. I've been taught that God's grace is abundant and that we can, in Him, *endure* whatever He allows to confront us. I was wrong to marry Townsend. I knew he was not faithful to God, so why should he be faithful to me? Now to jump out of my situation and expect to reap holiday cheer is immature."

"No, he stayed behind at Kea Lani," Zachary said. His voice turned sarcastic. "But his number one son, Silas, is here. Silas, that most seasoned and intelligent 'windfall-of-a-son' who arrived so unexpectedly from who knows where, is somewhere around, sneaking about, no doubt, with a deck of cards in his pocket."

Rafe showed interest for the first time. "You need to be cautious in what you say aloud, Zach."

Zachary jerked a shoulder to show his rebellious mood. "I have no proof yet, but I'll get it before this is over. And a whole lot more before I come out with it all. He says he's from Sacramento, and his mother was from the old silver rush in Carson and Virginia City. I think he's lying."

"Be careful," Rafe said again.

If Zachary's mood was any indication, the meeting between Townsend and his two sons at Kea Lani hadn't accomplished any good. Eden wondered if Ainsworth's sudden arrival had prevented the meeting.

"Ainsworth has a solid reason for coming here," Zachary said mysteriously.

Rafe shot a glance toward the plantation house, yet remained silent.

A solid reason? Eden drew her left hand behind her skirt, wondering. Grandfather Ainsworth wouldn't know that her engagement with Rafe was, as Zachary put it, "cracked in two." "What about Oliver Hunnewell?" she asked.

"Fortunately, he's gone on to Hunnewell Plantation to rest for a few days. Grandfather's giving a luau next week. Ol' Oliver will be there to begin his public courting of Candace. And guess what? Grandfather met up with someone else while in San Francisco," Zachary announced with sudden good cheer. "It turns out they all came home to Honolulu together. Just one big, happy family."

"Look, Zach, stop the theatrics," Rafe said. "You're worrying her. Out with it."

"Eden's brilliant father is here in the flesh—as gaunt and sober minded as a replica of Dr. David Livingstone."

Eden caught her breath. "My *father?* Dr. Jerome? He's *here?*"

"He is."

Dazed, she was nonetheless aware that Rafe tensed as he stood beside her.

Zachary turned on the saddle to gesture his blond head toward the big house. "If I'm not mistaken, that's Dr. Jerome coming off the lanai now to meet you, Eden."

Eden stared in near shock as a tall, thin figure in white came down the steps and walked in her direction.

"Eden?" he called. "Is that you, my daughter?"

It was, indeed, her father, Dr. Jerome Derrington. Her heart burst into unabashed joy from long-awaited expectation. With a laugh from deep in her soul, she dropped her medical bag and ran to meet him, arms open wide.

—☙❧—

Rafe watched Eden run to meet Dr. Jerome Derrington. They embraced and laughed. Rafe told himself that if he had thought winning Eden was difficult before her father arrived, the real struggle had only just begun. This moment would change everything.

Rafe looked up at Zachary astride the horse, expecting to see a typical smirk, but there was understanding in his blue eyes.

"My sympathy," Zachary said wryly.

Zachary drew the reins aside, and the horse did a fancy half-circle. "The Derrington patriarch wants to meet with you alone before he returns to Kea Lani," he said of Ainsworth. "You can bank on some important new conditions being added to the privilege of entering the Derrington family. Whatever they are, you'll need to wait and hear it from Ainsworth himself." With a two-finger salute to his brow, Zachary rode back up the lane toward the house.

Rafe stood in the tropical heat looking toward his plantation house. There was trouble ahead, and plenty of it. But he was no quitter. He would fight all obstacles to win what he wanted most. He was aware of the odds stacked against him, but that made the battle all the more important—and more interesting. What mattered was whether he was on the road of God's purpose or a path of his own making. A sure way to lose in the end.

Chapter Six
Dr. Jerome Derrington

den's enthusiasm over the arrival of her father, Dr. Jerome, remained undiminished throughout the day. Thus far, she hadn't mentioned the real reason for her visit to Hawaiiana, preferring to keep the matter of Kip and the Board of Health to herself and Rafe. Eventually, she would need to declare herself and her mission, since she could hardly keep the matter a secret when taking Kip away to Kalihi. She steeled her mind and emotions to endure what was ahead. She would need to explain to Noelani first since she was Kip's nanny. Later that evening, when she departed with her father in the buggy for Kea Lani, Kip would need to come with her. Perhaps the best time to bring Kip to Kalihi Hospital was when her father went to the Board of Health. He would need to give a broad report of his travels and research, since he'd been under the sponsorship of the deceased King Kalakaua.

Lunch was served on the lanai, the food arranged buffet-style on a long table with a bird-of-paradise flower arrangement. The family spent the afternoon enjoying refreshments and listening with interest while Dr. Jerome spoke of his travels.

Jerome's hair was thick and dark, and his long sideburns curving inward at the jawline were colored by the gray of age. His lean, craggy face, tanned and leathery from years of traversing the tropics of the world, wore a sober cast. His deep-set eyes told of a determination to achieve his goals, a single-minded spirit.

The dozen or so comfortable cane chairs were arranged casually. Eden became aware of her father smiling down upon her with undeniable pride upon learning of her successful ongoing studies in tropical diseases. Her heart, if only for a brief moment, was that of a young daughter, beating with the need to be cherished by her father.

The various dishes were cooked to everyone's delight, and even Eden, who thought she wouldn't be able to eat due to excitement, found herself enjoying the food. Her attention was riveted upon her father as he recounted his experiences with leprosy treatments in certain areas of India. She hardly stirred from where she sat near his chair on the breezy lanai. Fully absorbed, she continued to ask pertinent questions about the disease.

The other family members appeared to be interested, though they naturally would not share the zeal for medical knowledge that so engrossed Eden. If anything, Zachary looked bored and sleepy after lunch as he lounged in a wicker chair with his long, muscled legs stretched out before him and a small frown frozen between his golden brows. He looked as though he were recalling something unpleasant. He hadn't said whether he'd met with Townsend and Silas, and neither of them had come to Hawaiiana with Grandfather Ainsworth and Dr. Jerome.

Eden suspected Townsend's absence was out of deference for Celestine or, more likely, due to a wish not to encounter Celestine's rugged son, Rafe Easton, on his own property. Silas would have been welcomed, as Rafe had told her that morning, but Townsend remained a bully where Rafe's mother was concerned. Townsend knew well enough how his stepson felt about him.

Great-aunt Nora couldn't have weighed more than a hundred

pounds, but she was a tempest of energy when confronting matters she believed important to God and country—in this case the Hawaii Islands. Eden often enjoyed her vinegary facade, knowing that she had a tender heart, even if that tenderness was absent today. She sat as straight as a ruler in a fan-flared chair of white cane, one pale hand clasping a feather fan. Her crisp political gaze was fastened sternly on her brother, Ainsworth. It was apparent that she would prefer to interrogate him on his annexation meetings in Washington D.C., rather than listen to her nephew Jerome talk of exotic oils slowing the spread of leprosy.

Candace, with her flame-red hair braided like a wreath of nobility about her head, sat in outward Victorian repose, a tall, slim figure with a type of beauty that bordered on elegant plainness. The far-off look in her eyes told anyone who knew her as well as Eden, how her concerns were out wandering the pineapple fields with the handsome hapa-haole, Keno. Now and then Candace's eyes would sharpen on Grandfather Ainsworth like dueling blades preparing for a standoff.

Eden, with her spirits animated, found only one disappointment in the family gathering, and that was over her Grandfather's lack of enthusiasm for his son's research accomplishments. Accomplishments that Ainsworth labeled, kindly enough, as being "somewhat illusive." Eden was nettled by his attitude, just as she was affronted by anyone who failed to see the value of her father's sacrificial work.

Even so, Ainsworth's attitude didn't surprise her. He had found his younger son's dedication to a cure for leprosy a cause for concern from the beginning. According to Ainsworth, Jerome's jungle travels would end with his drowning in a river, being devoured by a tiger, or worse—contracting the dreaded disease himself. Ainsworth often stated that if he could have kept Jerome in Honolulu as he had Townsend, he would have done so. "Jerome is the son who should have run for the Legislature, not Townsend," he often said, "or if he wished to be the Lord's minister, why not lead a church in

Honolulu?" He affectionately called Jerome his "long-lost prodigal," and his travels, "a vagabond's penury."

To Eden, Dr. Jerome was the wise and noble traveler, the hunter and the finder of the golden grail, the hero who fulfills the divine quest and returns home with accolades. During lunch she tried to avoid looking at Rafe Easton, though she was fully aware of his presence. How could she not be? Unlike sleepy Zachary, swishing a pesky fly away from his nose, Rafe was not lounging at all, but standing, arms folded, and attentive to every word her father spoke. And it was Rafe who was asking Jerome the most knowledgeable of questions, so much so that her father looked surprised and altogether pleased.

Then something happened that changed the afternoon.

"Someone is coming," Candace said, stretching her neck to look over the railing at the wide court below. Eden, too, arose from her chair and went to the edge of the lanai. She feared it might be Townsend and Silas after all, which would throw new tensions into the mix. She glanced at Rafe. He stood watching the horse-driven buggy progressing up the dirt lane. Celestine came up beside Eden. Eden could feel the tension radiating from her.

"It's not Townsend or Silas," Celestine said calmly.

The buggy came to a stop below. A lone man climbed down from the seat and stood facing the plantation house. He was wearing a knee-length coat and a wide-rimmed canvas hat, and carrying a black leather satchel under his arm as though it contained gold bouillon. He lifted his head and looked up at them.

Dr. Jerome responded with a note of eagerness. "Why, it's Herald Hartley, my research assistant. This is a surprise!"

Jerome went on to explain that Herald Hartley had been detained in California, and that he hadn't expected him to arrive in Honolulu until the New Year. Hartley was in contact with a medical research colleague in San Francisco, trying to arrange a reunion between Dr. Jerome and a certain Dr. Chen. Jerome wanted Dr. Chen to appear with him before the Kalihi Board of Health to present their research. Both men were world travelers seeking to discover supplementary information on tropical diseases and herbicidal "cures," like chaulmoogra oil.

Herald Hartley looked to be in his late twenties, of pleasing appearance, with chestnut colored hair, a fashionable mustache, and steady, deep-set eyes of an unusual amber color. The moment he stepped onto the lanai he noticed Eden.

"My daughter, Miss Eden Derrington," Dr. Jerome said, then proceeded with other introductions. Rafe measured Hartley. Eden sensed Rafe's dislike from the first glance.

After introductions, Hartley was seated in a cane chair in the breezeway with refreshments, still clutching the black satchel. He then focused his attention on her father. "It is my misfortune to bring you tragic news. Dr. Chen, our colleague, has passed on. His death occurred last month at his Chinatown abode. It was a terrible accident. Terrible. He made the mistake . . . of bravery."

Dr. Jerome stared at his assistant. For a moment he turned ashen, then he leaned back into the cane chair in silence.

"My dear fellow," Grandfather Ainsworth suggested, horrified, "are you telling us that this ally of yours, Dr. Chen, contacted leprosy on his own person like Priest Damian of Molokai?"

Priest Damian, as Eden well knew, was now deceased. He had served for many years at the Kalaupapa leper camp and, in the end, had succumbed to the loathsome disease. Though Eden held the memory of the priest in honor because of his selfless dedication to the sick and infirm, she believed he'd been reckless in his approach. Damian had convinced himself he was invulnerable to catching leprosy unless God wished for him to suffer the ravages of the disease, and if not, he could take risks. He, therefore, took almost no precautions. He would drink from the same cup and eat from the same plate as lepers who were far into the final stages. He would smoke his cherished pipe, then offer it for a few good puffs to one of the lepers. The leper would puff on the pipe for a time, his mouth disfigured, and then hand the pipe back to Priest Damian, who would then replace the stem in his own mouth and puff on. He did this sort of thing for many years, which to Eden, was medically unwise. She would have scolded him had she been there, priest or no, but he remained one of her heroes, a Frenchman for whom she retained high respect. Few would live so selfless a life.

Eden recalled a nurse cleaning nauseating wounds of a leper, while a visitor stood afar looking on. "Horrible! How can you do that? I wouldn't do that for any amount of money."

The nurse, silent for a moment, said calmly, "Nor would I. But for Jesus I'll do it for free."

Herald Hartley's voice summoned Eden back to the moment. "Dr. Chen didn't die of *leprosy*. However, I suppose we could say . . . he died from his own research."

"What kind of research?" Rafe asked briefly, causing Herald Hartley to turn his head and take a long look at him.

"Why, he was testing the use of rare herbicides, Mr. Easton. Scarcely known on the mainland, and even less understood."

"The San Francisco authorities didn't mention any herbs by name?" Rafe asked.

"Offhand, I really couldn't come out and say. Dr. Chen took risks, as Dr. Jerome will tell you. Great risks, actually."

"Using herbicides on his own person? What kind?"

Eden looked at Rafe. Was he challenging him? Why?

"I don't know, Mr. Easton. There was . . . a packet of dried leaves found open on his research table, and an empty cup with residue. The authorities are working to identify what the leaves were. So far, they can merely guess. Personally, I believe the herb was from Tibet—not that I could identify it. I've not been there. It was boiled into a tea. The liquid is thought to be what took his life."

"A tragedy," Dr. Jerome lamented. "I would think Dr. Chen to have been more cautious."

"One would think so," Rafe said. "The Chinese are especially wise in the use of what we call *herbicides*. They know the difference between herbal medicines and outright poison. So it must have been a very rare packet of leaves. Wouldn't you say so?"

Eden tensed.

Herald lifted his water glass and squeezed a section of lemon into it, then stirred vigorously. His lower cheek and lip twitched. "Yes—yes. I thought so, too. I told the police so."

"Police?" echoed several surprised voices. "You were involved with the police?"

Herald looked at his water glass as though it bubbled up with information.

"Yes, it was an unpleasant experience for me. There was some question about his death actually, not resulting from accidental causes. I believe it's all cleared up now." He took a large, white kerchief and blotted his forehead.

"And to think I might have met with him in Chinatown before I voyaged to Honolulu," Dr. Jerome said disconsolately. "Unfortunately, when I arrived in San Francisco, he was unavailable. He had visitors, family from Shanghai I believe. I left Herald to stay on in California to see if he could arrange for Dr. Chen to come to Honolulu. When I met up with Ainsworth, we boarded the steamer for home."

Herald said with a heavy sigh. "Well, I ignored nothing, I assure you all. Had I arranged to meet Dr. Chen even a few days sooner, perhaps I would have noticed something that might have changed events, who knows? At least we would know more about his latest experiments with Tibetan lore."

"There's no accounting for hindsight," Grandfather Ainsworth said. "We would all live wiser lives if we knew the future."

"Would we? I wonder, sir," Rafe said. "Much of the future of the world is known, yet even those who understand often ignore it."

"Sadly so. Yes, you have something there."

Silence prevailed. Eden looked at her father. Dr. Jerome frowned, his lean, sun-tanned face creased with tired lines of age and possible illness. "Most astounding," he murmured, still benumbed by the loss of his ally. "Troubling, as well. We must make certain to uphold his name in our studies. Perhaps even name our new clinic after him. It would indeed be fitting."

Eden came alert. New clinic? Had her father returned to Honolulu to begin a leprosy clinic? Her heart began beating faster. It seemed that no one else caught the implication of what he'd said until she found Rafe watching her with a slight ironic smile. She looked away.

Great-aunt Nora picked up the pink feather fan from her lap and swished it around her face and throat. "Sounds like a lot of poppycock stew to me. Tibetan herbs, old wives' tales. Do tell me, Jerome, why do intelligent medical people, such as yourself, seem to think that if they travel to Timbuktu and hobnob with civilizations grounded in darkness and idolatry, that somehow or other, magical cures for all sorts of physical evils will sprout and abound?"

Zachary gave a short laugh.

So he isn't sleeping, Eden thought, irritated. *He's treating Father carelessly.*

"Maybe your Dr. Chen was victim of one of those mysterious tong wars," Zachary said lightly.

"Oh do be quiet, Zachary," said Candace.

"Lecture number six of the day," Zachary murmured. "Who said I was joking, old girl? It so happens I've been reading up on the tong wars. Gruesome, they were—or *are*. Depends. After all, Uncle Jerome just said he couldn't visit him because of visiting relatives from Shanghai."

Dr. Jerome appeared not to hear the chatter and went on gravely. "The grief I feel over Dr. Chen's death is not my personal loss alone. The loss is to the medical profession. He was to discuss his years of work with the Board of Health at Kalihi."

"Did I hear you correctly, sir, when you stated that Dr. Chen had recently returned from Tibet?" Rafe asked.

"Yes, though I couldn't tell you from where in Tibet," Dr. Jerome said. "Are you interested in the region, Rafe?"

Rafe smiled. "Not in particular, sir. My interests remain here, in Hawaii."

"Well, you have much on your hands," Jerome complimented.

Ainsworth looked pleased. "Good, good," he said to Rafe. "We need you in the islands."

Eden caught Rafe's eye. She arched a brow.

"In my humble opinion, there's too much interest in Hawaii. And I'm not speaking of you, Rafe." Great-aunt Nora turned her noble silver head toward her brother Ainsworth. "You haven't told us yet about your meetings in Washington, Ainsworth. Did Lorrin Thurston do any arm-twisting among the United States senators? I hope he found Uncle Sam daunting."

Rafe smiled, but Ainsworth looked at Nora with gravity. "No arm-twisting, my dear Nora, but discussions? Most beneficial. The Secretary of State proves to be a friend and ally of Hawaii. Just the same, we can discuss all that later. This is Jerome's hour. Go ahead, Rafe; what were you saying about Tibet?"

Nora stood to her feet, shaking her skirts out. "I've had enough talk on such depressing subjects as leprosy and murder. Coming, Candace?"

Murder! Eden began to feel a whisper of unease in the rustling of the palms and ferns.

Candace laid a hand on Jerome's thin shoulder as she went past into the house. "Sorry your homecoming was accompanied with unhappy news, Uncle. Welcome home nonetheless." She followed Great-aunt Nora from the lanai.

Eden noticed that Candace had not made the same departing "welcome home" remark to her grandfather. If Ainsworth had noticed, it didn't show.

"Murder? Rubbish," Dr. Jerome said, his cheeks ashen. "Accidental ingestion of poisonous herbs, if indeed that was the cause of Dr. Chen's death, is anything but criminal intent. I've almost made a mistake like that once or twice myself."

"Your aunt Nora misunderstood my explanation, I'm afraid," Herald Hartley said, his countenance apologetic as he looked from face to face.

"What was on your mind, Rafe?" Ainsworth persisted. "About Tibet?"

"Nothing in particular, sir." Rafe looked at Hartley. "Did you say earlier the medical report didn't disclose the plant that poisoned Dr. Chen?"

"I believe that's correct," Hartley said stiffly.

"Then you seem to be saying you don't know for certain that Dr. Chen actually died of some noxious herb."

"Well, yes, I guess that is so. I do not know for sure. The police wouldn't say. I suppose I am assuming somewhat."

"Although I was unaware of what he was working on in Chinatown," Dr. Jerome offered, "it does seem most probable it was a careless accident on his part."

"Even though I suppose his death may turn out to be heart failure from natural causes," Herald Hartley said. "Whatever the cause, it's a great loss."

Eden was listening intently. She grew restive. *Rafe's questioning of my father and Herald Hartley borders on a detective-like attitude. As if my father would know anything about Dr. Chen's death! Why should he?*

Eden stood abruptly. "You, too, have made many difficult journeys and risked your health in search of knowledge and cures. I suspect you know as much as did Dr. Chen. If you'll excuse me, Father, Dr. Bolton sent me to speak to Great-aunt Nora about her new medication. I brought it from Kalihi this morning." Without a glance at Rafe she turned and left the lanai.

_____C·Ω____

The afternoon ended peacefully enough, and the red-gold of sunset began to mingle with purple hues as dusk settled over Hawaiiana. The soft night whispered its arrival with the rustle of noble coconut palms making swaying shadows on the front lawn.

With Celestine requesting they all stay for a celebratory dinner to welcome Grandfather Ainsworth home and to celebrate Jerome's safe arrival from distant shores, Eden joined Candace in her guest bedroom. As they readied themselves for the elegant dinner, Eden wrinkled her brow, trying to recapture what it was about Herald Hartley's arrival that piqued her curiosity. The incident had come and gone like the rustle of the palms playing a theatrical interlude.

Candace's voice cut through Eden's reflection. "You haven't lost your earlier enthusiasm so soon, have you, Eden?"

Eden turned toward her older cousin of five years. Candace Minerva Derrington, with grave face, high cheekbones, and strong shoulders, stood watching her. Her auburn hair, so different from Eden's lush dark tresses, set them apart at any gathering. And while Eden's eyes were as green as gems, inherited from her mother, Rebecca, Candace had the sharp blue eyes of the Derrington men. She also had what Eden affectionately termed "a lean, hungry look" that complemented her sometimes overly strong opinions. Even the tone of her voice held the cool sharpness of a New England Yankee. If there was anyone in the family who had the emotional stamina to stand up to Grandfather Ainsworth, it was Candace. She was wealthy, having inherited all that belonged to her deceased father. As the only child of Douglas Derrington, Grandfather's firstborn son— and the son of his pride—Candace was destined to also inherit the lion's share of "all things Derrington."

Eden respected Candace for her convictions in the Christian faith. She was a sober woman who held interest in charity among the uneducated children of the sugar workers. She had always been unconventional, and thus it was no surprise when, instead of falling in love with one of the many sons of wealthy Island planters or businessmen, she'd fallen for a hapa-haole with no family to speak of and little prospect for owning large sections of land.

Candace was dressed for dinner in a blue dress of high Victorian fashion, lace to her chin and thin wrists. Her auburn hair was brushed clean and smooth into a sophisticated chignon.

"You're going with Uncle Jerome to Molokai, aren't you?"

Leave it to Candace to be one step ahead.

"He's not mentioned Molokai. He's more likely to resume his position at Kalihi," she said of the leper hospital.

"There may be trouble with Clifford," Candace said of Dr. Bolton. "Grandfather will naturally want Jerome to head up the Board of Health now that he's returned. That won't go over well with Lana, I'm afraid."

It was hardly a secret in the family, especially among the women, that Lana Stanhope and Dr. Bolton were in love, and had been for many years. Eden's preferences were torn between her father and Dr. Bolton, who had graciously granted her work in close alliance with himself and Lana.

"I shall avoid the battle, if it comes to one."

"I had no idea Uncle Jerome would return this soon after King Kalakaua's death. I wondered when the news might reach him."

Eden had wondered, as well. "Perhaps he and Herald Hartley were in San Francisco longer than we realize."

"Yes. With Kalakaua's death, will the royal funds for your father's leprosy research come to an end?"

Eden sighed. "I suppose so. The hospital research is separate, of course. That work is ongoing. I'm certain it's one of the main reasons my father is anxious to present his research before the Board next week. He needs funding to continue his own cause. That's the main reason I don't think he'll take, or even want, Dr. Bolton's position if asked. He's always been a singular man, as you know. His cause is Molokai—and Rebecca."

Candace nodded thoughtfully. "That's why I was surprised when he introduced the assistant, Herald Hartley. He's never worked with an assistant before has he?"

"He's never mentioned one to me. What did you think of him?"

Candace considered the question. "He seems dedicated enough to your father. I thought he appeared somewhat anxious at times." She smiled thinly. "He and Rafe didn't connect very well."

Eden glanced at her. Broken hearts often weaken one's health. *I should pray more for her.* Then she wondered about her own heart.

Other than the excitement over the return of Dr. Jerome there was actually little that brought daily joy. *Oh, Rafe.*

Turning to the mirror above the vanity table, Eden began arranging her thick, dark hair, decorating it with a few white blossoms that Celestine's serving girl had brought up on a tray. Eden had changed from her gray nursing dress and white pinafore into an evening gown borrowed from Candace, which almost fit. Candace was taller and thinner. Some would have called her "boney."

The stylish sash that Eden now tied about her waist did wonders for the fit of the pale apple-green watered-silk dress.

"Oliver's arrival was as unexpected as Jerome's," Candace said shortly. "It was quite unfair of him to return now."

Eden couldn't hide a wry smile over her cousin's indignation. "Would the time of his arrival in Honolulu ever be right?"

Candace sighed. "I wish he'd stay in the Bay City and take root like a mulberry tree. Even so, it wasn't fair of Grandfather to return with Oliver in tow, as though bringing me a new puppy."

"At least he won't be coming to dinner tonight. According to Zachary, Oliver went home to Hunnewell House."

"A small reprieve. The luau next week is more than soon enough. By then I may be able to convince Grandfather I've no intention of marrying Oliver."

The luau, as Eden recalled, was to announce the public engagement. Her heart knew a pang. There'd been a luau for her and Rafe as well. That warm and wonderful night of festivities under a big yellow moon was etched in her memory forever.

"I don't know how I'm going to convince him, but I must. *Good* marriages aren't made in heaven, according to Grandfather," Candace clipped. "They're made for land and money. Love doesn't enter in at all."

"Well, in fairness to the old ways of arranging marriages, the missionaries in 1820 married those who shared their hearts for the work. They were willing to give up material treasures for eternal reward. Love may have come later."

"I suspect it did. At least, they had respect for each other."

Candace seemed to be thinking of someone in particular. After a moment she said, "Poor Celestine. Who could respect a husband like Uncle Townsend. And springing Silas on her the way he did. It was odious."

"It was Celestine's decision to marry Townsend," Eden said. "And the reason had nothing to do with furthering the work of God."

"And now she suffers. But I have respect for her. At least she's taking responsibility and not making excuses. Well, *my* marriage will be made by heaven as they say, or there'll be no marriage."

Eden must have shown her doubt, because Candace paced restlessly. "I mean it, Eden. I'm not going to marry Oliver. If I respected him we could at least build a decent life together, or try. Maybe one day I could even love him as the father of our children. I'm sorry to say, I think Oliver's lazy and spoiled. He's inherited everything, and earned nothing. And he's willing to receive it all by agreeing to every wish of the Hunnewell family, and to Grandfather, too. Can you imagine the disagreements we'd have?" She placed a hand to her forehead dramatically.

Eden sympathized. She'd not cared much for Oliver, either, who was a boring elite, and worse than Zachary when it came to social prejudices. And of course, Oliver had little respect for Keno, whom he brushed off as unimportant. He could never understand why Candace would turn him down. "Grandfather would be shocked to hear you say you don't respect Oliver. If there's any name in Honolulu to which tribute is paid, it's Hunnewell."

"Oh, yes, *Albert* Hunnewell the minister, their great-grandfather. Along with our own *Jedaiah* Derrington, and *Wallace* Parker, good men, all. But their offspring? Some wear the name after the glory has departed. And to think we, like Oliver, are the offspring of some of the great missionaries of the past. They gave up family, friends, and security to come to the islands. They suffered from lack of food and became ill with tuberculosis in order to turn spiritual darkness into light. They received little if anything in return but a grass hut. And even that was slandered by the Honolulu business-men of the time as an act of greed."

"The businessmen were looking for excuses to condemn the missionaries. The truth is, they liked the money the whalers spent for their liquor, and didn't want to see the islands find morality," said Eden.

"They needed the Savior themselves, but didn't see it."

"*Would not* see it. They were comfortable dwelling in darkness." Eden knew well the story of how angry the whalers were because the Hawaiian women no longer swam out to their ships for sexual liaisons, but were keeping their bodies as dwelling places for the Spirit of God. Some of those whalers had lain waiting for Hiram Bingham to kill him, but a Hawaiian saved him from their clubs. The story reminded Eden of how the people in Sodom had sur-rounded Lot's house, threatening to injure him because he opposed their wickedness.

"I agree," said Candace, "and it saddens me. Even so, to convince the family Keno is a better choice will be nigh to impossible. For one thing he doesn't have a respected old family name, and he's not a landowner in Hawaii."

"It appears as if it doesn't matter what they sincerely *believe* in their hearts, just as long as they come from one of the old families. Oliver is a nominal believer. His faith doesn't influence his life at all."

Candace moved restlessly about the room, looking at some of the Easton family paintings on the wall. "To think I was born into such a missionary family, with Great-grandfather Jedaiah one of those early Christians. Yet, it wasn't until Keno—a *Hawaiian*—taught me the basics of Christianity that I fully understood the meaning of Jesus' death on the cross. Only then, did I claim His fin-ished work of redemption for *my* very *own*. Before that it was imper-sonal, just as it is with Oliver Hunnewell and many of us. It's so tragic. But Keno *isn't good enough* for me to marry."

Eden had understood all along that it was Keno's faith, brought to him through Rafe, that had won Candace's love and loyalty.

"Did you know Keno's the only one showing up at Ambrose's for the Monday night study? Of course Rafe's excused, with the new group he's started with the pineapple workers, but what about our own Zachary?" Eden remained silent about Zachary's tense relationship with his half-brother Silas. Even so, Candace was astute and must realize there was a problem.

"The Oliver Hunnewell I know wouldn't endure getting his shoes mussed by walking across a wet field to attend church. I shall tell Grandfather that, too. Make Oliver show he's a Christian by attending the Monday evening studies at Ambrose's. Let me see his love for our Lord, and his interest in Scripture. Grandfather will soon find out that Oliver's religious convictions are without foundation." Candace gave a brief mirthless laugh.

Her action took Eden by surprise. Candace sobered as quickly as she'd laughed. "Keno would walk through a thunderstorm to attend that Bible study. That's what I love about him. The muddy shoes and his old Bible. Facing the storm if necessary, all to be there. Don't you see what's ironic in all this? Are we not the magnificent Derringtons? The noble offspring of some of the first missionaries who left all in Connecticut and Boston to enlighten the Hawaiians? Grandfather Ainsworth keeps the painting of Great-grandfather Jedaiah in the hall at Kea Lani, doesn't he? The Bible Jedaiah used to teach his first Hawaiian convert is on the ledge beneath the painting."

"But Grandfather's proud of the work his father did here in Honolulu, as we all are."

"You're missing my point, Eden. He's proud of Jedaiah for the spiritual choices made in his time. When it comes to making spiritual choices today, however, the family frowns. Other than memorializing the painting, how does Jedaiah's work of faith inform Grandfather's present choices?"

The answer, of course, was painful, and Eden kept silent. She understood the tragedy for Candace in a marriage to Oliver. She'd never be content with him unless he became a *new man* in Christ.

What was it Pastor Ambrose had taught on a recent Sunday morning? It was on the same subject, but he'd applied it to all Christians in Hawaii, rather than just the old missionaries. "Are we like the ancient Israelites in the days of the prophet Jeremiah?" he'd observed. "They were the chosen people for the purpose of serving the God of Israel and making Him known to the peoples about them. Ah, Israel—the light of the nations, the one depository of *the* Truth!"

Ambrose had raised his worn Bible.

"Instead of leading the way for the spiritually blind about them, that generation of Israelites began to imitate their idolatrous practices. 'God will *never* permit Babylon to destroy Jerusalem, because we have the Temple,' they argued with Jeremiah. 'The temple of the Lord, the temple of the Lord!' they shouted. What were they saying? God would never bring Jerusalem to dust and rubble. After all, they continued their religious rituals, didn't they? Even if their behavior was like the heathen all around them, and far from the Holy One that the Temple was built to serve."

It had been convicting, and Eden wondered about her own heart. Did she desire to work with her father on Molokai for *God's* honor, or was her motive self-serving? The Derringtons liked to boast about their spiritual heritage as offspring of the great missionaries to Hawaii. They often boasted about *their* dedication, *their* work, and *their* faith. But what about *ours*? Ambrose was right.

"And what good is a painting of a family missionary hero, whose example we don't follow?" she murmured to herself. "We might as well put it in the museum."

Candace, who'd grown reflective, looked at her. "What were you saying about the painting?"

"Oh, just that it might as well be in the museum."

"Grandfather will never permit that."

Candace had misunderstood her reflection. Even so, she allowed the subject to fade. Probably no one in the family loved Grandfather Ainsworth more than Candace did. She had been chosen to receive most of his attention as they'd grown up. Not even Zachary, male inheritor until Silas arrived, had been so favored. Eden was sure Candace didn't speak this way out of disrespect, but in frustration. Even in Eden's own situation as a child and young girl, the silence in the family, which had cloaked her mother's leprosy had been permitted by the Derringtons, not for her good, but to guard the cherished family name in Honolulu and the mainland, where people often stigmatized any family with the sickness.

"Well?" Candace persisted, like a sharp-eyed bird honing in on its prey. "How does Grandfather's plan for my marriage harmonize with Jedaiah's sacrificial faith in God, which he honors so much? Would it not be a tribute to Jedaiah's memory for his great-niece to marry a *Hawaiian* who led *her* to the Lord? I believe Great-grandfather Jedaiah would smile with joy. What a great compliment to his missionary life."

Eden walked out onto the lanai, troubled. "You're right, Candace, but in fairness to Grandfather, he has allowed me to pursue studies in tropical diseases and work at Kalihi, though he wasn't thrilled about it."

"Maybe you were the fortunate one after all, to be born of a woman he thought so little about," she retorted. "He would never permit me such freedom, as you well know."

Eden ignored what could have taken as an unkind word about Rebecca. Candace was hurting deeply now, and she needed understanding. "Grandfather has his faults as we all do. Look at how my mother was chased off to Molokai and the truth kept from me all these years. I used to question whether I was even a Derrington."

"Yes . . . so did Zachary," Candace said wryly. "I'd be furious if I were you! About your mother, I mean. I've thought all along that you've borne that injustice very well, Eden. Like a saint, if you don't mind my getting sentimental. If that were my mother they'd sent away and allowed me to believe she was dead—well, perhaps we'd best not traverse that path."

"No," Eden said wearily, sinking into a chair. "I haven't behaved saintly at all. Many times I was furious, as you say, but I want to move ahead. And I shall. I'm going to work alongside my father, and no one will stop me."

Candace looked at her thoughtfully. "I won't try telling you what your heart bids you do, except to say that men like Rafe don't last forever. Parker Judson's niece had her eye on him when she was here last. I'm sure you noticed."

Eden wouldn't permit herself to dwell on that. There was too much to do, and all of it important. "Ainsworth has his reasons for doing things his way, and while I don't always agree," Eden said, "I won't believe callousness plays a part in his decisions."

"Callous? No, that he is not. I know he loves us and wants the best for our future, but I still recognize that the Derrington enterprise is his first love. I would be perfectly satisfied if I could marry Keno and live in a modest house by the mission church while he took Ambrose's place as lay-pastor."

Eden sighed. "You're noble, Candace, and knowing Grandfather, he'd think so, too. But as you say, the Derrington name and enterprise are more important to him than a humble mission church and a small congregation. And he's leaving the enterprise to you."

"And if he does leave the Derrington enterprise to me, it's not really for me. He will choose the man that he wants to entrust it to, and I just happen to be the means to turn Kea Lani into a larger enterprise. The Derrington-Hunnewell enterprise."

"So, then," Eden said with a sigh. "We're back again to Oliver P. Hunnewell."

"Rather, we're back to the huge Hunnewell lands." Candace was looking out past the lanai. "I'm surprised Rafe's been able to keep this pineapple plantation-in-the-making. Do you know how badly Grandfather and Uncle Townsend desire this new pineapple he's brought to Honolulu?"

Eden knew very well, indeed.

"I think Grandfather would offer Rafe most anything to buy out his partnership with Parker Judson. Or, at least, to acquire it through Rafe's marriage into the family." She looked pointedly at

Eden's left hand. "I'm not the only one destined to stand against the old lion on the marriage issue. What are you going to do when he learns the engagement with Rafe *and his pineapples* has been set aside?"

Eden recognized the wry note in her voice at the mention of Rafe's pineapples. Yes, Ainsworth had welcomed, even promoted her marriage to Rafe before he'd left for Washington D.C. He'd praised Rafe's strength and abilities, *and* his pineapples from French Guiana. Matters were not likely to go well when she let it be known that she was setting marriage aside for now to follow her vision of medical research with Dr. Jerome.

Candace scrutinized her. "From what you've told me it wasn't Rafe's decision to postpone, but yours."

"We agreed in unison," Eden said quickly.

"The only reason I'm mentioning it is that if Rafe decides to say anything tonight to Grandfather, you'd best be prepared. Grandfather's asked to speak to him alone."

Eden stood, alert. "Have you any idea what it's about?"

"Not exactly. Great-aunt Nora thinks it has something to do with annexation, and the Reform Party that Thurston started. But, one never knows. And if either Grandfather or Rafe mentions the engagement, the frog will be out of the pond."

Eden pondered uneasily. Maybe she was in for more trouble tonight than she'd thought. As Candace had observed, she herself could be held accountable to sacrifice for the Derrington cause: sugar and politics.

Or, maybe the meeting had nothing to do with her at all, and everything to do with Rafe's partnership with Parker Judson and pineapples. "Whatever the reason for their meeting, Rafe isn't likely to relinquish his part of the enterprise," Eden said. "Once the pineapple business looks successful, Rafe will be rewarded by being in charge of his father's Kona plantation, Hanalei."

Eden knew she was vindicating the postponement of their engagement by putting Hanalei on the same scale as her work with her father. She and Rafe *both* had separated to pursue their goals. Then how could Ainsworth hold her responsible?

Eden turned unexpectedly and fixed Candace with an inquisitive gaze. "Are you certain it was Zachary on the lanai you saw the other night?"

Candace's auburn brows lifted. "Yes, I'm certain. Has he explained?"

"I'm not sure anyone's asked him about it. Ambrose referred to it at the mission church earlier this morning. He mentioned that Rafe had come by and wanted to know if he'd seen Zachary around."

"Had he?"

"Apparently not. Rather odd, though, of Zachary to be on the lanai at midnight."

"That's why I mentioned it to Rafe this morning."

"And you're certain it was Zachary?"

"Eden!"

Eden smiled. "Yes, you're certain. Well, I shall leave you to finish dressing. I want to check on Great-aunt Nora before dinner." As Eden left the room, she was aware that Candace's eyes followed her out the door into the wide hallway.

Chapter Seven
Serpents in Paradise

$\mathcal{E}$den came noiselessly down the flight of stairs that fanned out at the bottom. She heard a woman's voice dimly resonating from the garden through the wide-open doors. Before she reached the doors, the banana plant in a green and gold pineapple-shaped planter pot moved, and for a startling moment Eden thought she saw a reptile coiling. She stopped short and looked again, then smiled to herself when a harmless green garden snake slithered out. She picked up an extra cane belonging to Great-aunt Nora and, managing to loop its body, carried it gently down the steps and deposited it safely under some ferns. "Next time you try sneaking indoors, I'll excommunicate you from the entire garden," she murmured to herself. Turning to leave, she heard a woman crying. She looked toward the lava stone walkway that wound through tall hibiscus flowers to a pond.

The woman might have been any of those in the house. Eden hesitated, wondering if she should offer a shoulder to cry on. Her concern got the best of her, and she walked in that direction. She had gone past the hau tree when she came upon a black lava stone bench behind some ferns. "Excuse me, can I help?" she asked, but when she came around the ferns no one was there. She was sure she'd just heard a woman crying.

Eden turned, scanning the spacious garden and breathing in the intoxicatingly sweet fragrance from the white gardenias with their yellow centers. Her steps made a faint sound on fallen petals.

Across the lava stone patio a flight of steps led through ferns and orchids toward the sandy, covelike beach. She thought of going down, certain now that whoever it had been, had gone there, but thought better of it. Evidently, the person had heard her coming and didn't wish to talk. Eden turned around and started back. She glanced toward the sea and saw clouds sitting there, waiting like an army for the signal to storm the island.

Except for the sound of her footsteps, silence pervaded the lovely tropical setting. The garden and mansion seemed to have withdrawn into secretive solitude. Then, unexpectedly, she heard Celestine's voice. "I won't stand by and see you take advantage of him again."

"Take advantage of *him?* You must be joking. That young man's one shrewd scoundrel! Look how he managed to come back to Honolulu with those pineapple slips."

"And you wanted them."

"Why not? He's my stepson! He should have come to me for a loan for this property, not Parker."

"You know very well you would have rejected his plans. You've never treated him like a son."

"Nonsense. I've treated him the same as Zach. What am I supposed to do? Go around tucking them in bed at night? Read them stories and pray with them? I'm not Ambrose."

"Oh, stop it. I'll go straight to Parker Judson if you try to stop the turnover of Hanalei to Rafe."

"The trouble with both of you Eastons is you can't get past Matt's death. Rafe's convinced I was to blame for that accident on Hanalei."

"Don't even bring that up."

"Rafe's always resented me. Jealous, from the beginning. Always praising Matt. Anything his father did was put on a pedestal. Hands off for anybody else. Now, see here, Celestine, you signed Hanalei over to my supervision when we married."

"An error on my part."

"And I've legal right to the plantation should Parker decide to back out of the lease. It was part of the deal. He can't transfer the lease unless I agree."

"You're known for scheming, Townsend. Ainsworth knows it, too. If you trouble Rafe again, either about Kip or Hanalei, I'll disinherit you completely from my will. If Ainsworth does the same, you'll be penniless. Then what? Do you think your foolish ways can sustain the lifestyle you're accustomed to indulging in? Not without everyone else's help, they can't. You'll be out cutting cane or harvesting coffee beans."

"That's extortion!"

"To protect what's rightfully my son's? To safeguard Kip? It's you who've extorted from Rafe's inheritance all these years. Not again, Townsend. Never again."

There came a loud slap, a woman's pained gasp, then silence.

Eden dug her nails into her palms. A sickening knot formed in her stomach.

Frozen to the spot, she stood unseen behind the palm fronds, her heart thudding in her ears. She'd been rudely awakened to an ugly side to her uncle Townsend. Fear jumped to her throat, and her heart thudded. *If Rafe ever learns that Townsend struck his mother . . .*

Celestine and Townsend mustn't know she'd overheard. The incident was between them and God.

Eden began backing cautiously away from the emotional quicksand she'd nearly blundered into and inadvertently bumped into something that moved. Whirling about she looked straight into the eyes of her cousin Silas Derrington.

He wore an unpleasant twist to his mouth. He took hold of her arm and drew her swiftly away behind some leafy trees.

Just then, Celestine hurried past where they stood concealed, and went toward the house. Eden made a move to go to her, but Silas's fingers tightened on her arm. He gestured with his head. A moment later more footsteps crunched over the sandy pebbles, and Townsend emerged from the shrubs, striding along the same path.

Silas looked after him, released Eden's arm, and shoved his hands in his pockets.

"It's not my affair, but if I were you, I wouldn't let either of them know you overheard."

"Eavesdropping isn't one of my pastimes, I assure you," Eden said shortly and might have wondered aloud whether it was one of his. *Where had he come from, among the tropical shrubs?*

"I don't know Rafe Easton well," he said, "but if what happened between those two gets back to him, he seems the sort that might want to teach Townsend a lesson on gentlemanly ways."

Eden remained judiciously silent when it came to commenting on Rafe's mother and her failed marriage. Uncle Townsend had long intimidated Celestine, who was so opposite her son, Rafe, in temperament that most people would never suppose she was his mother. Celestine was taken advantage of by Townsend and bullied into doing what he wanted. Eden remembered from growing up with Rafe at Kea Lani how angry he would become when he saw Townsend show disrespect to his mother or take advantage of the estate left to her by Rafe's father, Matt.

When Rafe had returned from his voyage to French Guiana and formed his partnership with Parker Judson, he'd suggested to Celestine that she could find a reprieve under his roof if she thought it necessary. So when Silas arrived in Honolulu two months ago, causing a great stir of gossip, Celestine quietly departed from Kea Lani late one evening with Eden's help. Eden brought her here to Rafe's new plantation house as she'd requested, and here she remained, keeping to herself.

So far, Townsend had left Celestine to her solitude. He carried on his life in Honolulu as usual, managing the Kea Lani's sugar business and occupying the Legislature seat he'd held since he'd been a young man in his twenties.

Celestine's public excuse for being private was illness. She needed the quiet, she told her friends. Eden was aware that she had also been assisting Great-aunt Nora with a book Nora was writing on Derrington family history.

Now, facing Townsend's son Silas, Eden remained silent. Would Rafe confront Townsend? When Eden had witnessed Townsend using his fists on Rafe at the beach, Rafe had refused to strike Townsend back. But, of course, back then it was Rafe being struck, not his mother, whom Rafe ardently respected as a true and gentle lady. Eden shivered to contemplate what might happen if Rafe had been here now, or if he should find out what happened. With a sick heart she folded her arms and looked back toward the plantation house. By now Celestine would have taken refuge in her bedroom.

What a mongrel Townsend turned out to be! Why was he such a selfish and ill-tempered man, when he'd been raised the son of Ainsworth? Although Eden's grandfather was dedicated to the sugar industry and to Hawaiian politics, he was not an unbeliever, nor was he a man who turned a blind eye to his son's immorality. Ainsworth had often rebuked Townsend for his disgraceful ways. How was it that his son had slipped through his fingers and grown up as he had?

Eden prayed for her uncle to change, but she was the first to admit that to pray for Uncle Townsend was one of the hardest prayer assignments she had, and all because she lacked the sincere fervor of Ambrose, who regularly prayed for the lost.

Dear Ambrose. She knew that Ambrose had Townsend's name on a special list of people he prayed for from deep within his soul. Ambrose would arise early enough in the morning to be single-minded, and three mornings a week he would take his special list of people with him while he walked along the beach "to talk with God, while our Great Intercessor Jesus Christ presents my feeble requests and pleas to the one and only Holy Father."

Eden was pondering all this when Silas's words pulled her back to the moment. "Looks as if I'm not the only eavesdropper in the family."

Eden sucked in a breath. Immediately she was tempted to lash out at Silas for insulting her. She flushed, furious with the irony that danced in his eyes.

Just like his father, Townsend. But was he?

Silas was in his late twenties, with chestnut brown hair and a well-trimmed goatee. He had the same light blue eyes as Zachary, but more grave. He wasn't as tall as his father or Zachary, and while of a husky build, appeared to have no particular liking for the outdoors. Even now, he wore crisp white linen, well-polished shoes of the highest fashion, and she noted his long fingers that often tapped and moved restlessly. Out of place on the Islands, but typical of Silas, he also wore a fine Italian silken vest embroidered with four-leaf clovers. His sideburns curved into his jawline and joined the goatee, all meticulously trimmed and, she imagined, perfumed. Silas was that sort of man.

"I wasn't—I mean—it was an accident," she protested. "It all took place so quickly I couldn't help but overhear their argument."

"A handy little excuse. No matter. I'll keep your secret."

"My secret! What were *you* doing here, sneaking around and coming up behind me like that?"

"Eavesdropping," he said, unabashed. He offered a rueful smile of apology. "Actually, I was out enjoying the scenery when I heard a horse riding on the road. When I saw it was my *father*," he said, speaking the word with light mockery, his southern accent as smooth as cream, "I followed him. I was planning to talk to him about something or other, but I guess it can wait till another day."

Oh, really?

"Then I saw Rafe's mother, Celestine, coming to meet him, or so it looked. I knew there was a whole lot of trouble between them over my arrival in Honolulu, so I was thinking I might apologize to her for the way I arrived on the lanai that day two months ago. I've been thinking about my behavior, and I'm sorry I chose to announce myself that way."

Was he speaking the truth? Zachary would scoff at this unexpected humbleness in Silas. Eden didn't know him well enough to judge his character. Until she did, she would be cautious. She had a tendency to feel sympathy for him. He could not have had a happy life while growing up, bandied about from relative to relative after his mother died. It was not until he was about fifteen or so that she'd heard how Townsend took a financial hand in his life and put him into a boys' private school somewhere in San Francisco, or so she assumed. The southern accent, however, cast doubt on where he'd been reared, at least for most of his life.

"Shall we call a truce?" Silas was saying. "I meant to eavesdrop, but I've heard you're quite a lady, so I shouldn't have teased you like that. After all, we are blood cousins and all that, even though I'm not much for the Derringtons to boast of."

She relaxed her guard a little, taken in by his boyish smile. Was it genuine?

"I'd say Rafe's mother made herself one big mistake in marrying my father," he said, and now there was no mockery in his voice. His face was sober, and a look of genuine pity was reflected in his eyes.

Indeed, who was the real Silas Derrington? Who was the man who had unpredictably decided to confront his father and family and, after demanding a place at the table by his mere arrival, had then refused to sit there, and had withdrawn. Although he'd been given a room at Kea Lani, he spent most of his time in Honolulu.

"What do you think of our Grandfather Ainsworth?" she asked, using the word "our" without undue emphasis. "I believe you met him, along with my father, Dr. Jerome, at Kea Lani this morning?"

"Actually, I haven't met them yet. Great-aunt Nora will have the honor of making introductions before dinner. I'm on my way to her room now. She's a fine lady and suggested I write some articles for the *Gazette*."

That would not make Zachary happy. He'd been running the newspaper for her since last year.

"I was told you'd worked as a journalist for the *Sacramento Times*."

"Oh, for a few years. Before that it was the *New Orleans Globe*."

"Then you come from Louisiana."

He smiled. "My accent can't deny that good news."

She tried to make sense of the details of his past. Some of them contradicted what she'd first been told by the family.

"If you're on your way to the house to see Nora, I'll join you. Before I forget yet again, I've an important package to bring her." She tried to keep the conversation on a lighter tone after that horrid scene between Celestine and Townsend, but it was difficult. "If Dr. Bolton knew I hadn't yet given Nora the prescription he'd sent with me, he'd berate me for slackness in duty. As you can imagine, the arrival of my father has eclipsed most everything for me. I haven't seen him in years, and his arrival was completely unexpected," she said, avoiding mention of how many *long* years it had been.

As Eden walked back toward the plantation house with Silas, she continued her questions, subtly, she hoped. "Then, if you didn't meet with Grandfather Ainsworth and Dr. Jerome at Kea Lani, was the meeting with Townsend and Zachary delayed as well?"

"So you knew of the peace conference. No, I haven't met with either of them yet. I arrived late, and the others were already on their way here to Rafe's."

Then Zachary's dour mood on the lanai that afternoon was not due to anything from the meeting.

Flowers and ferns grew in lush abundance, giving a thick fragrance and beauty to the coming dusk and soothing her revulsion over what had happened a short time ago. Yet there remained a dullness in Eden's heart that grieved over the way sin was damaging everyone and everything. A late-returning crimson butterfly with a six-inch wingspan lighted upon some wild white orchids and took cover among the blossoms.

"So this is paradise," Silas said. "There's a warning in that, I suppose."

"A warning?"

Malicious amusement shone in his eyes. "As Adam's children we might do well to remember that paradise isn't always as safe as people think."

She paused as they neared the steps of the plantation house. Twilight was upon them.

The wind rippling through the ferns brought a small chill. That harmless little garden snake she'd removed from the front hall came vividly to mind. Silas had a point. The fall of mankind had taken place in a paradise, the garden of Eden, and was soon followed by the murder of brother against brother, all because of jealousy.

A brief silence hung between them. Then Eden turned and rushed up the steps. A voice spoke from the shadows, where some rattan chairs and tables were cloistered.

"There you are. Great-aunt Nora is asking for you."

Zachary stood from where he'd been lounging, then noticed his half-brother, Silas. Even in the dim light Eden could see his muscular frame stiffen, the white shirt he wore tightening over his chest as he sucked in a breath of displeasure.

"So. You decided to show up after all," Zachary said to Silas. "Where's my father? Is he with you?"

"I don't know where he is. Am I allowed to step over this threshold, or no?" A note of maliciousness hung on his brief chuckle. "If not, I'll keep the snakes and insects company."

"Hawaii doesn't have snakes." Zachary hurled back the verbal dart. "Except those brought in from the mainland."

Silas chuckled, and Zachary turned and walked through the door into the brightly lit room.

Eden glanced over her shoulder at Silas, who remained below the lanai with one foot on the step, looking up.

"Come this way," she said briskly. "I'll take you to Great-aunt Nora."

To herself she thought, *Honolulu does have at least one snake. A green one. I carried it into the garden less than an hour ago.*

Chapter Eight
Two Brothers

W hen Eden entered the plantation house, Great-aunt Nora was not in her guest room but was waiting in the living room. Eden had always loved this room. She recalled the time when Rafe had shown her the house plans, saying he wanted her approval because it was being designed with her in mind—the bride who would reign here, as well as in his heart . . .

The room was walled on three sides, while the fourth had an archway with intricate wrought-iron scrollwork screen doors. The screened side accessed the lanai that faced an enclosed garden of tropical foliage, delicate ferns, and flowers. Her favorite tree was the poinciana, with blossoms in lush crimson, and there was an aged hau tree with a plethora of sunny yellow blossoms.

Through the background of thriving foliage Eden caught glimpses of an early moon rising in the tropical dusk, a gem from the Creator's hand, appearing nearly within her grasp. As she glanced about she felt the romantic loss of Rafe, but refused to yield to the painful longing.

Great-aunt Nora, according to Silas, was to introduce him for the first time to Ainsworth as his "unexpected" nephew from California, *the firstborn son of Townsend*. Just how Grandfather Ainsworth would respond to the occasion of a new nephew, Eden would not hazard to guess. It was widely known that Ainsworth frowned upon Townsend's immoral behavior. But the question remained; would he accept Silas on an equal basis with Zachary?

Townsend too, was supposed to be here with Silas as they faced the momentous introduction with Ainsworth, but Eden wondered if Townsend would show after that horrible episode between Townsend and Celestine that left Eden sickened. The introduction offered an opportunity for Townsend to position Silas as a Derrington with all rights and privileges, with Great-aunt Nora standing beside them, adding weight to the appeal.

Townsend was now absent, and only she and Silas knew why. His absence could not be explained easily without unmasking the tragedy that had occurred with Celestine.

Townsend's absence would give Ainsworth and Great-aunt Nora the impression of irresponsibility, which in Eden's mind was true, but emphasizing this would not help Silas. Sin, Eden thought, ruined whatever it came in contact with. It corrupted what God intended to be good and noble.

But in John's gospel Christ had taught, "*I am come that they might have life, and that they might have it more abundantly.*"

She wondered about Silas, unsure how to feel about his character and motives. Was he a cousin who should have her loyalty, sympathy, and support? Or was he shrewd and calculating? After the confrontation with Townsend and Celestine, Eden thought he might be misunderstood. At times, he seemed to have humility and a heart that could be reached, that would respond. But then, his remark at the doorstep about the serpent in the garden had come with a mischievous, even sinister amusement.

Now, Eden left Silas in the outer hall looking at the paintings of the Eastons on the wall above the stairway and, in particular, the painting of Rafe's father, Matt Easton. She entered through the archway into the living room, where Nora was seated in a rather royal-looking chair in front of the lanai. There was a magnificent vista of ferns, orchids, fragrant gardenias, and a quiet pond with white *kea* fish with diagonal designs in bright red, blue, black, and gold. Behind all this stretched the sandy beach, palm trees, and the ocean's waves softened by an offshore reef.

Great-aunt Nora had never accepted the notion that older women should dress primarily in dark blue or black. For the dinner tonight she wore a smartly tailored burgundy gown of silky texture, the color flattering to her fragile skin and platinum hair worn elegantly in the style of Queen Victoria. She smiled warmly at Eden, closed the leather-bound journal she'd been writing in, and placed it in a knitting bag. Nora could neither sew well nor knit. "Even as a girl of fifteen, I was all thumbs," she had said, "so as soon as I was old enough to do as I pleased, I gave up on handwork and turned to writing during my free hours."

Eden entered the living room and forced a smile, unwilling to worry Nora over Celestine at the present. "How's the book coming, Auntie?" she said cheerfully, looking pointedly at the knitting bag with the journal. Eden had a genuine interest in Nora's work. In the past, Eden had assisted her in gathering historical data. Sometimes she had even helped edit the manuscript before mailing it to the publisher. Nora's first book, written on the early Hawaiian history of the Kamehameha I monarchy, was completed during the time Eden attended Chadwick Medical School. On one occasion Nora had come to San Francisco and lectured at the historic Palace Hotel, where Eden, Zachary, and Grandfather Ainsworth had been in attendance. Rafe was there, while the pineapple slips were aboard his ship, and his first meeting with Parker Judson occurred there to bring about their partnership in the pineapple plantation. From that moment onward Ainsworth had groaned over the fact that he had failed to believe in Rafe and partner with him.

Eden hadn't read any of the manuscript Nora was working on, for she was too busy at Kalihi Hospital. For some reason, though, Nora seemed to be keeping the contents of the book wrapped in mystery. Eden did know that, unlike her first book, this one dealt more with family history than with the monarchy. She had learned that both the Derrington and Easton history on the Islands was written from Nora's perspective. Though Nora hadn't come out and said so, Eden suspected some of the information would not please Ainsworth.

"Ah, there you are, my dear. The new book? It's coming along too slowly. Celestine has the first chapters." She frowned. "I seem to have mislaid some of the later chapters though. I can't think what I may have done with them."

"Perhaps you left them at Tamarind House," Eden said of Great-aunt Nora's big house near Diamond Head, willed to her by Eden's Great-grandmother Amabel.

"Yes, that must be it. I won't worry about it now."

As Eden knew, Nora hadn't been strong recently, though she wouldn't admit to the fact, for it would mean she must be slowing down her routine. Eden scrutinized her for a moment through medical eyes and could recognize the signs of weakening stamina. She retrieved Dr. Bolton's prescription from her satchel.

"Before I forget, here's your new medicine. You're to take it before dinner. Dr. Bolton insists you take it twice a day, when you first rise and at bedtime."

Nora made a sound of impatience. "What is it? Heart medicine again? I don't need it. I told him so."

"Great-aunt Nora!"

Nora broke into a smile as though she enjoyed putting up a fuss just to see Eden's reaction. Eden came beside Nora to a koa wood table and set the bottle down with a decided *click*.

Nora winced. "You sound just like a nurse. They always set the medicine down with that certain *click*. Obey, or else."

Eden smiled. "Then I'll live up to the reputation of an efficient one. If I find out you're neglecting what's good for you, I'll tell Rafe. He'll make sure you take it as prescribed."

"Spare me. I won't have him coming here twice a day to play nanny."

Eden laughed at such a ludicrous image of Rafe.

Nora gestured at her empty coffee cup. "All I need is a good night's sleep, which is proving impossible with all this dreadfully strong Kona coffee he has here. Keeps me awake. I haven't slept soundly since I left Tamarind. I keep telling Rafe to grow *tea*. The rascal laughs at me."

Eden laughed, too. *Tea, in Hawaii.*

"I understand there was an early attempt to grow tea here and produce silk as well," Eden said. "I think sugar, pineapples, and Kona coffee are quite enough for one Island. And now, you must take the medication so you can stay strong enough to support the monarchy. You're running the *Gazette* now, too. With Zachary's help, of course, but he tells me you're putting in many long hours." Nora was considering making Zachary editor-in-chief, a position he desperately craved. Even now, he was the lead editor and writer.

"I must put in long hours at the *Gazette*. We're having financial difficulties. Zachary believes he can get us a loan, but he won't say who from, and I suspect it would come from Ainsworth, and I won't have it. So I've told him to forget trying. Somehow we will bring the sales up to pay off the debt I've incurred for the last two years. If not, I may end up needing to relinquish the *Gazette*. That, to me, would be a tragedy."

"Surely someone in the family can lend you money to pay the creditors?" Eden said, incredulously. The thought of losing the *Gazette* troubled her also.

"Ainsworth controls the Derrington purse, my dear, should you have forgotten. Townsend, too, is in debt, but for reckless reasons. Gambling. Ainsworth has finally refused to cover his debts."

So that was the reason for her uncle's desperation in wanting to reclaim Hanalei from the contract he'd made with Parker Judson.

"Anyway, Ainsworth's the last person I'll come to for a loan, though as his sister, I've as much right to the Derrington inheritance as he. Of course, I have Tamarind House and its sugar lands, but I should hate to let go of it. I want to leave it all intact, as an inheritance for one of my four nieces and nephews."

One of the four nieces and nephews? Apparently Great-aunt Nora had decided to accept Silas as a true Derrington. This would alarm Zachary.

"Oh, Ainsworth would be delighted to lend me money, by all means. It would grant him the leverage to interfere in what the *Gazette* prints. He'd expect me to have articles in favor of annexation. What I need is for Rafe to come back," Nora said wistfully. "Oh to have a few of those superlative articles he did a few years ago on the monarchy. He's been difficult enough to get along with recently. I can't get a simple yes or no out of him when it concerns supporting Liliuokalani. I do believe he's a writer, not a planter." Nora turned a sharpened gaze on Eden. "What's come over him, recently? I would think you, at least, would be able to influence him to work for the Queen. Really, Eden. What a shame you're delaying the engagement."

"Please don't mention the broken engagement in front of Grand-father or my father. Neither of them have said a word to me about Rafe. I want to keep the matter quiet until I know what his plans are."

"Jerome's plans? Or Rafe's?"

"Dr. Jerome's," Eden said, more familiar with the term for his renowned reputation than for the term for relationship as her father. "I want to know what he plans for his research work in leprosy."

Nora frowned. "Don't tell me you still wish to go traipsing about diseased jungles with him like some devoted gypsy. It's a dreadful risk to your own health. No wonder Rafe is difficult to get on with. He's worried about you, both of the plantations—Hawaiiana and Hanalei—and Celestine. If that weren't enough, Jerome arrives to sweep you off on some dubious research on rotting human flesh."

"Nora, dearest, *please*. I'd rather not talk of leprosy, Rafe, or my father's arrival now. I want the family dinner this evening to be a pleasant one."

Was she being naive? Could this evening's dinner actually be *pleasant*? She thought of Celestine's miserable meeting with Townsend and cringed.

If Rafe was concerned for his mother before, what would he think now?

Even though Silas warned her to not mention the incident to Rafe, she couldn't help feeling uneasy. What if Silas found something to benefit him personally from the unfortunate circumstance?

"I shall say nothing to Ainsworth and Jerome of the sad state of your relationship with Rafe," Great-aunt Nora said soothingly and reached over to pat Eden's hand. "I'll even thank you, dear, for coming here to bring me Dr. Bolton's prescription." She reached over to the table, took the bottle, and put it inside her knitting bag.

Eden squeezed her hand. "It's because we all love you. Do take it as prescribed."

"Well, I'm pleased somebody loves me. Yes, I'll take it, dear."

Eden wondered if she truly would. "By the way, Silas is waiting in the hall. Did you tell him you'd introduce him to Grandfather before dinner tonight?"

"Somebody must get them to face each other for the first time. Townsend's to be here as well, not that he'll be much help, that malingerer."

Townsend has returned to Kea Lani, thought Eden, but she couldn't say so without having to explain how she knew.

"I can't say I'm much pleased about Ainsworth returning from Washington so unexpectedly. He's boasting about winning over the U.S. Senate. Such audacity—he and Thurston, both. Those two are cut from the same piece of cloth."

Eden was about to tell her that she needn't be awaiting his arrival, when a voice came from the doorway.

"Am I interrupting?"

Silas walked over to where Nora sat and brushed his lips against the upturned cheek of the lady who expected regal recognition from all of her great-nephews and nieces, especially a "new" nephew. But now she cast him an irritated glance.

"I wish you wouldn't keep sneaking up on me like that, Silas. I could almost think you were deliberately eavesdropping," she accused.

After what happened earlier in the evening with Celestine and Townsend, Eden felt uncomfortable.

Silas grinned disarmingly. "Now, Aunt, what other kind of eavesdropping is there but *deliberate?* And what else would you expect from a man accused of gathering 'secrets' about the family for his own selfish ends?"

A second unexpected voice surprised them from the lanai. "And do you have 'selfish ends,' Cousin Silas?" Candace entered and stood looking at him. For a brief moment, Eden thought she caught a slight frown.

"Why, of course, *Cousin* Candace. Don't we all?"

"No," she said decisively.

"Well, I admit to having them—to win the warm affection of my new family. What else would you expect?"

"Yes, what else?" Great-aunt Nora repeated.

"Ah, dear Great-aunt! Always tart! But beloved nonetheless."

"Nonsense. You're a worse rascal than Rafe."

He looked at Eden. "You shouldn't say these things in front of Eden. You'll convince her I should be avoided."

"She doesn't need much convincing," Nora said. "And you'd better watch that tongue of yours around Rafe, or you might end up with a bruised lip."

"Ooh!" he winced. "Yes, well. Then I wouldn't want to offend my amiable host now, would I? Or is he also my brother?" He looked at Eden.

"I suppose he is, rather," Eden said.

"You may be more of a scamp than even I think you are," Great-aunt Nora snapped.

Silas looked amused. "You're the one in this family with a true sense of humor, Nora. I'm becoming extremely fond of you."

"Zachary would suggest it was my newspaper you've taken such fondness to."

"Ah, yes ... Zachary." He looked at Eden with a glint in his eyes. "Need I say more?"

"No," Candace said, walking around Nora's chair and laying a hand on her shoulder.

"Hand me my shawl, Candace, will you? That evening breeze can feel a little chilly for a woman my age. That's it—thank you. Where is Zachary by the way?" She glanced toward the front of the house.

"He was looking over that handsome horse tied out front," said Candace. "He thought it belonged to Uncle Townsend. Townsend was here earlier—but couldn't stay."

Eden looked at Candace. How did she know? Had she seen Celestine enter the house or spoken with her?

"Then Townsend won't be coming?" Nora asked, troubled.

"No, he returned to Kea Lani." Candace walked over to the lanai and looked into the garden, as though uncomfortable about something.

"The horse does belong to Townsend," Silas said unexpectedly. "I noticed her in the stables this morning. The stable boy told me Townsend bought the mare a few months ago to breed with Rafe's stallion. He had the mare brought over by ship. There's a fine breeder around Sacramento by the name of Wilder. I wonder if Rafe knows of him?"

"If there's a good breeder somewhere, Rafe will have heard of him," Eden said. "He and Zachary are both interested in fine horses."

"Anyway, Townsend gave me permission to ride her this morning," Silas said. "So I first rode up the lava slopes, then back here to Hawaiiana. The sights were incredible."

"Silas, I don't want anything unpleasant to occur between you and the other two young men," Great-aunt Nora warned, changing the subject.

"I'm willing to get along. It's Zachary who'd like to send me packing back to San Francisco."

"Never mind Zachary. You just do your part to avoid trouble, or it will upset Eden."

"I'm sure Eden has more important matters on her mind." He

looked at Eden as if he shared some little secret with her. His eyes were bright and curious.

"Such as my father's medical research?" She spoke quickly to hide her uneasiness, and with a shade too much emphasis.

"That, too, is very intriguing. I was thinking, though," his voice casual, "of Rafe's new support for the annexation movement. That must be upsetting to anyone supporting the queen. Some would call him a turncoat."

"Turncoat!" Eden said, momentarily disconcerted. He had her full attention. Rafe had told her earlier that day in the buggy that he hadn't come to any firm decision. Then she remembered his anger at the Board of Health over Kip and his words against the monarchy. Could Silas have met with Rafe since then?

Nora stood. "Pah! Whatever are you saying, Silas?" An anxious frown tugged at her white brows.

"And in Rafe's own house," Candace said crisply.

"Yes, whatever gave you the right?" Eden said. "Turncoat, indeed!"

"My dear ladies!" He placed hand at heart, as he looked from one to the other in what Eden saw as feigned regret. "I seem to have spoken too soon on the subject," he said. "I would have thought you all realized . . . but it appears I was mistaken. Perhaps we should let the matter go," he said with unexpected deference. He stooped and retrieved the shawl Nora had let slip from her shoulders to the floor.

"I believe you owe us an explanation, Silas," Nora said gravely, as he carefully replaced the shawl around her shoulders.

"You know how talk circulates," he suggested. "You're probably right, Nora; this isn't the right time or place to discuss Rafe's new ambitions."

New ambitions? Eden stared at him.

Silas lowered his voice. "I've heard from Townsend that Grandfather Ainsworth—if I may be so bold as to address him in that way—would like to see Rafe run for the Legislature as an annexationist. The other planters and certain haole businessmen will back

Rafe at the snap of a finger since they know he and Parker Judson are partners in this new pineapple venture. And what a venture, I might add. It's bound to become a tremendous success. Fresh, sweet pineapples to ship to California? The idea seems to be the envy of many a planter *and* investor."

Eden resented his insinuation that because Rafe was backed by Parker Judson, he no longer exercised independence. If Silas thought Rafe Easton was owned by the powerful sugar interests, he certainly did not know Rafe. If he did cooperate with them, it would be because he believed in what they were doing. She recalled what Candace told her earlier about Ainsworth and Rafe. Was this the reason her grandfather wanted to talk to him alone?

"If Rafe does humor the growers it means he's willing to come out against Liliuokalani," Silas reminded Nora.

"Have you heard anything about this?" Nora asked Eden, sinking back into her chair as though her legs would no longer hold her up.

Eden was tempted to vent her frustration by scowling at Silas, who had troubled the peaceful waters, but refrained. "Rafe has a keen interest in Hawaii's destiny, as we all know."

"But not as a member of the Reform Party," Candace observed.

"He's never favored annexation before," Eden agreed. "So I can't imagine why he would change his views now."

"People have a propensity for changing their minds when it benefits their bank accounts," Silas suggested.

Eden gave him a speculative once-over. "Yes, some people do, but not Rafe. He's not a man who can be bullied into taking a stand he doesn't believe in."

"Oh my," Silas said, leaning on the back of a tall chair. "You're not suggesting your Grandfather Ainsworth is a bully?"

Eden refused to be trapped by his words. She was beginning to dislike Silas. Whether he meant to jab with his words or not, the effect was the same.

"It looks as if we may have a new bully in the family," Candace said, walking about restlessly. "I would advise, Silas, that you not put words in Eden's mouth. She would never call her grandfather a bully."

"I do concede on that point, and beg your pardon. After all, it is for you, and not Eden, that Ainsworth is trying to arrange a marriage."

Eden held her breath as a perceptible silence froze the room. Then Candace eased matters by granting Silas one of her kindest smiles. "Yes, he is," she said. "I've been told Oliver P. Hunnewell has returned to Honolulu. But that is neither here nor there. I wonder what Grandfather will have in mind for you once he realizes he has a new nephew?"

"A boot, probably," Silas said with a grimace.

"I think not," Candace said. "Evidently you don't think so either, or you wouldn't have come to Kea Lani. I think you'll agree he'll not only welcome you, but will bestow generosity."

Eden thought she saw a fleeting expression of satisfaction in Silas's features. Well, why shouldn't he? Eden rebuked herself. It's not his sin that he was born out of wedlock, and he's as much a great-nephew of Ainsworth as Zachary, Candace, and myself.

Nora whisked the bright feather fan before her face. "I still think it's possible to gain Rafe's support. I haven't forgotten those articles he wrote for the *Gazette*."

Silas pursed his lips. "Well . . . what I've heard is something different. Disturbing, actually. How Townsend ran Rafe out of Honolulu for writing those articles."

"Uncle Townsend did not 'run him out,'" Eden said. "Rafe sailed for French Guiana on a business venture."

"Eden is right," Candace told him. "And it looks as if Rafe's foresight is reaping benefits. Townsend has regretted his impulsive decision to stand at odds with his stepson ever since Rafe returned with the new pineapples and won over Parker Judson's support."

"Quite a rich plum Rafe pulled out of the pie, eh?"

"And sour grapes for Ainsworth and Townsend," Great-aunt Nora acknowledged, with an energetic swish of her fan. "Townsend was hoping to get rid of Rafe and reap Hanalei from Celestine. Now Rafe is back to stay, and Hanalei is also headed his way, as it should; Celestine is his mother, and it was Rafe's father, Matt Easton, who built Hanalei."

"Yes, I've heard about Hanalei," said Silas.

Eden saw his gaze flick toward her, and she pretended not to notice. If he dared to say anything about what they'd overheard . . .

"I must hand it to Rafe," Silas went on. "He raked in the winnings all right in that venture to French Guiana. No wonder Grandfather Ainsworth has drawn up his political plans to include Rafe. Rafe not only has the plum, but the pie, and the Derringtons want a big slice. Can't say that I blame them."

"I do hope you're wrong, Silas," Nora said. "At any rate, I must discuss this with Rafe before I return to Tamarind on Monday."

Silas apparently decided he would do better with Nora on a topic more to her liking, so he brought up the *Gazette*. Nora had purchased the *Gazette* for the single purpose of defending Liliuokalani against the Reform Party, and a year earlier she had turned over the running of the paper to Zachary. He had hounded Nora for the position, and she'd relented. Since then, he hadn't taken a clear stand for the queen in the articles he'd written or in his choice of news stories for the front page, and subscriptions had tumbled, and now Nora was in debt. Although the *Gazette* had already been in a weakened state before Zachary took over, Nora's dissatisfaction was growing, and Zachary was sure to reap criticism.

Whenever Nora complained, Zachary became sullen, suggesting journalism should be unbiased. This, of course, provoked Nora, since she also defended journalistic freedom, but the debt continued, and so did her irate mood.

Eden suspected it wasn't Zachary's belief in unbiased reporting that caused him to be timid in coming out for the queen, but nervousness over confronting Townsend and Ainsworth. Not only did they favor annexation, but they would decide which son became heir to the Derrington enterprise now that Silas had appeared. So

Zachary was straddling the political fence, playing to both sides of the issue for as long as he could.

"It's really none of my business," Silas was telling Nora, "but being a newspaper man myself, I can't resist a comment or two on the way Zachary is running the *Gazette*."

"He's doing a fair job," Nora countered, but there was no enthusiasm in her voice. "We're getting a few advertisers, mostly planters."

Silas rubbed his chin. "That's just it. If the *Gazette* is ever going to compete in Honolulu and grab the hearts of the Hawaiians, it needs stronger fare than those watered-down articles on the monarchy and Reform Party. They don't convince either side."

Nora looked troubled. "Yes, state your mind, Silas."

"I think it's clear enough. You've seen what Zachary is printing. He hasn't had a strong story yet on why Hawaii should keep the royal line of Kamehameha."

Eden noticed the gray pallor of Nora's skin and was nettled that Silas had upset her.

"I admit Zachary's been overly cautious. It happens I'd already made up my mind to speak to him about the matter."

"Cautious? If I didn't know better, I'd have thought Zachary's articles were written by a member of the Hawaiian League."

A flurry of movement drew Eden's attention across the living room to the lanai entrance. The horizon behind the tall palms was streaked with angry vermillion. Zachary appeared, his icy blue gaze honed in on Silas, like a hawk on a dove. Eden's heart sank. It was clear that he'd heard Silas denigrating his journalism.

"What did you say about my *Gazette* articles?" Zachary challenged, striding into the room.

"Now, now, none of that," Great-aunt Nora warned.

Silas looked down at his shoes as though embarrassed. "Sorry," he said.

Great-aunt Nora went straight to the point. "Silas seems to think you're not doing justice to the cause for which I bought the newspaper and made you manager. He does have a point, Zachary."

Zachary's gaze remained fixed on Silas. Eden saw the pulse beat in his throat. "Maybe you think you can do better?"

No, Eden thought. *That's just what he wants you to say.*

Silas held up a palm of peace. "Don't get riled. I'm bound to have strong opinions on writing. I'm a journalist, remember? And," he said with emphasis, "I've had years of newspaper experience, whereas you—" He left the word to hang a moment, then continued, "Why, you are just now entering the newspaper world. I would think you'd look me up for pointers. What are brothers for?"

"One more crack like that—"

"What troubles Nora," Silas continued, "and I admit that it troubles me as well, is your writing lacks the zeal it needs for Liliuokalani. At times you even shadow-box with Stevens."

Mr. Stevens was the American Minister to Hawaii. Eden believed him to be a staunch proponent of annexation, working behind the scenes with men like Lorrin Thurston and Ainsworth. He was said to be almost in continuous communication with Blaine, the U.S. Secretary of State, about the troubled situation in the Hawaiian Islands.

Silas now took center stage as he paced, tapping his chin and gazing at the floor as though it held the answers to the Hawaiian dilemma. "Isn't it true that Minister Stevens is trying to learn from Secretary of State Blaine how far the U.S. president is willing to go, should circumstances warrant the overthrow of the monarchy?"

Eden heard her own breath catch. Overthrow Liliuokalani? That would never happen, surely.

"Rubbish," Zachary snapped. "What are you trying to say? That the Mainland government is in cahoots with Grandfather Ainsworth and the Reform Party to raise guns against the queen?"

"Not at all. The overthrow of Liliuokalani will be by 'an orderly and peaceful revolution,'" Silas stated with light sarcasm. "It must be 'orderly,' by all means, and it must be 'peaceful.' That will soothe their democratic consciences."

Silas looked at Nora with a satisfied smile. "Now, I ask you,

Nora, is that worthy news for the *Gazette* to come out with in morning headlines, or isn't it?"

Eden was speechless. She looked at Great-aunt Nora. Her face glowed pink with surprise and then outrage. She thrust herself up from her chair and stood, confronting Silas.

"Where did you hear this? If it's true, it's shocking news. Where is Ainsworth? I want to talk to him now. If anyone knows, he will." She walked briskly to the lanai, looking into the garden.

"He's out reviewing Rafe's pineapples," Candace said. "I think we should all step down from the present emotional level we find ourselves in. Let's wait until we know more about this."

Nora turned on Zachary. "What do you know about this?" she demanded.

Zachary reminded Eden of a trapped rabbit. Her anger at Silas began to burn. He was deliberately using rumors and falsehood to undermine Zachary before Nora. It was shameful.

"Rubbish, I say. I've not heard a whisper about this," Zachary said. "Any rumor of tactics for the overthrow of the queen is likely an outright lie." He pointed his hand at Silas. "The question is, just where did you hear such inflammatory information? Or did you steal it?"

"Zachary!" Nora rebuked.

But Silas merely smiled. "My, you don't think very highly of your humble half-brother."

"Should I? If you have access to inflammatory information, then it had to come from the office of John L. Stevens," Zachary persisted.

"Since when does a journalist disclose his sources?"

"Stevens wouldn't willingly give it to you. You're bluffing."

"Bluffing?" Silas turned to Nora. "I admit not every news reporter in Honolulu is able to unearth the kind of story that should be printed. But that doesn't mean the *Gazette* should settle for lax reporting, either." He snatched the morning edition of the *Gazette* from the table and held it up. "'Profitable sugar prices brought home to planters by Ainsworth Derrington.' Followed by the comments of Lorrin Thurston on his 'successful meetings with the powerful Secretary of State in Washington D.C.'" He tossed the paper down and looked from Zachary to Nora. "But not a commendable word on Queen Liliuokalani."

Zachary flushed with anger. He grabbed the paper from the table and shook it at Silas. "I reported the truth. Ainsworth and the members of the Reform Party *did* manage to work out higher prices in a treaty for Hawaiian sugar. *And* a treaty for a U.S. harbor at Pearl River, to be named Pearl Harbor. *And* Thurston held high-level talks with the U.S. Secretary of State, James G. Blaine, bringing greater American interest and control to Hawaii." He then tossed the paper aside. "These events actually happened, and we reported on them. So what about the 'planned overthrow' of Liliuokalani? Where did you get those *facts?*"

Silas shrugged, becoming languid. "As I said, old fellow, a journalist rarely reveals his sources. You should know that. The point, Zachary, is that it's true."

"Prove the accusation you've leveled against the U.S. minister," Zachary demanded, "and we'll print it. Won't we, Nora?" He stepped up beside her chair. "We will never rush to press with lies or intentionally start a political fire raging in Honolulu. If the *Gazette* prints sensational stories and half-truths, they'll become self-fulfilling."

Eden breathed easier. Zachary was making headway with Nora.

"If you print the sensational without having facts to back it up," Zachary said, resting his hand on the back of her chair, "the newspaper won't last through the year. They'll soon be onto us. You won't need to borrow money to pay off the debt. We'll be out of business instead."

Silas wore a faint smile as he watched Zachary with a spark of interest. Caught in a losing situation, Zachary had managed to turn things his way.

"Poppycock," Nora snapped. "You know me better that, Zachary. There'll be no rush to judgment. Still, what Silas suggests of Minister

Stevens sounds suspiciously like the truth. I've met the man on several occasions, and I never did trust him. He's certainly for annexation. He doesn't fool me. I want the full story on this, and I want it printed." She turned to Silas. "Well? Have you facts to back up your charge?"

Silas grinned. He walked to a chair and sat down comfortably, crossing his legs at the knee. "No."

There was an intake of breath and a moment of startled silence, then Zachary folded his arms and gave a humorless laugh. "Lies. I said as much. What are you trying to do, Silas, ruin Nora and the *Gazette?*"

"Not at all. The facts are there," Silas said, looking not at Zachary but at Nora. "It just takes a newspaperman to ferret them out into the open."

"Nonsense," Zachary scoffed. "What facts? Everything the Reformed Party is doing is legal and in the open."

"Is it? What about the Honolulu Rifles, the secret club for annexation started by Thurston?"

Eden recalled her brief showdown with Rafe over the club. Zachary's mouth tightened, and he made no comment. Silas smiled his victory. Nora watched Silas with sharp attention.

"If what you say is true, Silas, then go ahead and ferret out the facts. If you get hold of them, we'll print them for all to see."

"Nora—" Eden protested.

"Hush, Eden. Well?" Nora asked Silas.

"And if I do ferret the facts out?" Silas mildly challenged her.

The answer was plain enough. Eden glanced from Nora to Zachary. He must feel as though the ground were breaking up beneath his feet.

"And if you do," Nora said, "and prove them to be accurate, well then, the two of you will need to learn how to work together. That should stir up Thurston's Hawaiian League and put Ainsworth on shaky ground."

"That's all I was waiting to hear," Silas said, on his feet again. "A word of caution, though. This kind of unveiling will make you unpopular with powerful entities. They'll want to put you out of business in a hurry."

"Oh, I'm sure of it. But the *Gazette* is already in debt, so I've little to lose. Maybe the truth will attract more readers."

Silas turned to Zachary. "Together, my lad, we'll make the *Gazette* sizzle."

Zachary's jaw flexed. Eden, who knew him so well, guessed that he was already sizzling. He turned abruptly and without a word strode from the room.

"He'll get over his temper," Nora said.

"But not his injured pride," Candace said quietly.

Eden excused herself from the others. As she walked past Silas, she paused and looked at him. It was difficult to keep the disappointment and anger she felt from showing in her face. He had used clever tactics against Zachary before Nora, and at a time when the *Gazette* was in financial turmoil and needed an experienced leader. Zachary was right when he said it seemed that Silas had arrived on the Islands on a dark cloud. Pride and jealousy could slither into the heart and strike, leaving their venom to ruin and destroy.

Once in the wide hall she stopped. Zachary must have gone out the door. Would he even attend the dinner now? Would Celestine?

Except for the loud ticking of the great grandfather clock standing against the far wall, silence settled in, and adversarial voices faded. She walked across the polished wooden floor toward the stairway and begin to ascend, troubled. A figure moved below, and she paused to look down. It was Townsend moving down the hall. *He must be going to see Nora*, she thought and went on her way.

Father, enable us as Your children in Christ to live wise lives with eternity in view. And for those who don't know Your forgiveness and adoption, may their blind eyes be opened and their deaf ears hear what You are saying in Your Word.

She climbed to the upper hallway. There was no need to knock on Celestine's bedroom door, for experience told Eden that the older lady would not wish to lay her dignified head on a shoulder to cry out her woes. Her crying would be done alone, with God.

Voices were drifting to her from the nursery. She recognized Noelani's voice speaking rapidly to someone, certainly not to baby Kip. Eden straightened her shoulders. It was time she told Noelani about her mission here at Hawaiiana to bring the baby to Kalihi. It would break her heart, but if anyone would understand Eden's dilemma, it would be Noelani, the loving, faithful woman who had become a mother to her after Rebecca was sent to Molokai.

I need a miracle, Eden thought. But the miracle was to be found in the inspired Word of God. She must depend upon eternal truths. Historical changes and fickle fads of modern culture did not change the Truth. Truth would be the final judge of all. *What a comfort for those of us who love truth and fear the deceptions of darkness.*

Yes, the times were uncertain, and trouble grew like thorns in the loveliest of gardens, but she could walk steadily forward knowing she was not alone, knowing that the future was known by God and that the path of faith grounded in His Word would ultimately lead her to His purpose.

She would pray that Silas and Townsend—and all of them, really—would, like John Bunyan's Pilgrim, lay down their burdens in exchange for eternal peace.

Chapter Nine
Noelani's Warning

*T*he sound of annoyed voices speaking Hawaiian drew Eden toward the lighted nursery. She walked through the doorway and stopped upon seeing a young man in a white cotton shirt standing with his back toward her. Keno, tall and muscled, was talking to Noelani. Despite Eden's earlier concern for Candace, it wasn't unusual to see him around the plantation house since Noelani was his aunt.

Did Keno know about Kip? Had Rafe explained the dilemma? Perhaps there was no need on her part to tell Noelani.

Noelani glanced over and saw her. "Aloha, Eden dear."

"Am I interrupting?"

Keno turned at Eden's question. His quick smile greeted her. "Never, Miss Eden. I was just leaving." He moved toward the open back door of the nursery, where the stairway led down to the pineapple fields. "Ambrose sent me to ask if Noelani will have dinner here tonight as usual. Rafe says Noelani should attend the fancy dinner with Ambrose to welcome your father home from the wilds. She says no." He looked at Noelani.

Eden caught the scowl Noelani threw at her nephew. Keno kept smiling.

"Of course she'll come," Eden said amiably. "You must take your usual chair beside Ambrose. Rafe is correct. You are family—the only one I ever knew, until recently." She walked over and put her arms around the statuesque woman in the muumuu.

Noelani patted her arm affectionately, but shook her gray head. "No, I cannot come. Go tell Rafe." She waved a hand of dismissal toward Keno, picked up her basket weaving, and sat down on a cushion. She concentrated on her work, still frowning.

"Such a stubborn mood," Keno said with a smile as he nodded good-bye to Eden. They could hear his feet pounding down the outside steps as he departed.

Eden walked to the open door and looked down after him, but he'd already disappeared into the warm night. She could see small lamps burning in huts along the coast, and she watched the waves in the moonlight, foaming and curling a lacy edge along the sand.

The unpleasant task remained undone. She turned back to where Noelani was sitting, involved in her weaving. A door into the small bedroom where Kip slept was open a crack. Eden sadly looked in and saw the baby boy asleep in his crib, with a small lamp burning above casting a pinkish glow on the side of his face. *I promise I'll protect him*, she told herself again.

Announcing the painful news to Noelani would be almost as difficult as explaining the Board's decision to Rafe. She walked back to where Noelani sat, head bent, weaving the green palm leaf in her lap as Eden had often done as a child. Noelani had taught her to weave baskets, small rugs, and the leafy head crown that the Hawaiians also wore during their *hula*. Noelani's strong arms had often embraced her, consoling her after the loss of Rebecca, whispering comforting words in Hawaiian. On Eden's fourteenth birthday, Noelani even translated an English hymn into Hawaiian from the Foundling Hospital Collection of 1796 and had taught it to her on the ukulele:

Praise the Lord! You heavens adore Him;
Praise Him, angels, in the height;
Sun and moon, rejoice before Him;
Praise Him, all you stars of light.

Praise the Lord! For He has spoken;
Worlds His mighty voice obeyed;
Law which never shall be broken;
For their guidance has He made.

Praise the Lord! For He is glorious;
Never shall His promise fail;
God has made His saints victorious;
Sin and death shall not prevail.

Praise the God of our salvation!
Hosts on high, His power proclaim;
Heaven and earth and all creation;
Laud and magnify His name. Amen.

Noelani and her relatives worked long hours mending their nets, cracking oysters from the pearl lagoon, or drying ocean fish, seaweed, and coconuts to sell in Rat Alley, the Chinese district in Honolulu. She must remember to warn them to avoid the district for the present. Sometimes Noelani traveled miles inland with the younger Hawaiian women and boys to gather mountain taro roots to store and sell for poi, the staple food of the Hawaiians.

Eden sighed and sat down in a chair near the cushions where Noelani was at work. There were a few moments of silence, nothing unusual between them, but she was unprepared for Noelani's next words.

"Keno and Candace Derrington. What a tragic love affair." She shook her gray head. "Much worse than when I fell in love with Ambrose Easton. At least Ambrose was free to do as he wished.

Makua Matt, his younger brother, did not interfere. He had his own troubles with love not meant to be."

Now what did she mean by that? Eden had never heard of any failed engagement before the marriage between Rafe's father and Celestine. "It would be a blessing if Keno and Candace were free to make their own decision before God," Eden agreed.

"Yes, but they are not. Keno tells me Makua Hunnewell is in Honolulu. Now, it's too late for Keno. And so I told him, he must wake up and accept the painful fact that he will never marry the haole granddaughter."

"Candace is determined not to marry Oliver Hunnewell," Eden said. "There's still a chance, Noelani. Love may yet triumph."

She shook her head. "No, child, there is no chance. I wish you would tell Miss Candace to leave my Keno alone. She can do nothing but hurt him. She should never have let him think there was a possibility."

"But she loves Keno."

"Maybe so. And Keno loves her. As you say, left alone they would do well. But the Derringtons will not leave them alone. She will not marry Keno. Therefore it was wrong of her to let him fall in love with her. She should have known better. She's a wise girl. Out of her love for him, she should have gone away to San Francisco and left him to recover. Now he speaks again of going to sea with Rafe."

Eden looked up. Rafe is going to sea? But he couldn't go. Not when he had Hawaiiana to manage and Hanalei in his sights!

"Keno could have become a lay pastor to follow Ambrose, but he will never stay close at hand now, with Candace here and soon to be married to Makua Hunnewell. She will be driving around in fancy buggies and wearing big hats."

"Noelani! I've never heard you speak like this before. Why, you sound bitter and angry with us."

"No, child, not with you. You will always be my daughter. I am not even angry with Miss Candace. She is a fine Christian woman.

I'm only disappointed with events. Because she should have seen how it would turn out for Keno and moved earlier to keep both of them from getting badly hurt. Now that Makua Ainsworth is home, and the rich man Hunnewell, Keno as he says, might as well go to sea again. That means he will never be the lay pastor of the mission church. That was my dream, and Ambrose's since he was a little boy. Now? Gone. Ruined because of the haole woman, Miss Candace."

Eden was silenced. *This is dreadful,* she thought. "I had no idea you felt this strongly, Noelani. I'm sorry you are so hurt."

She shrugged and kept on with her weaving. "I shall heal. The Lord will see to my soul. Keno, too, in time. A shame, though, that so much time needs to be wasted on getting healed of hurts and disappointments."

Eden sighed deeply within. *How can I possibly tell her now about taking Kip?*

She could not. Not now.

"Nothing is wasted in the lives of believers. God will use the hurts, pains, and disappointments to burn the dross away from our hearts."

"Yes, He is faithful. But we must let Him, Eden. He will not force the growth in grace and knowledge of His Word. We grow when yielded, when obeying His Word. Too many times we refuse. Then we end up suffering eternal loss of rewards." She sighed and shrugged her strong shoulders.

Yes, we must yield. We must stay in the Word and act on what is written. "What is Candace to do?" Eden asked suddenly, allowing herself to become as frustrated with events as Noelani. "Is she to obey Grandfather Ainsworth? Or is she to go with her heart?"

"Neither, in my opinion. Candace needs to obey God. What does God say?"

"She's not to marry an unbeliever."

"She is twenty-three. She is fully mature. Has she not inherited Makua Douglas's inheritance?"

That was true. Silence overtook them. The tropical wind blew in through the door and stirred the cane blinds.

Eden stood slowly. "Dinner will be served soon. Are you certain you won't come down with me?"

Noelani looked at her for a solemn moment. "You, too, will go away. I sense it in my heart. The two that I love the most, like my own children, are being taken from me."

"Noelani, don't say that." She knelt on the cushion and put her arms around her. "I'm never going away from you and Ambrose. Not permanently. I'm not even sure I'll go for a short time."

"You will go. He will see to that, Makua Jerome. You, too, like Keno and Miss Candace, are making a mistake. They should separate, but you and Rafe should not. You must be careful. I fear you will lose Rafe if you play this game. You cannot keep him on a fishing line forever. If you try, one day he will become angry, break free, and never let himself be entangled with you again. Who wants to live with pain? You should marry him now. Forget Makua Jerome and leper island. That is all past. Rebecca will die in peace one day. She is a strong Christian. She would want you to live and marry, not risk your body and your life on Molokai."

The firmness of her words and the seriousness in her eyes convinced Eden that Noelani was baring her heart. Eden remained silent, unable to respond. Somehow, she knew it was true. And yet she could not break free of the tie that bound her to a cause. A cause she believed she must see through to its end. But what *was* the end?

Eden slowly stood. Noelani resumed her weaving, and Eden, after a long moment of silence, turned and quietly left the nursery.

Chapter Ten
A Ring for Three Days

*I*t was nearing the dinner hour. Diamond Head sat tinted with gold, and a brilliant tropic dusk silhouetted the tall coconut palms. Sweeping rollers from the coral reef brought a soothing ambience to the occasion.

Colorful lanterns decorated wide-spreading tree branches, casting greens and blues through tinted glass along the front yard and entranceway. Inside the plantation house, stalks of bird-of-paradise and wild orchids decorated the tables. The dinner table was laid with good fare: platters of smoked meats, fruits, cheeses, and a variety of juices served from crystal bowls.

Eden, dressed in an apple-green watered-silk gown, left Noelani and went downstairs in search of her father. As she entered the columned hallway and walked to the balustrade she saw Keno below, moving toward the kitchen and the back of the house. Then he had not yet gone to the bungalow to see Ambrose. Why had he gone around the house?

She walked toward the landing just as a familiar form dressed in handsome evening clothes was coming up the staircase. Rafe appeared to have more sobering matters on his mind than dinner.

He took the last steps two at a time, then stopped as she approached.

Eden wondered if her expression revealed her feelings after her serious meeting with Noelani, for he studied her carefully, then looked into the hall as if expecting to see someone behind her.

Eden was curious if he had any suspicion about Noelani's feelings on their broken engagement, and the idea brought a tint to her cheeks. She turned away from him and walked back to the balustrade, her gaze focused below in the hall, where one of the staff was coming across the floor with a tray, headed for the dining room.

"Hiding from the Derrington patriarch?" Rafe asked.

Eden smiled in spite of herself. "I understand you have a private meeting with him tonight. Are you on your way to see him now?"

She hoped Rafe would reveal the purpose of his meeting with Grandfather Ainsworth, but she received no illumination beyond a flicker of his energetic dark eyes and a light smile.

"Zachary tell you that?"

"No. Candace. She thinks you might be won over to the Reform Party. Great-aunt Nora is in a tizzy trying to figure out a way to get you back writing for the *Gazette*."

"Writing demands hours. More than I can give at the moment. But someday, perhaps. I've even thought about owning my own news-paper."

"It looks as if Zachary will need to share the *Gazette* with Silas. Nora hired him tonight to unearth some story about the American Minister Stevens secretly helping the Reform Party overthrow Liliuokalani." She arched a brow and scanned him as though he were hand in glove with the movement.

"No wonder Zach looks as though he's wired to a powder keg. Silas appears adept at elbowing his way into things. To change the subject . . . have you told Ainsworth our engagement is off? And has your father been told? Then again, did your father even know of our engagement since he's always away?"

Eden grew uncomfortable under Rafe's penetrating gaze. The remark about her father's absence brought a rekindling of tension with Rafe. Did he think Ainsworth wished to discuss the broken engagement? Perhaps Candace was wrong. The meeting might have nothing at all to do with annexation.

She became aware that she was rubbing her ring finger, a recent and uncomely habit. She placed her hands behind her back and straightened her shoulders, showing strength of purpose. His mouth turned with wry amusement. He folded his arms and leaned against the pillar.

"Why—I'm sure Ainsworth would have informed Dr. Jerome that we had become engaged," she said formally, "either in a past letter or on the steamer from San Francisco."

"But you have not told him, in any of your letters?"

She was surprised that the idea of her father not being aware of their engagement hadn't crossed her mind until now. It was Ainsworth's response that worried her, and Rafe knew it. Until this moment she'd been oblivious to what Dr. Jerome might think, either of a marriage or of a broken engagement. Everything was centered on Ainsworth. What he would think, what he would say, what he would do when he discovered the truth. That she hadn't worried what her father would say painfully revealed how uninvolved he was in her life. It was a sad reminder that sparked her anger. Rafe became the bully for bringing it up and making her see what she didn't want to see. He'd brought it up deliberately so she would focus on what Rafe called her devotion to a father image.

"Obviously we both understand it isn't my father, but Ainsworth who rules over the Derringtons. Dr. Jerome is master of one subject, his medical research, just as he, and I, would have it."

"So it seems. If Ainsworth informed Dr. Jerome on the steamer that he'd approved of his daughter's marriage to an Easton, then it's interesting your father's not commented to me about it."

"He only just arrived," she protested, though she had no wish for her father to speak to Rafe. It could be the means for Ainsworth to learn the engagement was broken.

"I beg to differ. They arrived this morning. There's been ample time. And it's natural for your father to seek me out at once and interrogate me on why I deserve—" he stopped, bowed, and continued, "*deserved* his only daughter."

Her heart beat faster with annoyance. Rafe said pointedly, "I spoke alone with Dr. Jerome while you and Candace were getting dressed for dinner. He is unaware of most things that don't coincide with his hopes for a clinic on Molokai."

"If you're hoping to cast my father in an unflattering light, it will do you no good. Of course his main thoughts are for his work. It's quite understandable. He's traveled the globe searching for a cure to save Rebecca. He's not in strong health. Anyone can see that. He's gaunt—and while he won't admit it, I'm sure he's plagued with malaria."

"I would agree that it's malaria. I've seen many cases in the tropics. Look, Eden, let's not fight about Jerome. It's Ainsworth that poses the chief problem. He believes we're still engaged. That means trouble for you."

"I know that," she confessed. "I've been concerned all day and keeping my ring hand out of view."

"So I noticed." The corner of his mouth tipped. "On several occasions I was about to suggest a glove."

"It's not amusing."

"It's exasperating. The entire charade could end now if you'd keep the vow you made to me that night on Waikiki and marry me."

"Rafe, please." She turned her head away, holding on to the banister. His hand closed about her arm.

"You're the most frustrating of womankind, do you know that?" he gritted.

"I'm sorry if you think so. It's not my intention. Do you think I enjoy bringing pain into your life? First, with what I must do about Molokai, and then with Kip?"

At the mention of Kip, his hand loosened on her arm and he drew back. She rushed on. "I was hoping Ainsworth wouldn't find out, for at least tonight." Her eyes came to his, anxiously searching.

"Rafe, I need a little more time to prepare a suitable explanation."

"My exact thought," he said smoothly. "I have decided to be mercifully generous with you. I agree that a little more time will help you survive tonight—in spite of how you threw my expensive engagement ring back at me."

She sucked in a breath. "I did not!" She knew he enjoyed the exaggeration and folded her arms. "I cried."

"I didn't cry. So I will become the magnanimous gentleman and, like Samson, let the pillars collapse upon me as I come to your rescue. I will say nothing about our separation."

Relief swept over her as she understood he was willing to help her. His maturity was overruling any revenge. "Oh, Rafe, it's generous of you to keep quiet. I feel dreadful about all of this."

"So do I," he quipped dryly. "I'll buy you more time to decide when and how you wish to confront the old lion. Zach won't say anything tonight; he's riled over Silas."

"Candace and Nora have promised they won't bring it up, either."

"They know the storm it will cause. And Candace has her own mountain to move."

"You've been more than fair with me, and I—"

"And you, my heartless one, have been a frustration to yours truly." He lifted her chin with one finger. His gaze dropped to her lips. "Ah, but love is patient." He opened his palm, and the diamond engagement ring sat winking in the evening lamplight. "Yours, my dear, for the retaking—at least for tonight, if not forever. Call me gallant, if you like." He placed the ring on her palm, then gently folded her fingers around it.

Eden felt a lump in her throat. She swallowed hard. The cold diamond began to warm, and if her imagination were rich enough, the stone began to beat with a life of its own, bringing her senses back again to Waikiki, the warm white sand beneath her feet, the wind, his arms around her, his kiss . . .

"Yes, I can be patient, but not so patient that I won't ask something in return," came his next words, jarring her back to the moment. Her eyes lifted quickly to his. Dark and vital, there was love and mystery mingled in their depths.

"So! There's a trap to this!"

"Not at all, my sweet." His smile was disarming. "I'm trying to help you, to protect you from the ire of Ainsworth—should he learn it was *you*, not your humble fiancé, who wanted out of our perfect love affair on its way to a happy home and many future children."

"My, how poetic you've become."

"I'm bighearted is all, and as you've said, you need time to prepare your case. And I, being the unrequited devotee that I am, offer you such—on one condition."

"I knew it."

"I want you to enjoy your dinner tonight with your beloved father, home at last to sit before the cheery fire crackling in the hearth—"

"In Hawaii?"

"So you can wear my ring freely tonight. Let's agree to three days, to avoid a showdown. By then you'll be ready for the gladiator arena."

"That's indeed bighearted of you, Rafe," she said sweetly.

He smiled. "For you? Anything. Now, we've got that settled." He glanced below. "Ainsworth's asked me to meet with him in the billiard room before dinner for a one-on-one chat."

"Yes, but it couldn't be about the engagement," she hastened, "because he doesn't know yet."

"Quite. He doesn't. However, there's no telling what might come up in that warm little confab. Who knows? I might lose control of my emotions and break down in bitter tears, telling all. All about how his most gracious of granddaughters, his most beautiful by the way—and that green dress is lovely on you—has broken my heart, as well as the engagement, and intends to follow the footsteps of her father, not to Timbuktu, but . . . to leprosy-infected Molokai."

She narrowed her gaze. "I always knew you were but an inch from behaving the scoundrel. You would have made a telling pirate."

"Perhaps."

"If I remember correctly, it was you—*you* who were anxious to take the ring back once I offered it, you nearly snatched it from my hand."

"Let's not quibble, my sweet. Look, you're not the only one who could use a little time to think through these unexpected events. I need time, as well. To think about Kip." He tilted his dark head. "To decide some issues that are important to me. So if you'll give me a few days to think about Kip—then, well, I'll say nothing to the old lion tonight. That's fair, is it not?"

She wouldn't have responded, even if she could. She studied him a moment, and when he lifted a brow, she let out a breath. "I must say, I'm surprised to learn your motive in all this is Kip. Are you saying you've changed your mind about turning him over to me?" Her heart melted a little in sympathy when it came to the baby. "I promised you I'd defend and protect Kip at all costs," she said fervently, "and I will."

"I believe that. But I haven't said I've changed my mind."

"Then I don't understand—"

"I've offered you a short reprieve with Ainsworth. We both need to catch our breath. As I said, I too, need to rethink this matter with Kip. When do you need to return to Kalihi?"

"Not until Monday morning. I've arranged it with Dr. Bolton and Lana so that I could stay the weekend at Kea Lani. Now that my father's arrived, though, I might manage an extra day. He'll return to the hospital with me, of course, to present his research to the Board."

"He'll want to gain their support for a clinic on Molokai?"

Remembering his words about following her father to Molokai, she grew uncomfortable. "Yes, certainly. Dr. Jerome's research must be a crucial treasure of information."

"Perhaps, but leprosy and tropical diseases are subjects I can't debate with you."

She smiled.

Amusement showed in his eyes. "Well, it would take an intelligent woman to break my heart. So, then, Dr. Jerome will assume his past position at Kalihi in research?"

"He hasn't said so yet, but I'm almost certain he will. He'll want to speak with Queen Liliuokalani, too. It was her brother who sponsored his world travels and research."

"Yes, I remember. Kalakaua had his strong points. All right, then, Eden. We agree to give each other three days."

She hesitated, unsatisfied, and yet his compelling gaze won out. "Very well. Until Tuesday, then."

He was about to say something when someone entered the hall below. Eden turned to look down the banister. Ainsworth Derrington stood, a tall, singularly slim man with silver hair, and a short V-shaped beard. He was dressed in tropics white, a somber man with eaglelike gray-blue eyes.

"Ah, there you are, Rafe. I hesitate to interrupt, but if we're to talk before dinner, we should begin soon. How about the billiard room?"

Rafe's fingers enfolded her arm, and they descended the stairs together, Eden holding tightly to the ring behind her apple-green skirts. He left her at the bottom stair and walked across the wide hall to the library. Rafe opened the door and waited until her grandfather passed through, then followed, closing the door behind them.

Eden watched, disturbed. So Rafe needed time to rethink the issues involving Kip. Had he decided not to follow through on discovering who had alerted the Board? Knowing Rafe, he would remain committed. Eden opened her palm and looked again at the engagement ring. She thought of the warning Noelani had given her. Then, soberly, she slipped the ring on, walked across the hall, and entered the living room.

I've stepped across more than one threshold this day. Were my decisions wise? Should I have put the ring back on knowing I'm being a little deceptive? Do I have the right to tell Rafe I'll wait about Kip? Is Noelani right about Rafe? Is it possible to lose him by waiting too long to assure him of my love?

What did the Lord expect of her? Where would her decisions lead, and what consequences awaited?

"Keep thy heart with all diligence; for out of it are the issues of life."

As she entered the room, Dr. Jerome looked over at her, and his countenance brightened. "Ah, there you are, my daughter. I was hoping to speak with you alone before dinner."

"Of course, Father." She responded swiftly, walking toward him. With his arm around her shoulders, they crossed the threshold into the large room.

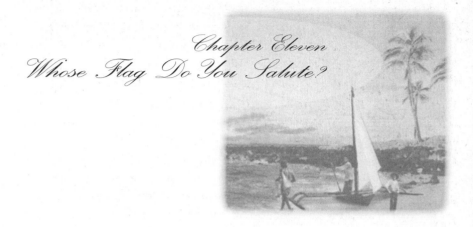

Chapter Eleven
Whose Flag Do You Salute?

*R*afe Easton watched Ainsworth Derrington, who stood in
white, staid and dignified. With concerted precision he lowered the satchel from under his arm, leaned over the glossy hardwood
table, and removed some neatly bound papers. Rafe thought him a
well-disciplined man, studious, frugal, and sober. Ainsworth looked
much like his missionary father, Jedaiah Derrington, with a smooth,
well-clipped beard and deep-set, pale blue eyes, very slim, and of a
Puritan mind-set. One large disparity separated Ainsworth from Missionary Jedaiah. While Jedaiah had been committed to teaching and
establishing the gospel in the Islands, Ainsworth was committed to
making his beloved Hawaii a part of the United States.

The years in the tropics had not changed Ainsworth as those
same years of travel under hot sun had seeped away the health of his
younger son, Jerome. Ainsworth was pleased with his work and too
disciplined to grow indolent in the Hawaiian tropics. His wife had
died many years ago, leaving him reasonably young, and he had
never wished to marry again. His energy went instead toward sugar
and the fate of the Islands.

Suddenly, the library door swung open, and Townsend burst into the room, closing the door behind him with just enough of a bang to express his frustration. His strong proportions were evident beneath the white cotton jacket and frilled shirt. In his early forties, he'd once been as handsomely golden as his son Zachary, but a dissolute lifestyle left its trademarks on his features and was reflected in his eyes.

Rafe mastered a swell of anger, but Ainsworth looked at his middle son with the steady gaze of an iceberg.

"Though I understand I'm not invited, I will be included in this meeting," Townsend snapped. "I've got to report to the League tomorrow on your Washington visit."

Rafe had become hardened to Townsend's bullying personality since his childhood years when he'd often climbed out of his bedroom window at night to run away to his uncle Ambrose at the church bungalow. Out of respect for his mother he'd learned in his teen years to restrain his emotions when it came to his stepfather. There had been times when he'd wanted to flatten him—but one night, when alone with Ambrose in prayer, he'd vowed not to lay a fist on Townsend. It hadn't taken long for his vow to be tested. He and Zachary had come to a showdown on Waikiki Beach over Zach's brash treatment of Eden. Zach hadn't believed Eden was his blood cousin and he'd grabbed her and tried to kiss her, ignoring her protests and refusing to turn her loose. Rafe had struck him down in the sand in view of Townsend, who had been driving by in a carriage. Townsend came bounding out of the carriage and across the beach to find out why his son was lying dazed, sprawled in the white sand. Zach had blamed Rafe, and nothing Eden said would convince Townsend otherwise. Townsend determined that Rafe, the bully, would be taught a lesson, and Rafe had endured the beating because of the vow he'd made while praying with Ambrose. After that, anything Townsend said was filtered through distrust in Rafe's mind.

Though restraining physical action required discipline, Rafe had confided to Ambrose that it was just an initial struggle. The real battle was with the anger, sometimes even rage, that kept churning on the inside. "That's the battle I can't handle. It wins most every time—no matter how I struggle."

"We must realize it's a spiritual battle," Ambrose told him. "And it's ongoing. You can win one day and fail the next if you're not aware of the danger and dressed in the armor of God. It demands spiritual weapons to defeat a spiritual enemy. Victory can come, but only by applying the Word of God and having confidence in the Holy Spirit who indwells you."

After bursting into the library, Townsend strode over to the large table, eyeing the stack of papers Ainsworth had carried into the meeting. For an awkward moment no one spoke. Rafe, showing respect for Ainsworth, turned his full attention upon him, ignoring Townsend.

"You wished to speak with me, sir?" he prodded politely.

"Yes, indeed, Rafe. I've some important matters to discuss with you." Looking over at his son, he added, "Since this is a family affair and the outcome will affect all present, it's not inappropriate that Townsend has *decided* to join us."

Rafe might have cocked a brow at that bit of rainbow-colored sentiment. A *family affair* since when? Eden had been treated as an outsider until she'd begun to mature, and until he'd returned from his voyage with the coveted pineapple slips, he'd been fit for little except to be "run out of Honolulu."

As Rafe considered this man who had bargained to allow him an engagement to his granddaughter Eden, he wondered what Ainsworth's response would be when Eden told him the engagement was off?

Ainsworth's icy blue eyes glinted in the lamplight as keenly as sunlight on the ocean swells. Rafe felt those eyes measure him anew, but they told him even less about what stirred around in his mind. If it was about Eden, he'd need to keep their secret awhile longer as promised on the stairway, no matter the personal cost. It was crucial for his own plans as well. In the end he may need to apologize to Ainsworth, but so be it.

Rafe kept his manner and words amiable, but formal and appropriate to the meeting. This was no warm social call, despite Ainsworth's mention of a "family affair."

"I spent some time in discourse and planning with Parker Judson while in San Francisco," Ainsworth continued. "We had a solid meeting. I congratulated him on the wisdom of backing you in Hawaiiana, and I let it be known that if I'd been more discerning as to your abilities, I'd not have failed to recognize the initial stages of a successful venture."

Though satisfying, the compliment made him uneasy.

Townsend began to move about restlessly. "Maybe, but Rafe could have come to us on his return and told us about those pineapples!"

"Gaining the pineapple slips was as much a stroke of good fortune as it was grit," Rafe said to Ainsworth.

Townsend laughed shortly. "Don't be so modest, Rafe. We know that's hardly how it must have been."

"It took courage, and it took ambition—the right kind, I may add." Ainsworth glanced meaningfully at Townsend, who did not seem to notice. "You had the insight to judge where Hawaii's success is likely to be in another decade or two. That's what the best of us struggle to determine, and I'm not the first person in Honolulu to recognize your accomplishment, Rafe."

"Good speech, Father," Townsend said with a bold grin. "Just tell Rafe you're sucking him into the whirlpool of a future Derrington-Easton conglomerate and save us all a lot of time."

Ainsworth scolded him with his gaze. Rafe remained unreadable. The intentions of the Derringtons were well known to him.

"Hawaiiana is sure to be a success," Ainsworth continued.

"Thank you, sir. Before I become too conceited over all this praise, there must be another reason you wanted to speak with me."

Townsend threw back his golden head and laughed.

"Another reason other than you're becoming my future grandson?" Ainsworth smiled faintly.

Here it comes. Keep Eden out of this as best you can.

"There is another reason. It concerns Parker Judson," Ainsworth continued.

Again Rafe remained quiet. *When near a precipitous ledge, move slowly.*

"Parker intends to stay on in San Francisco for some time. His sister, as you probably have heard, is incurably ill. She may not live much longer. The daughter, Parker's niece, I forget her name—"

"Bunny Judson."

"Yes, that was it, unusual name—she's taking the news with great difficulty, as one might expect. She was close to her mother, I understand. Parker wants to stay and help them through this ordeal, so he may be away from Honolulu for a year or more."

"Very commendable." However tragic the death of the mother may be for the Judson family, Rafe wondered what the matter had to do with him. Judson kept in contact with him by telegraph and mail, and Rafe wrote monthly reports on Hawaiiana's progress and expenses.

"You were the main topic in our meeting," Ainsworth went on. "Parker and I decided to settle the big question. Where each of us stood on ownership of Easton land in Hawaii, and when to return it to the heir."

For the first time Rafe was taken off guard. This was the last topic he could have imagined Ainsworth willingly discussing.

Townsend also appeared stunned. His gaze darted between Rafe and Ainsworth. "What's this?" he demanded. "What do you mean about Easton land returning to the heir? Are you referring to Celestine's property? That will be a snowy day in Honolulu! Why wasn't I consulted on this? What's been going on in San Francisco behind my back? I'm the one to handle Celestine's property. She's *my* wife!"

"Keep quiet, Townsend," Ainsworth said coldly. "One might argue those points in court. And as for Celestine, you've forgotten you even have a wife." He turned his gaze back to Rafe.

Ainsworth's stern rebuke mollified Rafe's anger. *Better he should*

The Spoils of Eden

say it than I. I'd take it a mile too far.

"Rather than waiting for Hawaiiana's pineapples to become successful in the market, Parker agrees that he should return the Kona coffee plantation to you immediately. What's more, it will be returned debt free."

His words might as well have been dynamite. Rafe hardly trusted himself to speak.

The return of Hanalei? Now?

Debt free?

When the dust finally settled, it was Townsend who reacted— by exploding in rage. He slammed his big fist on the table with such ferocity the lamp danced.

"Over my dead body! What the devil is all this about? I won't have it! Do you hear me?"

"The whole island can hear you. You have nothing to say about this. It will be up to Rafe whether we follow through."

Townsend froze in shock.

Rafe centered his gaze on Ainsworth. "I'd think this was a gambit on your part, sir. Except I know you to be a gentleman of sobriety."

"I assure you, Rafe, the details, with the exception of some papers needing Celestine's signature—and yours—are in order. The lawyers, Parker's and mine, will attend to that in Honolulu in the next several days. Naturally, you'd be wise to hire a lawyer of your own. You can soon be overseeing your Kona plantation, though you shall be a busy man. Parker wouldn't permit the possibility of finding a replacement for you here on the pineapple plantation."

It sounded genuine enough. Still, Rafe was reluctant to permit his emotions to seize the prize he'd purposed to regain since his father was killed at Hanalei—and *not by a mere accident*, as he'd said to Keno in the bungalow.

"Parker Judson is a business baron." Rafe spoke bluntly this time. "What cause does he have to sign over the deed to Hanalei before I'm producing pineapples by the shipload?"

Rafe's suspicion did not appear to disturb Ainsworth. He removed an official white envelope from the papers on the table. He tapped it against his palm. The crisp blue eyes glittered. "I prefer to call the return of Hanalei a just repayment of what rightfully belonged to Matt Easton, and to his son, in the first place. Hanalei belongs to you. This is the bill of sale."

"You can't do that!" Townsend nearly croaked. His eyes blazed. "I leased that plantation to Parker under the condition it would revert back to me, should he decide to get out."

"And if you could produce the finances to cover its debts," Ainsworth said in a quiet voice. "The matter of Hanalei is out of your hands now. The lawyers who handle our contractual agreements have been through the details with a fine-tooth comb."

Townsend's face turned ashen. He lowered himself into a leather chair that squeaked beneath his frame. His fingers curled about the arms like bird claws.

Rafe wondered, could Ainsworth's offer of Hanalei possibly be as straightforward as he had presented it? There had to be something valuable to both parties involved.

"You say Hanalei is debt free, but what of Townsend's gambling debts? He used Hanalei as collateral."

"Now just you wait a minute—" Townsend growled, springing up from the chair. "I poured good, honest money into Hanalei. It was Derrington money that built the new high mountain road. It took a year under my supervision."

"The incurred debt is paid," Ainsworth announced, sober faced.

Even Townsend ceased growling to stare at his father. "Paid? Paid in full? And yet you wouldn't loan me from my rightful inheritance to have paid that same debt? Had you done so, there would've been no need to lease the Kona property to Parker to begin with."

"How many times have you borrowed against your inheritance, Townsend?" Ainsworth asked calmly.

"What's that to do with it?"

"If you can't understand my serious concerns for the future

management of the Derrington enterprise, then explaining is a waste of time. Between your weaknesses for gambling and women, and Zachary's lack of management ability, is it any wonder I've decided to include Silas in the family? It may be that Silas will prove himself the leader I need."

Townsend, who'd been pacing like an angry tiger, stopped and looked at his father, speechless. "What did you say?"

"You heard what I said, Townsend. Will it help if I repeat it?"

Townsend's shoulders sagged for the first time. His face was colorless, and he looked as if he'd aged. He was silent a moment too long, then altered his emotional course. He stood up and strode to the door, threw it open, and looked back at Rafe, then at Ainsworth. "No, it won't help if you repeat your threats. I'm mighty proud of my son Silas, if you want to know. You won't use him as a threat against me. I'd like to see him brought into the sugar enterprise. Maybe you're right," he said shortly. "Maybe Silas will prove himself the leader we need." And he went out as abruptly as he'd come in, banging the door.

Silence gripped the room. Ainsworth shook his head in grief.

Rafe walked to the screened windows and gazed across the pineapple fields and toward the mountains. The moon was hovering, soon to dip behind the shagged palm fronds. Along the beach some boats with lighted torches bobbed in the dark waters of the lagoon. Palms grew thick along the bank, and from somewhere music filtered up to them.

He waited for the smoke to clear while Ainsworth composed his thoughts. It was several minutes before he addressed Rafe again.

"As I was saying, you'll receive the Kona property as soon as the papers are signed. Let me tell you, Rafe, Parker's got a high estimation of you. He expresses confidence in your future here in Hawaii and wants to invest in it for the good of the Islands. I've the notion if it weren't for my granddaughter Eden, he'd like to arrange a marriage between you and his niece, that Judson girl—what did you say her name was again?"

"Bunny. You know better than any planter in the Islands how long it would take me to make the Kona business productive. Why are you willing to do this?"

"If anyone can make the Easton lands financially viable again, you can. You'll manage to do it for Matt, if for no one else. I've not explained any of this to Celestine, but I've small doubt she'll be anything other than thrilled that Hanalei is free again—our own kind of Jubilee, you might say. You'll be able to inherit what Matt wanted you to own. That is all Celestine wants." He smiled in his faint, rueful manner. "And don't forget, marriage to my granddaughter makes you a grandson. I'll be able to add you to the list including Candace, Zachary, and now Silas."

Rafe was now obligated to let him know the engagement was broken. He walked over to the glossy wooden table where Ainsworth sat with the papers in front of him. "There is a serious issue you need to take into consideration before we go through with this. The trouble is, I'm not able to discuss it tonight."

Ainsworth looked puzzled, but surprisingly he was not so concerned; he replaced the envelope inside his jacket and called it a day.

"Then we'll discuss the issue when you feel free to do so. And . . . it will give you some time to consider a matter connected with the offer Parker and I are making you."

Rafe's gaze focused on Ainsworth. *I might have known it!*

Ainsworth wore a faint smile.

Rafe tilted his head. "What matter?"

"Rest assured, neither I, nor Parker, wish to trap you."

"That's yet to be demonstrated, sir." *Don't trust either of them.*

"Nonsense, it's not what you think. We're bestowing a political honor upon you."

Political? Since when had he been involved in politics?

"We believe you have the ability to run for the Legislature and win," Ainsworth said calmly. He folded his hands together, interlocking his fingers.

Rafe was taken off guard. *The Legislature.* "Sir, surely you're joking."

His white brows lifted. "No, indeed, we're absolutely serious. We're also confident you can win the race."

Rafe could see his earnestness.

"The Legislature," Ainsworth repeated, as though savoring the plan he had in mind. "Think of what we might accomplish with you, a planter, holding a seat."

"I know little about politics. And what I do know, I don't like. The corruption, the influence peddling—"

"You can learn the honorable way easily enough."

"A seat in the Legislature would tie me down in Honolulu. I can't manage Hawaiiana and bring Hanalei out of its financial losses, cooped up in a building in Honolulu."

"We're confident you will do better than you think. And we do not need your presence at Iolani Hale every day."

Rafe was starting to recognize that he would be expected to follow orders in the Legislature, the orders of the Reform Party.

"You can be convincing in speech, and you handle yourself well in matters you care about. That's important and, we have the seat in mind that's available. Parker Judson's."

Parker Judson's!

"It's this way, Rafe. Parker gave me a copy of a letter he wrote to Liliuokalani and her cabinet. Here it is." He handed it over from a folder in the pile. "He's resigning his seat in the Legislature. He wants you to fill in for the rest of his term. There's no doubt his request will be honored. Once you're in place, he'll decide not to run again." He went on, laying out the agenda. "You'll have a head start on any opponent. Naturally, those of us in the Hawaiian League will pay all expenses for running against your opponent. Many of the big planters will line up behind you." He unclasped his hands, pushed back his chair, and stood. "You have a great future ahead of you, Rafe."

Rafe was rapidly putting the pieces together in his mind. He thought he knew the bumpy road they had chosen for this long-distance trek, but again, what were they expecting to reap in return?

His caution mounted. Politics meant power. Power meant money. Money meant more power. On and on it went, one generation after another, until cultures rotted and empires fell.

"And Hanalei will be mine," Rafe repeated.

"Absolutely, free and clear. But we need you to join the Reform Party, to work zealously for annexation, to become one of the annexationist speakers in Honolulu, even in Washington D.C. You'll join Parker, Thurston, Hunnewell, me, and a few other planters who are well connected. As I said, we'll back you fully in the Legislature and use our influence to see that you're heard and elected to your own term."

"I'm a loner, sir. That means I don't care to be out front making speeches and getting headlines. I'd fail you with my first dud speech."

"I know better. You wrote those powerful essays on the rights of the monarchy for Nora's *Gazette* a few years back."

"That was different. I only wrote it."

"You could deliver much the same information in a speech. Those editorials wielded a good deal of attention and support." Ainsworth added with a touch of grievance, "Do you recall that unsettling debate you and I had at the dinner-ball for Candace after her return from Queen Victoria's Jubilee? If I remember correctly, you held your own on that night. And what greeted me the next morning at breakfast? Your editorial in Nora's paper."

"And if I recall correctly, sir, Townsend read you my editorial."

"He did," Ainsworth said stiffly. "But look here, Rafe. Surely you can see why we consider the absolute rule of the monarchy dangerous both to us, our future grandchildren, and the Islands as a whole."

"Then Townsend went down to the *Gazette* to rough me up, but I wasn't at the office. So the editor-in-chief, poor old Mr. Thornley, got pushed around."

"Thornley, yes, poor fellow, indeed. That was none of my doing, I assure you. He's no longer at the *Gazette*, is he?"

"No. Zachary's holding his position now."

"I'd prefer Nora kept Zachary. I've not kept up with the *Gazette* while away, but I'm told he's avoided all-out approval of Liliuokalani.

That he's managed to do so, in spite of Nora's support for the monarchy, tells me he's avoiding ire from the family."

"Silas has offered to heat things up for Nora by writing investigative articles in favor of the monarchy and against the Reform Party. I don't know what information Silas thinks he can uncover."

Ainsworth frowned thoughtfully. "Oh really? Hmm. Disturbing. Where did you hear this, Rafe?"

"Eden was in the room with Nora and Zachary when Silas pointed out weaknesses in the headlines and articles. He claimed he could write articles exposing annexation plans."

"Indeed. Well, I'll do what I can about it. As I told Townsend, if Silas wants to get on in the Derrington family, then he'll need to know which side of the annexation issue we stand on."

Rafe suspected that one of Silas's main reasons for coming to Honolulu was to worm his way into Nora's favor. If Silas was from San Francisco as he claimed, he would be well aware of Nora Derrington from her speaking tours in the Bay City. She went to the Palace Hotel frequently, usually to promote a new book on the history of the Islands. She was working on another one now, which his mother was editing.

Rafe wondered if he was reviving the big brother syndrome again where Zachary was concerned. But he did think Zachary deserved better. He and Zach had both suffered at the thoughtless hands of Townsend when they were children and in their teens. Zach would surely be troubled that Silas was so soon favored over him by Nora, and now that Silas was about to be grafted into the Derrington family tree, it appeared he would be a thorn in Zach's side from now on. First though, Silas would need to prove himself loyal to the family and an essential help to Ainsworth. When Townsend explained the possibilities open to Silas under Ainsworth's broad canopy, Silas would easily worm his way back from the *Gazette* and over to Ainsworth. *But what of me? Am not I being offered back the Hanalei plantation on the condition that I join the Hawaiian League?*

Yes, but I'll never fight for a cause I don't believe in.

As matters now stood, after the passage of time, Rafe had seen serious shortcomings in the monarchy. Those fiery articles he had written three years ago were no longer finding support in his own thoughts. For some months now, he'd felt himself edging toward annexation as the most secure answer to Hawaii's future.

Ainsworth was sounding pleased with his pronouncements. "An impressive young man of your character, ability, and accomplishments, who can write for the journals, can convince others of the necessity of securing Hawaii. The sons of the older planters who have yet to make a stand will listen to someone of their own generation. Many of them are already talking about your voyage to French Guiana for the new variety of pineapple slips."

Rafe measured Ainsworth, his one-time opponent and now ally. He remained silent, allowing him to make his case.

"We've got to do something to guarantee our generational rights and freedoms in Hawaii. We can't be left to the whims of future Hawaiian kings or queens. If we do, everything we've worked to establish since 1840 will be at risk.

"Queen Liliuokalani is neither weak like King Kalakaua, nor indolent. She's not one for gratifying a call for pleasure and play as many of the Hawaiian sovereigns before her. She knows what she wants for Hawaii, and she'll push to attain it. She has said in secret, 'Hawaii for the Hawaiians.' I shall take her at her word. However, it's for we haoles who built Hawaii into what it is today, to act for the preservation of our grandchildren's future. We, too, are Hawaiians. Most of us are second- and third-generation Hawaiians! We have strong evidence she and her allies in the Cabinet and Legislature are planning behind our backs to overthrow the '87 Constitution." Ainsworth moved about the room, hands behind his back. "Do you know what that means, Rafe?"

He did. He had also been offended by the notion that he was not a Hawaiian because he was a haole. As Ainsworth had said, Rafe was a third-generation Hawaiian.

The 1887 Constitution had been labeled the "Bayonet Constitution" by the disgruntled supporters of King Kalakaua. In reality, the Constitution was a victory for individual rights. The anger over that victory still simmered among supporters of the monarchy. Many of the haole businessmen, who in 1887 had grimly marched with Lorrin Thurston to Iolani Palace demanding King Kalakaua form a new government limiting his powers, were in 1891 supporting Hawaii's annexation by the United States.

Kalakaua had recognized his inability to stop the revolution of '87, so he'd cooperated and signed the new Constitution that limited his authority while granting more power to the new Legislature to write laws and curb wasteful spending, which Thurston and those with him had claimed was bankrupting Hawaii.

His sister, however, then Princess Liliuokalani, had been furious that the king had given in to the haoles' demands by permitting the new Constitution.

And therein was the problem. She was a firm believer in royal sovereignty, and it was this Constitution that she was about to overturn. The haoles feared they could not trust total authority to any one man, woman, or assembly without the legal right to appeal. Perhaps most of them did identify in heart with the Constitution of the United States.

This debate of supreme rule over the people of Hawaii had been at the forefront of their displeasure when Liliuokalani came to the throne. While she claimed it was her royalist supporters and the Hawaiian natives who wanted her to end the "Bayonet Constitution" and disband the new Legislature, she herself firmly believed that it was her duty to the Hawaiian royal family to have the '87 Constitution revoked in favor of her sovereign authority. Rafe could also understand her reasoning. He had once supported that premise.

"She's a headstrong woman," Ainsworth commented.

"She's also intelligent and gifted."

"Indeed, no argument there, but she is wrong."

In the meetings of Thurston and the Honolulu Rifles, Rafe heard enought from reports from spies and those in position to know that a royalist counterrevolution was a strong possibility. Whether or not the present controversy would end in armed conflict was constantly debated in the meetings of the Hawaiian League, also known derogatively by their opposition as the "Missionary Party," because the men in leadership, such as Thurston, Dole, Parker Judson, Hunnewell, and Derrington, were grandsons or sons of the early missionaries.

"Parker has told me you've attended several of the meetings of Thurston's Honolulu Rifles," Ainsworth said quietly. "So you're aware of what we fear might happen. We need younger blood in the struggle. If you fill Parker's seat to finish out his term, then you'll be in a key position in the Legislature to aid us, and others, in thwarting Liliuokalani's plans to overthrow the Constitution. If we can motivate you to join the movement, we'll make certain you have the seat. Who knows the difference your seat in the Legislature can make?"

Ainsworth's last words may have done more than anything he'd said thus far to grip Rafe. The Board of Health paraded across his mind. He thought of Kip, snatched from his control and sent off to Molokai without his having a word to say about the injustice of the act. Kip was not a leper. He endangered no one. Yet Rafe had not a word to say about the baby's fate.

"What if I told you I've already decided to throw in with the annexationists?"

"I should be pleased, indeed. I thought that you might come to the side of the Stars and Stripes, in the end. The dream of having that flag flying over Iolani Palace is a worthy aspiration, Rafe. Along with it comes the Bill of Rights, the U.S. Constitution granting individual rights for liberty, justice, freedom of religion, the right to bear arms, and the protection of United States government and military. I've heard rumors floating from Japan that they're interested in these Islands."

"Well said. I find myself fully committed to such laws and rule. I don't think we'll have them granted to us under any monarchy.

Kings and queens come and go. Generations pass, and who knows? Without a Constitution anything might happen. As you put it, sir, I like the idea of the Stars and Stripes rippling in the trade winds over Iolani Palace."

Especially when I've been robbed of my right to defend private property and keep Kip as my adopted son.

"That you're now on our side is the best of news. I shall write Parker tomorrow."

"Sir, you should know, however, I've also a personal reason for wanting a seat of influence in the Legislature. My rights to adopt Kip as my son have been denied by the Board. I intend to challenge that."

Ainsworth, puzzled, drew his white brows together.

"Oh, the baby. Your nephew, is he not?"

Troubled, Rafe took a turn around the room, paused, and looked over at him.

"Not exactly, sir. The 'nephew' idea was a way I came up with to bring him to my home. I found him on Molokai—with the rising tide of incoming waves about to wash him away."

"My word!"

"The details of how it all came about can be explained to you later, should you wish to hear them, but for the moment, you should understand he was born of a leper . . . and that the Board of Health, by enforcing unfair laws, is insisting I turn him over to Kalihi Hospital for indefinite incarceration. He's even a candidate for the leper colony. However, it is certain that Kip is not a leper."

Ainsworth's expression of horror encouraged Rafe. "What! Kip sent to Kalawao?"

Rafe threw out the details as bluntly and harshly as he could, but left Eden out of the Board's decision. Rafe carefully chose his words. "And that seat in the Legislature, besides giving me power to work for annexation of Hawaii to the United States, may give me the opportunity to help change a ruling that says a child born on Molokai of a leper, even though given a clean bill of health by the Board's own doctors, cannot be adopted or live freely in Hawaii."

Ainsworth listened attentively, and the sympathy Rafe saw in his face convinced him he'd made the right move. In the end, Rafe believed that if he worked for annexation, Ainsworth and even Parker Judson would stand beside him in an effort to save Kip.

Despite this hopeful sign, Rafe would take no chances now. Any law he might help enact would take months, most likely years to become incorporated into the laws of the Board of Health. This moment, however, was a beginning. He was surprised to find himself on the same side of the conflict as Ainsworth Derrington.

Where this still-shaky union would lead them, he could only guess. He would do what was necessary to win for a cause he believed both just and honoring to God. If it meant changing his way of life, he would proceed.

As for Eden, he suspected that if he appealed strongly enough to Ainsworth, he might gain the marriage he wanted, regardless of Eden's wishes to go with her father to Molokai. The question that gnawed at his heart was whether or not he wanted to force her into a commitment she wasn't ready to make.

He still wanted her, but he knew the union must be on mutual terms. If she didn't love him, need him enough to yield her heart and will to his headship—then, to Rafe, the concept of marriage and all that it meant would best be forgotten.

Regardless of the direction Eden would choose, the struggle he pledged to carry out both for Kip and for Hawaii would be a worthy effort. And the return of his Hanalei debt free, waiting serenely on the Big Island for his return, would be the treasure found—and Eden, the woman he loved . . . the missing jewel.

*E*den stood with her father on the living-room lanai, this one
of generous size, screened to the outside, and presenting a
view of the white beach below. The brief tropic dusk muted the
bright colors of Waikiki, while the sound of waves breaking on the
shore was a constant reminder of the blue-green Pacific.

Eden waited in the evening stillness for her father to speak. Her
anticipation heightened. What was on his mind? What would he tell
her?

Dr. Jerome, she knew, was fatigued by more than his voyage
from San Francisco. She believed he had tropical fever. He was
struggling against a prolonged sickness that he, apparently, did not
wish to discuss, perhaps because it might impede the realization of
his ambitions. Nonetheless, his emotions bordered on jubilation.

"This is a celebratory day, Eden, my dear. My plans to open a
research clinic on Molokai have been fortified this afternoon with
the arrival of Herald Hartley. I can tell you this, Dr. Chen's journal
adds a great body of research to my own."

Surprised, Eden turned. "Oh, then you have Dr. Chen's research journal?"

"Indeed, we do. What a bounty he has left to my charge. The greatest treasure I could have been awarded, and by Dr. Chen himself."

Eden listened intently while her father explained how Hartley's sole purpose in rushing here to Honolulu was to bring the journal to Dr. Jerome. Hartley had kept the journal a secret until alone with her father.

"Herald understood that Dr. Chen's journal of the past thirty years was priceless to me. A letter, though a separate issue entirely, was also in his care." Her father placed his lean hands on her shoulders and smiled wearily, but with twinkling eyes. "At any rate, my dear, we now own Dr. Chen's work, and I couldn't be more pleased."

So that's why Herald Hartley had guarded the satchel like it was a golden treasure! She almost laughed. She knew little about Dr. Chen or his research, except for what was disclosed earlier that day on the lanai, mostly through Rafe's questions.

"We've been richly blessed," he was saying. "I wanted to make my announcement to you first of all. In my long absence, you too, have endured privation. Therefore you share in the victory. Our mission is coming to fruition at last, and I want you to be a part of our plans, our success, Eden. I expect a mandate from the Board of Health to open a new research clinic on Kalaupapa."

Eden caught a breath and for a moment couldn't respond. *Our plans, our mission.* At long last she was linked with her father's invaluable calling, though for much of her life that work had been shrouded with mystery. The implication of his words warmed her heart. He recognized the emotional deprivation she'd experienced and was drawing her into the final success. She was the first person in the family that he was announcing his successful plans to. *A clinic on the island of Molokai, at the Kalaupapa encampment!*

Moved by his enduring love for her mother, she was thrilled to see her father's high spirits.

"I'm sure the Board's physicians will be as enthused as I am when

I present my findings before them," he said. "However, I'll still need your help with Dr. Bolton. Your grandfather's help with Liliuokalani will be needed as well. Kalakaua was in many ways a serious thinker when it came to the threat of leprosy on his islands. I'm not as knowledgeable about his sister. Liliuokalani may not be as willing to back me financially as was Kalakaua."

"I'm afraid Grandfather won't be of much help when it comes to Liliuokalani. She considers members of the Reform Party as enemies to her rule."

Jerome shook his head over the annexation question. "I've never been one for politics. I will leave the annexation debate to others more knowledgeable. At any rate, that isn't why I wanted to see you alone. It's about my Rebecca—your mother. Oh, Eden, my poor dear. I realize the deception placed on you as a child. Looking back, I should have insisted the truth be told to you. However, I fear I wasn't emotionally capable at the time . . . and I left the matter to others. It was important I begin the search for a means to save her, you see. That was all I thought about, all I cared about."

"As soon as I learned the truth, that she was alive, I began a search to locate her on Molokai," she said, lamenting. "I've run into one stone wall after another. It's been exasperating. There was a kokua woman, I know, but Grandfather couldn't remember who she was, and all my searching since returning to Honolulu was fruitless. The Board would give me but little information. I could have gone to Molokai myself to search for news of her, even her grave—but, again, the Board wouldn't grant me permission." She looked at him. He bore the expression of sympathy. "But now that you're here, there must be something we can do!"

"Eden, there's no doubt Rebecca *is* alive. Her life was what kept me pursuing my research far and near. There is yet hope. We may be able to help her recover to some form of a happier life. Perhaps, I dare to say it, even to leave the island of Molokai." He reached inside his coat and removed an envelope. "*This*," he said, showing her the envelope, "is what I wanted to see you about. This is the letter

Herald also brought me. It's a letter for you, dear daughter, from Rebecca."

Eden gasped. She stared, fixated on the white envelope, bright in the moonlight, in her father's thin, sun-browned hand. Her heart began to thud as she reached for the envelope.

"Her kokua wrote for her, of course," he said. "We have Herald to thank. He contacted her and explained how you now know the truth of her leprosy and wanted to meet her on Molokai. Herald is a fine man. You'll come to see that for yourself in time."

The trades whispered through the palms. The wind, like gentle, soothing fingers, played in her hair and cooled her cheek.

An actual letter from her mother, Rebecca. Her throat cramped. She blinked hard several times. Her fingers smoothed the envelope to make certain it was real. At last a word from *Mother* . . . the kind and loving woman from her childhood.

Eden remembered sitting on the seat of a carriage in front of a big house that had turned out to be Tamarind House on Diamond Head. The fringe on the carriage top jiggled cheerfully in a warm, sweet wind. Her own childish laughter had sounded in her ears, then suddenly—shouting voices! Her mother was running into some trees. Someone was chasing her! Fear had filled Eden's heart. "Mommy! Mommy!" she had screamed.

Later, many years later, after she'd grown up, she had learned from Rafe that it was her father, Jerome, who had been running after Rebecca—to hold and kiss her good-bye one last time before she boarded the steamer for Molokai. Her mother had run from him, in fear of spreading the disease.

When Eden first learned this, she had wept.

All that was over. She'd accepted and adjusted to the truth. She'd been praying over her dilemma for months, and now something impossible seemed to be happening. A dream was awakening to reality. But was the answer an end in itself, or the beginning of a process that would accomplish even more? Meeting Rebecca would lead to further understanding, but would the meeting bring her to the end of her heart's long search? No matter which way the road went or what obstacles stood in the way, she believed she would learn more of God's purposes.

"I suggest you wait to read the letter when you're alone," Jerome said gently. "Perhaps tonight, after we've returned home to Kea Lani. By God's good grace you shall meet her, Eden. If it's the last thing I do, you'll have your conversation with Rebecca."

⁓

Rafe left Ainsworth Derrington inside the library going over the legal documents to bring to Honolulu in the morning. Outside the library door, he glanced at his timepiece. There remained thirty minutes before dinner. That meant Keno would be returning at any time to bring Ambrose's message to Noelani.

Rafe walked to the living room; when he entered, Eden's voice wafted to him—

"The work on Kalaupapa is my dream, too, Father. I've planned for this opportunity, hoping and praying that somehow it would come together. I'll do everything I can to help."

"It is an ambitious choice. Then you're certain, my dear; you want to leave all this behind and go with me and Herald to Molokai? It won't be a simple task. There will be much sacrifice involved."

"Father, your clinic on Molokai is important to me. Now that I know my mother is alive and wishes to meet with me—nothing will stop me or cause me to change my mind."

"Then as far as I'm concerned, the matter is settled. Ah—is that Herald below in the yard?"

"Yes . . . I think it is."

"Excuse me, my dear, I've a short meeting with him on the beach before dinner . . . can I get down by way of these steps?"

"Yes, the stairs lead to Waikiki . . . be careful, though, going down. Perhaps I should go with you."

He chuckled. "No, no, your father is still quite fit, just a mild case, now and then, of tropical fever. I'll see you at dinner."

The trades rustled the wooden blinds as his footsteps faded in the direction of the stairs. Rafe waited, uncertain. He felt no qualm at having overheard. Though his own future was bound up in Eden's choices, there was such a thing as male self-preservation.

Should he step into the moment so obviously precious to her, or not? If they cared enough about each other to have once contemplated marriage, did he have the right to know where things stood?

He stepped onto the lanai and saw Eden standing there with her back toward him, looking toward the beach. The gentle breeze, the sound of the restless waves washing the shore . . .

She must have heard him, for she turned quickly. He read the excitement on her face. His gaze dropped to the envelope she held clasped to her heart. Their eyes met, hers green and shining in the lamplight. He read in their depths all he needed to know.

There's nothing now that will thwart her from joining her father's work. The letter from Rebecca is the final motivation for joining him on Kalaupapa.

Rafe turned and walked away, choosing to honor her time of joy by not interfering. He closed the living-room door behind him without a sound.

"*Rafe,*" Eden whispered and took several steps after him, then stopped, as though her legs would not respond. As the waves lapped at the shore below, she lifted the envelope away from her heart and looked at it.

Chapter Thirteen
Ten for Dinner

*T*he long, gleaming dining room table awaited the Derrington dinner guests. Ambrose did not show up. *Curious*, Eden thought. Ambrose and her father had been close friends when they'd been younger men, much like Rafe and Zachary now that the two "brothers" had moved beyond rivalries to trusting one another. Ambrose had told her that it was her father who'd first arranged for him to pastor the mission church before departing on his travels. And her father had chosen Ambrose to care for her during childhood. Why hadn't Ambrose come tonight to welcome her father home after years of absence? Because of Noelani's refusal to attend the dinner?

Odd, Eden thought.

Before she'd even entered the dining room, Townsend's voice could be heard on a political rampage. "If she burns the '87 Constitution, our rights will be trampled. We're dead fish! Years of work and sweat to build these Islands into the success they are today will all be lost!"

She saw Townsend pacing the hall with the drama of a politician. Broad-shouldered, tanned, and dressed in white, his blond hair streaked with gray. He wore the usual diamond stick-pin in his lapel. It was a wonder he hadn't gambled it away, Eden thought unhappily.

Silas and Herald Hartley stood listening—Silas with a pencil and small notepad in his hands. What did Silas think of his overassertive father?

Townsend resumed. "We—the haoles—built Hawaii into what it is today. We were the men who built the schools, the hospitals, the churches."

You mean the true missionaries did, Eden thought.

"We established the sugar plantations and developed the trade. The Islands were nothing when we arrived in 1820. The modern notion that Hawaii was a green, tropical paradise before we arrived is a fantasy. It was a desolate, swampy wasteland. We brought in the sugarcane, just as we're now bringing in the pineapples."

We? It was Rafe, whom he'd wanted to run out of Hawaii just a few short years ago, who had the savvy to bring in the pineapples. Suddenly she realized she was battling her uncle emotionally, working herself up into a temper and losing her spiritual perspective. She took in a deep breath and forced herself to be calm. There was little anyone could do to change Townsend.

"And now, with civilization and success all around us, are we to be robbed of our right to vote and sit on the Legislature? Not on my watch! We planters aren't going to put up with her meddling."

"What of the Chinese and Japanese?" Silas asked. "What if they rise up on the side of Liliuokalani? What would you do then?"

"Do? Why we'll request Stevens to ask the U.S. Navy to land troops."

"Mr. Stevens, the American Minister to Hawaii?" Silas asked, surprised. "Will Minister Stevens respond to your request?"

Eden came alert. *Now why is Silas asking that? It's almost as if he's asking a leading question to bait Townsend, hoping his too-ready tongue will say something that Silas can use in the morning headlines of the Gazette.* What had Silas boasted he knew about in the earlier meeting with Great-aunt Nora and Zachary? Hadn't he told Great-aunt

Nora that the American Minister Stevens was a staunch proponent of annexation working behind the scenes with men like Lorrin Thurston and Ainsworth? Silas had accused Stevens of a continuous communication with the U.S. Secretary of State, Blaine, regarding the troubled situation in the Hawaiian Islands. That in itself was normal in a time of crisis, but Silas had claimed Minister Stevens was trying to learn from Blaine just how far the U.S. president was willing to go, should circumstances warrant the overthrow of the monarchy. "An orderly and peaceful revolution," Silas had said with light sarcasm. And now Silas was coaxing Townsend to admit that plans were already in place for American troops to come ashore with guns. What a headline!

Silas was taking a great risk. Surely he was shrewd enough to realize that connecting Townsend's name in the *Gazette* with a scandal would abruptly end any position of favor within the family?

"The Chinese won't rise up. They've no reason to involve themselves. Their livelihood is with the planters. And if there's any rebellion in the cane fields they'll end up out of work and starve to death."

"I wish you wouldn't speak of death so lightly, Townsend," Dr. Jerome said as he came into the hall.

Townsend brushed the remark aside. "C'mon, Jerome. There's millions of 'em to spare in China."

"Millions, yes. In need of their Creator's forgiveness in Christ. Each one a unique individual, with hopes and tears and an eternal soul."

"You're off the subject," Townsend snapped. "The planters are determined, all right. Even some of the Englishmen and Germans are riled up. What's more," he went on, "if Liliuokalani thinks she's going to stack her cabinet with men in favor of tossing out the Constitution of '87, she'll have a war on her hands."

"War!" Herald Hartley said, startled. "Oh, surely not, sir."

"The Hawaiian League is talking about buying up every rifle in Honolulu just in case things blow up. Some of the monarchy supporters may try a revolution of their own to end the '87 Constitution.

I already have rifles and ammunition stashed away. If we need to teach them a few lessons, we will!"

"Can I quote you on that, sir?" Silas asked his father, with pencil and pad in hand.

"No," came a calm but firm voice. "You may not."

They turned. Ainsworth stood there, having come from the library. Tall and straight as a pillar, he fixed his cool blue eyes on Silas.

Silas looked like a schoolboy caught with his hand in the cookie jar.

"I don't think it wise or conducive to Hawaii's present circumstances to have your father on the front page of Nora's newspaper, threatening war. Do you, Silas?"

The noticeable emphasis on *father* surely spoke a veiled warning to Silas. He was either to show loyalty, or he would find the door to the Derrington family, with all its benefits, barred to him.

"No, sir, absolutely not."

"I'm glad to hear that."

Townsend flushed heavily. As if to save face for his blundering tongue, he thrust himself back into the debate with defensive energy. "We can't back down, Father. We don't want a monarchy breathing down our necks."

"Nor do we want to sound the trumpets of war."

Ainsworth looked pointedly at the intrusive note pad in Silas's hand, indicating that its presence was an offense at the family dinner. Silas must have come to the same understanding, along with a realization that he wouldn't be attending a second family dinner if he hadn't. He hastily stuffed it into his jacket. Eden thought they wouldn't be seeing Silas acting the nosey journalist again anytime soon, if ever.

"Well, shall we all go in for dinner?" Ainsworth suggested, glancing around. "Where's Rafe?"

"He's coming now, with Celestine." Candace, with her New England brittleness, came briskly into the room. She walked up beside her grandfather. He seemed especially considerate tonight of his favorite "firstborn" granddaughter, knowing her objections to marrying Hunnewell. Eden didn't think Candace had stood up for Keno yet, but she would. Oh, yes, she would!

Celestine arrived a moment later on the arm of her son, Rafe Easton, looking gracious in a simple evening dress with a crimson flower corsage. Eden had worried that there might be a mark on Celestine's face from Townsend's vile temper. She was relieved to see there was none. Either some feminine cosmetic had concealed a bruise, or it hadn't yet developed. Eden was upset over Townsend's presence at dinner, apparently more so than Celestine, for she showed no anxiety, and oddly enough, there was an excitement in her eyes. She hardly appeared mindful of Townsend. *Strange*, Eden thought, *am I imagining all this?*

Eden avoided looking at Rafe when at all possible, so handsome was he in his white dinner jacket, the only style for Hawaii. For his part, he ignored her. She had no right to be offended by his action, but she was. The engagement ring on her finger was a charade after the emotional drama that had occurred between them less than half an hour ago on the lanai.

Did Rafe think the dilemma between them was easy on her? Did he believe her to be playing the silly heartless creature who enjoyed controlling a man's emotions? *He should know me better than that*, she thought, despondent. *I should go back upstairs, change into my nursing uniform, and return to Kea Lani.*

But since her father was guest of honor, how could she leave?

Ah, yes, for your father you'll do anything, she could hear Rafe saying with a sting in his voice. *Always for your father. Yet when was he ever there for you? When we were growing up, who was it that came to your aid, time and time again?*

And of course, Rafe had always been there for her, even defending her against Zachary's melancholy moods and ardent missteps.

Eden entered the large dining room on the arm of her father. Even while her heart beat with excitement over the medical future she would have with Dr. Jerome on Molokai, she felt miserable over Rafe.

That Silas had remained for dinner suggested that his meeting with Grandfather Ainsworth, arranged by Great-aunt Nora, had gone better than expected. Eden was still hoping that Silas would find a place of acceptance at the proverbial family altar.

Who was the man in the book of Judges who'd been illegitimate, rejected by all his half-brothers, and barred from his family inheritance? Then, in the end, due to affliction by Israel's enemies in the land, they had sought him out to be their judge and to lead their army?

She pondered, trying to recall his name.

Zachary entered late, mumbling an apology as he took his chair beside Candace. His unfriendly mood also told Eden that yes, Silas was now accepted by the family patriarch.

"Jephthah," Eden said softly to herself, satisfied.

Her father leaned toward her. "You were saying, my dear?"

She smiled and whispered, "Jephthah. In the book of Judges."

He thought for a moment, then gave a nod and appeared to follow her thinking, for he looked at Silas, who looked subdued. He'd had his wings clipped tonight, but his eyes were alive, and he seemed content.

"Silas needs our prayers," Jerome told her in a low voice. "He and Zachary, both. Two brothers at odds are not good, or maybe I should say three brothers?"

Eden followed his gaze to Rafe, who was just then studying Silas with a pensive gaze.

"Now, what was the history on Jephthah—ah, yes," Jerome said. "I remember. In the end he made his family eat humble pie, did he not? He made a rash vow to God, however, the result being that his daughter would never marry. A tragedy in those days."

Eden wondered if there was a message for her as well as Silas in the history of Jephthah. *Am I going to Molokai to serve Christ? Myself? Or my Father? Whatever you do, do heartily unto the Lord and not unto men.* Meaning not for men alone, but to bring ultimate praise and honor to the One whose name alone was Good and Holy.

Search my heart, oh God. Lead me in the way I should go. You know I love Rafe, and I don't want to hurt him. You also know I feel drawn to Molokai . . .

But, who or what was wooing her? God? Or a strong conviction born of a need, or a quest? Was it *God's* quest?

—❧❧—

The table was complemented by a dozen oval-backed, dark-wood chairs upholstered with a woven tapestry in the warm colors of pecan, mango, ebony, and gold. Celestine's Viennese crystal lamps were lit and gleaming, and in the midst of the table there was a bird-of-paradise flower arrangement. The various dishes were cooked to everyone's delight.

"So, Silas," Dr. Jerome said in a friendly tone from across the table. "I'm told your home was in California for the last several years?"

"Why, yes sir, it was."

"I'd prefer you called me Uncle, or just plain old Jerome."

"Thank you, Uncle. Originally, it was Nevada. Have you heard of Virginia City, Reno, and Carson?"

"Indeed. Silver country. During the War between the States, the silver in the Comstock Lode helped finance the Union army."

"I see you've maintained an interest in American history even in faraway lands. Yes, you're right about the silver bonanza and the War between the States. Actually, I grew up in the South . . . so I don't know how I feel about the outcome of that war. As I told Cousin Eden earlier today, I'm also a Louisianan."

Zachary turned his golden head. His mouth curved. "You could also say those old western towns you mentioned all have something in common. Virginia City, Reno, Carson, New Orleans, are all gambling towns."

Eden tensed.

"You're so right," Silas said easily.

"Leave it to my young son Zach to fail to appreciate the wealth of experience gained by interacting in the real world," Townsend said with amusement.

Zachary's gambling slur had been turned against him. He said nothing.

Eden glanced at Rafe and saw his dark eyes flicker.

"Since when does tossing your money away over a deck of cards prepare anyone to handle the seriousness of life?" Rafe asked Townsend, a veneer of coolness in his voice.

Eden was amazed that Townsend did not attempt to counter Rafe's critical query.

"Well said." Candace spoke up, lifting her glass. She looked pointedly at Grandfather Ainsworth. "Oliver Hunnewell is known to attend gambling parties in Honolulu."

"Oliver? Nonsense, Candace. He's a church-going man. Always was."

She looked at Rafe. "Does Keno gamble, Rafe?"

Before Rafe had a chance to answer, Dr. Jerome said calmly, "I hope everyone realizes I'm not smiling upon the evils of gambling, but it is possible to play cards and still be a true Christian."

"*Please*," Great-aunt Nora said, snapping her spoon against her glass like a dowager instructor. The clear ring caused everyone at the table to look at her. Silence momentarily prevailed. "Let us not open a theological debate at dinner. Have we not problems enough? Ainsworth," she said, leaning past Candace to fix him with a steady gaze, "how friendly are you with that overly zealous American Minister Stevens?"

Oh no, Eden thought. *If Great-aunt Nora brings that up again, and after the episode in the hall between Silas, Townsend, and Grandfather . . .*

Eden said quickly, "Those particular towns you mentioned in California all have some fairly good newspapers as well," as though she hadn't heard Nora.

"Yes," Rafe said, backing her up. "Tell us about them, Silas. Where did you work as a journalist?"

Silas looked around the table. "About four months ago, I came to San Francisco, writing for the *Bay City Times*. Fortunately for me they needed someone to research the tong wars going on in Chinatown."

"Tong wars!" Zachary made a point of looking at Candace to vindicate his previous mention of them.

"We're fortunate to have Silas willing to spend some time writing for the *Gazette*," Great-aunt Nora chimed in, turning to Ainsworth. "I firmly believe Silas will be an asset to the Derrington name."

"By all means," Ainsworth said calmly. "I hardly think he'll find his place in the sun writing propaganda for the *Gazette*, however. I should probably announce that Silas also has experience managing a sugarcane plantation in Louisiana. Is that not so, Silas?"

"Yes sir, that is, I was assistant to the top overseer."

"So Silas will be working closely with Townsend from now on. He'll learn what it means to manage a real sugarcane plantation," Grandfather Ainsworth said with a smile. "We need to train the younger generation to take over the enterprise after us. Right, Townsend?"

Townsend grinned. "You've made the right decision."

Silas looked struck by lightning.

"Well." Great-aunt Nora set her water glass down with a tinkle. She lifted her head. "I'm shocked, Ainsworth. Is this not a bit hasty?"

"Not at all, not at all. I do not make hasty decisions, dear Nora."

"And I had such high hopes for Silas writing for the *Gazette*."

Silas finally got hold of his voice and said to Ainsworth, "Sir, I'm astounded at your generosity. Coming into the grand Derrington family like this to be a part of the sugar enterprise is more than I would have hoped for."

"You are a Derrington," Ainsworth said quietly. "You're my grandson. Besides, we need strength of purpose and fresh blood in the family. I can't very well expect my two granddaughters to run the Derrington Enterprise one day unless they marry good names, men of leadership. We're pleased about Eden and Rafe Easton, and now Candace and Oliver Hunnewell."

Zachary thrust back his chair and stood. He started to say something, but was hindered as Rafe, too, stood and caught his eye.

Herald Hartley, Dr. Jerome's assistant, mumbled a profuse apology as he recovered his water glass from the edge of the table where it had tipped over. It wasn't clear to Eden whether his hand had knocked it over, or Rafe's. The servant, Wong, quickly came to the rescue with a cloth.

"Oh, Madame, it was indeed clumsy of me, my deepest apologies," Herald Hartley spoke to Celestine, who now also rose to her feet, some water on her dress.

"It was my fault for not moving before it ran down, I fear," Celestine said. "No matter, Mr. Hartley, it was only lemon-water, but I think I'll run upstairs and change. Do excuse me, everyone?" she said to those around the table. "There's been too much excitement tonight, I think. Candace, dear, perhaps you could carry on? Have Wong arrange coffee on the lanai?"

"Yes, of course." At Grandfather Ainsworth's proud mention of Oliver P. Hunnewell, Candace had lapsed into a cool mood, as though she'd come indoors from a New England winter.

With dinner over, Eden's spirits, at a high point all day, now sagged. She'd held her breath when Ainsworth mentioned her marriage to Rafe Easton. That toppled glass had come at a fortunate moment—not only for her, but for Zachary who'd been on the verge of an angry outburst.

The mood at dinner had been appalling. The way in which Grandfather Ainsworth had nearly crowned Silas heir of Kea Lani in front of Zachary was heartless. Zachary seemed all but left out of the succession for controlling the Derrington enterprise in the future. And *he* was the legitimate son of Townsend and his first wife, a kind, Christian woman who'd died young.

Why did Grandfather make the announcement at the table? He wasn't a cruel man, but decent and reverent of God. So many of the things that had occurred during this momentous day had been in her mind. Odd.

She soon lost sight of Rafe. He'd slipped away like a shadow during coffee and dessert on the lanai, and had not reappeared when the hour came to depart for Kea Lani. Eden and Candace waited in the front hall for Candace's bags to be brought down from the guest bedroom she'd been using these past few weeks. Zachary had left immediately after dinner without taking desert, and Silas disappeared some twenty minutes after Zachary.

Horse hooves sounded out front as the large Derrington carriage drew up to the front yard. Grandfather Ainsworth and Dr. Jerome went down the steps together and were standing in the moonlight talking quietly while waiting for her and Candace to board.

"Isn't Nora returning with us to Kea Lani?" Candace asked. She glanced back up the stairway.

"She'll be going to Tamarind House," Eden told her. "She left a section of her manuscript there."

"Oh? I'm surprised she would have left it behind. Celestine is helping her arrange the chapters."

They expected Celestine to come down and send off her guests, but she'd not reappeared after the lemon-water accident. Perhaps the busy day was leaving her weary. Still, it wasn't like her Victorian manners not to make that final effort to bid her dinner guests good-bye.

Celestine justified her stay at Hawaiiana with her alleged poor health and a need for quiet and rest. While Eden knew Celestine was not strong, she also understood the deeper reason why she did not return to Kea Lani. For the last six weeks Celestine had been attending counseling sessions with Ambrose, studying the Word and wrestling over what to do concerning Townsend.

Eden wondered what she would decide. Could Celestine be forgiven for marrying Townsend, when all along she'd known he wasn't a committed believer? Then again, had Townsend *ever* been a genuine believer? And could a true believer live in almost constant disobedience to Scripture as Townsend did?

These thoughts were interrupted as Wong hurried in from outdoors, agitated and gesturing behind him into the yard. Addressing Eden, he called, "Ling Li outside make much noise. He very upset. Say number seven son very sick to leave Rat Alley. May die. He change mind, he say. He want haole medicine right now!"

"Rat Alley? You can't go there at this time of night," Candace said.

"No, I'll have to get a doctor to come with me. We must talk with Ling. Is he outside now?" she asked Wong.

"Ling outside, very upset."

"Tell him I will be right there. Then go ask Dr. Jerome to speak with Ling and learn whatever he can about his son's sickness."

Wong hurried out the front door as Eden turned and started up the stairway. Candace followed her to the bottom step. "Where are you going?"

"To find my medical bag and nurse's uniform," she called over her shoulder. "I'd forgotten about them till now." On the upper landing she looked down at Candace. "I intended to send a medical message to Dr. Bolton about Ling's son the moment I arrived here this morning. Now it's too late, so I must go myself and tell him."

Upstairs, Eden rushed to the bedroom. She was furious with herself. She'd been so emotionally involved with thoughts of Rafe and Kip and her father's work on Molokai that when a medical emergency was happening right where she lived, she'd allowed herself to become distracted. She quickly found her uniform where she'd left it when dressing for dinner, but where was her medical bag? She remembered having the satchel in hand when she'd visited Noelani in the nursery, thinking at the time she'd examine baby Kip.

Eden rushed down the hallway. While Ambrose hadn't shown for the dinner, Noelani might still be here, waiting for the night *kahu* to arrive, who kept watch in the nursery in the late hours.

The lamps burned. Noelani's weaving materials rested on the *lauhala* mats made from the leaves of the pandanus tree. The door to Kip's little room was closed, the boy fast asleep. Noelani must have stepped outdoors for a moment. Eden looked about for her medical bag and found it by a chair. Turning to leave, she noticed a drawer of one of the bureaus standing partially open and a child's blanket fallen on the floor.

Eden paused. She walked over to the bureau and opened the top drawer. Empty. She opened the other drawers. Empty. She whirled, hurried over to Kip's room, and opened the door. Darkness. The night lamp was not lit. Alarm seized her as she rushed to the side of the crib. *Kip was gone.*

Wait—think. Might Noelani have brought Kip to the church bungalow? She sometimes did that when there was no kahu to watch through the night. Could Ambrose have come for her and she'd simply not wished to disturb the group at dinner?

Yes, that must be it. It's the reason for Kip's baby clothes and blankets being missing. She turned and went out, closing the door with exaggerated quiet.

But so many clothes? So many blankets? Eden forced her emotions into a calm repose. Why should she react in such a panic? It was needless, really. There was nothing whatsoever to worry about. She would find Rafe and ask him.

Before leaving the room, she walked over to the bench-chest and lifted the heavy lid. The extra blankets and clothing kept in store were all missing. *Everything is gone.*

Eden stood still. A sparkle from the diamond on her finger caught her eye. "Time was needed," Rafe had said on the stairway. *Time.*

Wearing the ring tonight would buy her *time* to decide how to inform Grandfather Ainsworth she was no longer going to marry Rafe Easton. Rafe, as well, had bought himself what he had needed. *Time.* "I haven't said I've changed my mind," he'd said.

No, he hadn't changed his mind about turning Kip over to the

Board, and the delay was for a purpose that went beyond Grandfather Ainsworth.

Her heart thumped steadily. So, that was it. This had been his plan all along. To smuggle Kip out of the house while she gathered around Dr. Jerome, listening to his exotic tales. *Time.*

She hadn't expected the controversy over the Board's decision to go this far, but now that it had, it explained Rafe's behavior this evening.

Noelani and her nephew Keno had been in some sort of heated discussion when she'd first found them in the nursery. Keno must have been giving Noelani orders about Kip, orders from either Rafe or perhaps even Ambrose. Most likely, both men. In the end, Noelani must have agreed to help Keno, Ambrose, and Rafe in their plan to smuggle Kip out of the house—to where? To the mission church?

When she'd left Noelani and met Rafe on the stairway, he'd been prepared to bargain. And she went right along with it, thinking she was getting more from that bargain than he—three days. No wonder he'd been preoccupied at dinner!

No, she hadn't expected it to go this far, but now that it had, what would she do?

She could alert the Board of Health to Kip's disappearance at once, as soon as she went to Honolulu tonight to see Dr. Bolton about Rat Alley. She could storm down to Ambrose and Noelani's bungalow and demand to know where they were hiding Kip. She could even find Rafe Easton and tell him what she thought of his "bargain."

She stood there in the silence. Yes, she could do all of that, but in the end she did none of it. There were footsteps coming up the stairs, and voices. She snatched the blanket from the floor, stuffed it into a drawer, and closed the other drawers as well. She moved quickly to the middle of the room and turned, satchel in hand, when the door opened from the hall.

Candace stood with Dr. Jerome. Tension lines were etched on his brow.

Eden hurried toward them, ushered them out of the nursery, and closed the door behind them. "Father, have you spoken with Ling?"

"Yes, he gave me a description of his son's symptoms. Since he spoke with you this morning, his son has deteriorated. He has abdominal pain, vomiting, bloody diarrhea, and red swellings on his neck and underarms. Eden, this suggests much trouble to come."

She was struck by how rapidly these new symptoms had appeared.

"Dr. Bolton must be informed," he insisted. "We must go to Kalihi Hospital at once. Do you have everything you need? We should depart immediately."

"Yes, I'm ready." She turned. "Candace, let's not worry Celestine or Great-aunt Nora tonight over any of this. They've retired, and both need a good night's rest."

Chapter Fourteen
Rat Alley

hough it was late when Eden and Dr. Jerome arrived at Kalihi Hospital, Dr. Bolton was still on site, and they were able to meet with him about Ling's son before returning to Kea Lani for the night.

Early the next morning, Eden located a Chinese messenger boy and sent him with written notes for Rafe and Keno at Hawaiiana. She urged either of them to contact her at once with information about Kip.

By midmorning she was preparing for the incursion into Rat Alley when the boy returned. She took him aside and asked in a low voice, "Did you find Makua Easton?"

"I look under every palm, knock on every door. The *luna* in pineapple field tell me to go, or he put me to work plenny fast."

Rafe's silence is deliberate, she thought, frustrated. Not that she worried about Kip's safety. Kip must have been taken from the plantation house under Rafe's orders. What else could it be? As for Noelani and Ambrose, Eden felt she should avoid contacting them about Kip in order to not implicate them once the Board took up the matter of Kip's whereabouts, as they were bound to do.

Eden's hours were filled with turmoil and indecision. While half of her heart was concerned with the dilemma of Kip, the other half was burdened by the possibility of a new epidemic simmering at Rat Alley and spreading throughout Honolulu.

The information she'd delivered to Dr. Bolton about Ling's son was received with alarm among the physicians on the Board. There did seem to be at least one blessing in disguise for Eden, for with all the concern over Rat Alley, no one seemed to notice she'd returned without Kip. The reprieve wouldn't last long, but she was grateful for every extra hour granted her. In two days she would hear from Rafe. If she didn't, she had no other choice except to notify the Board that Kip was missing.

"What if it's cholera spreading in Rat Alley?" one of the staff cautioned.

"If it is, we'll soon have a horrendous crisis on our hands," said another.

"Are we ready for that?"

"Who is ever ready for a crisis when it happens?"

Dr. Bolton and Lana Stanhope were two of the most knowledgeable on staff in the identification and treatment of tropical diseases. Dr. Bolton requested that Jerome accompany them to crowded Chinatown, and Eden, serving as Lana's student-assistant, completed the sober foursome that set out to find Ling's son.

The Chinese had first signed labor contracts with the haole sugar planters in 1851, and just a few decades later there were as many as twenty-five thousand workers on the Islands. Many of the Hawaiian residents complained that an Oriental majority would soon populate the Islands and displace them. The planters, however, insisted they needed cheap labor to produce sugar, and as usual, economic considerations prevailed.

The Chinese were industrious workers who lived in tiny bungalows on the plantations, using exceedingly sharp knives to cut the cane. Sometimes those blades were used in murderous fights among themselves. When they fulfilled their labor contracts with the planters, some signed up again, while others returned to their homeland. A majority stayed on the Islands, however, moving into the outlying areas, particularly in Honolulu, forming what was called Chinatown. The municipal administration there was weak and permissive, and the Chinese workers endured what Eden thought to be abysmally distressing conditions. It didn't take long before opium, gambling, prostitution, and physical violence were unrestrained. Due to the language barrier and the absence of a Chinese consul in the Islands, trouble intensified in what became known as Rat Alley.

Not all was dark and dangerous, however. Many industrious Chinese opened little shops and businesses, and still others became farmers and street peddlers, offering valuable goods for sale.

Ling Li led the four of them from the Board of Health down one alley and then up another. The hovels were piled like ramshackle boxes on top of one another. Narrow, winding pathways meandered this way and that, like a serpentine maze. Chickens wandered about, skinny dogs yapped incessantly, and rivulets of raw sewage ran along the edges of the alleys. There were tiny businesses selling everything from fish to firecrackers. A merchant man with a long, black pigtail balanced a pole across his shoulders with baskets at each end filled to overflowing with lotus roots and eggplant. He moved at a light trot through the narrow streets, calling out his wares in a singsong voice, his conical woven reed hat pointing skyward.

Ling led them to a number of huts that formed a crowded building. Eden followed Dr. Bolton, her father, and Lana through a low doorway and into an open room. The floor was covered in palm mats, and a young Chinese lad of perhaps seventeen was sprawled under a blanket, his head on a rolled rug. A male relative with a long, white beard and black gown stood beside him.

Eden watched Dr. Bolton approach cautiously. She had great pity for Ling as he stood with shoulders stooped, watching the haoles. Ling's wife and six other sons were working in the fields at Kea Lani. Dr. Bolton stooped for a closer look. When he rolled the lids back from the boy's eyes, Eden suspected the worse.

"This lad is already dead."

"So quickly?" Jerome asked, also stooping to look.

Eden drew closer. "He must be unconscious. Ling left him alive less than an hour ago." She looked over at Ling. He and the old Chinese gentleman were in urgent discourse.

"The fever was very high—look at those puddles of perspiration." Dr. Bolton drew the blanket back to examine him. "Poor boy. It looks like—" he stopped abruptly, pulling his hand back from the boy's chest. Looking at Dr. Jerome, he said, "Do you see that?"

"Yes. God have mercy."

Eden stepped closer to look down over her father's shoulder. There were swollen, dark-purple nodules on his neck and under his armpits. His death had come quickly and horribly. Her heart wrenched with pity and alarm, and she glanced meaningfully at Lana. Lana's mouth had tightened, and she drew back toward the doorway. Eden followed, and they stepped outside.

"Show no alarm," Lana murmured as individuals began gathering. "We mustn't spread panic. I fear four haoles coming here carrying black satchels has already sounded an alarm."

"What could he have died of so quickly?" Eden asked, though she feared she knew. "Ling said he was alive just an hour ago."

"I'd rather not venture a guess. Whatever it is, it's out of my jurisdiction. It isn't like any disease I've ever seen on these Islands."

Eden believed Lana did know, but refused to make a professional comment until Dr. Bolton made his decision.

With solemnity they boarded a Honolulu horse buggy that carried them along the narrow causeway away from Oahu prison in Iwilei. When the buggy reached Kalihi Hospital, Dr. Bolton immediately called for the Board physicians to assemble for "an urgent confidential report." Behind closed doors, they heard the grim details.

Eden waited with Lana in her small office next to Dr. Bolton's. Through an open window she could see the waters of Kalihi Bay, which fronted the leprosy hospital on two sides, to the west and south. The natural anchorage that was then called the Pearl Lochs looked a deep green-blue.

Oh, Lord, what am I going to do? Strengthen me to make the right decisions where Rafe and Kip are concerned. And please stay the dev-astating hand of disease in Honolulu. Grant that the death of Ling's youngest boy will be used to bring him and his family to Christ.

"What happened with Kip?" Lana asked in a low voice.

Eden closed her eyes. *Oh, no, here it comes, and I cannot lie. What to do?* She turned and faced her grimly. "Oh, Lana—everything went wrong, at least for me. I should have stayed out of it, as you sug-gested. I thought I could make Rafe see what needed to be done, but it didn't work that way."

Lana looked as if she'd expected news of this sort. She rested her mussed blond head in her hand, elbow on the desk, and groaned.

"Lana, please, I need a little more time, just two days more. Only two. I assure you Kip is clean, and there's no danger to anyone."

"I've always believed Kip was clean. He's as free of leprosy as you or I. But that isn't the issue, Eden. The issue at hand, that we must deal with, is the law. We've been through all this before."

"Painfully so, yes. Please, Lana, give me two days. Surely in your high position you'll arrange it?"

Lana sighed. "I don't know. I can't promise you. You'll need to tell me what happened. I won't say until I judge the situation. This could affect your position, you know. And mine."

Eden paced, hands at her temples. "I know, I know." *This is all Rafe's fault*, she wanted to say in self-defense, but bit her tongue. Looking over at her aunt, she said, "I'll tell you everything. I know I can trust you." *And so can Rafe and Kip*, she thought.

When she'd finished the details, explaining how after dinner she'd gone up to the nursery and found Kip and his clothes gone, Lana moaned, shaking her head. "I knew it," she said, "I knew Rafe would resist with every fiber of his being." She stood from the chair behind her desk. "You've got to find out where Kip is, Eden."

The mission church, she wanted to say, but couldn't bring herself to incriminate Ambrose and Noelani. "I'll find Kip. Give me just two days more."

Lana drummed her fingers on the desk, staring out the window. The palms rustled, and a breath of fresh air blew in over the papers on her desk.

Eden prayed earnestly.

Lana finally looked at her. "The Board will be fully occupied with this crisis in Rat Alley. It's likely they'll not even think about Kip for a while. If Clifford—Dr. Bolton asks me about Kip, though, I'll need to explain. I'll do what I can to influence him."

Eden sank into a chair. "Thank you."

"Two more days," Lana said. "After that, I must report his absence. And that means Rafe Easton will be in more legal trouble than he may realize."

—⟨◦⟩—

Eden waited for Dr. Jerome to come out of the Board of Health meeting and join her. When he did, she read the forbidding news written in his severe countenance.

"We have all agreed," he said. "Some of us have seen the results of this sickness before. I saw it in China and India. The grotesque purple nodules on the neck, armpits, and loins . . . the loathsome odor from the nodules when they burst . . . the high fever, the hallucinations—" He shook his head as though the memory haunted him. "The boy died of bubonic plague."

Eden's mouth went dry. Tight fingers of horror gripped her. She'd feared it was the plague when Dr. Bolton drew her father's attention to the evidence on the body. The idea was staggering. There were thousands of people in Chinatown, all of them crammed together in tiny huts built on top of each other.

"How many others might there be who've been exposed?" she said in a low voice, for as yet the finding was not permitted for general discussion.

He gave a brief nod and, taking her arm, walked her down the hall toward the front door. "Is there anything to be done?" she whispered.

He said nothing. His tired face was gray in the late afternoon light. "The measures to be taken will be decided upon based on how many sick and dying the search teams discover in the next day or so." Eden's heart was heavy.

"Where this will end, we cannot say. The Board will handle things here for the day and evening. We must return to Kea Lani to inspect the huts of our own workers. Remember, Ling is one of our own, and his wife and children are on Kea Lani at this moment. If the youngest boy became sick yesterday, there could be more by now. This is an emergency, Eden. We'll need to call a meeting with the other planters so they can search their own workers' huts. We don't know where this will end, but it looks as if Kea Lani is the place to begin."

She thought of Rafe and Hawaiiana and all the workers that had contracts with him. They too, must be checked.

Kea Lani Plantation had not changed much in the years since Ainsworth and Nora inherited it from their grandfather Ezra Derrington, who had arrived from New England and settled in the Maunalua area near Koko Head. The land was not leased as much of the sugarcane land was, and to own land on the Islands was either a special benefit from the early kings or inherited through marriages to members of the royal families. For reasons unknown to Eden, Ezra's first plantation house had been abandoned, and he'd resettled in the Kalihi area, near Honolulu, hiring builders to ship materials from Europe to construct Kea Lani for his bride, Amabel.

The white-pillared, three-storied structure was a replica of Amabel's ancestral home in Vicksburg, Mississippi. When their granddaughter, Nora, had jointly inherited Kea Lani with her brother, Ainsworth, Nora had set about to transform Kea Lani's Southern mansion grounds into an island paradise. The magnolia trees so carefully shipped from Vicksburg to grace the long, shady lane leading up to the mansion were transplanted to Tamarind House and replaced with two rows of date palms. Nora's private grove contained banana, mango, and cherimoya trees, as well as guavas and one French Guiana pineapple slip that she'd managed to wrangle away from Rafe, which she said was growing "very well, indeed." Many of the trees and plants on Kea Lani were not native Hawaiian, but brought in from other tropical locations around the world by horticulturalists.

Ainsworth hadn't concerned himself with what his maiden sister was doing in Kea Lani when it came to her interests, which he'd called, "flowers, fashion, and furnishings." She was also interested in preserving the history of the Islands and the monarchy, something he found a thorny issue. Hawaii's annexation to the United States meant the fulfillment of America's Manifest Destiny and was therefore inevitable. He was determined to see the momentous occurrence take place in his lifetime. To that end he'd given his time, cultivating friendships in American politics and donating money to elect congressmen who were in sympathy with annexing the Islands. Ainsworth's other effort was focused on accumulating more land for sugarcane and, since Rafe's success with pineapples, contracting more Japanese and Chinese laborers to work the fields.

When Eden arrived home to Kea Lani from Kalihi Hospital, Dr. Jerome immediately called Ainsworth, Townsend, and the rest of the Derrington family to explain the dire news of the death of Ling Li's son, and why this had been declared an emergency by the Board's physicians at Kalihi.

"The boy died from bubonic plague."

A gasp came from Candace, while the others wore stunned faces. As they came to understand what this horrific announcement could mean for Honolulu, Ainsworth sat down weakly in a chair, head in hand.

Townsend's mouth turned hard. He immediately began to stride about the room, hands shoved in his white linen trousers.

Silas frowned, and his nervous fingers reached into his jacket for the skinny cigars he smoked. A glare from Candace, as she snatched up her fan and meaningfully swished it, stopped him from proceeding. He smiled regretfully with an accommodating bow of his chestnut head.

Zachary frowned, then his light blue eyes came alive. "What a story for the *Gazette!* I'll beat them all!"

He strode toward the front door. "I'm going to Tamarind House to find Great-aunt Nora."

Eden hurried after him, coming between him and the door. "No, there's a ban. There's not to be a word of this made public. A panic will result."

"Ban! Since when? Where's the freedom of the press? C'mon, Eden, that's nonsense."

"No, Zachary, Eden speaks the law," Jerome said. "If panic spreads, so will the sickness. We must do everything we can to avoid an outbreak. The Board has decided that the residents of Rat Alley must be confined, and the huts that are contaminated must be burned. This is the only way to stay the disease. If we're not successful, all of Honolulu will be at risk."

A silent shudder moved through the room.

"Is it legal to burn the huts in Rat Alley?" Ainsworth asked.

"Don't forget, you're dealing with the Chinese." Townsend cast the remark over his shoulder. "They'd as soon knife you as look at you."

"Oh, Uncle . . ." Candace chided.

"Now wait a minute, my dear," Ainsworth said. "Townsend could be right. These are their homes the authorities intend to burn."

"Homes, maybe, but still shameful shacks. We ought to do something about that slum. No wonder the rats accumulate."

"Shacks, yes, but still better than what they had when they first signed those labor contracts to come here and work," Townsend said.

"Most of the residents of Rat Alley have fulfilled their contracts and are now on their own, trying to create businesses. They would be right to wonder why we're willing to burn Rat Alley out from under them, but leave the haole districts untouched."

"They may misunderstand, but we still cannot tell the residents of Chinatown it's the plague. If we did so, they would panic and flee, bringing the disease with them wherever they go. You know what could happen. A catastrophe in the making!"

"They're always suspicious," grumbled Townsend. "They wouldn't hesitate to burn us out if it were the other way around."

"Regardless, this must be done with extreme caution and justice," Ainsworth said. "I'm sure the Board has carefully considered and debated the consequences, and they're probably working out the legality of the decision to burn at this very moment."

Jerome was ashen. Eden worried about him, but little she said or did seemed to influence him to take more concern for his health. She'd come to see that he was a driven man. Whether it was about Molokai or Rat Alley, he'd give himself to the cause. She realized her father's sacrificial attitude might one day lead to his own ruin.

"Ling Li's family lives and works here on Kea Lani," Ainsworth said, his emotions once again under control. "His bungalow must be checked to make sure no one else is sick. Has Ling returned?"

"He is to remain under quarantine for forty-eight hours in Honolulu, as is his family. Ling tells us his youngest son had been staying in Rat Alley for the last month with his great-uncle. Let's hope he came down with the sickness in Honolulu and not Kea Lani," Jerome said.

"God help us," Ainsworth repeated, shaking his head. "If it spreads throughout our sugarcane workers, it could mean not only the death of the workers, but judgment against Kea Lani's productivity for years to come."

"Judgment?" Townsend scoffed. "The very use of that word is outdated. What have we done to deserve ruin more than Parker Judson, Hunnewell, or Galloway?"

"You might search your own heart to answer that," Ainsworth said quietly.

Townsend mumbled under his breath and resumed pacing.

The others too, looked shaken. If the plague spread, it would show no partiality, from the poorest in Rat Alley, to the wealthiest in Honolulu. All were vulnerable.

"We're wasting time," Townsend said shortly. "At least send me to check Li's bungalow."

"Eden has requested to call on Ling's family," Dr. Jerome said to Ainsworth. "She can check the other family members while there. If there's anything suspicious, his bungalow will need to be burned."

"Why fool around? Let's just burn it now and get it over with!" Townsend snarled impatiently.

"Because Eden isn't a thoughtless tyrant like you!" Zachary shouted, startling not only Townsend, but the others.

Townsend's handsome face mottled with temper. He strode toward his son, his hands in fists at his sides. "You dare speak to me like that?"

"I've had a good teacher!" Zachary shot to his feet, and Townsend trembled on the verge of taking a swing.

Grandfather Ainsworth's voice cut into the ugly moment. "Townsend!" The sound of his father's commanding voice halted him. "Zachary! Both of you! This is no time for behaving like fools. There will be no burning of anyone's hut on Kea Lani until we have the facts at our disposal. Jerome will be the deciding voice in the matter as representative of the Board of Health."

Townsend stood there as if in a daze, then turned from Zachary. Zachary stumbled toward the door, thrust it open, and rushed out, not bothering to close it behind him.

Eden's breath slowly released. Her heart ached, pounding in her chest.

"Let him go," Ainsworth said quietly. "He won't go far."

Candace stood at the window, rigid, her face pale.

Eden looked over at Silas. He stared at his father, Townsend, whose back was toward them all. His jaw tightened, and for a moment Eden thought she saw a flash of some strong emotion but could not interpret it before Silas snatched a skinny cigar out of his pocket, as if in defiance, and struck a match. He stared at the flame for a moment as if transfixed, then held it to the cigar's tip and walked out onto the lanai.

Silence settled over the room, and Eden shut the door, her fingers stiff and cold. Townsend's rages always left her cold. As she stood there, her hand on the doorknob, she had an overwhelming desire to find Rafe; she wanted his strong embrace holding her close to his heart. Then she straightened her shoulders. *The Lord is my high tower, my hope, my joy, and all my tomorrows are under His watchful, gracious eye.*

Just then the thought came to her, *I must see Ambrose to call for prayer, not only for Ling and his family in the loss of their youngest son, but for my family, too. We desperately need God's grace.* Who knew whether He might heed their prayers and quell the plague from reaping a harvest of souls not ready for death? And whether He would send showers of mercy to those in her own family who did not know Him?

Eden hurried upstairs to her bedroom, grabbed her woven sun hat from the bedpost, and came back down. Grandfather Ainsworth had sent Townsend and Silas to call the area planters together at Kea Lani to hear Dr. Jerome's report. As they went out the front door, Jerome walked up to her.

"Father, you're weary to the bone. You haven't had much sleep since you arrived yesterday. Why not rest in your room until the other planters arrive?"

"I must call on Ambrose. We'll need many from the churches to organize and manage food camps for downtown Honolulu. This must be a widespread effort."

"I was going to stop there anyway. I'll tell him."

Her thoughts jumped to Kip. He was undoubtedly at the church bungalow with Noelani, who would be careful to keep him out of sight.

Eden took her medical satchel with her. She may need to

prescribe a sedative for Ling's wife, Hui, though she knew the woman was strong and rarely showed emotion.

This was going to be difficult. How did one knock on a door and tell a mother that her youngest son was dead? Could Eden comfort her in any way? Certainly with shared tears, but with what words of hope? *I have a solid foundation for joy in the future. We* "*sorrow not, even as others which have no hope,*" the apostle Paul had written. *No hope without Jesus.* There was no reincarnation, no refining purgatory, no second chance. Behold, *now* is the acceptable time; behold, *now* is the day of salvation. "Today if ye will hear his voice, harden not your heart . . ."

Eden walked quickly down the porch steps and across the yard toward the mission church road. She would ask Ambrose to go with her to call on the Ling family.

The mission church was ahead, waiting like a well beside a dusty road on a blistering hot day. Eden quickened her steps and brushed past the ferns. She came into the open yard surrounding the church—and stopped. The church door had opened, and Rafe walked out, settling his Panama hat. He stopped, too, as surprised to see her as she was to see him. Their gazes held for a long moment. Then Eden drew in a courageous breath and marched toward him, determined. Rafe closed the church door behind him and walked to meet her. He had the looks that once belonged to his rugged father, Matt Easton. His years of hard work, swimming while growing up with Keno, and their expert pearl diving contests, had muscled his form.

She stopped in front of him. "So, Mr. Easton. As I entered the nursery last night for my medical satchel, I understood the true reason behind your generous 'three-day' bargain."

His rich brown eyes taunted her beneath dark lashes.

"If I recall, I told you I hadn't changed my mind on turning Kip over to the Board."

"So you did. Though I had no idea you'd abduct him from his bed."

A brow lifted. "Oh, come, Eden. Abduct my own son? He *is*

going to be an Easton, you know. He'll be named Daniel, after the first Easton who set foot on Hawaii."

He was telling her plainly enough that he was rejecting the regulations of the Board of Health and pursuing his own independent plans.

"I gather you've used your reprieve to garrison your stand against Ainsworth?" he asked.

"The truth is, I haven't had a moment's peace to consider how I shall tell Grandfather. After what's happened to Ling's son in Rat Alley, I don't think Grandfather will be much concerned about my personal plans."

"I wouldn't count on that."

She looked past him toward the church and struck out boldly. "Is Kip inside with Ambrose?"

"Ambrose is out preaching somewhere like the faithful shepherd he is."

She met his enlivening gaze with courage, then looked away.

"Too bad about Ling's son," he said.

The mention of Ling took her by surprise. "How did you learn of Ling's son so quickly?"

"Zachary rode by here. He was on his way to Hawaiiana to warn me. I was here meeting with Ambrose. Have you been to Rat Alley?"

"Yes, with Dr. Bolton and Lana. Oh Rafe, it was dreadful. It was the first time I've seen a victim of the plague—"

"You didn't go inside!"

"I had to go in. I'm a nurse. Even more than that, a student of Lana's," she said proudly. "We thought the boy might have been sick with some tropical disease, but—"

"And I suppose you're going to be leading the way back into disease-ridden Rat Alley to search for the sick and dying?"

She wasn't sure how she felt about the frustration in his voice. "As a matter of fact, no. Sadly, there's little to be done for the sick . . . but I shall help my father, and Dr. Bolton at the camps. Oh, Rafe, they need to burn the houses. This could be more dreadful than we realize."

"Burning is the only way to stop it."

She looked again at the church. "Is Kip in there?"

He folded his arms and cocked his head, looking down at her. A brief smile touched his mouth. "Why would I keep Kip in the church? No, he's not here. Do you think I'd involve Ambrose in this? Then *he'd* need to answer to those despots on the Board."

So he understood the risks better than she'd given him credit for. "Then where is he? Do you realize the situation you've gotten *me* into with those *despots*, as you call them?"

"Do you really think I'd allow you to face the Board and be blamed for Kip's disappearance? You don't think much of me, do you, Eden? We bargained for three days. When the agreed-upon hour strikes, you can be assured I shall face the Board's questions. You won't be called upon to answer. I wouldn't be very gallant if I expected you to take the blame for losing their medical prey, now, would I?"

"You make out their motives sound so dreadful, when it isn't at all!"

"I'll be the judge of that when it comes to Kip. He's my responsibility. I took him on knowing full well what the repercussions might be. I'm not backing out of that responsibility now just because the cauldron's boiling. I consider him my son. And no son of mine is going to wander about the leper camp to be preyed upon by the lawless and corrupt."

She grew silent. Down deep in her heart she admired him tremendously, but dared not say so in her situation. "As if I'd ever allow that to happen to Kip."

"As I've said before, you won't be able to stop it. It's the Board's decision who gets sent to Molokai."

She had thought that she would take the heat for Kip's absence. She realized she'd misjudged him. Again. "Where *have* you hidden him?" she persisted.

"That, my sweet, is no longer your concern. You certainly have enough to worry about with this epidemic about to break. And if I had my way, you'd be safely tucked away at Kea Lani far from all disease, rats, and corpses."

She tried not to enjoy his concern, yet she did. "I desire to be involved with issues that are of eternal importance."

"You won't find me faulting anything so commendable. It's one of the virtues that drew me to you."

She was warmed by his compliment. "What were you doing alone in the church just now?"

"Why do you ask?"

"I'll take your word that Kip and Noelani aren't in there."

His mouth tipped up at the corner. "Why, thank you, Miss Derrington. I'm honored. If you must know, I wanted to be alone. Though I can be alone and pray anywhere, especially while riding out in the pineapple fields, I took advantage of the peace and quiet since I was already here."

She looked at him, liking what she heard. "By the way, I intend to visit the Christian women's group on Hawaiiana before I return to Kalihi. Unless you forbid me entry."

"Now, why would I do that?" His smile was disarming. "You're wearing my ring, after all. And haven't I been trying to get you to move in permanently?"

She avoided his gaze by absorbing herself with her hat. "I may not get back here for weeks, and someone needs to encourage them with the Scriptures—except I need to borrow Noelani's Bible. Is she in the bungalow?"

"No, but you're welcome to use mine. Shall we go?"

"Yes, thank you."

"Poor old Ling. This is rough news for him and his wife. Will you be all right calling on her alone?"

"Yes, I think so. I've spoken with Hui before."

"The meeting with your father is to begin shortly. Since you have your work cut out for you, I'll ride over to Kea Lani. By the way, do you know what had Zach so riled? When he rode by here, he was fit to be tied."

"He and Townsend had a terrible flare-up over burning Ling's bungalow. I'm worried about Zachary," she said. "He's been disturbed ever since Silas arrived in April, and matters are only getting worse. You heard what Ainsworth wants to do—train Silas alongside Townsend to manage the sugar enterprise. It was cruel of my grandfather to announce it at the table in front of Zachary."

"Yes, I couldn't understand why he did so until I learned from Zach that Silas had plans to use the *Gazette* against the annexationists. I think Ainsworth was forcing Silas to make a choice: either play Ainsworth's way, or pack up for San Francisco."

"Still, it was hurtful to Zachary."

"You're supportive of him."

"I learned it from you," she said glibly. "You always protected him growing up."

"Yes, even when he lay awake nights plotting my downfall," he said wryly. "Tell me this, if you can. Does your great-aunt have much control over Kea Lani enterprise?"

"You mean the sugar management?"

"That would be included, but does she own any part of Kea Lani?"

"Oh my, yes. She owns half of the entire estate. Plus Tamarind House, the *Gazette*—though it's failing financially—and," she hesitated, glancing at him cautiously, "and half of the old pearl fishery. The Easton pearl bed. When your mother married Townsend," she said quietly, knowing how it affected him, "she allowed him to sell half of it to Nora."

"He undoubtedly forced her into it."

"Yes, it came at a time when Townsend was in some sort of financial trouble."

She saw his jaw flex. "He's always throwing money away. He's wasted his own, and now he's wasting that of those he controls. He owed my father once. Owed him a great deal, in fact." He tapped his chin thoughtfully. "Strange . . . I'd forgotten about that. Townsend came over to Hanalei one night when I was a boy and begged Matt to help him. Whether or not he did, I don't recall."

Rafe had never before spoken of her uncle owing his father money. She considered that, uneasily, for she was well aware how Rafe believed Townsend may have been involved in his father's accidental death on Hanalei.

"Ah, the pearl bed," he said more lightly. "I'd almost forgotten it. Thanks for reminding me."

"After diving for the Black Pearl?" she said with a smile concerning a past pearl diving contest during the annual hoolaulei. "You never did tell me how you managed to get it away from Primo while underwater that morning."

He smiled, but said nothing. Then, "I think I'll soon be reclaiming that."

"The Black Pearl?"

"No, I used that to help pay for the *Minoa*. I mean the pearl bed my father found and developed."

She arched a brow of friendly pessimism. "You'll reclaim it along with Hanalei?"

Rafe smiled. His gaze searched her eyes as if looking for something. Evidently he didn't find it. Was there something she should know? He seemed so optimistic. Then he said simply, "We'd better be going."

Rafe had said he would give the name Daniel, to Kip on adoption. Daniel was a special name in the Easton family, for it dated all the way back to before the Derringtons arrived in Hawaii. Rafe had an ancestor among the original missionaries of the 1820s, though there was no official historical record of an Easton being among the first couples who arrived. There was some talk that the missionary Daniel Easton had come from England. He'd also come from the failed missionary attempt on Tahiti, where, sadly, the first single male missionaries had succumbed to the intrusive carnal temptations of the Tahitian women. Thereafter, the mission board made it a rule that only married couples could venture to Polynesia. Just as the mission church here at Kea Lani was a family original, there was also a missionary church founded by Daniel Easton on the Kona Hanalei plantation on the Big Island, the result of Daniel's preaching, at about the time when Hiram Bingham had preached and brought in the first widespread island revivals.

Chapter Fifteen
Rebecca's Letter

*I*nside Kea Lani plantation house the urgent meeting with the planters arranged by Grandfather Ainsworth and Dr. Jerome was drawing to a close. Grim-faced, they listened to Dr. Jerome tell of the dangers.

"I've seen entire villages wiped out in Asia and India," Dr. Jerome cautioned the planters. "What happens in Chinatown is not to be treated lightly. If the plague spreads beyond Rat Alley to Honolulu or the plantations, the health authorities will be coming here to set all the huts afire. It's imperative to have every hut examined to stop the rampage before it begins."

"I can have a barricade in place around the workers' huts in a few hours if I move at once," Rafe said. "So can the rest of you. We need our most loyal men to search every hut. If we start now, we should be finished by tomorrow morning."

"How many guards can you round up to safeguard the barricade here at Kea Lani?" Ainsworth asked Townsend.

"Enough. Silas and I will make sure no coolie breaks through this plantation, or he'll get a bullet hole," he said, then went out, calling for Silas to join him.

—ᕬᕱ—

For Rafe Easton, the long hours following the decision to search for any sick among the workers were heavy with turmoil. Toward early morning, when silence permeated the rosy dawn, he sent a brief message to Ambrose, Dr. Jerome, and Ainsworth at Kea Lani: "Hawaiiana is free of the plague."

At Kea Lani, despite their weariness and sorrow over the accident that had taken place with Eden and the Ling family—their bungalow had mysteriously caught fire and nearly burned down around them while Eden was meeting with the family—there was a prayer of thanksgiving made to God for Rafe's plantation being free of the plague. Ambrose had returned earlier in the day with Jerome, his friend from youth, and they had spent much of the early evening praying and reading the Scriptures. "I credit the mercy of God for the safety of Eden, the Ling family, and the rest of our workers," Ambrose said.

Slowly and one by one, the other reports also trickled in from the various plantations in the region: "Plague free."

—ᕬᕱ—

When the sun came up, bright and glittering in Honolulu, Dr. Jerome and Eden wearily boarded the carriage for the ride back to Kalihi. When they arrived, Dr. Bolton greeted them with a sober face.

"Twelve dead and several sick. There's no longer the remotest doubt we're dealing with the plague."

Briefings were held, and the dire news announced. "The fires will need to begin in Chinatown to purge those houses where either the sick or dead were discovered during the search. The fire department, with those from the Board overseeing their work, will proceed with the burning at noon."

Ambrose and Candace arrived with a number of Hawaiian men

and women from the mission church who were working with other churches in Honolulu to see that food, blankets, and other needed supplies were available at the various camps set up at different locations. Those driven out of Rat Alley fled to the safety of the camps, leaving all behind for the cleansing flames.

"Kawaiahao Church is packed," Candace told Eden, when they met in the large tent set up near one of the camps on the slopes of Punchbowl, the volcanic crater that rose on the edge of Honolulu. "So are the other churches. The people are in bewilderment and fear, though others have a sober realization of the reason for the flames."

Still, the response hadn't turned out as badly as Eden had feared. "Who else is here from the family?" Eden didn't like to think of the Derringtons being exceeded in charitable work by any of the other missionary families. The Eastons of course, through Ambrose, and Rafe's cousins were all involved, using their resources and time for the emergency, as were the Judsons, the Galloways, the Bellingtons, and the Hunnewells.

"Silas and Zachary are around, keeping order in the camps, and most everyone else is here, too, except Great-aunt Nora. She's still at Tamarind. Poor Nora. She's altogether frustrated because she can't seem to locate a section of her manuscript. And Uncle Townsend . . ." Candace let her voice trail off.

Eden was stacking sterilized white cloths into a transportable cupboard when Candace paused. The mention of Townsend brought an uncomfortable moment. "What about Uncle Townsend?" Eden looked over her shoulder. Candace was staring into space. "Is something wrong?" Eden pressed for an answer.

Candace blinked and looked at her. "What? Oh, it's just Uncle Townsend. He was thrown from his horse and is recuperating back at the plantation house. And Grandfather and Rafe are at the Legislature—"

Eden dropped the towel she had in her hands, turned, and stared in shock at her cousin.

"What did you just say? Rafe is *where?*"

Candace arched her cinnamon brows. "Do you mean to tell me, Eden, that you of all people, don't even know what Rafe Easton's up to?"

It was rather hard to keep up with Rafe, she wanted to say, but didn't.

"Parker Judson gave up his seat in the Legislature to stay with his dying sister and Bunny in San Francisco. He wrote to Liliuokalani saying he wanted Rafe Easton to fill his seat, then to run on his own."

The Legislature!

Candace picked up a large bag of boiled towels and began to fold them neatly. "Rafe was sworn in yesterday."

Eden remained stunned at the news. Rafe, sworn in to the Hawaiian legislature—and she'd known nothing about it. For a fleeting moment she imagined herself there as he took his oath and wished ardently she'd been invited to watch. An emotional letdown descended upon her. Why hadn't he told her? Why couldn't he have stopped by Kalihi yesterday and picked her up to bring her and Dr. Jerome to the ceremony?

"I'm surprised Rafe agreed to settle down," Eden commented a bit testily.

"I'm not," Candace said, shooting a glance her way. "He's wanted to settle down *with you* for a long time."

Eden considered. "Maybe. He still speaks of making another voyage."

"Keno says Parker Judson and Grandfather got their heads together in San Francisco and made their plans. They both agreed Rafe Easton would be the perfect candidate to run for his seat when his term is up. Filling in for Mr. Judson now will give Rafe a head start in next year's race."

Eden still couldn't get over her surprise. Rafe entering politics was the last ambition she would have expected of him. Perhaps she didn't know him as well as she thought?

Then again, why not politics? He certainly had a magnetism that could influence and draw people. She remembered his zealous editorials for the *Gazette*, except back then they'd been written in *favor* of the Kalakaua monarchy. She had no doubt that under the right circumstances, Rafe could stir a crowd with his words and pleasant countenance. Ainsworth and Parker Judson must have thought they'd found a political goldmine for their cause.

She recalled the conversation between her grandfather and Rafe in the library. Was that when her grandfather had laid out their plan? Probably. And no doubt Ainsworth had pledged the full support of the Hawaiian League.

"Will he run as an annexationist?"

"Without a doubt. To finish out Mr. Judson's term, he'd need to be a member of the Reform Party."

"Great-aunt Nora will need smelling salts for the first time in her life."

"We'll be hearing much about Rafe Easton in the Legislature from now on, I think. You should be proud of him, Eden."

Proud of the man she loved? Yes, she was, indeed. But she wasn't at all happy about Rafe's abilities being utilized to support the annexationist call for Hawaii to become a territory of the United States.

Then again, knowing Rafe as she did, there must be something else motivating his new convictions about Hawaii's destiny in the world. Grandfather Ainsworth knew how to sway men's minds, but Rafe wouldn't have been easily won.

A memory renewed itself. On the morning she'd told him of the Board's decision about Kip, Rafe had become frustrated with the laws of the Board of Health. He'd declared their decision to arbitrarily seize Kip as tyrannical and unjust. Could this experience have motivated him to accept Ainsworth's and Judson's political backing? Evidently the offer had come at the right moment, or they would never have gotten him involved.

"You've been so busy here," Candace said, "that it's little wonder you haven't kept up with all that's happening."

Eden hadn't heard a word of anything else developing in Honolulu except the epidemic, the fires, and her relief work. Not even Ambrose had told her Rafe was to fill Parker Judson's seat in the Legislature. Ambrose was as busy as she, with prayer meetings, Bible teaching, and comforting the fearful and bereaved. She'd seen Ambrose several times talking with Silas, and it looked to her as though Ambrose were discussing eternally serious topics.

Could so much have happened in just three days?

Three days. With a start she came alert. Today would complete the bargain she'd made with Rafe. Although the Board was overburdened with the Rat Alley epidemic, in spite of everything she may still have been called before them to account for Kip. Thus far, Lana Stanhope was the only one at Kalihi who knew Kip was missing.

She would, in addition, need to return the ring—and then break the news to Ainsworth, who was sure to be provoked. After her grandfather's well-laid political plans for his future "grandson-in-law," Ainsworth would be greatly displeased.

"I haven't seen Kip since the night of the dinner at Hawaiiana." Candace pulled at an earlobe. "Kip . . . strange situation, isn't it? Yet Rafe doesn't appear the least bit worried. Most strange." Her eyes met Eden's, a mischievous gleam flickering. "Did you have anything to do with Kip being taken?"

"Me?" Eden said. "I was as bewildered as anyone else." *Maybe more so*, she thought. She certainly hadn't expected Rafe to whisk Kip away somewhere.

Aunt Lana stepped through the tent door, carrying a medical box. At the sound of Kip's name, she looked from one to the other.

Eden, taut, waited. She was nearing the deadline for the reprieve Lana had granted her.

Lana took out a key and unlocked a red metal cabinet, then went about her business of re-supplying the medical bottles.

"So far the Board remains too occupied with what's going on in Honolulu to inquire about Kip's whereabouts. I can't say how much longer it will remain so. If either of you see Rafe, tell him to contact me. I'll try and arrange a private meeting between him and Dr. Bolton."

Candace looked from Lana to Eden. "So, then, what I've heard from Ambrose is true. You were sent to Hawaiiana to take Kip away to Kalihi?"

Eden sighed and gave a small nod. Wearily she leaned against the cabinet. "I should have let Lana handle it. She was right. I'm much too involved with Rafe."

"I'm sure you handled it in the only way it could be handled," Lana said.

"I'll probably get into trouble saying this, but I don't blame Rafe for taking Kip," Candace said. "In his position I may have done the same thing. We all know Kip doesn't carry leprosy."

"I won't comment on the moral right or wrong of it," Lana said, stacking bottles with brisk efficiency. "And actually, we've no proof that he did take Kip and conceal him."

Candace walked over to the tent door and looked out. "Rafe was here at the camp less than an hour ago. He was looking for Ling Li."

Eden turned, uncertainty nudging her. Had Rafe heard what happened at Ling's family bungalow on Kea Lani? Even if he had, what made Rafe think he could find Ling here, in this particular camp?

"Ling was released yesterday," Lana said.

"Did you speak with Rafe?" Eden asked Candace, trying to keep concern from dictating her tone of voice.

"Only for a moment or two. He saw me, asked if I'd seen Ling, and when I said I hadn't, he rode on without comment."

Eden's thoughts settled into a bed of worry. Why had Rafe shown up here? What did he wish to see Ling about, if not the fire?

Candace appeared to have lost interest in either Kip or Ling and walked over to Lana, watching her work. "It must be either wonderful or maddening to work closely with the man you love."

Lana was startled at the bluntness so common with Candace, then she relaxed and laughed. "If you're asking whether the long-delayed romance between me and Clifford is reheating after so many years, the answer is yes."

"I thought so. I'm so pleased for you both."

Lana stopped what she was doing and searched Candace's face. "How did you guess? I thought I was being discreet, and I know Clifford is."

"Women know these things," was all Candace would say. "Well, I'm glad love is working out for one of us."

Lana and Eden both looked at Candace with sympathetic sobriety.

"It's so wrong," Candace said, sitting down on the edge of a canvas cot, chin in both palms. "Keno is such a good man, strong, committed, loyal—and Oliver is so, well, so ordinarily wealthy, stuffy, and common. Do you know that old Mr. Hunnewell had to poke him with his cane and threaten to whack him on the head if he wouldn't get up off his hammock to come here and dirty his hands? When Oliver did arrive, he was wearing a white watered-silk vest and an expensive derby hat. Imagine. White, in this smoky atmosphere. So insulting to those who've lost all they had, which was mostly nothing to begin with!"

"Many young women would stand on their heads to marry a wealthy man like Hunnewell, even if he is stuffy, common, and meticulous with his fashions," Lana said with a small smile.

"I don't mind being different," Candace admitted. "Keno's been here since the beginning, sleeves rolled up, making a sacrifice to do his part, courteous, strong . . . and *handsome*." She looked off in the distance meditatively.

Eden exchanged amused glances with Lana. "Anything else?" she teased. "You mustn't allow yourself to be modest with your praise."

"Rafe, too, has been working long hours in the crisis," Candace went on. "Whereas Oliver . . ."

Rafe? Working in the camps? Eden wondered. Why hadn't she noticed him? She'd caught sight of Zachary and Silas several times, and too much of Herald Hartley. He was often at her elbow, often when it was unnecessary. She had a vague suspicion her father hoped she might find Herald a comely gentleman. It was true they shared much in common, but when it came to men, she was much like Candace. There was only one man that thrilled her.

Later, when Candace and Lana left the large tent, Eden too, went outside for a few moments of respite. She glanced around for Dr. Jerome and decided he must be busy elsewhere, for only Herald Hartley was in view, his shirt sleeves rolled up, his hat crammed low on his head. He walked toward her, his face tired and his brow damp.

"Miss Derrington, have you seen your father about?"

"I was coming to ask you the very same question."

"I've not seen him since this morning. Ah, well, then. He must've gone off with the plantation owner, Rafe Easton. He rode up asking about the good doctor about an hour ago."

So Rafe was here as Candace had said. Perhaps he was asking Dr. Jerome about Ling. Her curiosity grew. She turned to go, intent to locate them, when Herald cleared his throat.

"Ah, er, Miss Derrington—I was wanting to ask you if you, er— if you had received the letter from Mrs. Derrington?"

For a moment Eden became confused. She'd rarely heard Rebecca called Mrs. Derrington before. "Oh, my mother—why, yes." She smiled. "Dr. Jerome passed it to me when we were at the Easton plantation. I've been meaning to tell you how appreciative I am of the effort you made to carry out my father's wishes. I do apologize for not mentioning my gratitude."

"Oh, no apology necessary. I wanted to be sure the good doctor passed it on to you, is all. As you say, we've all been so immersed in this dreadful situation that almost anything could go unnoticed."

He used his hat to swish the dust off a nearby cane chair he drew up for her to sit upon. To refuse the gesture would be unkind, though she was anxious to find her father and Rafe and to discover what the interest in Ling was all about.

She tucked her skirts in and sat down. Perhaps this was as good an opportunity as any to ask the myriad questions she had about Hartley's involvement with Rebecca's kokua. The letter from her mother was nothing at all like she'd expected it to be. Perhaps Rebecca had thought it unwise or even useless in the present circumstances to write emotionally as one would naturally expect a mother to write to her daughter after many years apart. Perhaps the emotion was so ponderous there was no way she could ever express her feelings. Perhaps she was no longer able to speak clearly . . .

Eden found her fingers knotting into her skirt.

Yes, what could her mother say? How could she find words to tell her of her broken heart, lost dreams, shattered happiness, the suffering both physical and mental. How could she describe what it was like to be a young woman torn from her husband and daughter and brought to a hellish leper camp without much law and order, and without the hope of waking up on the next sunny morning to find that it all was just a passing nightmare?

How would she fit it all in one letter? How she'd prayed for her these past years, how she took satisfaction in knowing Eden had grown up well, had gone to Chadwick Nursing school, and was now working at Kalihi showing help to other lepers . . . ?

Eden had imagined the letter she'd *expected* to receive a thousand times. But the letter she *did* receive simply read, "Not a day has gone by that I haven't remembered you, prayed for you, and taken pleasure in knowing you were safely cared for by the Derrington family. I knew Lana would intervene for you. I knew she would be the mother I couldn't be."

Actually, those circumstances with Lana hadn't worked out quite the way her mother had expected, but Eden had no intention of writing to tell her. Rebecca's notion that somehow her younger sister, Lana, would step up to become the new mother to her little girl was probably unrealistic considering the emotional needs and troubles Lana herself had faced. But the idea that she would do so had been a comfort to Rebecca in her dreadful situation.

One thing Eden would never do was add more disappointment to her mother's expectations by explaining what had gone wrong in her life without her. Some issues of suffering and loss were better left unspoken. What good would it be for Rebecca to learn of disappointments Eden had felt while growing up? Had she not enough suffering of her own? Eden had made the decision that when at last she was allowed to speak to her mother, she would say nothing to increase the load of unhappiness upon her shoulders after years of trial on Molokai.

I shall go there to bless and minister, not to receive. I shall go there to make her proud of me so when her hour comes, she'll know her daughter, at least, turned out well enough and has a future in Hawaii.

Surely, at this stage, that would be about all her mother would want to know.

Realizing Herald Harley stood watching her with a quizzical tilt of his auburn head, she managed a smile.

"I intend to answer her by letter just as soon as life here gets back to normal. Tell me, how was it you were able to go to Molokai and locate my mother's kokua?"

"Ah, a long tale, Miss Derrington. Suffice it for the present to say simply how I, personally, owe Dr. Jerome my very life. He found me in India, abandoned, sick, and without any place to go." As his mind went back, Eden saw a flinch of unpleasantness. "I was hopeless at the time. My reputation was in ruins." He blotted his face. "He nursed me back to health, then took me on as his assistant. I am indeed greatly indebted to him."

"What manner of illness did you have if you don't mind my asking?"

"Oh, no secret, none at all. Tropical fever. A very sore case, indeed."

"My father has it now, does he not? I recognize the signs."

"Yes, I'm sure you would. He's recovered from the worst, but it appears it can return under certain conditions. Stress, perhaps? I am not a doctor, so I cannot say for sure. Well, to go on, there's little that means more to Dr. Jerome than a clinic on Kalawao. I thought if I could find Mrs. Derrington there and have her write a letter to Dr. Chen, then your father could have the means by which to appeal to the Hawaiian Board of Health, for Dr. Chen was highly respected for his research. Though I think your father is a far better and wiser physician. I managed to visit the leper camp, and I had the name of the kokua from your father. I found them both quite easily, explained my mission, and received their well wishes and support. Dr. Jerome had mentioned you to me on several occasions, so I thought that if Mrs. Derrington were willing to write you, I should ask her kokua to broach the subject. Well, you see, it all worked out rather well." He looked at her with anxious interest. "Then you do intend to go with us to Molokai?"

"I wouldn't think of missing the opportunity to meet my mother and to be of benefit to Dr. Jerome."

He nodded in approval. "Very wise of you, very wise indeed."

When Eden left Herald, she remained thoughtful, trying to remember what more he'd said on his first arrival, about San Francisco and Dr. Chen. She'd been so excited that morning with her father's arrival it was difficult to recall the details. Perhaps it didn't matter.

he trades were blowing, clearing much of the smoke and haze from the fires that had turned the Rat Alley shacks into smoldering ash heaps.

Eden walked toward the private tent she shared with her father for meals and a few hours' rest away from prying eyes. The tent had two sections, the front for normal activities and the rear where extra medical supplies were kept along with their personal belongings.

So much had happened. Her father's arrival, Kip's disappearance, the death of Ling's son, the plague in Rat Alley, and now the purging flames. It seemed to her that a month should have come and gone, rather than a few brief days.

Eden's concerns for Dr. Jerome grew. The longer she spent in his company, the more convinced she'd become that he had contracted some serious tropical malady. His symptoms might be the result of malaria, dengue, yaws, scrub typhus, or yellow fever, perhaps from his last visit to the Brahmaputra river region of India or even South America.

Eden had studied the prevention of such diseases, but cures

remained elusive. Emetics were used, the most effective being ground cinchona bark, called Peruvian bark, first used in South America by indigenous tribes. Wine was sometimes used, and snakeroot, mercury, or arsenic compounds. She remembered a question from a quiz Lana had given: "When had quinine sulfate first been extracted from cinchona bark?" The right answer was 1820. Quinine worked best for malaria in bringing down fever, as was commonly known by now. Mustard plasters and hot baths were used to help the circulation, and mercurials to clear the intestines.

Eden had noted among her father's personal medications, from which he treated himself, both quinine sulfate and artemisinin.

In her studies under Lana and Dr. Bolton, she'd found it interesting that a dozen years earlier, a French army surgeon, Charles Laveran, had discovered parasites in the blood of patients suffering from malaria. But what could it mean? How did parasites get into the blood? *Someday*, she thought, *we will discover the answer.*

That morning she'd seen something new among her father's personal medications: "glyceryl trinitrate," or "trinitrin", which were terms used to avoid alarming patients who, taking nitroglycerine for angina pain, might otherwise correctly associate it with dynamite. She had noticed signs of a heart condition; after breakfast, when out of breath and stressed, he'd placed a small tablet under his tongue.

How would this affect his plans for Molokai? Knowing her father's determination, she believed nothing would hold him back. Her love and respect for him only increased, and she would pretend not to notice what a medical student with her training would surely understand.

Eden walked past some tents put up by Kalihi staff and the Honolulu police. These were used for the injured, the old and infirm, young children, babies, and expectant mothers. Everyone else was kept away, confined to guarded public camps, or they went away from downtown Honolulu on their own, toward the more desolate northeastern section of Iwilei, past the Oahu prison and toward the Koolau mountain ranges.

Here in the camp headquarters for Kalihi, small tents housed food, medical supplies, and other necessary provisions for the displaced. Farther up on Koko Head, Eden could see a large number of people camped.

She wondered again why Rafe had come here looking for Ling, who'd been released from quarantine yesterday. By now he would have returned to Kea Lani to console his wife. He would also have discovered the tragedy that his family hut had been burned to the ground and heard Hui voice her fear that the fire hadn't been an accident.

Yet how could it not have been an accident? Despite her uncle's moral failures, he wouldn't have tried to take someone's life, would he? Even so, the memory of that moment in the hut, with all of the potential for utter destruction, shivered its way through her mind. If it hadn't been for Silas . . .

As she approached Dr. Jerome's tent, she was startled by a young boy bursting from it. In his haste he nearly ran into her. His cheeks were flushed, his brown eyes wide and excited.

"What's wrong?" she demanded.

"Doctor grab his chest like this." He reenacted the scene. "I helped him go inside the tent. He sits on a chair now. I find the wahine nurse—"

"I'm the nurse."

Eden rushed into the tent, straight past Dr. Jerome and into the rear, and cast a quick glance around for Jerome's medical bag. With his bottle of nitroglycerine in hand, she went back into the front section to where Dr. Jerome was seated in a chair, his face haggard. Hurrying to his side, she shook out a tablet and placed it under his tongue. She knelt by the arm of the chair to take his pulse and waited.

After a minute he said, "I'm all right now."

She watched tensely until she was certain the medication was working. "This will teach me not to go anywhere without my medication. The angina—a small problem." He reached to pat her shoulder, managing a weak but confident smile.

Small? Indeed.

He'd had little sleep, and his gaunt appearance was emphasized by loose-fitting clothes.

"Father, you're working much too hard. If you don't take care of your health, there won't be an opportunity to open that clinic at Kalawao."

He sighed and gave a nod. "Yes, I'm aware of that. I've decided hereafter that I'll take a reprieve from all this and leave it to Dr. Bolton and his staff. He's already told me he believes we've done what we can for the most part. I think I'd better concentrate now on the cause for which I've come to Honolulu."

She was pleased he'd grappled with the issue and decided his course of action. Perhaps the angina episode had lifted a veil. "You relax," she admonished. "I'll go to the cook tent and find us some tea." She put the bottle in his pocket and left through the front flaps.

Some fifteen minutes later Eden was carrying a canteen of hot tea and Hawaiian sugar. As she walked toward Jerome's tent, she recognized Rafe's golden horse—the handsome, pampered stallion he rode everywhere—tied nearby under the palms. She quickened her steps, intending to enter through the tent flaps, when Jerome's words struck like a thunderclap.

"I gave you my response on how I feel about Kip when you met with me in Tahiti."

"And in Tahiti, sir, you encouraged me to proceed with my plan. Adoption was a viable recourse."

"I'm sure I must have considered your intention of keeping him merely casual rhetoric."

"I do intend to adopt him."

"Rafe, you know the laws. He's better under my jurisdiction. As for my daughter, Eden, she's committed to the same ideals as Rebecca. She's not ready for marriage. She's coming with Herald and me to Kalawao."

"You never liked my father, did you? Perhaps that's why you're against me, his son."

"That's outrageous!"

"My father tried to talk you out of bringing Rebecca to Molokai. She had no interest in medicine, and you know it. She was a teacher. She had expected you to settle at Kea Lani, pastor the mission church, and raise a family. But you couldn't see it. Like the obedient, godly wife she was, she set aside her calling at the school and went with you to Molokai. And when she contracted the disease, you became a guilt-ridden man. You've spent all these years traveling the world, searching for the miracle cure that doesn't exist. To this day the memory of my father disturbs you. That's why you don't want Eden to marry an Easton, and it's why you're now against my plans to adopt Kip and make *him* an Easton."

There followed a heavy silence. Then came Jerome's choked voice. "Yes, Rafe, it's true about Rebecca. I've never forgiven myself for bringing her to Molokai. It haunts me day and night. And it's true about Matt, as well. He'd had feelings for Rebecca, but it never went far. Then he fell in love with your mother, Celestine. But he retained a friendly, Christian interest in Rebecca, and he warned me to not bring her on such a horrendous pilgrimage. He said that she wasn't prepared for that manner of onslaught, and that it was no life for a gentle girl like Rebecca."

"And you resented him for it?"

"Yes I did, even to this day. I knew he was right, you see. I didn't care to admit it. I was jealous that he seemed to understand her better than I, her own husband. Then, when his warnings were realized, I couldn't face it. As you put it, I traveled the world in search of my 'miracle cure.' But this is where you're wrong, Rafe. The cure *does* exist. It will be found in Dr. Chen's work, and we will soon be able to help those now held captive on Molokai!"

Another long silence ensued. Eden stood transfixed just outside the tent.

"Sir, I am honored and humbled that you would confide in me as you have. I allowed myself to speak in anger, and for that I request your forgiveness. However, I am not here to question your commitment to Rebecca. It is Eden I'm concerned about. Eden and Kip."

"I've already discussed the clinic with her," Jerome replied, an edge back in his voice. "Her heart is the same as mine. She received her letter from Rebecca, and her 'commitment' is the same as mine. We're going to Molokai."

"And Kip?"

"I want Kip under my own authority."

"It's disappointing enough after what happened to your wife that you're willing to risk your daughter to leprosy, but will you also bring Kip back to the leper camp? The mother of the baby did not want Kip in the camp. If she had, she would have kept him there."

Jerome's chair creaked and his voice increased in timbre. "Kip is my responsibility, and I will do what's best for him."

"Sir, I respect you, and your work. The fact that you are Eden's father makes it doubly so. You have no reason to fear me. I'm not trying to steal Eden or Kip away from you. Or trying to keep you from your lifelong goal on Molokai. But I will do everything in my power to protect Kip. And if it means working to change the law of adoption in the Legislature, I will. I intend to keep him."

"If that's the way you would have it be, then I, too, should let it be known that, as a son of Ainsworth Derrington, my reputation in Honolulu is respected. I have leverage."

"I'm well aware of that, sir."

"Then be aware that if I choose to do so, I can use that influence. I'm a doctor specializing in leprosy research. I could make an issue out of holding you accountable for removing Kip against the wishes of the Board. It's not what I want to do. However, you could find yourself in grave trouble, should I make your actions a public controversy."

"Yes, you could do all of that, sir. Maybe more. You could turn Eden against me as well. It doesn't mean that I'll knuckle under. It is their welfare I am most concerned for."

"I'd rather not do it, Rafe. Apart from this difference of opinion now over Eden and Kip, you have all the qualities of a fine young man. Matt would indeed be proud of you. And if it weren't for the clinic on Molokai—and the necessity of having my daughter with me, I could accept a marriage between you and Eden. Any conflict Matt and I may have had in the past is over now. Matt, too, was a good man. You're wrong if you think I still hold some unchristian malice toward him because of Rebecca."

"I'd like to believe that. But there are unanswered questions about my father. There's the matter of how he died on Hanalei. To this day I've not been able to satisfy myself with the accidental-death ruling. There's more to it than I've been told."

"My word, Rafe! You're not suggesting that I—"

"No, sir. I'm suggesting there may be some small piece of information you haven't mentioned about that day."

"I wasn't at Hanalei that day."

"Something you've shut out of your mind and refuse to consider. You may have seen something, heard something later, that your Christian mind wants to reject."

"This is beyond me. I've no wish to even discuss such vileness."

"A Christian knows better than most what evil lurks in the brightest gardens. We know that fallen sons of Adam are capable of far more than murder. Why try to behave as if sin doesn't thrive all around us? Sin reigns supreme in the unregenerate heart. And even in the regenerate hearts of Christians, the sin nature has not yet been eradicated. It still demands its pound of flesh."

"Matt's death was an accident. I've no cause to think otherwise."

"And the fire at Ling's hut?"

"The fire—why, an accident! What else could it be?"

Silence held command for a long moment before Rafe spoke.

"I can see I'm wasting your time and mine. But about Kip: this is the third day of his absence. Tell your daughter she needn't concern herself. I will handle matters directly with the Board."

"Eden? What has she to do with Kip?"

"From this moment onward, sir, nothing. Tell her I went to the Board of Health this morning and met with Dr. Bolton. Kip is no longer under my care at Hawaiiana. In fact, there is no child to turn over to Kalihi. And one thing more. You may not know it yet, but Ainsworth Derrington is making a public stand on my side of this controversy. So are Parker Judson and the rest of the big planters. Whether it works or not, time will tell. They're all urging the Board and the Legislature to support a change in the law that will permit me to adopt Kip."

Silence again prevailed. Then . . .

"I'm not surprised Ainsworth is using his influence with the Board in the matter. He has high plans for your political future. I'm also well aware he wishes my daughter to marry an Easton. Whichever way this struggle unfolds, Rafe, I intend to go on with my life's work. It's all-important to me. That clinic *must* be opened at Kalawao. Regardless of the Derrington thrust behind you, I don't believe there's anything you or Ainsworth can do to keep Eden from working at my side."

"In that, sir, you are undoubtedly correct."

Shaken to the core of her soul, Eden stood in frozen silence. How could all this be happening?

What did it mean? Puzzlement clutched her heart. How was it that her father appeared to know so much about Kip's past? Jerome spoke with a knowledge that went back to an earlier time, to Tahiti. He'd spoken to Rafe as though they believed some right of control belonged to Dr. Jerome. Why then was he just now making an issue about Kip's adoption?

Just how *did* Rafe find and rescue baby Kip at Molokai? Was there more to Kip's story than she'd realized? Why was it being kept from her?

The mother of the baby hadn't wanted Kip left at Kalawao, Rafe had suggested, words which repeated themselves in her mind. Mention of Kip's mother had seemed to stagger Dr. Jerome. Why? What mother *would* want her newborn left to the pollution of Kalawao?

Why then did the mention of this particular mother seem to send a painful blow to her father? Had her father not seen babies and small children abandoned on Molokai or sent back to Kalihi for care? Certainly he had. Then why had Rafe expected his words to make a strong impact on Dr. Jerome?

Eden stood still, drained of emotion, her heart thudding in her ears. She wrestled with the impossible.

It couldn't be. No, it just couldn't be.

Keno, she thought. *I've got to talk to him alone.* Who could arrange it? Candace. Yes, if anyone could bring Keno to a meeting, Candace could.

Keno could shed more light. He'd been with Rafe on Molokai when Rafe found the baby boy. He'd also been with Rafe in Tahiti. Maybe he'd been in the actual meeting between her father and Rafe.

A stronger conviction bound her. Was there another reason to go to Molokai with her father—to discover the secret she believed was being kept from her? Dare she even think it?

Was *Rebecca* Kip's mother? *Then who was his father?*

No, it couldn't be Jerome—then there'd be no disagreement between him and Rafe over who owned the baby. And it couldn't be Rafe. Though Rebecca was not too old to still be a mother, she was old enough to be *his* mother. And beyond all that, it was unthinkable that Rafe would go to a leper compound to indulge in immorality!

Weary, worn, and stunned by the notion that Kip might be her own half-brother, she needed to see Ambrose. And she needed time with her Lord in prayer.

Chapter Seventeen
A Call to Tamarind House

*I*t had been a month since the fires in Rat-Alley had died out, and the winds had swept Honolulu clean, bringing fresh hope as rubble was slowly cleared to make room for rebuilding. There'd been no new cases of plague reported in weeks, and the emergency mode at Kalihi had simmered down to normal duties and daily routine.

Eden's daily routine, however, was filled with more than "normal duties" as she also assisted Dr. Jerome in his ongoing struggle to gain permission from the Board of Health and Queen Liliuokalani to open his clinic on Kalawao. What had initially seemed a straightforward endeavor was now thwarted by various obstacles.

Ambrose listened sympathetically when Jerome came to him with his recent burdens. "Perhaps the timing is not quite ready for our God to act. Let's continue to wait on His wisdom," he exhorted Jerome after the Sunday service at the mission church. "We surely know our compassionate God has heard our pleas. Then again, let's not underestimate enemy spiritual forces who stand against any work that will glorify Christ. We'll continue to pray, rely on His

Word as our light, and patiently wait."

Patience was a fruit far removed from Eden's anxious spirit in those long days and weeks. Her heart was torn between a strange longing for Rafe, whom she hadn't seen in over a month—since he was said to be on the Big Island at Hanalei—and concerns about Kip, her father, his clinic, her mother at Kalawao, Candace's broken heart, and on and on it went.

How can I be so torn? she cried to herself one day. *There's a part of me that longs to run into Rafe's arms and walk away from everything else, and another part of me that struggles to reach Molokai!* On that day Eden went to see Noelani for an hour of rest. She sat in Noelani's bright kitchen, enjoying coconut cakes and coffee.

The door stood open, airing the kitchen from fried coconut oil. A flight of wooden steps wound down a little hill, where a passion fruit vine meandered toward the beach. Through the open doorway Eden watched the waves. They were rough this afternoon, foaming over the white sand.

"I already told you what I think you should do, honey," Noelani said, pouring Eden a cup of coffee. "Marry that handsome Rafe Easton. Every girl in the Islands is watching him, and the richer he gets, the more they will want him! Go live on Hanalei and have lots of green-eyed sons and daughters. Then you'll be happy."

Eden laughed for the first time in weeks. "Maybe you're right. But Jerome is counting on me."

"So is that Herald Hartley, if you want my opinion. You watch out for that one. He looks innocent enough with that boyish grin and red looking hair, but he's been around plenty, so I think. He's been all over the world, including India. That tells me he's no innocent little fellow dedicated to God."

"Noelani, sometimes you say the most outrageous things. Why wouldn't Herald be dedicated to God? Look how he adores my father and his work. He's rolled up his sleeves and has been working hard at his side ever since he arrived."

"Oh, yes, I know. I'm not saying he doesn't respect Dr. Jerome.

He seems dedicated more to Jerome than anyone else. You should ask your father why that is. How did he meet Hartley in India?"

"Herald told me he was at wits' end when my father found him and gave him a new start. He's just being grateful."

"Humph. He sounds suspicious to me. Here, have another coconut cake. Rafe used to love them. He hasn't been around in a long while, and you're losing weight each time I see you. You and Candace both. Nothing but skin and bones, worrying me all the time."

"Noelani, where is he keeping Kip?"

"Now don't go asking me that. I don't know. I don't want to know."

"What about Kip's origins on Molokai? Have Rafe or Ambrose ever talked to you about them?"

Noelani's face turned immobile. She shook her head.

"Did you know Rafe met my father on Tahiti and talked to him about Kip?"

"Why should Rafe tell me that?"

"I don't suppose you would encourage Ambrose to tell me anything he remembers?"

"You're right. I won't. Enough, now. Here, eat up. That's a good child."

Child. She felt like anything but a child. Even her bones ached.

As the weeks had passed, conflicts of various kinds appeared to escalate in all realms. There was tension between Townsend and Grandfather Ainsworth over the lifestyle he was living, not to mention the breach that had formed between Townsend and Zachary since that conflict over the burning of huts. Zachary was now spending most of his time away from Kea Lani at Great-aunt Nora's Tamarind House on Koko Head. He was also writing boldly in favor of the royal monarchy, much to the aggravation of Grandfather Ainsworth. Eden believed Zachary was deliberately supporting Liliuokalani to get back at his grandfather and Townsend.

"If you expect a loan to save the *Gazette*, you won't continue supporting the corruption of a monarchy gone wrong," Ainsworth had recently told Nora and Zachary.

Nora had scoffed. "Corruption in politics, my dear? Selfishness and greed are the mainstays of the annexationists in the Legislature."

"Need I remind you, Nora, that the Legislature is not supporting the opium trade or gambling in order to dig Hawaii out of its financial hole," Ainsworth bit back.

"Now that we've brought up gambling," Zachary said, "why should my inheritance be cut in half to favor Silas? It wouldn't surprise me to find he's working with the gambling cartel in Louisiana to get the monarchy to give them a larger slice of pie in the Islands."

Eden considered what motivated each of the two brothers. Rafe had changed his political agenda due to genuine beliefs in Hawaii's future with the United States. Zachary had changed, not on merits of the issue, but because of his offended self-realization.

Eden came back to the present as Ambrose spoke. "The Derringtons' conflicts come mostly from spiritual struggles in their hearts. If the heart is right, other things in our lives usually fall into place. But where jealousy and envy are, there is striving. The harvest is needless personal struggle, resentments, and discontent."

Noelani said, "Townsend mentioned once that God intends for His children to be rich in this world's goods." Her eyes smiled at her husband.

Ambrose laughed, a hearty almost joyful laugh that Eden loved.

"Oh, he did, did he? Well, now, the great apostle Paul might disagree with Townsend—and any other so-called minister who's uttering such mush. 'And having food and raiment let us be therewith content,' Paul wrote. Can you imagine Paul entering cities in the book of Acts and standing up to preach that God wanted them all to be wealthy, successful, and healthy? Paul, who stood in basic clothes, owned neither gold nor Mediterranean resorts, and had a body scarred with lash marks? He must have been stiff and aching after the stoning he took. And Paul said clearly, 'Be ye followers of me, even as I also am of Christ.'

"Paul is an example for the church. He preached that all men are sinners. Without sin there is no meaning to the gospel, and no reason for the sacrifice of Christ at Calvary. No wonder Townsend doesn't want to hear it. 'For I determined not to know any thing among you, save Jesus Christ, and him crucified,' Paul said. He told them the remedy for sin, not a course on feeling good with an abundance of this world's goods."

⸻

During the long weeks that followed, Candace occasionally poured out her heart to Eden. "At least the epidemic had thwarted the luau Grandfather intended to give as a public show of Oliver courting me. For that I'm grateful."

Oliver P. Hunnewell called at Kea Lani twice a week, bringing Candace everything from flowers to books, which she loved, boxes of chocolates, and other pleasant things, all of which Candace had refused until Grandfather Ainsworth scolded her sharply.

"I was taught at New England School for Ladies not to accept gifts from men," Candace had told him loftily.

"*This* man is Oliver P. Hunnewell, son of the wealthiest planter in California *and* Oahu," Grandfather corrected her. "You are permitted to accept *his* boxes of chocolates and books."

Zachary, too, found his love life detoured in unwelcome directions. Oliver's younger sister, Claudia Hunnewell, was to become engaged to Zachary after her return from a one-year grand tour of Europe. The day was growing ever nearer. Zachary, however, wanted the cool, fair-headed, and restive Bunny Judson, who was now in San Francisco with her uncle, Parker Judson, while her mother approached her last days on earth.

"*Maybe* I should just pack up and go to the Bay City," Zachary told both Eden and Candace one morning at breakfast on the Kea Lani lanai. He frowned. "*Maybe* I should try to work for the *Bay Times* there. Show Silas he's not the only one who can write for a newspaper in San Francisco. *Maybe* Townsend would regret my leaving Honolulu ... and Grandfather, too. The way they badger me and praise Silas, you'd think they *wanted* me to leave the Islands. Who knows, *maybe* Bunny would come to see *me* as the man she could turn to in her time of sorrow."

"Maybe," Candace said wearily. Eden smothered a laugh.

———✿———

The days crawled by, and when Eden's thoughts turned to Rafe, she struggled with the ongoing conflict that lay between them, growing daily. The engagement ring was still on her finger. She'd kept it on, so she told herself, because she'd had no opportunity to give it back to him. There was much on Eden's mind, but now that she was working with her father at Kalihi, there was little time to search for answers to the questions hounding her. Had Rafe ever found Ling? What had happened to Ling? He was no longer seen on the road with his hackney, waiting to drive her and other hospital staff around Honolulu. Did he remain at Kea Lani with his family, pining for number seven son? Her heart was heavy for him, and she prayed for him, hoping to again have the opportunity to bring him to the Savior, where he would find the source of eternal life.

As soon as I return to Kea Lani, I must make an effort to locate him.

Eden was proud to see Dr. Jerome welcomed back to his long-vacated position in the research department of Kalihi Hospital with glad handshakes from Dr. Bolton and all those who had known him in the past. His return, she knew, was needed to provide a base from which to influence the Board of Health to grant permission for the clinic on Kalawao. He'd brought Herald with him to the hospital as his personal assistant, though there were questions about Herald Hartley's medical credentials from Dr. Bolton's staff, which Eden had discovered quite by accident. Mentioning this oddity to her father, he merely patted her shoulder as he was accustomed to doing when he thought she was unduly upset about something unimportant. He told her Herald had gotten his certification in India, and somehow the records had been destroyed in flood waters during the monsoon season.

When it came to Herald's "vocalizations," promoting Doctors Jerome and Chen's research to the Board members, her father couldn't have found a more enthusiastic supporter. Herald showed no timidity urging Dr. Bolton and other physicians to recommend to the queen, her cabinet, and the Legislature that the Derrington-Chen clinic should receive immediate sponsorship.

The cool manner of the Board showed that they found Herald's assertive conduct offensive. As Lana told Eden, "Herald would do Dr. Jerome a favor by keeping silent. These Board members are highly educated physicians from well-known medical schools. They look down upon Herald's credentials. Dr. Bolton has only permitted his presence here out of respect for Dr. Jerome."

While her father continued to push Dr. Chen's research journal upon the Board, the Board, except for Dr. Bolton, a close ally of Jerome, resisted what they called "herbal cures and kahuna-like healings." This angered Dr. Jerome.

"Chen's journal isn't filled with old wives' tales or mystical herbs. Chen was a physician. He was in many ways equal to any of us seated here today." He thumped his hand on the table where the long-faced Board members sat unmoved, some with eyes cast down, others looking with a kind of pity at her father. Eden was startled by their manner.

There'd been others who had tried to cure leprosy, as well. She'd studied about Kainokalani, the Hawaiian priest, the Americans with their patent medicines, the Indian named Mohabeer, Sang Ki and Akana from China, Goto from Japan, and Eduard Arning, the German bacteriologist who'd received permission from King Kalakaua to intentionally infect a condemned murderer named Keanu. None had solved the mystery of leprosy, nor had anyone found a cure.

"Now, look here, Clifford," Dr. Jerome said to Dr. Bolton, whose head rested in his hands. "When can an audience be arranged for me to see Queen Liliuokalani? I shall make my final case to her!"

Bolton shook his head. "I don't know, Jerome. I can send another message to her cabinet minister, but she's been away recently, traveling through the Islands."

Jerome looked sharply at the skilled men sitting soberly around the table in Bolton's office. "After all, gentlemen, was it not the queen's own brother, King Kalakaua, who first sponsored my research travels? Does she not wish to hear what I've discovered? This research journal was thirty years in the making. It deserves to be printed and studied."

"That's part of our dilemma." One of the physicians spoke up, his voice sugared with sympathy. "It is Dr. Chen's journal, not Dr. Derrington's."

Eden's breath paused. She couldn't bring herself to look at her father. She felt indignation rise in her heart. Was the doctor hinting at something unseemly? But her father apparently saw no insult in his colleague's words.

"It is indeed Dr. Chen's journal. And I've worked hand in hand with him on many of these same techniques for the last five years. Because this journal is mostly Chen's research, it gives reason for the Board to fund its printing. Was Chen not correct about chaulmoogra oil before one of our own colleagues incorporated its usage?"

Eden had studied the findings from the chaulmoogra, an East Indian tree, which gave a brownish-yellow oil, or "soft fat," that was taken from the seeds of the tree and used in the treatment of leprosy and skin diseases. She'd even heard of certain cases of leprosy where the patient had actually experienced a reversal of symptoms.

"That is true, Jerome. No complaint is intended toward you or the deceased. Nevertheless, we cannot rush this matter through, just to have you open a clinic next month. This matter will take time, effort, and *money*."

"We'll do what is possible," one of the leading physicians said calmly. "We'll hold another meeting next Monday. Liliuokalani will have returned by then. Isn't that so, Dr. Bolton?"

"I believe so. I'll contact members of her cabinet first thing tomorrow morning."

The meeting ended in a dull thud as the prized journal slipped from her father's hand and dropped to the floor. Eden scooped it up and handed it to him. His hand shook as he took hold of it and placed it inside his satchel.

Lana spoke to her privately, later in the afternoon as the working day drew toward its close, and buggies and carriages were gathering out front to bring the leading staff to their homes in Honolulu. "Matters don't look promising, Eden."

Eden agreed, troubled and disappointed. "At least Dr. Bolton agrees with him on the need for the research clinic."

It was out of friendship with Jerome that Dr. Bolton was trying to make a case to the members of the Board to sign the recommendation and send it on to the Legislature and ultimately to Queen Liliuokalani.

"Clifford's a missionary doctor at heart," Lana said. "He always was. I think he'd be a more contented man serving under an American mission board than the Hawaiian government. He has great compassion for lepers." Her eyes sparkled with life as she spoke of the man she had once almost married. Then the lines on the bridge of her nose tightened. "Oh, Eden, sometimes I worry so about all of this. I think Clifford takes too many risks."

"You mean by supporting Dr. Jerome?"

"No, not that. I, too, support Jerome's efforts. But this morning I found Clifford in one of the leper wards having coffee with one of the newer patients. He has the tendency of 'touching and comforting,' which reminds me of the errors made by Priest Damien. It scares me."

When Eden returned to Kea Lani it wasn't lepers she had on her mind, but Ling Li. She hadn't seen him around the hospital or Kea Lani recently. She tried to remember when she had see him last. Perhaps it had been around the time of the Rat Alley alert.

It troubled her that Ling was nowhere to be found on Kea Lani.

She'd even gone to the new bungalow where Ling's family lived, and she had spoken to his wife, Hui. Strangely, Hui too, had not seen him.

"Ling not come home," Hui had told her tensely. "Have not seen him since after fire. He go to find Mister Easton. I worry. You help find where Ling is?"

Where could Ling be? Was this related to the fire?

"I tell you Ling in trouble. Fire bad luck. Plenny bad fortune. Should have stay in Shanghai running rickshaw. Better than fires everywhere. Dead son. Bad fortune. Stars say much trouble."

Eden had stood with Hui outside the grass hut located near the cane fields. She put a consoling hand on her arm. "Remember what we talked about in the Bible class, Hui? Don't trust the stars for guidance and blessing. Trust the Maker of the stars. You'll come again this Sunday?"

"Yes, I come. Much worried."

That next Sunday, after Eden attended worship service at the mission church, she took the horse and buggy and her Bible over to the Hawaiiana pineapple plantation. The promise she'd made to teach the wives of the Christian Chinese cane workers was well into its third Sunday, and thus far the meetings were progressing. Her lessons were of necessity quite simple because the ladies and children knew only what was called "pidgin English."

Eden discovered that if she taught simple Bible stories, the children could understand; the women, too, responded with full attention. She brought drawings with her in a large portfolio, some made by the artistry of Great-aunt Nora when she was younger and before she'd turned from painting to writing history. Eden used these drawings to clarify stories from the four Gospels, such as when Jesus raised the young daughter of Jairus, the son of the widow of Nain, and Lazarus. These profound acts of Christ raising the dead held them spellbound. Over several months she would ultimately teach up to the crucifixion of Jesus on the cross and His bodily resurrection from the rock-sealed tomb. Then, she would emphasize God's forgiveness of sin through Jesus' sacrificial death. "The blood of Jesus Christ his Son cleanseth us from all sin," she would have them memorize.

It was a warm and breezy morning with a topaz sky, green foliage, and a green-blue sea. Eden secretly hoped she might "accidentally" run into Rafe Easton, but he was nowhere around Hawaiiana. Keno, too, she hoped to meet. The questions she wanted to ask him about Kip were ever in her heart. But she didn't see Keno near the bungalow for the men's class. There was a young Hawaiian teaching from a Bible, a relative of Noelani. *Keno is undoubtedly with Rafe on the Big Island*, thought Eden.

After the class, Eden was putting her materials back into the buggy when a horseman appeared from the trees alongside the road. Eden paused and shielded her eyes from the glare. Uncle Townsend. Had he come to see Celestine at the plantation house?

Townsend rode up, a muscled form in white clothes and hat, a whip fastened to the side of his saddle. Eden hated the whip. What he did with it, she didn't know. She suspected it was decoration that harmonized with his personality.

"Good afternoon, Uncle."

"Eden, do you know if Rafe is anywhere about?"

"I haven't seen him since Rat Alley. I believe he's on Hanalei."

He gave a nod, his cool blue eyes busily taking in the huts and pineapples growing in the warm sunshine, as far back toward the hills as the eye could see.

"Most likely. Is Celestine with him?"

The question surprised her. Where was Rafe's mother? It dawned on her that she hadn't seen Celestine in weeks either. She'd taken it for granted that Celestine might be deliberately staying out of sight because of Townsend. Was she well? Could the bruises on her face have anything to do with her keeping out of view?

"Why, I thought she was up at the plantation house," Eden said, hiding her unease. "She hasn't been well. She wasn't at church this morning." *Or for a number of weeks, come to think of it,* but she kept that quiet. "Noelani comes up nearly every day."

"I just came from there. Noelani claims she hasn't seen her."

We seem to have a lot of missing people recently. Do they have anything in common?

"If she's up at the plantation, she won't answer the door or return my messages," Townsend complained.

"Then she must be on the Big Island with Rafe."

"Then maybe I'll need to go there." His face hardened. "Rafe would like that. He'd like to show me around his new plantation and boast of his father's enterprise of planting Kona coffee."

Eden kept silent. Why shouldn't Rafe take pleasure in his father's accomplishments? It hadn't been all that long ago when Townsend himself had boasted of Hanalei, having contributed nothing to its establishment.

"The nurse in me must ask how your injury is coming," she said, gaining the boldness necessary to ask the question that had troubled her since the fire at Ling's hut.

His broad brow furrowed, as though at first he didn't understand her question. Then, she saw the corner of his mouth drag. His steady gaze held her to the spot. "That was a terrible accident, Eden. Thank God you and the others got out safely. I swear I didn't know you were inside. I hope you believe your uncle wouldn't go burning the roof down over your head!"

"Of course not, Uncle."

"I admit I got carried away. That's one of my problems, you know. Anger. Can't control myself sometimes. Well, you know about that. But that filthy plague was a threat, and it was Ling's son who died. I was keyed up to get rid of anything that might threaten us at Kea Lani."

"Yes, of course, Uncle. Was it your knee you injured when the horse bucked you?" His injury had been the reason why he couldn't come to help them get out of the hut. It had been Silas who'd come at the right moment.

"My back and shoulder. They're improving now. I can ride comfortably again. If you do see Celestine, tell her to respond to my messages. It's important I talk to her."

He turned his horse and rode back toward the road in the direction of Kea Lani. Eden watched him ride away. *Now there,* she thought sadly, *is a deeply troubled man.*

When Townsend was gone, Eden walked around and climbed into the buggy, still in thought, when Zachary walked toward her from out of the trees and growth. "Wait up, Eden. I've got a letter for you from Candace."

She waited, seated in the buggy, holding the leather reins in her gloved hands. "Where did you come from?" she asked.

"The trees, where I was concealed. I was coming up from the mission church when I saw my father. I thought it best not to be seen."

"You still haven't made amends with Townsend?"

"He's not in an agreeable mood, as you should have been able to tell. He rides around with that whip like he'd enjoy using it—probably on me."

"Most likely on anyone who stands in his way."

"So you noticed. What did he want by the way?"

Eden looked off toward the plantation house of Hawaiiana, white and wonderful in the sunlight, thinking again that this might have been hers if she'd married Rafe. A sadness rode the rustle of wind in the palms. Everything was so silent. And Rafe, gone.

"He was asking about Celestine. She doesn't answer his messages."

"I don't blame her," Zachary said.

"Have you seen her recently?" she asked curiously.

He shook his golden head. "Not since the dinner two months ago. But then, I never did see much of her after she came here to be under Rafe's protection. She must be at Hanalei."

"Townsend is going there," Eden said uneasily. "This could mean trouble."

"Townsend usually means trouble. But Rafe can take care of himself and Celestine. I've been thinking about the fire at Ling's shack," he said. "Strange how Silas came on the scene not a moment too soon."

"The Lord was gracious," she said.

"Yes, it was by God's providence, and it might also mean Silas knows more than he's telling. He may have been suspicious of Townsend setting it on purpose, and kept out of sight to see what happened. When it did happen, well, then . . ." He jerked a shoulder and frowned. "Strange, all of it."

Was he actually suggesting his father had deliberately tried to harm them? She kept silent, troubled by the direction of his thoughts.

He looked at her soberly. "I talked to Rafe. He's doing well in the Legislature. He has a natural gift for leadership. He's already getting things moving on several issues he's interested in. By the way, he knows about the fire, and he too thinks it's strange how Silas got you out of the hut."

"I hope you didn't mention it was Townsend that lit the fire."

"He already had guessed that."

She studied him, alert. "Why?"

Zach shrugged, began to say something, then stopped. "Here comes Ambrose, walking."

Eden turned in the seat to look over her shoulder, feeling a jab of guilt, for she'd taken Ambrose's buggy and horse.

"Something's up," Zachary said. "Let's hope it's good news. Oh—here's the letter from Candace. She's gone over to Tamarind to stay with Great-aunt Nora. Ol' Oliver is getting more serious about his courting, so Candace ran off. Don't blame her." He walked to meet Ambrose.

Eden took Candace's letter and put it aside while she turned her attention to Ambrose, whose silvery hair glinted in the sunlight.

Ambrose was notorious for forgetting his hat. A large-boned man and tall, his stride kept pace with Zachary's.

He greeted Eden and pretended to be out of sorts that she'd run off with his buggy and horse. "Don't you know this is my calling day? Why, I've got a dozen families to see before we hold service again tonight. And you ran off with my nag and buggy."

"Sorry, but I expected to be back before you missed your nag and buggy," she teased back. "Uncle Townsend delayed me, asking about Celestine. Then Zachary brought me a letter from Candace. She's at Tamarind."

"Hiding from Hunnewell," Zachary said. "Great-aunt Nora's asking you to go see her, Eden."

"Is she ill?" Eden asked worriedly.

"Something's bothering her. Maybe more than her health."

"Then I'll go. But I'll need to meet my father at Iolani Palace when Dr. Bolton arranges a meeting with members of the Legislature." She wondered whether one of those in the Legislature would be Rafe. "I'll drive you back to the church, Ambrose," she said cheerfully. "I left some things at the bungalow."

"Don't listen to her excuse, Ambrose," Zachary said with equal good cheer. "Eden just knows Noelani's got Sunday chicken and pineapple cake with coconut waiting."

"Then you'll need to get there first before she eats it all," Ambrose told him, climbing up into the buggy and taking the reins from Eden.

Zachary ran toward his horse, and Eden laughed. For a little while at least, it seemed that happier times had returned.

Ambrose drove the buggy back toward the mission church. Eden tied her hat in place and relaxed in the refreshing afternoon breezes, looking out at the expanse of sea. "Ambrose, how much do you actually know about Kip's background? Do you know who his mother was?"

Ambrose was quiet for too long. "Rafe's my nephew. He's more like a son. But he's also my spiritual son in the faith. I'd betray the trust between us if I spoke of matters I've no right to discuss without permission." He looked at her, his dark eyes earnest. "Rafe's the one to ask about Kip."

"I intend to ask him," she said firmly. "I have several questions that should be answered."

"I agree. You can tell him I said so. I've some other news to discuss," Ambrose told her as they rode along. "I've been in touch with Rebecca and her kokua. There was a young Hawaiian fellow recently sent to Kalawao with beginning leprosy. His name is Kelolo. I've known him since he was a boy. He has leprosy in one ear. Maybe you recall him?"

Eden thought hard but in the end couldn't place the name or the young man.

"He may have many years of independence left at the camp," Ambrose said. "He's a Christian lad, with a habit of reading adventure books, though I'd rather he read books like *Pilgrim's Progress*. I wrote Rebecca about him and asked her to keep an eye on him for a few weeks until he adjusted. He was naturally depressed when he left. Her kokua found him and introduced him to Rebecca. Rebecca's been kind, as she always was, and rather mothering in nature. She's suggested Kelolo become useful to the Lord during his better times there. Since he's interested in books and writing, Rebecca wants to start a little newspaper for the colony, with Kelolo running it and writing up stories. But we need a printing press. Now, if we can get a printing press, I can teach Kelolo how to set up the running of it and the typesetting. If you remember, I used to help Nora with the *Gazette* early on, till I took over the mission church."

Eden, excited, smiled. "That's a splendid idea, Ambrose! Why, think of the encouragement a news journal could be to the colony. And Kelolo could print Bible messages, too."

"So we thought. Maybe some children's stories and other helpful materials as well. The problem is the cost of the printing press and then delivering the machine to Kalawao. No easy task, as you well know. It would take some real skillful handling of ship and men to get the press delivered dry."

Eden frowned. "With the money we Derringtons and Eastons have, it shouldn't be a problem to buy a printing press."

"They are very expensive, Eden. The problem is, the Derringtons and Eastons may have money, but unless Ainsworth or Nora is willing to put it out, it won't do us much good."

"I know Nora is already having financial troubles. She needs a loan for the *Gazette*. All her wealth is in land, houses, and such like. Grandfather Ainsworth could afford a printing press, but he's not likely to be much enthused about it. He takes scant interest in the doings at Molokai."

"Well, we will begin a printing press fund," Ambrose said. "We'll spread the word around and see what may turn up. The Lord is our provision. We'll make it a matter of prayer. Prayer will involve the hearts of the Hawaiian Christians, and that is good. They can have a part in something that brings Christ to Molokai."

Eden didn't know how much inheritance she would receive from Grandfather Ainsworth—maybe little or nothing once he discovered her willfulness in not marrying Rafe. "I'll mention the printing press to Jerome, too," she said. "If Rebecca wants it for Kelolo to have a cause worth living for, I'm sure my father will take an active role in helping make it a reality." Eden, too, wanted to get the printing press to Molokai in honor of her mother. "But how to deliver it once we have one?" she asked.

Ambrose rubbed his chin thoughtfully. "I've been thinking of Rafe's ship, the *Minoa*. If anyone could deliver a printing press and see it delivered dry, my vote would be on Rafe and Keno."

Eden remained tactfully silent. Yes, she'd place her vote of confidence in Rafe as well. But would he be willing to involve himself with Kalawao? Still, could the printing press be a legitimate reason to visit Hanalei where she could also talk to Rafe about Kip and Ling?

When they arrived at the bungalow and gathered with Zachary in Noelani's cheery kitchen, smells of Hawaiian chicken and fresh Kona coffee greeted them. Eden opened Candace's letter and read it to herself. Zachary was right when he'd said Candace had run off to Tamarind to be free of Oliver.

I need time to think and pray alone. If there's any place with a lonely atmosphere and plenty of empty rooms to sit and brood, it's Amabel's house here on Koko Head.

Great-aunt Nora has been quite ill. We don't know why. She's asked me to write and tell you to come for a few days if you can get away from Kalihi. "I want to talk to Eden," she tells me. So come when you can. Zachary can bring you on the ferryboat since he's coming back.

Grandfather's becoming alarmingly persistent in wanting to announce my engagement to Oliver this year. Instead of a luau he now wants to give me a "Queen Victoria ball." He's offered me gifts galore to marry into the Hunnewell family, even a second grand tour of Europe. I don't want any of his presents. Grandfather is getting desperate. I fear he has come to the point of making an ultimatum that will chain me to Oliver for the rest of my days. Grandfather has something on his mind. I'm worried that I can't hold out forever. By now he knows I'm here at Great-aunt Nora's. I expect a sober letter from him any day now, putting forth the bleak details of his strategy. I keep wondering what it will be. I'm sure I'll be able to tell you the dire outcome when you arrive. Remember me in your prayers, Cousin, as I remember you, and "you know who."

Oh! I shall end this letter with happy news! Yes, there is some good news. Guess what? Your aunt Lana Stanhope and Dr. Clifford Bolton are announcing their intention to marry this year. Isn't it marvelous? A love affair that worked out after many years of delay. There's even time for a family of their own.

Is there time for us, I wonder?

Candace

Eden smiled. *A prayer answered,* she thought. She'd been praying that Lana and Dr. Bolton would marry ever since, as a student at Chadwick, Lana had told her the sad story of their breakup. Now, at last, the day arrived.

Eden found Candace's parting words, "Is there time for us, I wonder?" to be a sobering reflection.

Chapter Eighteen
Seeking the Open Door

As the weeks went by, Eden worked diligently toward helping Dr. Jerome gain the Board's approval to open a new
research clinic on Kalaupapa. Lana, too, lent her influence, along
with Jerome's friend and chief adherent, Dr. Bolton.

Despite all their efforts, they were discovering that labor and conviction alone were not enough to win the approval of the Hawaiian
Board. Eden was convinced that a few of the members were critical
of his research for personal reasons, and that the more Dr. Bolton
tried to sway them toward Jerome and Dr. Chen's work, the more
resistant they became. Herald Hartley's vociferous arguments in
urging the proud physicians to act at once proved to be irritating,
Lana told her one day.

"He's becoming a garrulous champion of your father. Dr.
Phillips in particular is offended. You know how haughty he is when
he thinks anyone of lesser credentials questions his judgment."

Although they needed Dr. Phillips's support, Eden couldn't help
but smile as she pictured the scene: Dr. Phillips with his tall lankiness,
meticulous silver beard, and stuffy manner.

"Dr. Phillips is thinking of having Hartley reprimanded or even sent away from the hospital. Do tell your father to put a damper on his assistant."

Eden did so, and Dr. Jerome put Herald Hartley to work writing a comprehensive compilation of exotic horticulture from Dr. Jerome's notes as well as Dr. Chen's herbal remedies recorded during his wanderings from Nepal to the Amazon. They dealt with everything from heat rashes to nail fungus. Herald felt he was doing great work, so much so that Eden felt somewhat guilty. Dr. Phillips, however, was mollified and thereafter more patient with Jerome.

Eden found this late summer morning to be one of somnolent peace, suggesting little threat of increased trouble ahead. Her confident footsteps quickened across the polished wood parquet floor to the front door, where she left the hospital for the Iolani Palace area.

In these busy days, while spending much time with Jerome, she wanted to ask him what he knew of Kip and about his meeting with Rafe in Tahiti, but his harried demeanor and ongoing frustration with the Board kept her from raising the issue. Rafe was the one to ask, when she managed to see him again. At present, she was late to join Dr. Jerome, who'd finally been granted a meeting with representatives from the Hawaiian Legislature. She wondered if she would see Rafe in the Legislature.

Outside in the warm yard, a waxy-green banana tree waved its leafy arms in the trade wind off the aquamarine Pacific, as if offering a song of thanksgiving to its Creator.

She walked along the volcanic stone path toward the dirt road lined with rustling coconut palms. The tropic sun blazed, and the balmy breeze ruffled her dark hair. Eden's green eyes under a fringe of lashes squinted. She lifted a hand to shade her view of the road. She could almost envision Ling and his hackney waiting as they had for so many months, but she should have been able to stop another hackney going her way. Ling still had not been seen, and no one appeared to know where he was, including Hui. Strange, though, that Hui no longer seemed to worry as she had a few weeks ago. Was it her growing interest in Christ? Or did she know something of where her husband may be? Eden refused to believe that Ling was dead—of course not! "Put such things out of your mind," she told herself aloud.

After the meeting with the Legislature, Eden needed to visit Great-aunt Nora at Tamarind House, located on Koko Head, overlooking Maunalua Bay. Tamarind had a ominous reputation since Great-grandfather Ezra Derrington had the grand house built there for his wife, Amabel. When Amabel met an accidental death, the native superstition was reinforced. Amabel had left Tamarind to Nora in her will. Since then, Nora had refurbished the interior, bringing more tropical light into the rooms, and altered the landscape to her liking. She'd hired a gardener to help her cultivate the rare orchids she loved and a boatman to bring her back and forth to Honolulu. Nora's message to Eden was, "Come as soon as you can. I want to speak with you alone."

Eden could only guess at what was disturbing Nora. Was it the *Gazette's* indebtedness? More than likely she wished to discuss Liliuokalani and Rafe's support for annexation—especially now that he sat on the Legislature.

Eden had requested leave from Kalihi and arranged to join both Nora and Candace there at Koko Head that evening. She would have departed that morning, except her father had wanted her to meet him at Iolani Palace garden before his speech to the Legislature.

"To Iolani Palace," she told the driver.

The driver maneuvered his public buggy along crowded Merchants Street past Spreckels Bank, Bishop Bank, the W. O. Smith Law Offices, and onto King Street.

The historic Kawaiahao Church, its first pastor having been missionary Hiram Bingham, was a short distance from the palace and the Ali'iolani Hale building. As the church came into view, with its cemetery in back holding the remains of many of the early Christians, Eden felt an emotional tug at her heart. They had given up much to come here and had been criticized by the world for their dedication to Christ. But one day when eternal rewards were given at the judgment seat of Christ, they would surely hear, "Well done, thou good and faithful servant!"

Bingham and those with him had not only brought the gospel of Christ, but they had introduced a written Hawaiian alphabet that was used to give the Hawaiians a Bible and textbooks they could read. They had built schools and medical facilities, and had taught the women that their bodies were temples of honor, to be treated with respect by men. Satan, of course, hated these pioneer missionaries and to this day was using unregenerate minds to cast verbal abuse upon them. How differently God weighed the spirits of men! What was mocked by the Devil and those men blinded by him, was considered gold, silver, and precious stones by the sovereign King of kings.

The driver neared Iolani Palace and stopped the buggy on the side of the street. The name Iolani meant "royal hawk," and swaying in the trade wind beside the palace on a tall pole, Eden saw the Hawaiian flag with eight stripes symbolizing the eight principal islands.

The handsome palace stood in the center of Honolulu on a wide square of verdant lawn surrounded by a parkland of trees, shrubs, and sweet-smelling flowers. The building was primarily of stone, with tall, slim pillars painted white, and was embraced on its two levels by long lanais with wrought-iron railings. Across the street from the palace were a small military barracks, Central Union Church, and Washington Place, the longtime private residence of Liliuokalani.

As Eden stepped down from the buggy, her feet scarcely touched the ground before a Hawaiian guard hurried up.

"Miss Derrington? Dr. Jerome's daughter?"

"Yes. I'm expected to attend Dr. Jerome's meeting with members of the Legislature. I hope I'm not late."

"I regret to inform you that Legislature has canceled the meeting with Dr. Jerome. He asks you meet him in the park near the mammoth banyan tree."

Canceled again! Frustrated, Eden walked the parkland to the banyan tree, which was the oddest shaped tree she'd ever seen. Its lower branches sent down into the ground many pole-like roots to form a wide and oddly shaped trunk. To Eden it looked like the tree was growing upside down, its roots sticking out.

Not far away on the quiet walkway a yellow poinciana was in bloom, along with what were called monkey pod trees and a kapok tree that cast pools of shade, bringing relief from the long hours of sunlight in the tropics.

She paused, troubled by the news. *Canceled!* Ahead she saw her father pacing to and fro in front of a white, wrought-iron bench.

He was tall and lean and garbed like the many other haole businessmen in Hawaii, in white trousers and a cotton shirt. His solitary oddity was that, even though it was humid, he would almost always wear a longer knee-length coat of some dark broadcloth, with a cutaway flap in the back. Also, instead of a derby hat, he wore his usual woven cane hat with a band of ribbon encircling the wide brim. He swung his familiar walking stick, with an ivory globe bearing his initials in gold, a gift imparted to him long ago by King Kalakaua.

Eden remained where she was, on the outskirts of his mental world, for a moment longer to consider him. His craggy face, with its strong jawline, wore a troubled frown. Here was the father she had always wanted but was denied. Then, like a fairy tale come true, he had returned home, declaring victory from his long, health-destroying journey. He believed he held secrets that could help not only Rebecca, but other hopeless victims of leprosy, and he'd never doubted that his honorable request would be granted.

After his return to Honolulu, Eden's expectations had soared at the possibility of building a relationship with both of her parents. She envisioned meeting Rebecca, healing the wounds both of them had suffered after such a long separation. There would be loving conversations and long strolls with her father along the white sandy beach as they shared medical information, though yet unproven, which supposedly held ancient secrets for the remission of leprosy.

Did she believe all this was possible? She felt she must in order to assist her father! For as she had discovered, Dr. Jerome's thoughts were never far removed from his medical work. Even though he intended his research to reach out and embrace all those afflicted with the "dread curse," as he often put it, it was Rebecca that filled his mind, even at times (dare she think it?) *haunting* him. The singular goal was targeted for mainly one purpose, that Rebecca would recover and live.

Eden remembered the conversation between her father and Rafe, as well as Rafe's stunning words: *When she contracted the disease, you became a guilt-ridden man. You've spent all these years traveling the world searching for the miracle cure that doesn't exist.*

Eden stood there. She had soon discovered that if she wanted to communicate with her father and gain his attention and respect, she could only do so by becoming as dedicated as he to his cause. This she'd been more than willing to do. She understood his dreams about Rebecca and wanted to keep them alive, not for him only, but for herself as well. At times the energy that drove him brought her unease. It was Rafe who had warned that Dr. Jerome's good cause of so many years had since turned into an obsession.

There were times when cold reason whispered that optimism must, in the end, be folly if not built on a sure foundation of truth. Dedication must be motivated by sound knowledge. Conviction alone, however noble, could become unbridled fanaticism. And fanaticism was like the Pied Piper that led his followers off the well-trodden path to the cliff's edge.

No sooner would Eden think these things than rebuke herself for disloyalty. Who was she to question her renowned father? He had suffered from his own self-exile these hard years in order to discover help and hope, and would she walk away from him now, when he had at long last come home and asked for her assistance?

She had made her decision. She would see it through to the end.

As though coming awake, Eden walked toward the banyan tree, and her father turned at the sound of her footsteps. She smiled. "Sorry, Father, did I keep you waiting long?"

He came toward her. "No, no, my dear, not at all." He took her arm, looping it through his own and patting her hand reassuringly. "I needed a little stroll and some time to think. I'm afraid we've run into another disappointing hurdle."

She was frustrated to see the disillusionment on his brow and in the slight stoop of his tired shoulders. The cauldrons of annoyance were set to flame in her heart, so that she could have burst into the Legislature herself and demanded a hearing for Dr. Jerome Derrington.

"This is becoming a habit with these gentlemen," he said.

"How can they turn their backs and simply go about their business? You're a man more committed to good than most any in the Legislature."

"More than likely their business is plotting annexation of the Islands."

"What happened this time?" she asked, trying to keep her patience. "Why are they delaying again?"

"It wasn't the Board of Health this time. Dr. Bolton did all he could. Even Dr. Phillips wrote a commendable letter in my favor, for which I owe him my gratitude. It was certain men in the Legislature who held matters up. They desire more information on Dr. Chen."

"Dr. Chen?" She was cautious.

"Yes. I was surprised that several men rallied two of their fellow planters to cancel the meeting at the last hour."

Eden's heart thudded with suspicion. Did Rafe Easton have anything to do with this? She realized it was unfair to think this of him, but . . .

"This is the second time the opportunity to present your case has been canceled," she said unhappily.

"I suppose we can blame the delays on the political unrest between the haole Legislature and the queen. A stubbornness has set in so that cooperation between the two is sometimes thwarted. Using politics to undermine a worthy cause, however, is most troubling. We need friends in the Legislature who also believe in the clinic," he remarked as Eden sat down on the bench.

Eden watched him pacing, his hands in his coat pockets. She wondered why the younger son of the respected Ainsworth Derrington should be lacking supporters in the Legislature to back his research, especially with the Derrington name so powerful in Hawaiian politics. Could it be that her grandfather, who was on Rafe's side when it came to Kip, as well as their assumed-to-be-impending marriage, might also not want her joining Dr. Jerome on Molokai? But perhaps she was assuming too much. So far her grandfather had said almost nothing to her about her engagement with Rafe. She might have Candace to thank for that, since it was her marriage to Hunnewell that commanded his full attention.

"Even if it takes six months, we'll go forward," Dr. Jerome told her. "I've struggled too long to give up now."

They left the parkland at Iolani Palace and walked back to the waiting horse and buggy.

—◦◦—

The buggy jolted along the street between some sweetly rustling palms. The morning had been busy, but Eden wanted to hold back the rush of her father's concerns. The royal blue sea came into view. Dr. Jerome motioned eastward, where they could make out the greenish-blue haze that was the glove-shaped island of Molokai with its leper settlement, Kalaupapa.

"Queen Emma Kaleleonalani in the 1870s had a cousin who was a leper. Peter Young Kaeo lived at the settlement on Molokai until his unexpected release in 1876."

Eden surprisingly had never heard of this and was immediately interested. "But how was that possible?"

Dr. Jerome smiled faintly. "Peter's leprosy was supposedly

'arrested.' He was even allowed to resume his seat in the Legislature. He died a few years later. Naturally doubts arose as to whether he was actually cured. There's little a queen cannot do for a relative, my dear."

Her father was silent now, lapsing into one of his isolated moods. Eden accepted the silence and leaned back into her seat, intending to grant him a few undisturbed minutes before the buggy brought him back to Kalihi Hospital. The mention of Queen Emma and Peter suddenly sparked her imagination with new energy.

"Father," she said suddenly, turning to him. "If anyone can arrange for a meeting with Liliuokalani, it's Great-aunt Nora. She's friendly with the queen and fully supports her rule. And the queen thinks fondly of her. She told Nora how she appreciates the favorable articles in the *Gazette*." She took hold of his arm, her eyes pleading. "Why not come to Tamarind with me? We've done most everything we could except turn to Nora. Perhaps we should have appealed to her earlier. Besides, you're exhausted. You could use a few days' rest away from the all the stress of Kalihi."

In the end she'd convinced him, and by the latter part of the afternoon the plans were in place to visit Great-aunt Nora at Koko Head and discuss any ideas Nora might have for gaining the queen's support for the clinic.

Chapter Nineteen
Candace's Sacrifice

They met Zachary at the wharf to take the ferryboat around Waikiki and Diamond Head to Maunalua Bay by Koko Head Crater. It was around twelve miles down the coastline to Tamarind House. Clouds were accumulating over the Pacific, reminding her of an invading army, and the wind was warm and damp with the feel of oncoming rain.

Arriving at the wharf, Eden and Dr. Jerome walked along the wooden planking to where boats, large and small, were anchored. The wind smelled heavily of the sea and fish. Shells were piled here and there along the beach where fishing nets were spread.

Her father motioned ahead on the wharf toward the *Kilauea*, an older boat that was now being used for ferrying. There was a sign over the cabin that read, "Tickets." Zachary appeared on the boat, the wind tossing his blond hair and pale blue jacket. He waved at them. "Over here!"

Soon after boarding, the captain gave the order to free the boat from the pier, and it was rowed a safe distance away before the crew raised the sails. They began moving through the swells as the boat pitched, giving Eden a sense of unsteadiness. She clung to the side rail as the water parted beneath the hull and the sea breeze dampened her face.

"How did Uncle Jerome's meeting with the Legislature go?" Zachary asked.

She was surprised he knew of it. "Who told you about the meeting?"

He shrugged. "I ran into Rafe last night coming out of Hillsdale's house. He mentioned it."

Clark Hillsdale was a leading annexationist and a close friend of Parker Judson. "Rafe is in Honolulu?" she asked, trying to sound casual.

"No, not today. When I ran into him last night, he was on his way back to Hanalei."

"Are you hinting that Rafe may have had something to do with the Legislature's delay in authorizing the clinic?"

He shrugged. "I don't think it's much of a secret. He's already told Dr. Bolton and anyone else who'll listen that he doesn't want you going with Jerome to Molokai."

Was that the reason Rafe had seen Clark Hillsdale on the eve of her father's appointment with the Legislature?

She watched the green foliated hills on her left, which rose steeply out of the Pacific. The water was less rough as they sailed past Honolulu Harbor with the Koolau Mountain Range in the background, which isolated them from windward Oahu. As they sailed past Waikiki Beach, Jerome pointed out Diamond Head crater towering above the coastline. The ancient Hawaiians still called it *Lae Ahi*, or "Cape of Fire."

When they sailed past Diamond Head into Maunalua Bay, Koko Head Crater appeared in front of them. Tamarind House was at the end of the bay.

"Another half hour," Zachary spoke into the stirring wind. Above the bay were mounds of mist-shrouded hills, covered with tropical growth and palm trees.

"Amabel wouldn't stay at Tamarind House," Zachary said. "She feared the kahunas and claimed there were evil spirits. So they moved toward Kalihi and Waikiki, and built Kea Lani on good red volcanic soil. Excellent for sugarcane."

The kahunas were self-proclaimed priests of the Hawaiian gods of earth, water, and sky. The first Christian missionaries had called the kahunas "witch doctors." Although the old religion was banned by King Kamehameha II in 1819, a certain segment of the Hawaiian population continued to listen to the kahunas with reverence and, sometimes, fear. It was not unusual to see some aspects of Christianity (which they said they adhered to) mixed together with Hawaiian religious beliefs in an unbiblical alliance.

Eden agreed that there seemed to be a shadow across Amabel's bridal house. Ever since Amabel, young and newly married, had fallen and lost the baby she'd been expecting, she'd been frightened by the kahunas and departed from Tamarind House, never to return.

Eden also understood why Zachary didn't like the house. As a small child she had fallen down the stairs at Tamarind on a stormy night and, for a time, had been unable to walk. Her mother, Rebecca, had departed for the leper colony from Tamarind House, and Eden had grown up with tragic nightmares of the incident.

But Eden didn't believe in superstitious "curses." A house was an inanimate object made of wood and stone. If evil was lurking in a house, most likely it was due to the sinful nature of those living there. No, she wasn't superstitious. These circumstances were merely coincidental. Her life rested in the powerful nail-scarred hands of the Son of God. Jesus was alive forevermore, seated at the right hand of the Father.

"Evil spirits," Dr. Jerome said, "do exist. But we've nothing to tremble about. The Holy Spirit, who is in us, is greater than Satan, who is in the world. 'Greater is he that is in you, than he that is in the world,'" he quoted from 1 John 4:4.

Dr. Jerome went on to repeat the tale. "Amabel became emotionally upset one day, and instead of reading the Scriptures and calling on her Lord, she ran from the house and tripped, hurting herself. She had begun to plant hundreds of acres of cane on the plantation. Some missionaries were there too. They had built a bungalow church near the now-abandoned cemetery, but after she fell, she became even more afraid of the *kahunas*, believing they had cursed her, Tamarind, and the bungalow church. The *kahunas* told her that Kane, their idol-god, did not want the Christian God there. Unfortunately, Amabel feared all this."

"Bats in the belfry," Zachary said ruefully. "I wonder if I've inherited any of her bats."

"Oh, nonsense," Eden told him, laughing. "There's nothing wrong with you that a pleasant evening at a merry luau wouldn't cure, especially if Bunny Judson were there to smile at you."

Zachary grinned. "Ah, you know me too well, Eden."

"Bunny Judson?" Dr. Jerome drew his brows together, thinking. "I thought you were all but engaged to Hunnewell's daughter; what was her name?"

"Claudia," Zachary said woefully. "Yes, I'm supposed to be."

"Supposed to be? You mean you're not?" Jerome said with an amused smile.

"Not yet, fortunately. Not ever if I've got anything to say about it."

Eden quickly changed the subject. "Oh, look. I can see the top of Tamarind House."

Zachary swiftly backed her up. "Yes, I caught a glimpse of its red tile roof."

Eden clung to the railing. *For Amabel to attribute a simple accident of tripping while she ran in haste as the curse of a heathen god, seemed rather immature of her. Amabel couldn't have been much of a testimony to the omnipotent God of the universe if she trembled superstitiously before the kahunas and ran away to Kea Lani!*

Eden shaded her eyes as the ferryboat came to the landing near Kuapa Pond at Maunalua. The wind was rising and the palm fronds shifted and fluttered their welcome. They left the boat landing and walked toward a hill with a vine-tangled path and thickly growing palms. Zachary led the way, pausing to make certain she and her ailing father were able to follow.

"It isn't too far," he assured Dr. Jerome. "Once we reach the horse road, there'll be a buggy waiting. Candace said she'd have one for us, even if she had to pay the driver to camp out. If not, I'll go up and get one and come back."

"I'm doing fine," Jerome called up. "These legs have brought me to many a village."

As they climbed the modest hill, the path, once rough in places, had been smoothed for easier walking. She thought of Amabel with regret. She, as well as many Christians, viewed tragedy beyond their control as from the forces of darkness, seeming to forget their Savior was all-powerful.

True to Zachary's word, a buggy and driver were waiting. The driver was dozing under his cane hat, and Zachary boyishly enjoyed scaring him awake.

The ride to the house was longer than she'd remembered. As they rounded the bend in the road, the house emerged into view on a terraced hillside with a wall of leafy tropical trees. A magnificent structure, she could see that it loomed wide and tall, perhaps three stories high. The buggy came to a stop in the lava rock court, and both Candace and Great-aunt Nora came out the front door to welcome them.

"Whatever has troubled your health, my dear Aunt Nora?" Jerome asked, scowling his concern over her fragile appearance. Eden, too, noticed the change and was alarmed.

"Have you been taking the prescription I brought you from Dr. Bolton?" Eden asked. "You should be needing a refill by now."

"That medicine, my foot," Great-aunt Nora scolded. "That's what put me in bed for what seemed weeks and nearly brought me under till the Resurrection."

Eden, startled by the unrealistic description of the heart medication, waited for an explanation, but Nora was having none of that just now. She turned from Eden to welcome her nephew, Jerome, and her great-nephew, Zachary, chattering away about trying to regain her strength so she could return to Honolulu to see how well Zachary was managing her newspaper.

"Well enough," Zachary said. "This is the first week I've not written any articles. And the others were all welcomed by the monarchists and loathed by the annexationists, including Grandfather. So I must be doing something right."

"You'll need to tell me about your health problems, Nora," Dr. Jerome insisted as they climbed the steps into the large house.

Eden was still pondering Nora's response to the prescription when Candace followed her inside and closed the heavy front door. Candace's eyes were troubled.

"Has Nora seen a doctor?" Eden asked.

"Not in the three days I've been here. You know how she is . . . insists she feels well enough. I need to talk to you alone a bit later," Candace said in a low voice, "about another matter."

Eden nodded, and as the others turned toward them, Candace managed a smile and greeted her uncle Jerome with kind affection. *So Candace is worried about something other than Nora. What could it be?*

After their bags were brought in and placed in their rooms, refreshments were served in a dining room full of fine wood furnishings and carpets, glass, and fine paintings. It wasn't until after dinner that Eden and Candace were able to meet. Candace, who believed fresh air and long, brisk walks would cure most anything, insisted they walk along the cliff to watch the sunset.

They climbed the smooth path until they came to thick ferns in rich, damp earth where orchids grew over rocks. The wind among the palms and rocks, the distant roar of waves crashing to shore, and the smell of ocean, flowers, and decaying bark saturated her senses. The path wound its way to an open area where foliage disappeared. A gust of warm, damp wind struck them. Eden caught sight of the ocean and the white sandy beach far below. The waves pounded and splashed their spray upon the beaches.

Eden caught her breath at the wondrous sight. A glorious sunset mixture of crimson and gold swept along the far horizon as the last of the sun's rays glittered on the crests of incoming waves. She looked at Candace, smiling her pleasure and expecting to see a smile in return. She was startled to see that her cheeks were wet with tears.

"Why, Candace, what is it?"

Candice swallowed hard and pulled a rumpled, folded sheet of paper out of her pocket. She handed it to Eden, found her handkerchief, and blew her nose. "Grandfather has won."

Shocked at the implication of her words, Eden opened the paper, trying to hold it steady in the gusts. She skimmed the affectionate introduction by Grandfather Ainsworth, along with an excuse for the extreme measures he was taking to bring to pass her marriage to Oliver P. Hunnewell. Ainsworth insisted he needed to do this for the Derrington enterprise and for future Derrington generations.

Then the words that Candace had spoken of leapt off the page: "I will make Keno successful with a plantation of his own on one of the islands if you'll make the sacrifice and marry Hunnewell. Candace, my dear, you must show yourself to be generous to Keno for his own sake, if you love him as you claim. This is a superb opportunity for Keno, and something he wants more than anything else. His own land. His own cane workers. Respect for his hardworking ways. His future will be full and fruitful. I promise to see this through. Isn't this your desire for the man you claim to love? And now I am handing it to him on a silver platter. He will know nothing of our private bargain, or he would naturally refuse it. The land, the plantation, will be arranged through a third party so that he will never know either of us had anything to do with his future success.

"If you won't go along with what is truly best for both of you and your family, I'll have no choice except to make certain he will never know any success on the Islands, and your own inheritance will be placed under the control of either Silas or Zachary."

The words wound on, leaving emotional rubble in their path. Eden was speechless for some time, then she looked at Candace.

"You're not going to agree to this?"

Candace was her calm self once more. Her lips thinned, and her cheeks were pale even in the bracing wind. "Yes, I am going along with it."

"Candace, you can't! It's impossibly unfair. Why, I can't believe Grandfather would be this dictatorial, this selfish. He's dealing in bribery and extortion!"

Candace merely shrugged her thin shoulders and stared out to sea. The sunset was fading. "We'd better start back. There's no moon tonight."

"Candace—"

Candace turned and walked back toward the house, and Eden, clutching the letter, followed after her. She protested and argued all the way back to the house but, Candace remained resolute.

Ainsworth had known how to win, not by forcing Candace to give Keno up, but by playing on her devotion to him. It was dreadful.

When they reached the house where the lights now burned brightly in the windows, Candace paused and faced Eden. She smiled wanly and put a hand on Eden's shoulder. "I knew you'd be outraged. I could count on your understanding for the injustice done me. I wanted to enjoy your sympathy for a short time, before I turn away from it once for all. That's why I wanted you to know the truth. But you will promise me not to say a word of this to anyone. Not to Rafe, not to Grandfather, Zachary, Uncle Jerome, Nora, Ambrose, Noelani—and not to Keno. To no one."

"I won't promise!"

"You will, dear Eden. Because I love Keno more than I love myself. I want him to have what he can never have with me, though I'm a Derrington. I don't want Keno to be forced off the islands he loves. I want him to have that grand plantation, a family of beautiful children to enjoy it after he's gone, and yes," her voice held firm in Candace's brittle way, "a lovely girl to marry and eventually love. I want him to forget me. I'll be able to do that for him by turning away from him now."

"Oh, Candace . . ."

"My decision is made. You'll do as I ask and say nothing. This secret is ours alone. Someday, when we're old, maybe the truth can come out."

Eden had no words. She felt weak, for she knew Candace better than anyone knew her—except perhaps Grandfather Ainsworth—and she knew that arguing with her would only strengthen her resolve.

Chapter Twenty
Suspicion!

*E*den waited in the hall near Great-aunt Nora's sitting room where she had expected to speak with her alone that evening, as Nora had asked, but the opportunity was delayed when Dr. Jerome insisted Nora retire early so he could ask about her illness and check her heart. Before dinner, when he came from her room, he was scowling, his stethoscope still hanging about his neck.

"Her heart is steady. She appears to be getting stronger. She should be doing even better in the morning."

Eden sighed with relief. "What do you think made her ill? A stomach indigestion perhaps?"

Dr. Jerome remained pensive and noncommittal. "A number of possibilities," he said, offering Eden no help at all. Then he soothed her concerns by saying the vomiting and dizziness had all passed. "The worst, according to her, was a week ago."

"She should have seen a doctor."

"Candace would have seen to that, but she hadn't arrived yet. Nora loathes doctors and all the fussing that goes with them, as she puts it. By tomorrow, I imagine, she'll be up and walking in the garden."

"What about the heart tonic prescribed by Dr. Bolton?"

"I doubt it was the prescription. I'll know more once I've spoken with Dr. Bolton. He can tell me what it was he prescribed and the dosage. From what Nora remembers, it sounds like one of the older medications. That's rather curious, as to why he would go to an older medication. I believe those medicines used to contain a bit of arsenic."

Eden stared at him. "Yes, I believe you're right. Can you read the label?"

He wrinkled his brow with amused toleration. "Nora thought it had gone rancid. She claims she threw it away as soon as she became ill."

The next morning Eden entered the dining room early, hoping to find her great-aunt up, for she was an early riser. The room greeted her with unhurried silence, as no one had yet come to breakfast. The massive fan-shaped window faced the sea that lulled peacefully in the distance, while clusters of puffy, pearl-gray clouds drifted by. Then she heard her father speaking to someone on the lanai. He hadn't seen her yet and was standing beside Great-aunt Nora.

"I'm sure there's a reasonable explanation, Nora."

"No doubt, but I've every intention of delving into this."

"Maybe you should wait to speak with Ainsworth."

"I'd rather speak with Rafe Easton, since it concerns him."

Jerome noticed his daughter. "Oh, hello, Eden."

What was that all about? Eden knew she was interrupting something important. Great-aunt Nora turned her head away and remained at the railing, looking across the rocks to the sea. Jerome came into the dining room. He gave no hint of what they'd been discussing. With a pat on her arm he pulled a chair out for her, then another for himself. Eden looked toward the lanai. "Great-aunt Nora? Are you joining us for breakfast? I do hope you're feeling stronger."

"Yes, I'm fine today, dear. I'll be there in a few minutes. Go on without me, both of you."

Eden turned her attention to her father. She knew him well enough now to recognize the thoughtful glimmer of concern in his eyes. Was it over Nora's health or over the subject they had been discussing?

"I don't suppose you've been able to talk to Nora yet about Liliuokalani's support for the clinic?" she inquired.

He stirred his coffee. "We've mentioned it briefly, and she is enthused. We intend to map out her plans on how to proceed in the next few days."

Eden was pleased to hear it. "Then I was right about Great-aunt Nora. I thought she might be on our side."

"We'll need to take the tortoise route, I'm afraid. There is no ignoring the Board of Health. Even so, Nora believes that if I'm able to explain my travels these years to Liliuokalani and interest her in the findings of Dr. Chen, the Board's approval should follow sooner or later. I understand the new queen has an inquisitive mind. A few more friends on our side from the Legislature won't slow matters down either."

Eden thought of Rafe. If only a man of his drive were on her side. Parker Judson had two influential friends with seats in the Hawaiian Legislature whom she'd mentioned to her father, and though he'd met with them over luncheon on Punchbowl Street, neither had promised his support.

"Father, there's something that interests me about Herald Hartley, something that seems rather strange."

"About Herald?" he asked surprised.

"Yes, it was something he said at the camp near Rat Alley a few months ago. He said you had helped him in India. What did he do in India when you met him?"

Unlike Herald, her father showed no caution in discussing India. "Why, yes, he was in India. I thought I'd mentioned that he'd worked for Dr. Chen in Calcutta. Unfortunately, Herald got himself into a financial difficulty and began to drink too much. He was dismissed by Dr. Chen, and his reputation was ruined. When I noticed him on the street one day, he appealed to me for help. I brought him to a Christian mission. With time he came to trust in Christ. I gave him a new start in research by taking him on as my assistant."

Eden was quiet a moment. "So far he hasn't disappointed you?"

"Disappointed me? No, why should he? I'm almost sure he's sincere in his faith."

She noted the hesitancy. "Almost? But not altogether?"

"Until a few weeks ago, Eden, I would have said altogether. Something occurred recently that has raised a doubt. I intend to look into the matter further, but for now I'd rather not discuss it. You'll understand, I'm sure."

She did of course, but would rather have discussed it.

"Is it wise, Father? To have Herald Hartley involved in what you're doing with the clinic?"

"So you also have doubts about Herald. I don't think we have anything to be concerned about," he said. "Until I met him in India, he knew only the rejection of his colleagues and his family. We need every friend we can get, so let's not forget to be a friend to others who are in need." He reached over and squeezed her hand. "We've got Rebecca to think of. There's no time to worry about Herald's past."

She wondered if that was wise, but kept silent and accepted her father's decision.

She quickly changed the subject to Ambrose and Rebecca's hope for a printing press, and was relieved when he showed support and pleasure at the idea. She didn't tell him she intended to bring it up to Rafe Easton when she saw him at Hanalei. She'd already made up her mind that she was going to the Big Island to see him before returning to Honolulu.

Eden was still in the grip of her emotions when the servant entered to see if they were ready for the first course of their breakfast.

"Where's Zachary?" Candace asked, coming into the dining room. Dr. Jerome stood and pulled out his niece's chair. "Good morning, my dear Candace."

"Thank you, Uncle. Good morning."

"I haven't seen Zachary since dinner last night," Jerome said.

Nor had Eden. She excused herself for a moment and went to find Nora on the lanai, but she wasn't there. She peered over the rail and saw her great-aunt below. She had a pair of binoculars and was looking toward the trees on the nearby hill opposite the garden. Eden watched her until Nora lowered them, stood for a few moments without moving, then came back across the yard toward the lanai steps, then looked up and saw Eden watching her.

"Breakfast," Eden called down with contrived cheerfulness.

"I'm coming." Nora came up the steps, slowly and a little out of breath. She returned the binoculars to the wrought-iron shelf where she stored them for bird watching.

Eden smiled. "See anything interesting this morning?"

"Oh, just a bird."

Eden watched her go inside the dining room. Candace watched Great-aunt Nora, too. There was a slight puzzlement between her brows this morning. Eden thought that if she hadn't told her about Ainsworth's letter last night, she would never guess the crushing decision Candace had made.

Nora was seated at the table as primly as a queen. "Zachary went for a hike this morning," she said when Jerome inquired of his absence.

"Zachary?" Candace asked, surprise in her voice. "I've never known him to be much of a walker."

"He took some brunch with him, and a canteen of coffee," Nora went on, making no reference to the unusualness of Zachary's decision to hike.

Was it Zachary whom Nora had seen a moment ago in the binoculars? If so, why wouldn't she simply say so? What was there to conceal? Nora had said she'd been watching a bird, but—

Her thoughts were interrupted when Nora turned her head and looked pointedly into her eyes. "Eden, my dear, the reason I asked you to come see me is about Ling Li."

At the mention of Ling, the clink of utensils around the table came to a sudden halt.

"Ling!" Eden said, surprised. "Is he here? Does he know every-one at Kea Lani is looking for him, including his family?"

"Yes, he most certainly knows. No need to concern yourself for his wife. Recently he had his own way of letting her know he was well. Li's people are most mysterious, you know. Very intriguing."

"Why didn't he let *us* know he was well?" Candace asked bluntly. "The last time I saw Rafe at the camp near Rat Alley, even *he* was looking for Ling."

Dr. Jerome frowned thoughtfully.

And Rafe evidently did not find Ling, Eden thought. She glanced at her father again. Was he recalling that awful debate with Rafe in the tent?

"Where is Ling now?" Eden asked Nora. "I want to speak to him."

"He's not here. He showed up a few days ago, most upset, poor fellow, begging to find Rafe Easton. He fled here, he told me, not knowing where else to hide himself until Rafe could be contacted."

Both Dr. Jerome and Candace joined Eden in staring at Nora. "Hide himself?" Dr. Jerome repeated. "He works for Kea Lani. Why would he need to hide himself from us? If he cannot fulfill his work-ing contract, I'm sure Ainsworth would arrange for something more lenient. Is he sick?"

"Oh, no. Quite healthy, in fact. I've yet to see a fellow so lean and wiry, and quick on his feet."

"Perhaps the death of his youngest son has affected his mind," Candace said.

"No, I don't believe he had the death of his son on his mind just then. I arranged to send him to Hanalei to see Rafe or Keno. They are both at the Kona plantation."

"When was this?" Eden asked.

"Before I became so ill. Oh, by now he's on Hanalei and safe, I'm sure."

"Why wouldn't he be safe at Kea Lani?" Dr. Jerome asked impa-tiently.

"I believe his perceived lack of safety had something to do with his hut being burned down," Nora said too casually, immediately alerting Eden.

Eden remained silent, but her grip tightened on her napkin. She thought she knew why Ling felt himself at risk. The burning down of his family bungalow was accidental, but Ling was always superstitious, as was his wife, Hui.

Dr. Jerome considered this. "Ling," he said, as if to himself, "was looking for Rafe Easton. And Rafe was looking for Ling at the camp. Perhaps Ling believes he has something of import to tell Rafe. More than that, he must believe what he has to tell Rafe somehow puts him personally in an insecure position. Interesting." He drummed his fingers, staring into his coffee cup. "Most interesting. I don't suppose there was any suggestion of what that was?"

"No. He considered it an urgent matter, however."

Nora and Jerome looked at one another for a long moment.

Eden did not know how she realized it, but she thought, *Father's just remembered something that makes him uneasy. And it's connected with Ling and Rafe. Nora, too, knows what it is.*

"Zachary is going to the Big Island in the morning. He mentioned you were going with him," Nora said to Eden.

"Ambrose is hoping Rafe can use the *Minoa* to bring a printing press to Molokai. That is, should we raise the funds to buy one. He asked me to speak with Rafe about it."

"A printing press?" Nora asked, showing interest. Eden told her about Ambrose and Rebecca's plans, and of the young Hawaiian Ambrose wished to train.

"I'll certainly contribute," Nora said.

"So will I," Candace said.

Great-aunt Nora looked toward the lanai as though she'd heard something that caught her attention. She stood up and walked there, looking out, first in one direction and then the other. She went to the rail and peered below.

When Nora came back to the dining room, she merely stood in the opening.

Eden, seated next to Candace, heard a small intake of breath. Eden looked at her. Candace had the strangest expression on her face as she sat staring at the lanai. "Oh," Candace said softly, "I see."

"See what?" Eden asked, frowning.

Candace got up and walked to the lanai, and stepped out into the morning light. She stood perfectly still.

"Do you see Zachary coming?" Great-aunt Nora asked her.

"No. I don't see Zachary."

Dr. Jerome appeared lost in his own thoughts for some time. Then, without a word, as though he were unaware of the others, he left the dining room and went upstairs, soon followed by Nora. Candace's steps were heard going down into the garden, no doubt for one of her long, healthy walks.

Eden, alone at the table, arose and stepped out on the windy lanai. *What odd behavior*, she thought. The palm fronds rustled, and the air was tangy with the salty fragrance of the sea. She walked over to the shelf and saw the binoculars there. She picked them up absently.

Earlier, Nora said she'd been looking at a "bird." Nora never used the generic name for the winged creatures she loved so much, as a novice would. Something was still troubling Nora.

Eden lifted the binoculars and refocused them, studying the sea, the trees, the road. She saw nothing unusual. Below, Nora came out through the front door and walked toward the banana trees. She paused there, with her back toward Tamarind, then strolled out of sight.

Eden lowered the binoculars. They had all behaved oddly this morning. And that conversation between Nora and Dr. Jerome earlier, before breakfast, had suggested something about there being a "reasonable explanation." Explanation for her medication? Nora had said she was determined about "delving into" the matter. But Jerome had urged her to wait to speak with Ainsworth. "I'd rather speak with Rafe Easton since it concerns him," Nora had responded.

Eden continued her musings until the bushes and trees shook

and Zachary burst through and strode purposefully toward the front door. He, too, was acting strangely, she thought. *If he's arranged a boat trip to the Big Island, I'm going with him*, she thought, clamping her jaw. "This time I'll *demand* answers from Rafe Easton." She was certain he knew exactly what was going on. She whirled from the lanai, and rushed out of the dining room to waylay Zachary.

When she entered the front hall, he was coming in through the front door and saw her. There was a tenseness in his face that should not have been there after his supposed "little hike in the tropics." He'd been up to something.

"I'm going to the Big Island right away, Eden. I was going to wait until tomorrow, but I think I need to see Rafe today. If I start out now, I can be at Hanalei late this afternoon."

"I'm going with you. Do you have a boat?"

"Laweoki owns the *Lily of the Stars*. He'll bring us. I've already spoken to him."

"I haven't much to pack. Did you see Nora out front when you came in?"

"Yes, I told her. What about Uncle Jerome? Is he coming with us?"

"He wants to remain with Nora for a few days. He's waiting for Dr. Bolton to come over."

"And Candace?"

Eden hesitated. Keno was at Hanalei. Candace would not relent on her heartrending decision.

"No," she said quietly. "She intends to stay here with Great-aunt Nora."

───❦───

Beneath a gray-blue sky that appeared to stretch forever, Eden walked with Zachary along the wharf until they came to the *Lily of the Stars*, a white and green yacht that had been turned into a houseboat. Captain Laweoki, in white knee-length pants and shirt, cheerfully welcomed Eden and Zachary aboard.

"Aloha. Your sore knee all better now I see."

"My knee?" Zachary questioned, then, as if remembering, he looked flustered. "It's fine," he clipped, obviously unwilling to expound. He began to walk away.

Laweoki was not to be put off. "Should never have gone inside Tamarind House that night. That house is cursed by the *kahunas*. Especially when nice wahine Nora Derrington not there."

Eden looked from Laweoki to Zachary, confused. Zachary hadn't injured his knee at Tamarind House, but at Hawaiiana in Honolulu, and that was back in early June. This was late September. Why would he even connect Zachary with Tamarind?

Zachary avoided Nora's house as much as he could. Even today, after just one night there, he'd been anxious to leave for Hanalei. For years, he had blamed himself because Eden had fallen down the stairs while he'd been chasing after her. Eden had hoped his guilt would disappear when he'd become a Christian over a year ago. Evidently mental shadows clung like cobwebs in his subconscious. *Only saturating the mind with the Scripture could chase those memories away,* she thought.

But Zachary was not showing a Christian spirit now. His blue eyes snapped at his Hawaiian friend Laweoki. "Never mind about Tamarind House. My cousin is well aware of its history." He strode across the deck to the steps and waited for her to follow.

Laweoki refused Zachary's indifference. "Bad place," he repeated to her in a low voice.

"It's just a house," she responded soothingly. "Zachary could have tripped and hurt his knee anywhere, even on this boat."

"Yes, he could have," he said gravely, "but he didn't."

"Were you with him when the accident happened?"

"Me? Ha. You won't find me in mile of that house."

"Then how did you know he injured himself at Tamarind? Maybe it was at another house."

Laweoki raised his brows. "Maybe. He was limping a little, I guess when I bring him here from Honolulu late one night. Cost him plenty of money too, for me to risk dark waters to come here. When he comes back, I see him with both of my eyes, limping." He pointed to the beach. "He came from there. All 'riled up,' as haoles say it."

"Hey! What are you two chatting about? You'd better wait down here, Eden. It'll get awfully wet on deck before we reach the Big Island," Zachary called to her. "Laweoki? Can you send us down some coffee?"

"Yes, yes, I send you coffee. Cost you extra," he called with deliberate mischief and winked at Eden. "But you rich Derrington. Won't hurt to dish it over."

Eden walked across the deck to the steps, where Zachary waited for her. She looked at him evenly. He was frowning.

"Be careful as you go down. We don't want any more reasons to fuel Laweoki's superstitions."

"You have some explaining to do," she said flatly and went past him down the short, wooden steps.

Below, there was a small enclosure, cramped and holding crates. Zachary had to duck low as he followed her. She faced him. His mind was on something that bothered him. There was a pinched look about his mouth, but she didn't think it was because of the discussion about Tamarind House. He'd been under a great deal of strain recently.

Eden carefully removed her hat and set it down by a barrel, along with her overnight bag. The gathering clouds outdoors darkened the area, and Zachary turned up the wicks on several lamps that Laweoki had already lit.

Eden accepted the few minutes of reprieve and thanked the other Hawaiian boy, maybe Laweoki's son, for the mug of Kona coffee. She found her mind wandering back to Rafe. She hadn't seen him in well over a month. *I'm not supposed to miss him this soon.*

She sat down, pensive and worried about Zachary, wondering about his strange behavior. Had Zachary injured his knee that day in June on the lanai at Rafe's pineapple plantation, as he'd said, or here at Tamarind as Laweoki insisted?

Nora must have been watching him with the binoculars, but why? When he'd come rushing in the front door after she and the others had finished their breakfast, he had looked nervous or . . . afraid, perhaps? "I must go to the Big Island *now*," he'd said.

"Silas is a schemer," Zachary said unexpectedly, putting his mug down on the table with a thud.

Schemer. Was he? She frowned, uncomfortable with his mood, back to jealousy of Silas.

"Notice how he flatters Grandfather for his leadership in the annexation movement? When almost immediately beforehand Silas was lecturing me and Nora about uncovering a story to hurt the annexationists."

She remembered well.

"He was all about scalping me for being too pro-Hawaiian League," Zachary went on. "But as soon as Grandfather practically assures Silas he'll be heir of 'all things Derrington,' well, then old Silas is suddenly for annexation."

Eden rubbed her temples, feeling a headache coming.

"Remember the night at Hawaiiana when Candace said someone was prowling around Hanalei on the lanai?" he asked abruptly.

She came alert. "Yes, all of us remember it quite well. Even Ambrose was brought into it." She felt cross about all of the problems piling up around her, like faggots waiting for the flame. "Why didn't you just come out and admit it was you on the lanai whom Candace saw? She did see you, Zachary."

He drew back, offended. "Me! It was not me she saw loitering outside Nora's guest room! It was Silas. He came sneaking over from Kea Lani that night, and I followed him."

She looked at him, puzzled. "Are you sure?"

He made an impatient sound. "Absolutely sure."

"Now, Zachary. Candace saw you. You leaped from the lanai, and injured your knee in the process."

He frowned and was silent a moment. "Well, I did leap over the lanai—but so did he."

292

"Laweoki just told me you were not only at Hawaiiana that night, but he also brought you here to Tamarind. He believes you injured your knee *here* and blames it on bad fortune from the old *kahunas.*"

"I know. He talks too much nonsense."

She did not think it was nonsense this time.

"Evidently it just took a while before my knee swelled and was sore," he said. "You know how an injury can be. Sometimes you don't even know you hurt yourself till the next day."

She turned her mouth ruefully.

"Now, wait a minute," he protested. "I admit I was on the lanai at Hawaiiana, but it was Silas who was doing the prowling, and it was Silas Candace saw up to no good."

"She *did* see you. Stop fibbing."

"Fibbing! Are you calling me a liar?"

"You were at Hawaiiana that night in June. You injured yourself in your haste to escape when Candace saw you. Then, for some reason, you're saying it was really Silas. Afterward, you came here to Tamarind on Laweoki's boat and went up to the house, knowing full well that Great-aunt Nora wasn't here, but back at Rafe's. If you insist on telling me this is all fabricated, I'll say you're fibbing." She folded her arms. "Tell me the truth, Zachary. I want to know what's going on."

He looked at her with a sullen face and jerked his shoulder. "Well, I did admit to being there, didn't I? I told you, I followed Silas from Kea Lani to Rafe's. It was nearing midnight, so I knew he was up to something that was smelling rotten."

She closed her eyes. "So. You admit it was *you* Candace saw. That's a beginning, at least."

"I don't admit it was *me* she saw." He leaned his face toward hers. "Because there was someone else on the lanai sneaking around. It was your little cousin Silas. I think he was spying on Great-aunt Nora."

"Why think the worst? I mean, even if he walked from Kea Lani

293

to Rafe's and went onto the lanai near Nora's guest room door, so what? Nora is *his* great-aunt, same as *ours*."

"Silas goes to see an elderly lady at midnight?"

"Well, you were there at midnight."

"That's different. I followed him."

"Why follow him?"

"I don't trust him. Somehow he's involved in something. I think it's a gambling and opium cartel that's supporting Liliuokalani."

"If you have proof of that, go to Rafe. He's on the Legislature now. I don't believe it, Zachary. As for Great-aunt, midnight, and the rest of it, what could Silas possibly be looking for?"

The corner of Zachary's mouth dipped down. "He likes her money and her newspaper. At least he did—until Grandfather got the big idea of suggesting in front of the whole dinner table that Silas might become his main male heir."

"Grandfather did that to keep Silas from writing against the annexationist movement in the *Gazette*, though I thought it horrid when he said it all in front of you." She thought of what Grandfather was doing to force Candace to marry Oliver Hunnewell. "Grandfather is not living with Christian principles governing his decisions, and it will all come back one day to plague the Derringtons."

"Well, maybe so. But Silas took Grandfather's golden bait and purred like a fat cat with a sardine."

"First something rotten, now sardines. I'm feeling woozy. And this rolling boat isn't helping . . ."

"Silas will do anything to please Grandfather now."

Money. How people fretted and fought over it! How family members "bickered" over who "deserved" more of it. For love of money people murdered, destroyed reputations, lied, and stole.

Eden could have reminded Zachary that at one time he, too, had been willing to use Great-aunt Nora for the same reasons he was now accusing Silas of. Zachary had become a Christian since those days, though he wasn't behaving with much grace toward his brother now.

"Silas was there at Hawaiiana all right," he insisted. "And he knew that Nora wasn't at Tamarind House. That's why he came here to Koko Head. I followed him. That's where Laweoki came in. He brought me."

"And Silas?"

"On another, smaller boat, of course. Laweoki always knows these things."

"Are you certain it was Silas?"

"Almost certain."

"Almost. But you could be wrong?"

He said nothing and finished his coffee, looking adamant in his conclusion.

"Well, even if he came here to Tamarind House, why should it matter?"

"I think you know why."

"Why not ask him?"

"Because he doesn't want anyone to know he was snooping on the lanai at Rafe's and then coming here to Tamarind in the dead of night, that's why. He came here to Nora's to find something."

"How could you know that?"

He tossed his napkin down on the table. "I can see whose side you're on. It was a mistake to even talk to you about it."

"Zachary!"

He sighed. "All right. I'm sorry." He ran his fingers through his hair. "Because I entered through the front door the same as he did. He left it unlocked. He had a key."

He had a key!

"When I was inside, I heard footsteps on the second floor." He looked at her a little sheepishly. "At first I thought it was my mind playing tricks. I'm no coward, as you know. But there is this 'thing' about Tamarind that gets to me. Anyway, the wind begin to blow, I remembered the past, and," he stopped. "Well, you know how it goes. Maybe I'm going crazy."

"Everyone is afraid of something. You're troubled by fears from your childhood. But you need to keep telling yourself that God has taken care of the past, just as He'll take care of the future. We can trust Him with both."

"Well, I guess I need to work at that," he said wearily.

Her doubts grew. Had he actually seen Silas? Had he heard someone upstairs, or had it been the wind? Since Zachary didn't trust Silas, his own heart may have encouraged him to think that Silas was the unwanted intruder. Was Zachary suffering from some sort of complex? He seemed to think the family was "out to get him."

She watched him, keeping her suspicions from showing. He'd grow worse if he thought she was doubting his story. *I've got to see Rafe about all this. He's always been understanding toward Zachary. He'll know what to do. He can talk to him and settle his fears about Silas scheming against him.*

He looked at her. "Today, did Great-aunt Nora hint anything about seeing Silas around Tamarind these last two weeks?"

The boat creaked and groaned as it surged through the water toward the Big Island of Hawaii. Eden gathered her thoughts. She wanted to be careful about what she said, otherwise she might strengthen his suspicions. She gestured indifferently. "No, she didn't mention Silas."

He looked at her evenly. "You're not on his side, are you?"

"Be reasonable. I'm not on anyone's side. I want to be for both of you. Silas is my cousin too, even if it was his misfortune to be born out of wedlock. Really, it's not his sin but his parents'. Why hold Silas responsible?"

"That isn't what's troubling me, Eden. It's Silas himself. He wants to replace me. My own father has plans to replace me. And if Silas convinces Grandfather I'm not well—he *will* replace me."

"Is Silas hoping to convince Grandfather of that?"

Zachary shrugged. "It's just a suspicion of mine."

It may be that he has one too many suspicions. "Grandfather would never disinherit you altogether. Especially if you needed medical treatment."

"Medical treatment!" he repeated, frustrated.

"Anyway, you're a child of God now," she hurried on. "No one, not even your blood father, can rob you of your position in God's family." She smiled encouragingly. "Zachary, there's really nothing to be afraid of."

"Dear Eden, how little you know!"

She sighed, searching his eyes. "Tell me, did you actually see Silas walking around inside Tamarind House or, for that matter, even on the lanai at Hawaiiana?"

"So, now you think I'm imagining things—seeing ghosts."

"I didn't say that. I want to make certain, that's all. Have you mentioned this incident to anyone else? Nora? Candace?"

"No, I've talked to no one. You're the one person I thought would take me seriously." His gaze accused her.

"And I have. I'm very concerned."

"About my 'medical condition,' or what I've told you?" he asked unpleasantly.

"You haven't told me very much," she soothed.

Zachary banged his cup down.

"Maybe it was a servant you saw instead of Silas," she suggested. "Maybe even the new gardener."

"Oh, come on, Eden. The gardener? Coming out of Nora's room? It was Silas."

Out of Nora's room! Now that information did surprise her. "Did whoever it was, see you?"

Zachary's eyes were on her again, bright and pensive. "No."

"You still haven't explained yourself, Zachary. What did you actually see?"

His glance flickered to her face and then away. "I saw someone. At Tamarind the sound was coming from Nora's bedroom, so I went upstairs. There was lamplight shining from beneath the closed door. I didn't imagine it."

Then there had been some light to see who it was . . .

"The hall floor creaked under my footstep and alerted him.

When I opened the door, he rushed past me like a storm, knocking me over. I couldn't see his face in the hall shadows. But I'm almost certain it was Silas."

Almost. Almost certain.

"Did Laweoki see him?" she asked quietly.

"Of course not. He was back here at the boat. Anyway, he believes in spirits tramping about. So he'd just say it was a ghost or something dumb like that. I tell you Silas knocked me down to the floor. He ran down the stairs and out the front door. I started after him. But by then my knee was really acting up from when I jumped from the lanai at Hawaiiana earlier in the night. Anyway, I got over the hedge. But he got away." A rather ugly look crept over Zachary's face. "So I can't prove a thing. But," he said coldly, "*I know.*"

Zachary admitted, finally, that he hadn't seen Silas's face. However, Candace had seen the man on the lanai. And she claimed it was Zachary.

Eden's tone was gentle, "What reason would Silas have for snooping about Nora's room?"

"He was searching for something, of course."

"The question is, what?"

"I wasn't able to check her room later because of my knee," he said as if reading her thoughts. "I don't know if anything is missing. We'll need to wait for Nora to miss something."

"The only thing Nora has missed is part of her manuscript—" she stopped.

His eyes flashed. "The manuscript. The family manuscript she's working on. Of course! What a dolt I've been. There must be something written Silas doesn't want revealed—"

"Or someone *else* doesn't want revealed. I think Rafe should know about this. Are you willing to discuss your suspicions with him?" She faced him with a challenge.

"That's the reason I'm going to Hanalei. Even with our early start, we're bucking a headwind today. It's a good hour to Hanalei from the bay."

"When we get there, I want to talk to Rafe first," she urged.

"You want to prepare him?"

"I think it best, yes."

He nodded reluctantly.

"I don't think we should say anything about this yet to Nora or anyone else."

"I don't intend to upset her. I'll wait. In a few weeks, I'll have all the facts I need to nail Silas's coffin."

"Zachary! Please don't say things like that."

"Oh, I know what you think, Eden. That I'm jealous of Silas and want to ruin him. That's not it. What if I'm right, then what?"

He expected no answer, for he went up the steps.

Eden looked after him. Her heart weighed heavily and the creaking boat and rush of the swells added to her sense of uncertainty. *Yes, then what?*

That evening the *Lily of the Stars* anchored at Kealakekua Bay on the west coast of the Big Island, or "Orchid Island," as it was sometimes called. The hour being too late for the long drive out to Hanalei coffee plantation on the slopes of Mauna Loa, Eden arranged a room at the small Orchid Hotel, and Zachary arranged to sleep on Laweoki's boat.

Early the next morning Zachary rented a two-seater buggy. By the time he met up with Eden, it was a warm, lush day, with just the right amount of breeze to ripple the sea and sway the palms along the Kona Coast. She boarded the buggy, and Zachary drove along the shore road toward the Easton coffee plantation.

From the bay they passed through Kealakekua village and Captain Cook, where the British explorer was killed on the beach by Hawaiian natives in 1779. From there they headed for lovely little Kainaliu.

Eden had mixed feelings about visiting Hanalei and seeing Rafe again. She had every intention of keeping her emotions restrained, but *could* she? There was no use denying the strong passion she felt in her heart for Rafe Easton. And recently, with all the burdens she had been carrying, the diamond ring that still graced her hand was feeling more and more at home.

I'll marry him one day. He feels the same way about me. I'm the only woman he ever wanted enough to marry. He wouldn't be able to forget me that fast. I'll make him see that working with my father on Molokai is something I must do for now. But our own chance for a life of our own, perhaps right here on Hanalei if not Hawaiiana, awaits us on the sunny horizon. After all, are not Lana and Dr. Bolton going to get married soon?

Eden resisted the small voice of Noelani that arose to oppose her confidence. *You'll lose him if you convince him you're playing a game. You cannot keep him on a fishing line forever.*

As she looked toward the glittering sea, she saw clouds gathering—just a few at first, and then more as the morning wore on.

"Looks like a rainstorm," Zachary said, gesturing. "It's a good thing we're arriving at Hanalei early."

Eden lapsed into silence and tried to enjoy the beauty of the island. From what Rafe had told her through the years, the entire Kona Coast had produced coffee continuously since the early 1800s, and she glanced around at the dark volcanic slopes of Mauna Loa, somewhat confused as to what to expect. She had never been to Hanalei before.

"Where is Hanalei?" she asked.

Zachary smiled. "You're looking at it." He gestured. "Welcome to Kona land."

Her brows lifted. "You mean the coffee grows on the volcanic slopes of Mauna Loa?" She had expected to see flat or rolling sugarcane-type land, like Kea Lani.

"And behind us, on the slopes of Hualalai. As Rafe will tell you, it's the best soil and altitude for growing coffee. I keep forgetting you've never seen the Easton place. I've been there a few times with Townsend."

Rafe had talked to her about Hanalei since they were very

young, but she'd been so involved in trying to learn about her mother and find her own identity in the family that she'd only paid moderate attention to his descriptions. She said rather defensively, "He didn't think he had the right to bring me here. Until just recently, not even Matt's son and heir was welcome on Hanalei."

Did Zachary forget how Townsend had wanted to run Rafe out of the Islands altogether? Uncle Townsend would never have stood for Rafe taking up residence on Hanalei. "Townsend still isn't happy about Rafe getting back Hanalei," she said.

"You'll soon see why, when you get your first glimpse of what your future husband owns," Zachary said with a wry tone.

Zachary flicked the reins. The horse quickened its jaunty trot down the shore road from Kealakekua toward Captain Cook, Keei, and Honaunau.

The shore road had very old coconut trees lining its route and their tops were swaying in the wind. Eden glimpsed large houses, here and there, set back among the palms, some with ornate gates and long driveways. Always, there were flowers, frangipani, pink, orange, and yellow plumeria, pink and cream hibiscus, and heady gardenia.

Toward the sea, the morning brightness lingered above the horizon as heavy clouds gathered like gigantic billowing dragons above the sea, their cheeks puffed and rimmed with silvery gray. The humid wind blew against Eden's face, shook her dark hair, and ruffled her white cotton dress that she'd changed into at the hotel before starting out.

Soon the road climbed higher. From Eden's mental deductions they were somewhere on the western backside slope of Mauna Loa volcanic range, with the sea behind them like a placid, blue jewel amid a setting of lavish green.

Ahead, the robust color of the mountain announced: "Kona coffee country."

The air was tepid, the sunlight shining through a rainbow-like mist, making sparkles of predominantly amethyst and ruby. She felt the misty rain on her face but enjoyed it. She laughed at Zachary, who hunched his shoulders and lowered his hat. Somehow the intoxicating tropical atmosphere made her wish she was sharing it with Rafe.

"Rains every afternoon," he said.

Zachary told her that the acreage of Hanalei, the largest coffee-growing estate on the Kona Coast, was farther up the gradual slopes, while the mansion, or Great House as it was sometimes called, was closer to the village of Honaunau, near the beach, and built on an incline so that its windows and lanais overlooked the ocean.

When at last Zachary slowed the buggy on the narrow road clustered with palm, banana, and monkey pod trees, Eden was not disappointed. She caught her breath.

Zachary turned the horse onto a second avenue and they stopped before a pair of black lava stone gateposts. Eden's eyes fastened on the bold name:

Easton's Hanalei

Zachary said with malicious amusement, "Shall I go back to Tamarind House and tell Uncle Jerome you won't be going to Leper Island to bandage sores and help bury the dead?"

Eden swatted his shoulder, then turned back and stared.

"Oh," was all she could say. "Isn't it splendid?"

"I told you it was. Now you know why Townsend's fought like a starving rat to keep his prey."

"You shouldn't speak of your father in that way."

"You're right. I shouldn't."

"Oh, don't spoil this moment by talking about Uncle," she whispered. "This is Easton land. All the hard work and planning of Matt Easton and now Rafe."

"Anything you say, Cousin." He followed the carriageway for some distance to the front of the Great House.

Where was Rafe? She hoped to see him at once, not just to discuss Zachary's concerns, which they had debated on the boat as they'd come here to the big island of Hawaii, but about all of the other questions, including Kip, Ling, and the printing press.

For a minute she sat, drinking it all in, imagining Rafe as a child before his father died, before Celestine had erred in marrying Townsend Derrington from Oahu.

Eden stepped down onto the grass and stood looking up at the mansion. On the breeze she could whiff the exotic aroma of the waxy gardenia. What would Rafe do when he learned she was here?

Was Kip inside, happily planted in the nursery with Celestine at hand?

"Look here, Eden," Zachary said. "I doubt Rafe is in the house. Knowing him, he's out working with Keno. Why don't I find out? I do know there's a smaller house toward the hills, because when I came here with Townsend some years ago, that's where he'd bring me. He'd meet with the manager and check on things."

Eden's eyes thanked him silently.

Zachary jogged to the front door and used the bell chimes. A minute later the door opened and a Hawaiian in white spoke to Zachary. Zachary motioned toward Eden, and the serving man smiled and nodded, then pointed in the distance. Zachary jogged back to her.

"He says Makua Rafe is out riding his horse. He'll be coming back to the house any time now, because there's the feel of a storm in the wind. Take the buggy, and go meet him. He'll have a surprise when he sees you. I'll go find Keno. He's around back somewhere."

Eden climbed back into the buggy. Once on the seat, she flicked the reins, and the horse started down a secondary lane, lined with young macadamia trees. Someone was shouting from behind her, and she pulled over, looking back. A young Hawaiian boy came running up, smiling.

"Wahine looking for Makua Rafe?"

"Yes, do you know where is he?"

He nodded vigorously, but pointing at the buggy, he shook his head. "Path is too skinny to drive buggy." She could take the buggy if she wanted to travel the route used by the donkey wagons that brought the coffee cherries down from the mountain, he said.

"But Makua Rafe will come by the skinny path, not donkey road. I bring you a horse?"

She glanced toward the horizon, where billowing clouds churned restlessly, then told herself there was plenty of time to find and talk to Rafe. "How long to bring me a saddled horse?"

He snapped his fingers and ran off. Where the boy had the horse, she couldn't imagine, for within a few minutes he was back, leading a fine golden horse with a white mane, recently brushed. He put a hand over his mouth to hide a smile as he glanced back over his shoulder.

Now what was this about? "Is he safe?"

He sobered. "Very, verrrry safe!"

She climbed down from the buggy, ignoring her long dress. The boy held the reins as if she were a princess, while she stepped on the stirrup and mounted the saddle. After arranging her skirts, she took the reins. He was friendly enough and more than anxious to tell her which way to ride.

"Wahine be there in ten minutes. Remember, that way!" He pointed for emphasis. "That way."

Eden turned the horse's reins and looked down at him gravely. "If I find this is a prank, young man, I shall return and give you a switching myself."

He smiled and placed his hand against his heart. "Jesus keep your way safe, Wahine."

She smiled warmly and his eyes twinkled at her pleasure. "I see, I misjudged you." She turned and rode away, handling the horse with expertise.

Chapter Twenty-Two
Love's Challenge

*E*den's busy gaze took in snow-clad mountains with high peaks and volcanoes that could spew fire. The lush vegetation, the rainfall that made the white and purple-black orchids bloom, the cattle ranches and coffee plantations, all of this and more described the Big Island—Hawaii—the island from where Kamehameha the Great had gone forth to conquer the other independent island kingdoms around him and to form one kingdom, his own, that he named after his island homeland, Hawaii.

The earth was red in some places, with ebony sand covering large areas. Eden had not ridden far when thudding hoofs sounded behind her. She slowed her horse and looked over her shoulder. Rafe, astride an auburn-brown stallion with white hoofs rode up beside her. Rugged and good-looking as ever in hat and jacket, his lively dark eyes challenged her.

"I was riding back to the house when I saw you leaving in the buggy. I caught up with Zach. He said you were looking for me. Something about a magnitude of questions you want me to answer. I need to warn you though, I've a few of my own to ask."

"Who was the boy suppressing laughter when he brought me the horse? And such a wonderful horse!"

"He is. Zach will be jealous over this one. The boy is Koko. I sent him to hail you, so we could ride the paths together without Zach as chaperone. At any rate these paths are too narrow for the buggy."

"So that was Koko. I wondered what he thought was amusing."

"He was amused over my reaction to the arrival of such a stunning girl. That I would arrange to waylay you on the path will bring no end of laughter. They call me 'stone heart' around here. I have to protect myself from all their sisters."

"Indeed. Well, there's nothing like conceit." But she smiled, letting him know she knew he was most likely accurate, though telling her was just his way of goading her supposed lukewarm feelings toward him.

"Is this one of your many questions," he asked smoothly, "or do you have more dangerous ones?"

She picked up his veiled reference to Kip. "First, I want to tell you how pleased I am that you've regained Hanalei. Finally, an injustice has been made right." She looked around. "Rafe, you never told me it was this wonderful."

"Yes, Zach just told me you'd have married me a year ago if I'd shown you Hanalei."

"Oh, he's dreadful, sometimes." She felt the warmth rise to her cheeks. "It's been a long time since I've seen you around Honolulu."

She looked across at him and saw the spark in his energetic dark eyes. He smiled, still goading. "Does this earth-shattering admission in any way suggest you've missed me?"

She played along innocently. "Oh, yes, Rafe. Amid twelve-hour days and nights at smelly Rat Alley, problems mounting for every conceivable member of the family, from Zachary's suspicions, to Silas, Candace, Townsend, and Nora—yes, I did miss the long talks we had walking on Waikiki."

"Zach's suspicions may not all be that far off. But let's not get into that just yet. For the moment I'll bask in the fact that I've won the competition over such miserable circumstances as Rat Alley. Though I'd think walking the white sands of Waikiki under the Hawaiian moon might evoke more interesting things than long talks about Jerome's clinic."

"And then, there is Ling."

"Ah, yes, Ling. He's here, by the way. He's decided Kona coffee beans are more interesting than Derrington sugarcane, especially with Townsend stalking him. Townsend, that amiable bully of one and all. I'm anxious to meet Townsend again. Preferably alone. I want the details on how the fire started in Ling's hut with you, among others, inside. I fear I'll need to go to Ambrose afterward and tell him I've broken a vow."

His disarming countenance changed to such determined hardness that she held her breath. "What vow?" she asked cautiously.

He smiled unexpectedly. "That's not for this pleasant interlude. I won't complain about your ponderous list of questions, either. I've every intention of answering them, if I can. Shall we talk as we ride?"

Eden glanced around her to the mountain slope, then down toward the sea, taking in much of the estate. Her eyes came back to his. He'd been watching her. She smiled. His brow lifted.

"Yes, let's ride. I want to learn a little about your prized coffee."

His eyes narrowed thoughtfully, as though he were considering a certain course of action and whether or not he should risk it.

She looked away.

"If that's what you want," he said silkily.

"Yes, anything you suggest."

"You're very congenial all of a sudden." He turned the reins and gestured to the path they would take.

Eden ignored his light remark and turned her horse to ride along. Together they moved off down the path.

"Let's not talk clinic now," she said with a smile. "Let's talk coffee."

He turned his dark head, and his eyes held hers a moment. "I'm always obliging. Ask away."

Eden looked around at the greens of high distant cliffs contrasted with dark boulders streaked with garnet and mauve. On the slopes she saw the myriads of coffee trees. "Well . . . what are those workers doing now?"

He followed the direction she was pointing.

She was aware that the brick wall between them had again crumbled. She sensed their emotions touched, unwillingly at first, but once the contact was made, Rafe was once again reachable.

"My father got hold of some of the finest coffee-growing soil on the west Kona coast. A limited, choice land strip extending from the villages of Holualoa to Honaunau. Because of the ideal climate on the mountain slopes of the Hualalai and Mauna Loa volcanoes, it grows the best coffee."

"You can't grow Kona coffee on lower elevations?"

"The name 'Kona' applies only to coffee beans grown in north and south Kona. The beans produce the best flavor on trees and bushes between eight hundred- and two hundred-foot elevations on the volcanoes."

Eden thought she could understand why as she gazed about her. The tropical sun-drenched mornings, the humid rainy afternoons, the mild nights, all made ideal growing conditions for the trees, and also for other exotic plants, as well. She could see many other fruit and nut trees flourishing, including some nut trees from Australia.

"Like most everything else on the Islands, this nut was brought here to the Big Island a decade ago, by seed. The nuts haven't made a real name yet, commercially, but they will eventually."

"Are they as good as, say, walnuts?"

Rafe smiled. "Roasted and salted, these macadamias will become the king of nuts."

After they had exhausted what could be seen by horseback, Rafe stopped beneath some trees. Eden heard a mild roaring sound and turned to look at him with pleasure.

"A waterfall. Can we reach it on foot?"

"Yes, but you'll need to climb down a mountain path to see it.

Are you up to it?" He looked at the shoes she was wearing. "Not very substantial."

"I'll take them off. Let's see it, Rafe; it will be such a splendid sight."

He came around to assist her down from the saddle, and they started on the path.

The afternoon was filled with shadows by the time they reached the side of the cliff where he told her there was a hidden lagoon below, a natural offspring from the waterfall.

"There's a pearl bed there," he told her, explaining how Matt Easton and his original partner from Tahiti had transported the original black-lipped oysters to the quiet lagoon. "It's been a secret. Not even Townsend knew of this one. If he had known, he would have cleaned it out long ago for his gambling debts. I learned recently that Rebecca's black pearls came from here."

Rebecca's? She still retained Rebecca's black pearl necklace among her jewelry at Kea Lani. That held her attention, especially when she coupled it with the conversation she'd heard between her father and Rafe in the tent. She gave him a sideways glance. He was staring thoughtfully at the lagoon.

Should she hint of Matt and Rebecca's friendship and see what Rafe said?

"The black pearls came from here? Are you saying Dr. Jerome bought them from Matt Easton for Rebecca?"

His gaze came back to hers. "No, I've discovered recently that my father gave them to Rebecca 'once upon a time,' as they say. But 'a time for love,' as mentioned in Ecclesiastes, never worked out for them. She married your father—and I'm glad she did," he added, "or you and I would be related."

"Yes, how pleasant that God controls when we're born, to whom, and even why."

Eden remained determined to climb down to the waterfall and visit the lagoon. Rafe looked up at the lowering sky, where clouds steadily accumulated.

"I'm not sure the rain will hold."

"Let's risk it, Rafe. It's so enchanting."

"The path is slippery in places. Better take hold of my hand."

His hand clasping hers said that they belonged together. At the moment, she had no wish to argue.

They began the narrow trail. Eden breathed deeply of the inevitable and evocative smells of the tropics: damp, rich earth, ferns, and flowers, all intensified by the tropical warmth. Birdsong and the relaxing sound of the waterfall filled the early afternoon air. Tiny jewel-like hummingbirds darted here and there among deep-throated crimson trumpet flowers. Lazy frogs, unseen, croaked.

Rafe led her along the narrow way, avoiding rocks, skirting tall ferns, and ducking trailing vines. The hour was filled with contentment. For a timeless space neither of them spoke, and the enchantment weaved its spell around her heart.

He motioned ahead. The silvery blue waterfall plummeted down the lava rocks to lose itself below in green lacy ferns. Eden followed Rafe under a canopy of vines and came out where the water tumbled and splashed its way over twisted formations of black- and ocher-colored lava rock.

The path grew more slippery from the perpetual mist, and Rafe held on to her arm. She saw orchids and scarlet fuchsia. A few more minutes passed, and he gestured below to the quiet lagoon.

"The man-made pearl bed?"

He nodded. "I used to swim there with my father when I was quite young."

Eden felt reckless. "Let's do it now!"

Rafe considered, glancing up at the sky again. "That storm is gaining on us fast. I'm not even sure the path is still accessible. I haven't spent time here since I came back. It's probably overgrown with ferns by now."

She faced him, arms folded. "What an excuse from someone who thrives on risk and adventure. It seems much too wonderful not to enjoy it."

He turned to look at her. "With you? Yes . . . I'll agree to that." He looked at her a long time. "All right. Just remember, this was your idea."

He led her to what appeared to be a path descending right beside the waterfall through a carpet of flowering vines. "Hold tight," he shouted above the roar. "It's slippery."

They started down toward the lagoon through pink wood-rose flowers and star jasmine with small white flowers sending off a light sweet fragrance. Ferns, green and thick, were everywhere. So were plumeria and yellow alamanda. But it was the light blue orchids growing in a profusion of queenly glory that lent the most heavenly aura to the beauty that surrounded them.

Even before they reached the bottom, where the sandy beach waited in solitude, they were wet with spray. Eden saw shells of various colors, sizes, and shapes, including some of what Rafe had earlier called "black-lipped oyster shells." Eden stood taking it all in, turning and looking up at the cliff sides surrounding them. For a brief interlude it seemed, indeed, to be a little paradise. She shut out everything unpleasant from her mind and allowed only her heart to respond.

"Enchanting, isn't it?" she heard him say as he stood close beside her.

She didn't need to answer. They understood, and their hearts met, if not forever, at least for that moment in tropical paradise. Her eyes sought his.

"Almost too enchanting," he said softly, still holding her hand, his fingers closing about her wrist. Then, suddenly, he released her, breaking the spell deliberately. "The serpent likes to spin his enchantment too. This is a good place to keep a clear mind. Everything is too intoxicating." He looked up at the gathering clouds. "Come, we'd best go."

"What? Without dipping my feet in the pool?" she cried indignantly.

On both sides of the waterfall there were ivory beaches, untroubled by man, and Rafe pointed toward the opening to the Pacific, guarded by treacherous reefs. "See that? Every diver, including Keno and me, knows to avoid that area. The reefs can slice through you as sharply as a blade. I never saw any sharks as a boy, but one would be wise to be careful anyway."

She nodded and looked toward the warm, crystal waters of the lagoon. Rafe removed his shirt, dropping it on the warm white sand. Eden was not blind. He was in superb physical condition, but it didn't dawn on her until this moment just how tempting the rendezvous could be. She looked away quickly. *Don't be such a stuffy moralist*, she told herself. *You're a nurse, aren't you?* But Rafe wasn't just *any* man. It struck her suddenly that perhaps this little isolated paradise weaving its enchanting spell around her emotions wasn't such a wise and safe place after all. Rafe was right. And as he'd warned, this had been her idea.

"Don't worry. I've no wish to take advantage of the situation," Rafe said unexpectedly, as though reading her thoughts. "I think we can go for a swim with our clothes on and without compromising. If it troubles you, however, we can head back now."

"No," she found herself saying for reasons even she couldn't understand. "No, go ahead and swim, Rafe. I intended just to get my feet and hands wet." And to prove it, she ran to the edge of the lagoon, knelt, and splashed the unusually warm water on her face. It was delightful, and she looked at the deeper water longingly.

Avoid tempting situations, Ambrose's distant voice echoed in her memory, from a recent service at the church.

Abstain from all appearance of evil. What would Candace say if she saw them here alone—Rafe with his shirt off?

Flee from youthful lust. Flee? Eden had walked straight into it. And now that she was here, it was so tempting she didn't even want to fight it, but to enjoy it! Eden's self-discovery brought the heat of shame to her cheeks, and she splashed her face again.

"All right . . . I'm going in." Rafe announced. He emptied his pockets and walked over to the waterfall. "If I don't return," he called back with a taunt, "a shark got me."

Eden smiled to herself and didn't respond. Only an average swimmer herself, she was thrilled to watch him dive off a rock below the waterfall. His tanned, muscled torso cut through the water as cleanly as a knife.

She glanced up toward the cliff from where they'd come down, almost guiltily, as if her father, Dr. Jerome, or maybe Great-aunt Nora or Ainsworth stood watching, scowling. She could picture Claudia shaking a finger at them with a giggle. But in her heart she understood that it wasn't the eyes of a gossipy girl or her family or even friends that truly mattered, but the *holy and loving* eyes of the Lord watching His two children. That solid scriptural truth, instead of frightening her, brought unexpected peace. Yes, He was here. The Creator of it all. Their Redeemer. In times of temptation they could depend on His Holy Presence.

As she sat on the sand near the lagoon's edge, she slowly became aware of how quiet it was. Her eyes scanned the water. Rafe was nowhere in view. He had walked to the waterfall—

She jumped to her feet. Could he have slipped and struck his head on a rock? He'd just been teasing her about a shark, but what if it actually happened? Unreasonable fear gripped her heart. For a moment she let slip through her fingers everything about dependence upon God that she'd been thinking of.

"Rafe!"

Eden ran toward the silvery, splashing waterfall and climbed cautiously out onto a rock, becoming drenched in a matter of moments. The roar was deafening. She stared into the dancing white bubbles. Panic began to set in.

Don't be foolish, she told herself. *He can take care of himself. Remember how he dove for the black pearl at the lagoon near Kea Lani?*

"Rafe!" she shouted again. Frightened now, she clambered out onto still deeper rocks, the water's thunder filling her ears. The spray splashed up, and she dashed a hand across her eyes. She knelt on the rock and looked into the water, when—

She gasped as someone caught her hand. Too late! Rafe reached

315

up, caught her waist, and hauled her down into the warm water.

She gasped with laughter as the warm water swirled around them.

Holding on to her arm, he swam with her into the calm lagoon and brought her over to the beach. She stared at him, her eyes growing languid, and then they were in each other's arms, his searing kiss awakening dangerous passions. Surprisingly, he deliberately drew away, and with their hands still entwined, he walked her toward the path to the horses.

"We should never have come here like this," she whispered guiltily, but Rafe didn't appear troubled.

"You're afraid of your own feelings, Eden. You've been hiding behind your father's dreams. I knew what I was doing when I agreed to bring you here. I said you were safe being alone with me like this, and I meant it. If I'd thought differently, I'd never have brought you here, no matter how much you wanted to come."

He drew her into his arms. Her eyes came to his. His arms were around her, and she could hear his heart beating with her own. Her head went back, and his lips evoked a kiss that would be remembered long after their afternoon interlude at the lagoon had ended.

"Admit you love me," he whispered.

"Rafe—please—"

"Say the words. I want to hear them again."

"Yes, you know I do."

"I want to hear you say it."

"I love you! I need you!"

She kissed him back, her arms holding on to him tightly.

They stood entwined in an embrace and became part of the warm, fragrant wind that moved across the lagoon, stirring the orchids among the ferns.

They were still holding on to each other when the first drops of rain landed gently against them.

Rafe lifted her hand so that the diamond sparkled, watching her alertly.

"I do—want to marry you," she choked, haltingly. "Yet I promised my father I'd stand with him to get the clinic operating on Molokai. Oh, Rafe, please understand. It's so—important to him. To both of us. To Rebecca. It won't be forever. Just a while longer—" she stopped, and fell into confusion because she could see the warmth in his eyes flicker out like dying coals.

"And you want me to wait. To agree to another long waiting period, is that it?" He dropped his hand from her arm.

"It does seem more convenient," she began uncertainly.

"Convenient," he repeated. "For which of us?"

"I'll be so involved, so busy." Her voice became dull. Her gaze faltered.

"I understand perfectly." He walked over, snatched up his shirt, and put it on impatiently. "Let's go," he said quietly. "It's getting late."

She stared at him, swallowing the misery in her throat. "Rafe, please! Don't be angry with me."

"I'm not."

"I don't want to disappoint you—"

"You just don't want to disappoint Jerome's idea of a clinic on Molokai even more. I understand perfectly. Don't worry about me, *dear*. I wouldn't want that."

Eden didn't know how to answer. Her tired mind wandered to her father and the clinic on Molokai . . . while her eyes drifted back to Rafe. He stood, one hand on his hip, the wind billowing his open shirt. "You think I don't know what's on your mind?" he asked. "I know your heart very well, Eden, my love. But commitment can't be parceled out to make more than one man happy at a time."

"How can you be jealous of my father?"

"No, not of Jerome, but of your blind adherence to *his* dreams. You've had them since we were in our teens. You know just as I do that those dreams can never be."

"I don't know that." She turned a shoulder to him, shivering now, cold and depressed.

"By the time you do know, Eden, it will be too late for us."

"Rafe, please don't say things like that. I do love you. I always have. I do want you." She threw her palms to her temples and began to cry.

He came to her, holding her, stroking her wet hair. "I'm sorry, Eden. Don't cry. It's all right. I love you, and I always will."

And I always will.

"Oh Rafe, please understand my duty toward him. Don't make me choose. I love you, but I love him too, and he needs me."

"So do I, Eden."

"But you're strong. You're stronger than he is—you just proved it—and more independent than he is—my father isn't well. This clinic means so much to him. He's traveled the world over to find a cure for Rebecca. I know he can't cure my mother. It's been too long. I know that. *But he doesn't.* He's given his life to this search. I could lose him anytime. At the camp, he had an angina attack that proved to me how weak he is. Please give me more time, just a little while. Give *us* more time."

The wind was now whipping about them, the rain falling in heavier, more frequent drops. She held him tightly, hoping to convince him that her love for him was real and undying.

"Just a little while," she said again, her eyes pleading.

He was silent; then, his voice was calm. "All right. A little while longer," he said, but she could see he was troubled.

Relieved, loving him even more for his apparent understanding, she drew his head down to hers and kissed him. "My heart is yours," she said. "You must not forget that."

"Is it?" he asked quietly, but he did not expect an answer, and slowly her arms came to her sides. Rafe walked over and picked up her shoes. "Better put these on."

She said nothing more. Emotionally drained, she sank to the sand and put them on. He walked to the edge of the lagoon and looked out. His face was quiet now, the moment of decision between them seemed to have come, settled, and passed by like the billowing clouds.

He flipped a shell in the air, catching it absently.

She stood, the wind blowing against her. Now that he'd agreed to wait, she looked at the engagement ring.

"Then may I leave the engagement ring on, Rafe?"

"Yes, leave it on," he said simply. "It saves us both from explaining to the family. Besides," he confessed dryly, "I really don't see it matters much now. You have your commitment to Jerome, and I have work to do in the Legislature, as well as at Hanalei and Hawaiiana. I think we'll both have enough to keep us busy for a while." He turned and looked at her, his head tilted, one hand on hip. "We've agreed to meet again in around—what? A year? Two? Longer? We'll see how we feel then."

"You make it sound so—so pragmatic."

"I'm only giving you what you want."

"But you seem, well—businesslike."

He laughed unexpectedly. "For the life of me, I struggle to understand you sometimes. I told you I'd settle down if you married me. But we've mutually agreed to wait *again*. So why are you making something of my restraint? I thought that's what you wanted."

She seemed caught by her own words.

He walked up to her. "I've been in love with you since I was sixteen. I've waited for you all this time. So I guess another year or two won't rob us of too much. Unless," he said maliciously, "next time you want to wait until we need rocking chairs."

"Very amusing." She folded her arms, cold in the wind.

"Time isn't likely to end things between us. What does it say in Scripture? *Love never fails.* Love lasts an eternity, Eden, though this life doesn't. It's brief. The days, the weeks, the months pass quickly."

"Yes," she said, "of course our love will never die." Her throat was dry. She tried to smile. "Our love will last forever."

His eyes flickered with amusement. "Then, again . . . maybe not. I might forget you on Kalawao. Some pretty girl might show up and tell me how wonderful I am. In my loneliness she'll comfort me. And then, who knows? She may make me forget your frustrating ways."

Eden, her emotions sore and frayed, allowed her tears to spring to her eyes. "Don't say that. Don't even joke about it."

"Eden—" He wrapped her tightly in his arms and kissed her temple. "Don't you know yet that I will never stop loving you? You are the love of my life. You always have been. No one could ever take your place."

That was just what she wanted to hear. *But could promises, well intentioned, go astray?*

Time had slipped by, and the wind was increasing noticeably.

He smiled. "Even as children, didn't I love you and save you from Zach?"

She traced the tiny scar on his chin and knew it was there because he had, even as a child, fought to save her from harm. She didn't know whether she wanted to cry or laugh.

"Yes, you've always been there," she said. "You may have to come back and save me again. But not from Zach. Don't go far, Rafe," she said soberly, her hand tightening on his.

He scanned her face. "Who is the big, bad wolf this time, or don't you know?"

She shook her head. "No big, bad wolf. Zachary has turned into a lamb. One I try to protect." She attempted to speak with a mood of lightness, but her eyes, she knew, revealed a sense of gravity.

"What is it about?" he asked soberly.

"We better go back. The storm will worsen."

"Yes, but I want to know what's behind this sudden sobriety of yours. We'll talk at Keno's house. It's not far from here. We need some dry clothes anyway. Then we'll go back to the plantation house before dinner. Keno can make us some coffee."

She nodded as they started back toward the pathway.

"It concerns Tamarind House," she said, unable to hold back some of the details. "And Hawaiiana. And Silas."

"Don't tell me you've been seeing ghosts in the Round Room again on stormy nights." But he spoke gently, without mockery, and it gave her reason to take heart.

"No. I haven't been up there since Great-aunt Nora had the house refurbished. But Zachary claims to have seen flesh-and-blood beings. He brought me here in his friend's boat. He wants to discuss it all with you, but first so do I."

A brow lifted. He watched her alertly now. She knew once again, as she always had, even in moments of uncertainty, that Rafe was the one man she could turn to for help. Just as he said, he'd always been there for her.

"Zachary knows I've come here to see you about his suspicions and a whole lot more. He intends to talk to you himself later."

"It all sounds mysterious and intriguing, but we can't stay here. We should have left before now."

Clouds had rolled in from the tops of the surrounding mountain and settled above the lagoon. The rain began to fall in torrents.

With her hand in his, they climbed up the path near the waterfall.

"Hold on," he shouted above the wind.

They struggled upward, grasping shrubs and branches, keeping to the lava rocks and trying not to slide.

The rain struck her face, blurring her vision, while mud trickled down the path. He gripped her forearm, pulling her up after him. She missed her footing and slipped, the mud smearing her. Her wet hair plastered against her face and neck. Her skirt ripped on a shrub, and her knee scraped against a jutting stone.

Eden thought her arm might get sprained as he kept hauling her forward, trying to keep her from sliding backward.

"I can't—" she gasped, every muscle straining with effort.

His arm clasped her waist. "Yes, you can, darling! We can, *together*. Keep going!"

He climbed, making steady progress, and Eden followed in his steps, gasping. At last they reached the top of the path, where the full force of the storm lashed the rain against them, so that Eden could hardly walk. He drew her to his side, his arm around her. Then, with heads lowered into the wind, they started toward the horses.

"Keno's place is about a mile from here."

The storm turned the afternoon into an eerie twilight as her horse plodded forward behind Rafe's. Eden huddled toward its strong neck. She wondered how Rafe could find his way back, but he seemed to know where to go.

"We're almost there," he called over the wind, yet Eden thought they'd never arrive, were totally lost, and would soon be swept away in an avalanche of volcanic mud. Then, she heard him say, "There's the house ahead. Keno's lit the lanterns."

The golden light shone as a beacon of hope and refuge. Rafe came around and helped her down and, with an arm about her waist, walked her to the house.

Rafe banged on the door. It opened immediately, and there stood Keno. He looked startled, then ignoring all propriety, he threw back his head and laughed.

"Out from the raging storm come ghostly visitors awash in tropical dew. Come in, and *aloha!*"

Eden stumbled inside. Keno rushed about, gathering towels and a small rug for them to stand on.

"Take care of her, will you?" Rafe told him. "I'll be back in a moment. I want to get my horses in your stable."

Rafe hurried back out, the door banging behind him in the wind.

Even in her misery Eden thought, *How Candace would love even this little house to settle in with the man she loves.*

Chapter Twenty-Three
All Things Considered

*K*eno lit several more lanterns and the living room brightened to a warm, golden glow that revealed entrances to several other rooms, a kitchen, and bath. There were koa and teakwood tables, intricately carved with Keno's artistic talents, and lauhala mats on the wood floors. He had brought Eden and Rafe some big towels, and Rafe would borrow a shirt and trousers from Keno, for both men were much the same build. Drying her face and hair in privacy, Eden gave thanks to the Lord for getting them safely to a place of refuge and for bringing their mutual love to a hope of future happiness.

There was a heavy teakwood trunk in one corner, and Rafe lifted the lid and rummaged around briefly. He pulled out a blue garment and handed it to her.

"How do you know Keno approves of your rummaging through his personal things?" Eden said.

Keno laughed and looked at Rafe. "If I didn't approve," Keno said in mock gravity, "he would take it anyway. He always takes my things. Right, Rafe?"

"Everything but this." Rafe lifted the carefully folded garment. He shook it out and held it up by its shoulders. It was an oversized muumuu, much too long for Eden and far too wide, with a splashy blue hyacinth and bright yellow hibiscus flowers on the print. Rafe looked at Keno.

Eden, weary beyond stopping herself, burst into silly giggles.

"Noelani's," Keno said gravely. "A birthday present. And if it weren't for lovely Miss Eden being soaked due to your waywardness, I would wrap it delicately and put it away."

Rafe turned to Eden with a smile. "You heard him. Better get out of those wet clothes and into this. You can draw that curtain across the bedroom door."

When Eden returned, lifting the hem of the muumuu in order to walk, Rafe had already changed into a pair of black trousers and a clean cotton shirt. He took her in with one glance and laughed.

"You're about to taste some of the best coffee in the world," Keno said, as the pots and pans rattled in the kitchen.

Who is making coffee? Rafe and Keno were in the room with her.

"Easton Brand," Rafe stated. "How does the name sound? Think it will go over on the Mainland?"

"'Easton Brand,'" she repeated musingly. "Well . . . actually, I think it needs a little more 'Island' sound."

There was amusement in his voice. "All right. How's this—A Taste from Eden? Make you want to try it?"

"Yes, I think I might, especially if I lived on a farm in snowy Minnesota."

"Wake Up to Paradise," Keno joined in.

"Coffee all ready," announced Ling Li, walking in with a wicker tray and three cups of steaming Kona coffee.

"Ling!" cried Eden.

He grinned. "Been here plenny time now. I stand between two big man. They keep me safe from—"

"Later, Ling," Rafe interrupted calmly.

"Yes, Ling talk too much."

"Until recently not enough," Rafe countered.

Ling looked sheepish. He nodded. "Ling afraid of big haoles. He just come from China to work. Best keep tongue for eating." He put the tray down and, smiling at Eden and giving a traditional bow to Rafe, returned to the kitchen, where the pots and pans, then continued to rattle contentedly.

Eden was pleased to see Ling safe and, as he put it, kept safe with the bodyguards Rafe and Keno. So that's why Ling had been searching for Rafe. He had important information that he'd thought might endanger him.

"Are you going to tell me everything?" she asked quickly.

"Everything worth telling, my sweet, and all in good time. Are you hungry?"

"No—"

"Rafe is always hungry," Keno said. He got up and went into the kitchen and said something to Ling. A brief time later fruits and breads were brought out, and some hot food wrapped in brown bundles, chicken pieces stewed in coconut milk, and some shrimps.

With the wind and rain still howling, and the enticing aroma of coffee adding a touch of cheer to the room, Keno stood and slipped into a hooded jacket of oil-slick.

"Are you sure you want to risk it?" Rafe asked, but did not appear worried.

"What's a little rain? I'll go to the big house and let Zach and the others know Miss Eden is here, safe."

"Knowing Zach, he'll be pacing the floor," Rafe said. "The sooner he knows we're here, the better. Tell him he and I will have a long talk later tonight."

"By the way," Keno said, lingering at the door a moment and focusing on Eden. "Miss Candace didn't come with you from Koko Head, did she?"

Eden felt her spirits sink. She said quietly, "No, she remained at Tamarind with my aunt and father."

He gave a nod, as though he understood, and opened the door, with a gust of windy rain blowing. A moment later he disappeared into the afternoon weather, as though he were used to it.

After he'd gone, she must have shown something of her sadness over Candace and Keno because Rafe looked at her. Part of the tragedy facing Candace was that she forbid her to explain, even to Rafe, about her upcoming decision about Oliver Hunnewell.

"Will Keno be all right finding his way?" she asked.

"This is nothing to Keno. We faced far worse at sea."

Rafe must have mistaken her mood over Candace as worry over the matters at hand. "Let's begin with Zach," he said. "At the lagoon you mentioned the suspicions he'd talked about on the boat. What's troubling you, honey?"

She loved the way he pronounced the word "honey." It had a warm, caressing note that gave her the feeling of belonging to him, without too much romantic tension. With marriage well over a year away, they both wanted to avoid intensity.

"And what's going on at Tamarind?" he inquired, his expression inscrutable.

Rafe already understood the cause for the jealousy between Zachary and Silas, so it was only necessary to explain Zachary's latest suspicions. She did so in meticulous detail, including the accusation that Silas was the man Candace saw on the lanai at Hawaiiana.

"The boatman, Laweoki, made it clear to me that he'd brought Zachary to Tamarind on that same night, and that Zachary had returned to the boat sometime later, nervous and limping."

"Did Laweoki admit to following another boat with Silas presumably aboard?"

"Yes. He was sure of what he stated."

"Did he mention the name of the boat or anything by which to identify it?"

She sighed. "I didn't think to ask him that. Is it important?"

"Well, if we knew the boat supposedly bringing Silas or someone else to Koko Head, we could check with the captain for proof. I'll ask Zach later."

"What could Silas have been searching for in Nora's room?" Eden concluded.

Rafe stood. "My guess? A section of family history. She'd made up her mind to reveal a matter. A secret, most likely. One she's been keeping for years."

Eden turned her gaze to meet his. Rafe already knew something important.

"But," Rafe countered, "did Zach actually see Silas? And if Silas found what he wanted, the question is, what good was it? Nora could easily rewrite the missing section. So if it was Silas, he took it as proof to the person he intended to extort money from. Or to protect himself."

"But why the need to protect himself? He's only been on the Islands since April."

"So he says. I assume that part's true, but what if Silas is not a Derrington after all? And Nora knows it?"

She stared at him. "That, I hadn't thought of. But somehow, I can't say why, I always felt it was Nora who'd sent for him to come to Honolulu."

"Maybe. But what would she get out of his arrival? He's not been any help to her on the *Gazette*. He's turned annexationist."

"For financial reasons. You heard Ainsworth promise him a place in the Derrington fold."

"And warn him, if he didn't become a good little Derrington. Well, in that regard Silas has my sympathy. I've had a taste of Ainsworth's warnings about what would happen if I didn't cooperate with him. It just so happened I wanted that seat on the Legislature to help Kip. Otherwise, I may have walked out. Then again, there was Hanalei."

"Yes, but you do truly believe in the annexation movement now," she said, "and Silas doesn't. He's not a true Hawaiian. He's not one of us. I don't think he cares either way."

"You've read him correctly. Even if he wasn't the man Zach saw,

I believe Silas is untrustworthy as to his motives for coming to the Islands. But I owe him for coming to your aid in Ling's hut."

Thinking back to that moment on Kea Lani brought a shudder. "Yes, he came to my help. I mustn't forget that." She frowned. "It would seem Silas must be a Derrington. He looks like his father and Zachary."

"He's sure to be related. The question is whether or not he's the firstborn of Townsend as they both claim, or a cousin? Then again, Townsend should know if Silas is his son or not. Did Nora ever tell you she was the one who'd brought Silas to the Islands?"

"No. It was just a feeling I had."

"I don't think she did. She'd have a stronger hold over him otherwise. She could battle Ainsworth over whose side Silas should be favoring. If you remember, she made a fuss at the table, but not enough of one to warrant her sponsorship in bringing Silas here."

She sank into her chair, tired. Rafe was probably right. "Then who did suggest he come here?"

"Good question." He looked at her and smiled. "Maybe no one did. No one in the Derrington family, that is. Did Nora ever find the section of her journal that was missing?"

"She never mentioned it. She was still recovering from the illness when I arrived at Tamarind."

Rafe poured another cup of coffee. "Yes . . . the sickness. It's what troubles me most. It's also the reason I can't accept Silas as the man."

She wondered why he would come to such a conclusion.

"My father was quite disturbed about what made her so ill, but tried to hide it from me."

"Did he?" He looked at her thoughtfully. "Is that why he stayed at Tamarind?"

"Yes. He kept the matter casual, but he asked me about the prescription I'd brought Nora from Dr. Bolton."

"Ah, then Dr. Jerome is onto it."

"Onto what? I'm the one who brought her the medicine some months ago."

"But it wasn't always under your supervision was it?"

"Well, no—Rafe! You're not suggesting someone deliberately changed the medication?"

"That will be left for physicians to decide. Is it out of the question? No. It's quite within reason."

"But that would mean—" She could not go on. She remembered her father asking about Dr. Bolton. Almost wearily she confessed, "Yes, you could be right. Oh, this horrible. I've just remembered my Father has sent a message to Kalihi asking Dr. Bolton to come to Tamarind to discuss the medication." She jumped up from the chair. "Even so, we both know how Nora is when it comes to health and doctors. Even though she promised me she'd take it, she probably set it aside and refused to bother with it."

"Maybe. Then, at Tamarind, she might not have felt too well. Something caused her to take a dose. And once she did, whatever it was put her in bed. If she'd kept on taking it, well—" He looked at her and must have noticed how upset she felt. "Let's wait for your father's and Dr. Bolton's conclusions."

She cast him a despondent glance. "I'm afraid they'll have a problem coming to a certain conclusion."

He set his cup down abruptly, frustrated. "Don't tell me she tossed the bottle?"

Eden nodded.

"Regardless of what Zach says about Silas, I've decided he's not our man after all."

Eden rubbed her forehead. Now why did he come to that conclusion? Rafe had said that Nora's sickness disturbed him the most. Why? Because it implied someone could actually hurt another member of their own family? She looked at him quickly. He watched her alertly.

"Then you don't think Silas has the unbridled evil in his heart to murder?"

He folded his arms. "Well done. Exactly."

"The question then is, who does?" she asked quietly.

"Yes."

Silence gripped the room.

"My little suggestion about Silas not being Townsend's son isn't one that I believe. I think he is who he claims to be."

"But, if he is," she said, "what's there to fear from Nora's revelation?"

"Something important enough to risk putting Nora to sleep and burning down Ling's hut with his wife inside. To protect his reputation. To keep the truth about Matt Easton quiet."

Perhaps she had known it all along. "It wasn't Silas that Zachary saw . . . *it was Uncle Townsend.*"

"Exactly. It was Townsend on the lanai at the pineapple plantation. And it was Townsend at Tamarind searching for Nora's work. He had to discover if what he feared was true. That she knew and was about to mention certain facts in the history that would shine the light toward him. Well, she did know. Townsend killed my father."

She sank into a chair, sickened. She had always known Rafe believed this, but somehow it was never real to her, but an idea that floated in the background.

"I've known it all along," Rafe continued, calmly enough, "but I couldn't prove it. I still can't. But now, if we're right about Nora's revelation in her history book, Townsend must own up to his evil. Was it premeditated? I don't know. At times, I don't think it was. But he's guilty of letting my father die. Could he have saved Matt? I don't know that either. Maybe not. But again, he deliberately let my father die. He refused to go for help. He walked away and left him badly injured."

She looked up, horrified. "How do you know this?"

"Ling. He was a witness."

"A witness!"

"Townsend knows Ling is a witness, too. First, Townsend had to discover if his fears were true. It was Nora he feared. Did Nora know all along? Was she going to reveal it? He had to get hold of her work and see for himself. He must have succeeded. Then Ling became the big problem. Ling could testify to what he saw. Ling's the big piece of the puzzle. After Rat Alley, when he returned to Kea Lani, he found his hut burned to ashes. When he discovered from his wife what happened and heard her story of why she believed Townsend set it on fire deliberately, with her inside—Ling knew Townsend would no longer be content to ignore him. Not with Nora's history coming out. People would begin asking too many questions. Newspaper men would come prying, offering little prizes to Ling for his story. I can only guess, but once Townsend knew for sure Nora intended to include my father's death in her history, he had no recourse in his own mind except to rid himself of the one actual witness. Ling."

Eden stood still. "How did your father die? You never told me."

"Matt fell from one of the lava mounds. Some of the rocks were sharp. He was injured and trapped there."

Rafe went on to tell her of a terrible argument over his mother, Celestine. "Townsend was trying to start an adulterous affair with her. She refused him, naturally. She told Matt. Matt confronted Townsend. There was an argument. When Matt turned to walk away, Ling saw him stumble and go over the mound.

"At first Townsend reacted in his better nature. He ran to the mound. But then he did nothing. He stood there for some time. Ling actually heard my father calling for help. Townsend watched. Instead of running for help, he sat down and watched him.

"Ling was hiding, but he hurried away for help and found Nora in the garden. Whether she understood Ling's speech back then is doubtful. He'd only just arrived from Shanghai. But he did manage to convince her to find Dr. Jerome."

Eden turned her back, depressed, as Rafe explained how Ling brought Jerome to his father.

"Townsend was nowhere to be seen by then. And no one ever knew he'd been on the plantation. My father went into a coma and died shortly thereafter."

"And Ling was afraid to speak," she said dully.

"Time passed, and everything was forgotten."

"And later, Uncle Townsend married Celestine and gained control over the Easton enterprise and Hanalei," she said wearily. "Why did she ever marry him?"

Rafe shook his head sadly. "For one thing, she never knew until recently about Matt's death or about Townsend. Secondly, I don't like to say this, but you already know. My mother was weak back then. Townsend was a bully. He dominated her, and she allowed him to do it."

Rafe's silence closed the door. She might have asked, "What do you intend to do about it?" But that question seemed unnecessary. It was obvious Ling was being protected now to be the star witness in the case.

"What about Celestine?"

He walked up to her, placed his hands on her shoulders and turned her round to face him. She was surprised by the calmness of his gaze under such dreadful revelations. He must have known most of this for so long that it was almost old news.

"Celestine is in San Francisco with Kip."

She caught her breath. "So *that's* where you brought Kip!"

"Keno and I managed to bring him to the *Minoa*. Ambrose later brought Celestine, and she boarded with Kip. She wanted to get away from Townsend and think about her marriage. She felt as I did about Kip, so agreed to take him with her. They're both doing well on Nob Hill, in fact."

"Then Noelani did know where Kid was that night?"

He nodded. "But she wouldn't help by bringing Kip to the ship as Keno tried to get her to do. She would keep silent, she said, but have no part in it. Ambrose, however, did have a key part. So if you're angry at me, you must include Ambrose."

She sighed and shook her head. "It doesn't matter any longer. I'm glad I escaped involvement in bringing him to Kalihi. But how will this change things? The Board will still be seeking Kip. And as a Hawaiian, you won't be able to adopt him."

"It so happens things are turning out better than even I had hoped. Ainsworth, Parker Judson, and others are interceding with the Legislature, of which I am now a member, to pass a law permitting me to keep Kip."

"Who do you think sent that message about Kip to the Board?"

"Townsend. Undoubtedly to get even with Celestine over seeking protection at Hawaiiana, and with me for guarding her from his bullying. The good news is that I have every reason to think this will work out for the good. Kip is going to become Daniel Easton after all."

She smiled tiredly. "I'm happy for you, my darling."

He cocked a brow. "Darling? Do you know that's the first time you've ever used that word?"

"But it won't be the last."

"I'll hold you to that promise."

The rain was diminishing, and the darkness was fading. As the clouds thinned, the sun began to shine.

*E*den returned to Hanalei with Rafe and eventually rejoined him and Zachary in the living room after changing into her own clothing. Zachary was now pacing up and down the floor. Keno sat watching, and Rafe stood, arms folded, calmly trying to convince him he had not seen Silas but Townsend at both Hawaiiana and Tamarind.

"Now look here, Rafe. I ought to know what I saw." Zachary's jaw was set stubbornly.

"The mind can play tricks, especially when the heart knows what it wants to see."

"And I wanted to see Silas? Nonsense."

"All right. Let's go through this again."

Eden joined them. "Tell them exactly what you saw, Zachary."

"Silas broke into Nora's room to steal some diamonds she keeps," Zachary said firmly. "I know, because she told me she keeps them there. If anything happened to her, she said, they were to go to Eden, because she hadn't included them in her will."

"Silas wouldn't risk his future for so small a treasury," Rafe said. "He has much greater treasure on his mind."

Eden looked at Rafe with surprise. Rafe was beginning to sound like Zachary. Rafe ignored her frown and continued.

"You were there at dinner that night when Ainsworth all but crowned Silas the golden boy of the Derrington legacy."

Zachary ran his fingers through his hair. "Yes, how could I forget? And now all that remains is for Ainsworth to hand him the crown jewels."

Rafe looked at him sharply. "Exactly. So ask yourself why Silas would risk the Derrington crown by breaking into Tamarind to steal a few diamonds—a brooch or some earbobs."

"If it is Townsend, as you insist, wouldn't I have recognized my own father on the lanai, and at Tamarind?"

"I thought you were tackled by someone coming out of Nora's room?"

"I was!"

"You told me the lights went out when he opened the door, is that right?"

Zachary stopped pacing, and by his scowl it was clear that Rafe's reasoning was becoming feasible.

"Then, also," Rafe said, "it may have happened too fast for you to see his face. Right?"

"Well—yes. It was dark." His voice calmed. "But on the lanai at Hawaiiana, I got a look at him."

"You must have been a good twenty-five feet away from him on the lanai, Zach," Rafe said.

Eden looked at Zachary. "Candace insists it was *you* she saw on the lanai outside Nora's sitting room. I made a point of asking her."

A light rain again begin to rap on the windowpanes.

"Well, why shouldn't she have seen me on the lanai?" Zachary said uneasily, looking from Eden to Rafe. "I was there—" he stopped short. "Wait!"

"What's wrong?" Rafe asked.

Zachary looked pale. "She *couldn't* have seen me. Because I was on the far side of the lanai, near those flowering vines, and I couldn't see Candace's room."

"You're right, Zach. From the guest room where Candace stayed, you can't see the far side."

"Yes! When I first followed whom I thought was Silas up to the house, he went one direction, toward Nora's room, and I climbed up near the vines to keep out of sight."

"Candace must have seen Townsend," Rafe said, "covered up with a jacket and a hat. And his posture can look a lot like your father's, especially at that distance."

There was a rapping on the front door. A minute later the Hawaiian serving man entered with Ambrose.

Ambrose, his frock coat wet and his hat askew, looked at Eden, then scanned the room with a grave face.

"I've news that wouldn't wait, so I had Liho bring me over on his boat."

"Cousin Liho, where is he?" Keno asked.

"Still on the boat. He preferred to stay."

Rafe took his uncle's hat and wet coat. "What news, Ambrose? It must be important for you to come here now."

"It is." He looked at Zachary, who stood tensely watching. "It's your father. It isn't pleasant news. Why don't you have a seat, Zachary, my lad."

"I—I don't expect anything good from him. Go ahead. I can handle it."

Eden's heart was thudding.

Ambrose looked at Rafe. "It is as we thought all along. Townsend was responsible for Matt's death, just as Ling said."

Rafe stood perfectly still.

Eden's hands tightened. She moved to Rafe's side, her hand on his arm.

How had Ambrose known about Ling? Rafe must have told him. She shouldn't have been surprised. Ling had been here at

Hanalei for some weeks, and Rafe was in Honolulu at the Legislature a mere two days ago.

"I was with Ainsworth at Kea Lani, preparing him for the onslaught I knew would be coming, when Townsend burst in," Ambrose said. He shook his head sadly. "Townsend was in a bitter foment. At first he denied everything we put to him. Then he became arrogant. He admitted deliberately setting fire to Ling's hut to silence Ling and his wife. He's admitted the worst, Rafe. When you were a lad, Townsend left Matt to die in the lava bed where he'd fallen in an argument over Celestine. He claims he didn't think Matt would live anyway, but even if it wasn't murder, it's willful contributory neglect toward manslaughter."

"He wanted my father dead." Rafe's chiseled jaw set. "He wanted Celestine and Hanalei. Where is he now?"

"He's fled the Islands."

⸺◈⸺

In the days following, evidence against Townsend accumulated. Eden received a letter from Great-aunt Nora and Candace. Candace wrote that she'd seen the truth about Townsend while they'd all been having breakfast at Tamarind the morning before Eden and Zachary set out for the Big Island.

When I stepped out on the lanai, Great-aunt Nora called from the table, "Do you see Zachary below in the garden?" I was about to answer, "Yes, he's here now," when I realized with a shock that it was Townsend ducking behind the trees. It struck me like a flash that it had been Townsend I saw on the lanai outside Nora's room.

I never thought much about the lanai incident after I told Rafe what I'd seen, until the night of the dinner. Eden, you were so insistent, wanting to make absolutely certain it was Zachary that I saw. I remember watching you leave the bedroom, and I thought for the first time, Am I certain? As it turned out, I was wrong.

After I told this to Great-aunt Nora here at Tamarind, she confessed that she, too, now believed it was Townsend. Nora has sadly told Uncle Jerome and me that, "It was my own nephew Townsend who'd exchanged Dr. Bolton's heart medicine."
I'll let her finish this letter.
Candace.

⁓

That afternoon when we were at Hanalei, I remained in the sitting room off from the guest bedroom after everyone left me. We'd just had that dreadful row between Zachary and Silas over the Gazette. *After you, dear Eden, left to go up to the nursery to see Noelani, I sat there thinking how dreadful jealousy can be. I must have dozed off for a few minutes, for when I awoke, I found Townsend standing there by my chair watching me. He had the saddest look on his face. Unusual for Townsend, as we all know.*

Where did you come from? *I asked him rather sharply, for he had startled me. He claimed he was looking for Celestine. Perhaps he was. I stood up to leave and get dressed for the dinner that night when I dropped my knitting bag. Townsend insisted on picking it up, along with some items that had rolled out. I believe it was then that the evil idea took root in his heart—and he must have slipped the prescription bottle into his pocket in order to change the medication. Later, in my room, when I looked for the bottle in my knitting bag, it wasn't there. But strangely, after dinner, it was in the bag again. At the time I thought I must have previously overlooked it. Now, unfortunately, I realize I hadn't.*

Then, weeks later after I returned to Tamarind, on more than one occasion I saw Townsend about the property watching the house. At times, from a distance I thought it was Zachary. Remember the binoculars? Well, this time when I saw him I wanted to make certain. It was Townsend. I believe he was waiting for me to take the medicine and pass from this world. (I do so hate saying, "waiting for me to die from the poison." It's still painful for me to think of Townsend that way.)

It may be he wasn't planning to hasten my death, but to permanently weaken my health so I would turn over my financial assets to him. I had once mentioned doing so, but after he became such a tyrant to Celestine, I changed my plans and altered my will, though I never informed Townsend.

I believe he learned I was writing about Matt Easton's suspicious death in my Derrington family history book. I remember having seen Townsend walk out to meet Matt in the field on the day of his accident so long ago on Hanalei. However, after Matt's death, Townsend claimed he'd not been there on that day.

Why would he say such a thing? I wondered. It caused me to recall that at the time Ling worked for Matt. Ling came running up to me speaking Chinese-English that I couldn't quite understand. Later, of course, I realized he was trying to say, "Townsend and Matt Easton."

Unfortunately, I've waited much too long to deal with this apparent injustice done both to Matt and dear Rafe.

Nora

The next morning Eden left Hanalei for Honolulu with Zachary and Ambrose. As she boarded the *Lily of the Stars*, it was with a heavy heart. Rafe stood on the wharf, a handsome, robust figure who seemed to be offering her a paradise of their own, if only she would stay.

Ambrose came up and stood beside her, putting an arm around her shoulders. "Cast aside your gloom, my dear," Ambrose told her with a warm, encouraging voice. "The onward path, so full of obstacles, still leads God's children in the way that is everlasting. As for our earthly fathers, they are not always what we wish for them to be. How much more wonderful is our heavenly Father, who is never absent and never late, always knows every detail of the problems we confront, and has determined to work His perfect will in all things."

Tears came to her eyes. She blinked them back, still looking toward Rafe.

"By God's grace you'll both arrive where He intends. Believe that, Eden. I know Rafe does. He told me so this morning."

Eden thought of the others in and out of the family she loved. She trusted they would have their arrivals, too. *They will—if they surrender their plans and desires to the will of the Father. In His will there can be perfect peace.* "These things I have spoken unto you, that in me ye might have peace." The peace that passes understanding— even in the midst of the storm.

That faithful promise alone was enough to sweep her heart clean of the recent dark concerns.

Before she boarded the *Lily of the Stars*, Rafe had taken her left hand and looked to see that the engagement ring was still there. "Aloha, my sweet. Till we meet again." His energetic dark eyes had spoken far more.

Aboard the boat Eden lifted her hand to wave at him. "Aloha," she whispered into the trade wind. "Till we meet again—don't ever forget I love you."

THE END OF BOOK ONE

Read more about Eden and Rafe, Candace
and Keno, Molokai, and the Revolution
in book two of The Dawn of Hawaii series.

THE FAMILIAR STRANGER

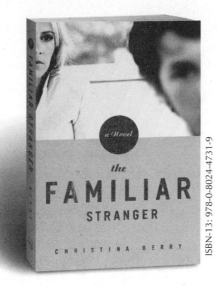

ISBN-13: 978-0-8024-4731-9

Denise wonders why her husband, Craig, has been so distant. Was it his job? The family? Her? When she gets the phone call that he has been in an accident, she rushes to his side. While keeping vigil by his bedside, she determines to make the marriage work. Perhaps this is the chance for a fresh start.

And when Craig regains consciousness, he appears to want the same thing—except for one small problem. He doesn't remember who she is; nor does he remember anything about their life together, their children, or his career.

As he struggles to regain his memory, ugly secrets begin to emerge. Can Denise deal with what she learns?

MOODY
PUBLISHERS

moodypublishers.com

Please visit our blog at www.moodyfiction.com

RAISING RAIN

ISBN-13: 978-0-8024-8734-6

Raised to be a "new woman" by her mother and three college roommates in the 70s amid anti-war protests, feminist rallies, and finals, Rain Rasmussen discovers that putting her career first has left her overdrawn at the egg-bank, and her baby fever has now driven off her significant other.

When her terminally ill mother demands a Celebration of Life before she dies, they all confront ghosts from the past on a stormy weekend in Monterey. Bebe, the roommate closest to Rain's heart, revisits choices that made the most impact on Rain, raising doubts about God's—and her own—willingness to forgive and to be forgiven.

MOODY
PUBLISHERS
moodypublishers.com

Please visit our blog at www.moodyfiction.com

LATTER-DAY CIPHER

ISBN-13: 978-0-8024-5679-3

When rebellious Utah socialite Kirsten Young is found murdered in Provo Canyon with strange markings carved into her flesh and a note written in 19th-century code, questions arise about the old laws of the Mormon Church. Journalist Selonnah Zee is assigned the story—which quickly takes on a life of its own. Even before the first murder is solved several more victims appear, each one more mysterious than the last.

Adding to a slew of other distractions, Selonnah's cousin Roger has recently converted and is now a public spokesperson for the Mormon faith. But paradoxically, Roger's wife, Eliza, is struggling to hold on to the Mormon beliefs of her childhood. If something is really from God, she wonders, why does it need to be constantly revised? And could the murderer be asking the same questions?

MOODY
PUBLISHERS
moodypublishers.com

Please visit our blog at www.moodyfiction.com

THE MISSIONARY

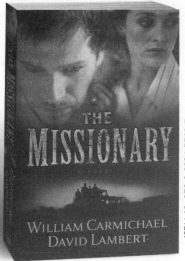

ISBN-13: 978-0-8024-5569-7

David Eller is an American missionary in Venezuela, married to missionary nurse Christie. Together they rescue homeless children in Caracas. But for David, that isn't enough. The supply of homeless children is endless because of massive poverty and the oppressive policies of the Venezuelan government, led by the Hugo Chavez–like Armando Guzman.

In a moment of anger, David publicly rails against the government, unaware that someone dangerous might be listening—a revolutionary looking for recruits. David falls into an unimaginable nightmare of espionage, ending in a desperate, life-or-death gamble to flee the country with his wife and son, with all the resources of a corrupt dictatorship at their heels.

MOODY
PUBLISHERS
moodypublishers.com

Please visit our blog at www.moodyfiction.com

MISS FORTUNE

In 1947 Allie Fortune is the only female private investigator in New York City, but she's kept awake at night by a mystery of her own: her fiancé disappeared in the war and no one knows if he's still alive. When there's a knock on her office door at four in the morning, Allie suspects trouble as usual, and Mary Gordon is no exception. Mary claims someone is following her, that her apartment has been ransacked, and that she's been shot at. Allie takes the case, and in the process discovers an international mystery that puts her own life in danger.

ISBN-13: 978-0-8024-6926-7

MISS MATCH

FBI agent Jack O'Connor receives a letter from Maggie, a woman he used to love, saying she's in trouble in Berlin. The FBI refuses to get involved, so Jack asks Allie Fortune to help him investigate. Allie and Jack pose as a missionary couple who want to bring orphans back to the United States. A child finds important documents that everyone in the city—Soviets and allies alike—want for themselves. Maggie refuses to tell Jack what the documents are, saying if things go wrong, they are better off not knowing. Through the course of the search, Allie's past is brought back to her, half a world away from home.

ISBN-13: 978-0-8024-6927-4

MOODY
PUBLISHERS
moodypublishers.com

Please visit our blog at www.moodyfiction.com